Freedom at Missionary Ridge: A

A story about a lawman, a solitary soul living in an age where the world was closing in all around him. New settlers were arriving more and more each day. All here to get rich, but most simply die trying to.

Thieves and highwaymen infest the West, and the west is where the gold is at. The gold is all a man needs, or so it seems. No amount of gold matter! If you out here on these plains come first frost, and you ain't got it together

Well, history goes on, doesn't it?

Law! hell, when it came to the law, your gun had to be quicker and more accurate than most. You must have some cunning about yourself, or end up laid out like them pilgrims who weren't prepared.

Well, God did send Bass Reeves, yes, Bass Reeves. Where do you think the character "The Lone Ranger" came from? Look here, this man could fire from both hands equally as deadly and accurate. His steady grip on his rifle enabled Bass to, as he put it, "Break a neck" at distances of 200 yards free-standing.

No sir! Belle Star herself got word that Bass had her bounty, and she turned herself in to the authorities.

This book is about that man! With my spin on the story. Hey! It's not a documentary, but you're gonna love it!

James E. Shaffer

Author/Filmmaker

This is the part where the author is appreciative of all his supporters. There are a great deal of people I could thank, but truth be revealed! One person has been my help my support, and worthy of dedication, and that person is my wife. For whom I am extremely grateful, Thank you baby!

Acknowledgment

Malikai Shaffer, Nick Norvell, Prince Davis, Myti Brown, Tyrone Williams, Mike Munroe, Charles Young, David Hauser, Trent, William Horton, Lynus Hinston, Mark Headley & last but not least, Michele Shaffer!

Contents

Missionary Ridge, Tennessee

December 1864

The air split with the thunder of cannon fire. Shrill screams pierced through the thick veil of gun smoke and Howitzer exhaust that hung heavy over the land like a shroud of death. Down at the base of the hill, a Union platoon was pinned in the mud. Dug in deep, shaking, cold in shallow trenches, their uniforms soaked through with fear and blood.

There was no safe route forward, and the only path to the ridge was a brutal uphill assault, exposed to every squirrel-hunting southerner's barrel this side of the Mississippi.

Up top, the artillery crews worked without rest. Beside the 12-pound Howitzers sat buckets filled with nails. Poured down the barrels when shells and shot needed wider patterns. You know, close-up war! When fired, the nails exploded outward in a ragged storm, tearing through flesh and uniform alike. Each blast sent iron screaming down the slope, a hail of death meant to shred any Union soldier's bravery or desperation.

The Confederate cannons fired in a steady rhythm, a constant percussion that beat back every advance with unrelenting fury. Smoke rolled over the hilltop like waves of ash, and with each thunderous recoil, the ground shook so hard men fell and screamed from the deafening percussion.

Pinned below the ridge, Colonel George Reeves crouched behind a fallen log, his face streaked with sweat and soot. A rugged man of thirty-five, maybe forty, he bore the hardened look of someone who'd long made peace with death. In the midst, he stood in stark contrast to the chaos around him.

He stared up the hill, eyes narrowed, lips pressed in a grim line. The path forward was suicide, and holding this position meant certain death.

Colonel George Reeves stood upright for just a moment, defying the bullets that sliced the air around him. His voice rang out over the thunder of artillery.

"Retreat! Retreat!" he roared, signaling with a frantic wave of his arm.

Sergeant John Doe stumbled toward him, his face streaked with mud and fear. In his mid-to-late twenties, the young sergeant was almost startling in his appearance, blond hair matted with sweat and dirt, piercing blue eyes wide with panic. He skidded to a halt beside the colonel, shaking his head.

"We can't, sir," he shouted. "They'll cut us down!"

Before Reeves could answer, the world erupted. An explosion tore through the earth in front of them, kicking up a geyser of dirt, fire, and iron. A screech of metal followed a sharp and sickening howl of misplaced air.

Nails, and shrapnel fired from the Howitzer's maw, & ripped through the air.

Reeves ducked instinctively, but Doe wasn't so lucky.

Several nails struck the sergeant with brutal force, one embedding in his neck, others peppering the left side of his face. Blood streamed down in long, dark rivulets, painting his collar crimson. He swayed on his feet, eyes wide with the weight of reality settling in.

"We're all gonna die here, sir," he whispered hoarsely, the fire in his voice replaced by something quieter. Resignation.

Halfway up the blood-soaked slope of Missionary Ridge, Bass Reeves moved like a shadow across the dirt, low to the ground, silent due the thunder overhead. His bare, muscular torso glistened with sweat and grime, the fabric of his Union-issue trousers soaked at the knees and thighs from crawling through mud and blood. At six feet one and solidly built, he was a formidable figure, even on his belly, built for war.

Moments earlier, he had paused at the edge of a shallow rise, sketching quick calculations into the earth with a stick, figuring range, angle, and cover in the thick of battle like a man solving a riddle under fire. He wiped the dirt from his hands, then slipped forward again.

Now, he crept along a flanking route, breathing steadily, his eyes locked ahead. He moved in a low crouching jog.

Just beyond the subsequent rise, a foxhole lay nestled in the hillside. Inside it sat a lone Confederate soldier, overweight, winded, and unaware. His uniform strained at the seams, and his rifle rested lazily across his lap, the look of fatigue etched deep into his face.

Bass stopped just short of the hole, eyes narrowed. There was no time for mercy, only decisions.

Bass moved with the precision of a panther stalking his prey. He lunged into the foxhole, wrapping his powerful right arm around the Confederate's neck. Before the man could scream, Bass twisted his jaw sharply to the side, and a sickening crack split the air. With his left hand, he brought the blade across the man's throat in one swift, fluid motion. The knife, sharpened in the way of the Chin (Qing) dynasty blacksmiths, nearly severed the head completely off. Blood sprayed across the hole as the soldier collapsed, lifelessly.

Bass exhaled once, steady and quiet.

He worked quickly, stripping the dead man of his uniform shirt and pulling it over his own bare torso. The fabric was damp with blood and huge across the shoulders. He didn't bother to clean the blood from his arms.

From a pouch on the dead man, Bass pulled a bundle of dynamite fuses and began knotting them into a long, single line with practiced hands. His fingers moved fast, his lips murmuring a steady count beneath his breath.

"One one-thousand, two one-thousand, three... four... five... six one-thousand... seven... eight... nine... ten one-thousand."

He cinched the final knot tight, eyes cold with focus. The ridge still thundered with cannon fire, but Bass knew he had turned this hunt around.

Bass leapt onto the back of a startled horse, seizing the reins with one hand and gripping the dynamite-laced rope in the other. With a hard kick, he drove the beast uphill, charging toward the ridge line behind the Confederate Howitzers. His body rocked with the gallop, the stolen shirt clinging to his frame, streaked with blood and dust.

As he crested the ridge, a Confederate soldier spotted him and raised a rifle, squinting down the barrel.

"I's comin', Massa! I's comin'!" Bass shouted, voice twisted into a child's ability to speak expected of the enslaved.

It gave him just enough time.

Behind the line of cannons, the first blast roared to life. The dynamite fuse he'd laid below ignited in a chain of thunderous explosions. Fire and iron filled the sky as Howitzer gun crews, and earth flew into the air in a grotesque ballet. One blast after the other went off near his path, shaking the ground and spooking his horse. The beast reared with a panicked fury, then cried out, throwing Bass hard into the dirt.

He hit the earth hard, rolling through the smoke and shrapnel, stopping at the boots of a Confederate soldier who had rushed to help what he thought was a fallen comrade.

The soldier bent to lift him, concern flickering across his face, until his eyes caught the blue-striped Union pants, then they widened in realization. His hand shot to his holster.

But Bass was faster, inhumanly so.

His knife flashed upward in a single, fluid motion, thrust deep under the man's chin, driving clean into the brain. The soldier's body stiffened, eyes rolled back. His hand, already holding the pistol, spasmed in death and discharged wildly, the shot striking a fellow Confederate in the distance, who dropped like a puppet with cut strings.

Bass staggered to his feet, the knife slick in his hand, blood soaking into the hillside soil. In the distance, you could hear Col. Reeves commanding his men to charge!

Bass looked skyward, breathing heavily.

"What!" he shouted, half-laughing, half-defiant. "I can't miss today!"

He stood still for a moment longer, eyes scanning the heavens.

"Well... here we are again, wit you savin' my tail."

A quiet moment in a storm of death. The ridge still burned, but Bass Reeves stood, alive, and was as deadly as ever.

The battlefield, though scarred and stained by war, now held a quiet sense of reverence.

The smoke had long cleared from Missionary Ridge, and the Sun hung low in the November sky, casting long shadows across the churned earth. Soldiers stood in formation, Black and white men alike, dressed in varying states of uniform, their eyes fixed on the figure before them.

Colonel George Reeves stood tall in his full Union dress blues, the brass buttons gleaming in the sunlight. His posture was formal, but his voice carried warmth as he addressed the assembled company. Off to the side, Bass Reeves tended to a pair of horses, his hands steady as he adjusted their harnesses, though his ears never left the colonel's words.

Behind the ranks, a modest brass ensemble of the honor brigade struck up the familiar chords of *The Battle Hymn of the Republic*. The music rose with slow majesty, stirring the hearts of the men and lifting their weary spirits.

Colonel Reeves raised his voice above the tune.

"We are gathered here today, in the year of our Lord 1864, November 24th," he said, his voice clear, resolute, "in the aftermath of the battle of Missionary Ridge."

A wave of applause and cheers rolled through the crowd. He lifted a gloved hand, gently quieting them.

He turned his gaze toward Bass, who had paused his work and now stood upright, silent and attentive.

"Sir," the colonel continued, "you have today earned the respect and the thanks of every soldier on that field. It is due to your actions that we're standing with our lungs and full hearts. It is due to your bravery that we are breathing."

He reached into his coat and withdrew two documents, folded and sealed.

"I have, on this day, drafted your honorable discharge papers, along with your free-man papers."

A hush fell over the company. The words hung in the air, heavy with meaning.

Bass met the Colonel's eyes. No salute. No smile. Just a nod, quiet, proud, and unflinching.

Bass Reeves stood at full attention, his uniform tattered and stained by battle, the fabric clinging to his powerful frame like a second skin. Though his clothes bore the marks of war, his bearing was precise, disciplined. Every movement he made was crisp and intentional, a series of formal maneuvers executed with the dignity of a seasoned soldier. He marched forward with steady purpose until he stood before Colonel George Reeves.

He stopped.

His boots struck the earth one final time as he came to a halt. Then, in perfect form, he raised his hand in salute, sharp, proud, unwavering, the gesture of a man who had earned his place.

Colonel Reeves stepped forward and extended the documents, folded, official, and life-altering. Bass took them with care.

"Thank yah," he said quietly, voice low and gravelly, touched with the dust of Tennessee and the weight of history.

The colonel smiled and turned toward the gathered soldiers. "Say something, Sergeant Major!"

Bass nodded slowly. He looked out over the men, some grinning, others solemn, all changed by the blood they had spilled together on that ridge today.

He cleared his throat. "Since on this here day we won the freedom to be American. To be one nation under God... I reckon I'll be headin' back off to the Arkansas Territories directly."

He paused, his voice catching just slightly.

"I got no better words than the ones my momma taught me. *'He that is slow to anger is better than the warrior; and he that rule his spirit better than he that take a city.'"*

He let the words hang in the air for a moment, "Proverbs sixteen, verse thirty-two," he added gently.

A hush settled over the field. No drumbeats, no horns, just silence and sky.

Bass turned, tucking the papers beneath his belt, and gave one last nod to his fellow soldiers.

"So y'all go on, finish this here up... so America can be who she's meant to be."

Then he whistled once, sharp and high.

"Hey up, Silver!" he called out.

From the edge of the camp, a proud gray horse trotted toward him, mane catching the light like smoke in the breeze. Bass swung into the saddle with effortless grace, cast one last look over his shoulder, and nudged Silver forward, riding off into the rising sun, a freeman in a divided country still learning what freedom & liberty meant in this nation.

The moon beginning to rise over the Arkansas countryside, casting a soft silver glow across the winding dirt road. Dust stirred beneath the hooves of Bass's horse as he rode Westward.

The chill of night settling him in.

The stars stretched wide and bright overhead, a quiet reminder of how far he'd come, and how far he still had to go.

Ahead, a wooden sign leaned slightly at the roadside, the paint weathered but legible:

WELCOME TO ARKANSAS.

Bass tipped his hat as he passed beneath it, a smile tugging at one corner of his mouth.

Not long after, he spotted a wagon pitched at an awkward angle just off the road. Its back wheel had sunken into a rut, and beside it stood an old man and a teenage boy, straining uselessly at a worn plank of wood wedged under the wheel. The mules snorted and pawed at the dirt, confused and impatient.

Bass pulled on the reins and brought Silver to a stop.

He swung down and approached the wagon with the easy stride of a man who knew how to handle himself and how to offer help.

"Hey, old man," he called out. "Let me give you a hand. Looks like you boys could use one right about now."

The old man straightened, wiping a sleeve across his brow. He was somewhere near seventy by Bass's guess, sun-darkened skin and a straw hat beaten down by years of use. His name, as Bass would later learn, was Ted Coon.

"You come here and push," Ted said, nodding toward the wheel. "And I'll guide the mules up front. This way we get some grip on both sides."

The teenage boy offered Bass a hopeful look, stepping aside so the big man could take position behind the wheel.

Bass nodded and rolled up his sleeves. "You ready?" he asked.

Ted was already gripping the reins, his voice steady. "On the count of three," he called. "One... two, !"

Bass Reeves planted his boots in the dirt and pushed with all his weight against the wagon's wheel, muscles flexing beneath his worn uniform. The wood creaked. The mules brayed. Just as the wheel began to lift, a sudden whoosh split the air.

Everything went black.

When Bass came to, the world was spinning and his head throbbed with pain. Cold iron shackles clamped around his wrists and ankles, heavy and tight. He was chained alongside a small group of Black men and a child. Each of them was gaunt, bruised, and barefoot. The scent of fear and slavery hung thick in the night air.

Two towering white men stood over him, both armed and grinning. One of them, a brute of a man with a thick neck and the bulk of a grizzly bear.

"We got 'em, Daddy!" the younger man cried. "We got his Black ass!"

It was Jim Bob Coon, Ted's son. About twenty-three, six-foot-four, and easily two hundred twenty pounds of mean muscle emerged from the shadows behind them, his hat now tipped back, revealing cold, calculating eyes. "Take it easy, boys!" Ted snapped. "Don't hurt the livestock. We ain't out here wastin' time catcthin'em for nothing."

Bass tried to sit up, but the chains bit into his wrists. "I'm not a slave," he said through gritted teeth. "I'm Sergeant Bass Reeves. Newly retired Union Army. A freeman, headed west."

Ted sneered and spat in the dirt.

"Sure you are, nigger," he hissed. "More'n likely a runaway who robbed and killed Sergeant Reeves, escapin' west like some dog. What's he reachin' for, boys?"

Bass froze. "No, sir. I got my papers. Right here in my pocket,"

Jim Bob took a step forward, rifle leveled at Bass's chest.

"You move to that there pocket, and you're dead, River Cricket, free or slave," he warned.

"Billy!" he barked over his shoulder. "You the only one who can read any got-damn way, get them papers."

Billy Coon, the youngest of the clan, sidled forward. Wiry, barely nineteen, with filthy fingernails and tobacco packed in his cheek, he chewed lazily as he eyed Bass like a curiosity.

"You move, boy... you die," Billy muttered, then reached into Bass's jacket and pulled out the folded documents.

He squinted at them under the lantern light, sounding out the words like a child.

"Well, Daddy," Billy said slowly, "looks like we got ourselves some kinda special Medal of Honor jig or somethin'."

Ted snatched the papers from his son's hands, crumpling them without reading.

"Ain't no honor in that God-forsaken Union Army," he spat. "Letting devils like *him* kill good white men."

Billy frowned. "Well, that's what this here paper says, Daddy..."

"The hell with that paper!" Ted roared. "And the *Medal of Honor* son of a bitch it rode in on! Chain his Black ass up with the rest of the runaways!"

Bass raised his voice, defiant even in chains. "Now boys, *I was nom.*"

Before he could finish, Jim Bob's rifle butt came down hard against the side of his skull.

Everything went dark again.

Bass Reeves awoke to the sting of sunlight piercing through the canopy of trees above. The warmth of morning bathed his bruised face, but his body ached, stiff and throbbing. His head pounded from the blow that had silenced him. A metallic taste of dried blood clung to his tongue.

His arms were stretched awkwardly, wrists bound in heavy iron shackles. A rusted chain ran from his cuffs to a thick pine tree behind his back. Around him, six other Black men, thin, sunburned, silent, were likewise chained to trunks, stumps, and wagon wheels. A boy, maybe ten years old, sat among them. His eyes were wide and unblinking, hollowed out by fear far beyond his years.

The road they were beside was narrow and deeply rutted, cutting through dense southern Arkansas woods.

Bass recognized it now; this was the slave road leading south, the trail used to funnel captured runaways and kidnapped freemen to Mississippi, often passing through the trading post at Fort Hindman.

The air was thick with heat and pine sap, heavy sweat, blood, and damp earth. Birds chirped carelessly overhead, unaware of the suffering below.

Bass clenched his jaw and took a breath through his nose.

He had survived worse.

But he also knew the war wasn't over.

Not yet.

The wind whipped across the plains surrounding Fort Hindman, carrying the scent of dry earth and distant campfires. Within the makeshift encampment, **Wind of the Gods** sat with an aura of quiet regalia, despite the rugged surroundings. He was a man of impressive physique, a muscular Moor with a cascade of long, black hair. At six feet three inches and two hundred pounds, he exuded an almost kingly presence as he sat cross-legged, observing the return of Bass.

"As Salam-Alaikum, dear brother," Wind of the Gods greeted, his voice a smooth, resonant baritone. "So, our war hero returns to us from the place where death is as close as a relative."

Bass, bound and weary, bristled at the implication of his captivity. "Hey! You boys are making a mistake. I'm free. I'm not a slave, I'm Sergeant Bass Reeves of the Union Army."

Twenty feet away, around a simmering pot of stew, one of their captors, Ted, responded, his voice laced with menace. "One mo' word outta you, Fredrick Douglass, and we gonna have ourselves a good ole Mississippi picnic. You know what a Pic-a-nig is, boy?"

Ted rose, a long blade glinting in his hand, and slowly approached Bass. "It's where ya pick a nig for a lynchin', hanging, or cutting off some special parts. I think them Medal of Honor nuggets would be mighty powerful on this here fertile-li-zation necklace." He pulled back his collar, revealing a grotesque necklace of shriveled, strung testicles, before turning and ambling back to the fire.

Wind of the Gods' voice was low, a warning. "Keep yo mouth shut, brother, these dogs bite."

But Bass's resolve hardened. "I'd rather die than be a fucking slave."

A faint, knowing smile touched Wind of the Gods' lips. "Don't worry. I have a cure for this disease. At around midnight, they stop and settle in. When I start removing this rotted meat, you just do your part with that old man who sleeps in the wagon." He subtly displayed a small nail, perfect for picking locks.

Bass's eyes gleamed with a rekindled fire. "You got-dern right."

Night's Escape

The moon hung high, a silent sentinel in the inky sky, as the band of captors settled into their camp for the night. Soon, the rhythmic rumble of Jim's snores filled the air. Skinny, a gaunt figure, detached himself from the group and approached the line of chained captives. With a chilling casualness, he unfastened a young boy, no older than thirteen, from the end of the chain and vanished with him into the surrounding darkness.

A faint click, almost imperceptible, broke the night's stillness. Wind of the Gods had freed himself from his restraints. With swift, practiced movements, he then liberated Bass and the four other souls shackled alongside them. The moment their chains fell, four of the freed captives bolted, scrambling into the night without a backward glance. Only Wind of the Gods and Bass remained.

Bass moved with stealth, casual, quiet steps, and determination towards the wagon where the old man slept. He found him disarmed, his gun belt set aside but nestled precariously between the buckboard and his sleeping form. Bass reached into the wagon, his fingers closing around the hilt of a Davy Crockett knife, still in its sheath, on the old man's belt.

Night's Deadly Dance

As Bass drew the Davy Crockett knife from its sheath, the old man in the wagon stirred, his eyes snapping open. Seeing Bass standing over him, weapon in hand, the old man's mind raced, calculating his chances of reaching his pistol before Bass could strike.

Just as Ted lunged for his Colt .45, Bass threw the blade. It spun through the air, finding its mark directly in the old man's spine the instant his hand closed around his weapon. With a gasp born of sheer defiance or perhaps pure hate. The old man twisted and fired a single shot that went wide, and then crumpled, passing on into the darkness.

The gunshot ripped through the night, jarring Jim awake. He barely had time to register the sound before Wind of the Gods was on him, moving with terrifying speed.

"Billy!" Jim bellowed, his voice thick with alarm.

"He will not be coming to your aid, demon," Wind of the Gods replied, his voice a low growl. "Tonight, you have the honor of dancing with Wind of the Gods."

Jim lunged for his rifle, but Wind of the Gods' foot lashed out, kicking the weapon into the murky water nearby.

"I am your way, your truth, and your Concierge to the afterworld," Wind of the Gods declared.

Despite Wind of the Gods' formidable presence, Jim had a few inches on him and charged, tackling him. They tumbled, rolling over the rough ground before springing back to their feet. Jim rushed forward again, but Wind of the Gods sidestepped, delivering a powerful punch as Jim passed, momentarily throwing him off balance. In that brief moment, Jim scooped up a handful of dirt from his fall and flung it into Wind of the Gods' eyes. Blinded, Wind of the Gods stumbled back as Jim unleashed a brutal flurry. Left and right hooks that would have felled a prize-winning bull at the Carson County Fair. And yep, Wind of the Gods fell hard onto his back. Jim retrieved his own blade from the ground and walked over, salivating over the fact that he gets to drive a blade into him. In a little girls voice, Jim says, "I'm Wind of the Gods". Then back to full-grown grizzly voice.

"Hell, if this is dancing with Jesus!" Jim snarled, raising the knife. "Tell 'em he's a shit of a dance partner."

As Jim plunged the knife downward towards Wind of the Gods' chest, Wind of the Gods, still on his back, blocked the blow with crossed arms. With a sudden surge of power, he kneed Jim from beneath, flipping him over his head. Scrambling to his feet, Wind of the Gods wiped the dirt from his eyes.

"Who the hell says Jesus was trash?" Wind of the Gods spat, his voice laced with renewed fury. "You dance with a student of the Qing (.,chin) Dynasty. Tribal enforcer of the Muhammad Ali Dynasty."

"Yeah, yeah, fuckin' hell," Jim muttered, lunging forward with the knife again.

But this time, Wind of the Gods was ready. He caught Jim in an arm bar, twisting the limb until the knife Jim held was rested against his own jugular. With a simple slap to the handle, Wind of the Gods drove the blade deep into Jim's neck.

"Tell Shai'tan that it was I, Wind of the Gods, that sent you," he whispered, "and I'm coming for him next."

The Aftermath

From behind Wind of the Gods, the frail figure of the little boy appeared, a bloody knife clutched in his hand.

"That evil man will spend the rest of his life without these," Lil 1 said, opening his hands to reveal a grisly display of severed human testicles. Maybe his daddy can wear'em on his, Mocking Ted Coon Lil 1 says "Fetile-lie-zation Neckalce". In the distance, the fading sounds of a man moaning in terrible pain drifted on the night air.

"We need to go back to Fort Hindman," Bass stated, his voice grim. "When someone discovers these bodies, the hunting party will be thirsty for blood."

"We'll use the Indian trails and runaway camps, staying off the main roads to get back to Indian Territory," Wind of the Gods replied, his gaze scanning the darkness. "I do not believe that what is behind us will find us welcoming either."

"Okay, okay! Let's bury these rednecks, gather up these here guns and ammo," Bass commanded, already moving. "When we're not in the camps, I'll be commissioned out of Fort Richardson for collecting deserters. The boy will be my helper, and you'll be the deserter. That'll get us through any more slave catchers.

Once we're in Fort Richardson, we will report what took place here today."

Tales on the Run

"Yes, yes!" Wind of the Gods declared as they moved swiftly through the night. "So, as we travel, let us get to know one another, my friends. We have a head start on you, and your story, Bass Reeves, a war hero."

Bass scoffed softly. "That's what they keep going on about, but truth be told, what else could I have done?"

Wind of the Gods' voice was firm, almost a declaration. "You are a hero, my friend, and that is because you just do what heroes do. It is the ability to take action in moments of fear, to rise above. They make it through, they survive, and the really great ones save lives." He paused, then turned his gaze to the youngest among them. "And you, Lil 1, what is your story?"

Lil 1's small voice was steady, though the words carried a heavy weight. "Massa killed my Mamma. I be somewhere near eleven years old when Massa killed my mamma. Well, it was actually Mrs. Missy who took a shotgun to my momma's head. Blood was everywhere, my momma's brains was on my clothes. Daddy tried to run, they caught him, and tied him to some horses."

"You don't need to speak on it if you don't want," Bass interjected, a note of concern in his voice.

"Nawh, it feels better said," Lil 1 replied, his gaze fixed on the path ahead.

"No, no, it's okay, we get it, really," Wind of the Gods reassured him. "Slaves can marry into the family to whom they are indentured. If they accept Islam, they are set free in Egypt."

"Now, as backwards as that sounds," Bass began, a hint of trepidation in his tone, "I'm kind of scared to ask, but Wind of the Gods, what's your story?"

"Do you know the Muhammad Ali Dynasty?" Wind of the Gods inquired.

"No, shh, what in the world is that?" Lil 1 piped up, genuinely curious.

"A Dynasty is a Kingdom, a heritage line of Rulers," Wind of the Gods explained. "Muhammad Ali, born in 1769 in Kavala, Macedonia of the Ottoman Empire. When his Dynasty took control of Egypt, I became an Enforcer for the regime. I am on special envoy to find a child related to His Majesty's cousin. A high-ranking diplomat was visiting the Americas with his cousin, aunt, and uncle, and they disappeared. It is believed that he had somehow been sold into slavery in the Americas. That's how I came to be on that lost chain of souls. My investigation led me to those particular slavers due to their young male fetishes."

Lil 1's face clouded with understanding. "What about the boy? Where is he?"

"You remember telling me about Beetle Bug? The friend that died before our hero arrived?" Wind of the Gods asked, his voice softening.

"That was him, huh? The Beetle Bug boy?" Bass realized, a grim understanding dawning on him.

"I'm afraid I was too late to save that one, but hey, look at us. We're free and alive, right, Lil 1?" Wind of the Gods attempted to lighten the heavy air. "We can fight another day, breathe the air, eat the marzipan, and baqlawa, basbousa, you know, marzipan, crushed almonds and honey?"

Bass and Lil 1 exchanged quizzical looks.

"Egypt, Africa, whole other place," Bass stated, the words a mixture of wonder and disbelief.

The End of a War and a New Beginning

The Arkansas road was a ribbon of cracked earth and red dust, winding through a landscape of dense, humid forest. After seventeen days of travel, the rhythm of the journey had settled into a weary hum. The rickety wagon, with its squealing wheels and protest-prone axles, was their entire world. Atop the driver's seat, Bass, a man whose quiet strength was as vast as the land they crossed, felt the air shift. It wasn't the wind. It was the palpable energy of a hundred armed men, moving with the practiced precision of a well-drilled army.

They came into view around a bend, a Platoon of soldiers rounding up runaways and what looked like holdouts from the Confederate army, a ragged band of men with defiant, haunted eyes. Bass tightened his grip on the reins, his gaze sweeping over the scene. His traveling companion, Wind of the Gods, a man of profound stillness and sharp wit, sat beside him, his chained but not locked hands a grim reminder of their recent ordeal.

"It's all right," Bass said, his voice low and steady, a calming counterpoint to the nervous tension in the air. "They're Union Army out of Richardson, I bet you."

He spoke with an authority born of experience, a deep-seated knowledge of the symbols of power in this new, uncertain America. Just then, the group of soldiers came to a halt. Leading them was a figure who commanded attention without a single shouted word. Major Alexander Augusta. He was a clean-cut African American man in his thirties, his slim build belying an immense, almost regal, air of complete control and authority. He sat on a horse that was as black and polished as a freshly shined boot, his uniform crisp and impeccable, as sharp as all the soldiers in his platoon. He marshaled his troops, about one fifty black soldiers and twenty-five white ones, with an effortless grace.

"Ho! Sergeant," he called out, his voice ringing with a calm command that cut through the humid afternoon air.

Bass's eyes found the insignia on the man's shoulder, a single, gold leaf denoting his rank. Without a moment's hesitation, Bass jumped down from the driver's seat, the movement fluid as practiced, coming to a stiff attention. "Sergeant Bass Reeves, Major, Retired!" he announced, his voice carrying the weight of his rank, the rank he had earned and, for a time, had to put aside.

He extended his papers, the official documents, a passport to a world of recognition and respect. As he did, a new figure stepped forward: Sergeant Jonas. He was a short, chubby, sloppily dressed African American man, somewhere in his forties or fifties. He had an uncaring swagger, a weary indifference that seemed to coat him like dust.

"Platoon at ease!" Major Augusta's command rippled through the ranks, and the soldiers relaxed their rigid posture, a collective sigh of relief.

"Yes, Suh," Jonas mumbled, the words a perfunctory chore.

"Would you be so kind as to retrieve the gentleman's paperwork?" Augusta said, his tone polite, but with an iron edge that was impossible to miss.

Jonas mumbled under his breath, just loud enough for Bass to hear. "Yes, suh... If and he got his papers... shit... can't we just get on to camp."

He moved slowly, dragging his feet off his horse as if the simple act of dismounting was a monumental effort. The twenty-foot hike to Bass felt like a mile.

Major Augusta's voice, though still calm, sharpened. "Move with some haste about yourself, Sergeant. You appear horribly out of shape."

A wave of chuckles rippled through the ranks, a small release of the day's tension. Jonas's pace picked up, his grumbling growing louder now that he was out of the Major's direct hearing, but still within Bass's.

"I don't know why dis horty torty ass man goin' so hard anyway, the war is over," he muttered, his words laced with a weary disdain.

Bass's head snapped up, his ears pricking to the words he'd just heard. "Did I hear that right, Sergeant? Did you say the war was over?"

Jonas paused his slow, reluctant walk, his eyes widening slightly. "Yep. As of May 9, 1865. Lee surrendered to General Grant at Appomattox, Virginia. We's all free now. Ain't you heard?"

Bass's mind reeled. Free? The war was over? The words hit him with a force that almost buckled his knees. He walked toward the Major, Jonas following behind him, the papers now held out in his hand.

"Did I hear the sergeant right, Major? This war is over?" Bass asked, his voice a mix of disbelief and overwhelming relief.

"Yes, you did, Sergeant. And there's still a few pockets of renegades who refuse to give up. Jesus Wales and a couple other holdouts, but the war is over," Augusta confirmed, his expression softening as he looked at Bass. His eyes then shifted to Wind of the Gods, still chained and sitting in the wagon. "Whose he? A deserter?"

"Oh, no, sir," Bass said quickly, shaking his head. "We were kidnapped by some slavers. In making our escape, the three of them were killed. We devised a plan for him, Wind of the Gods, to be a runaway, and I was returning him to Fort Richardson or Smith for hanging."

A genuine smile touched Major Augusta's lips, a rare light in his serious demeanor. "No need for all that now! What's your name, Sergeant?"

"Reeves, sir. Bass Reeves. This is Wind of the God, and… well, boy, I really don't know his name. We call him 'Lil 1'."

"You say, Bass Reeves?" Augusta's voice held a new, respectful note.

Wind of the Gods, always a man of dignity, interjected. "It is Wind of the Gods. Of the Gods."

Bass gave a small, weary chuckle. "Yes, sir, and okay."

Major Augusta's eyes narrowed in thought, a flicker of recognition in their depths. "Bass Reeves, who fought at Missionary Ridge, with Colonel George Reeves?"

"Yes, sir!" Bass answered, a flicker of pride in his chest.

Major Augusta's face broke into a broad, genuine smile. "Company attention! Present Arms!"

The soldiers, who had been lounging lazily, snapped back to attention, their rifles raised in a perfect, unified line. They presented arms to Bass, a man who had been a runaway, a would be slave just moments ago, now a hero.

"Boys, this man here is the ranger that saved his entire platoon at Missionary Ridge!" Major Augusta announced, his voice booming with pride.

Sergeant Jonas, the weary cynic, couldn't believe it. He leaned over to a non-described soldier and whispered, "This nigga here? This the Lone Ranger?"

Cheers erupted from the ranks. "Hip hip hooray! Hip hip hooray!" The sound was a roar of genuine admiration and respect.

Amid the celebration, Wind of the Gods, ever pragmatic, spoke up. "If we all done spooning over Bass, can someone release me from these chains?"

A chuckle escaped Major Augusta's lips. "Sergeant, remove those chains." He turned back to Bass, his expression friendly and inviting. "Where are you boys headed, Bass Reeves?"

"Out to Grayson County, Texas," Bass said, the destination feeling less like a goal and more like a refuge.

"Then on to Indian Territory, away from all this hate and death."

Major Augusta nodded, understanding in his eyes. "Why don't you boys bed down with us this evening? Get a good meal, some music, a drink, and some fine women. We're by a runaway camp/Indian reservation. I swear they musta run from God's plantation 'cause they got some heavenly bodies over there."

Wind of the Gods' eyes lit up. "Sounds like the perfect place for God's Wind to be."

Bass smiled, the weariness of the road melting away, replaced by the promise of warmth and fellowship. "Lead the way, sir."

"Platoon, Hi Ho!" Major Augusta commanded, and the company set off, their new companions following close behind.

They passed through a shanty of a town, its wooden structures crooked and faded, before arriving at a saloon, a beacon of light and music in the gathering dusk.

The air smelled of woodsmoke, cheap liquor, and something sweet, like a promise.

The saloon was a cavern of noise and motion. The swinging doors creaked open to a cacophony of laughter, conversation, and a pounding, fast-paced piano tune that seemed to possess the dancers on the floor, their bodies sweating and gyrating in time with the melody. The air was thick with the scent of cheap rye whiskey and the earthy smell of hormonal excitement, vibrant, alive.

Major Augusta led them to the bar. "Bass, we've all heard of the Ranger at Missionary Ridge, and proud as hell when we heard he was a Negro too. Crippled a dozen 12-pounders. Killed the dynamite flanker and the rest of the enemy forces with a Bowie knife."

Bass took a sip of his whiskey, choked a bit, then a wry smile appeared on his face. "Well, all of that ain't like it was, but I for sure would do it again."

Laughter and drinks were shared among the men, the sound of their camaraderie a balm to Bass's weary soul.

Wind of the Gods, ever observant, surveyed the room with a wide smile. "Ooh we, there are sure some heavenly bodies on earth tonight."

Major Augusta, a paternal warning in his voice, said, "These girls ain't barmaids, boys, so be respectful."

Wind of the Gods, a scholar of the Quran and a connoisseur of beauty, responded with a quote. "Oh, Ahki, Alldiah Qalaika Fasawah! Indeed, Allah has created in due proportions! I shall respect every wiggle of dat sweet brown jiggle."

Bass's eyes, however, had found their own focus. They locked with a young lady, no older than twenty-one. Her big brown eyes seemed to reach out and grab him from within, holding him in place, rendering the rest of the world to a blur of noise.

"Wow, who is dat over there, Major?" Bass asked, the question escaping his lips before he could stop it.

"Oh, dat there is Jennie Morning Star," Augusta said, following Bass's gaze. "Her daddy is the chief of the Quapua. The largest tribe in the whole state of Arkansas."

"She's got to be the most beautiful woman in the world," Bass said, his voice barely a whisper.

Augusta laughed, a full-bellied, joyful sound. "I can say you gotta taste for the finer thangs, young man."

At a table with her friends, Jennie Morning Star sat, a slim young woman with a full figure, her skin the color of warm caramel. Her big, beautiful brown eyes met Bass's. She gave a small nod and a shy smile that melted Bass's tough exterior, forcing him to notice her in a way he couldn't ignore. He had to introduce himself.

Taking a deep breath, Bass walked over to the table full of beautiful Black Native American women. The music and laughter seemed to fade as he approached.

"Good evening, ladies," Bass said, his voice uncharacteristically soft. "My name is Bass. Bass Reeves. Speaking now in her native tongue, "I could not help but notice you and your friends and how amazingly beautiful you are. May I have this dance?"

Jennie's eyes sparkled with a playful challenge. "I do not normally dance with strangers. Are you Quapua?"

Bass took a step back, the challenge fueling his desire to be known. He had never been a man of many words, but now they flowed. " No, Ma'am, I was born on a plantation in Tennessee. Where a man named Reeves let my parents work as sharecroppers to earn money to move back out West. Also, bring his slaves to Texas to work the harvest season. It was supposed to be a partnership. My daddy came over to America to find his path, but found it uninviting, free or not, for a Black man's success in this country. Well, Mr. Reeves became fond of my daddy and allowed us a life there on his plantation, as long as we made money. I joined the military with him, won a few battles, and now here I am, asking you to dance with me, not a stranger."

Jennie's playful demeanor softened into a genuine smile. "Now it seems like I've known you all my life. Excuse me, girls, while this young man entertains me."

Her friends giggled. "Gal, I wish that handsome som-n, som-n was entertaining me all night." The female voices from the table sighed in unison, a chorus of "Unh, unh, unh, Lawd, Oooh."

Just as they entered the dance floor, the music changed from the frantic, fast-paced melody to a slow, melodic tune, a bluesy serenade that seemed to have been written just for them.

"If I didn't know better," Jennie said, her eyes twinkling, "I would think you had me set up or somethin."

"Ma'am, I wish I could take credit, but I ain't never been so smooth," Bass said, a genuine, easy smile on his face. "Would you remind me, though, to thank the Major when we're done?"

Jennie leaned into him, her hand light on his shoulder. "I don't normally slow dance with strangers. Since you are a war hero and all, I guess I'll do my patriotic duty."

"Well, ma'am, what is your other going to say about tonight's dance card?" Bass asked, a shy curiosity in his tone.

Jennie stopped dancing, looking him dead in the eye. "If you tryin' to figure if I got a man, the answer is no. You ain't gotta play sheep-wolf."

Bass, flustered and a little stumbled over his words. "No, ma'am, I, uh, I, uh... ain't sneaking up on nothing. I just didn't want to get bushwhacked."

"You, uh, what?" Jennie's laugh was a melodic, bubbly sound. "If you wanna ask me out, just ask."

"Do you wanna go out with me?" Bass said, the words a jumble, a lifetime of training for war falling away in the presence of a beautiful woman.

"No," Jennie said, her smile broadening. "Not until you learn how to ask a lady out."

Bass took a deep breath, his mind racing. He had faced down dozens of armed men, but this simple task felt more terrifying than any battlefield. "I'm sorry, ma'am. I've just been around guns and men screaming for so long, I forgot my manners. Ms. Jennie, may I take you out to dinner?"

"Well, sir," Jennie said, a soft, teasing light in her eyes. "I couldn't ask for a more eloquent proposal."

"Proposal!" Bass said, his voice a panicked gasp, his mind racing. "Hold on there now. Can I taste the milk before I buy the cow?"

Both of them laughed out loud, the sound a beautiful, simple moment of connection.

"It's getting late," Jennie said, the smile still on her lips. "This is no place for a lady after 10 o'clock. I will see you, sir, tomorrow at 8:00 a.m. You can call on my father at the livery stables at first light."

Bass's face fell. He had hoped for another moment, another dance. "Ma'am, first light call on your father?"

Jennie's smile became a firm, undeniable line. "If you plan to court me, Mister, I suggest you be there!"

"Yes, ma'am, yes, ma'am," Bass said, watching her walk away. "I don't know what I was thinking!"

He watched as Jennie's full, well-fed bottom wiggled and shook its way through the saloon doors. She glanced over her shoulder with a shy grin, catching him in his perverse stare. He quickly turned his head, a hot blush spreading across his cheeks even though you couldn't see it.

Wind of the Gods, who had been watching the entire exchange, walked up beside him. "Now, that there will make a man beg for many a child!"

Bass and Wind of the Gods heartily laughed, their laughter a sound of a new beginning, a sound that rang in the warm smokey saloon air. They headed toward the bar, sitting down to a few glasses of rye whiskey, trading war stories. As they talked, Bass's eyes scanned the room, a new sense of contentment in his heart. His gaze fell upon three men, fresh off the trail. They were dirty and dusty, looking mean Jand ornery and clearly looking for trouble. The biggest of the three pushed a town drunk to the floor, his voice a low growl.

"Mr. If you'n ain't up and outta my way, I's kill ya where ya stand!" a big man snarled, his words thick with menace.

A Marshall's Calling

A barmaid, a woman with kind eyes and a tired smile, stepped out from behind the bar. "Leave ole Bill alone, he ain't mean no harm," she said, her voice soft but firm.

The biggest man, a hulking figure with a cruel glint in his eyes, grabbed at his crotch. "Bitch if you got something to say, it better be about putting this love stick in your mouth. To fetch a couple bits."

Wind of the Gods started to move, his body tensing, his eyes blazing with a righteous fury, but Bass's hand shot out, holding him in place.

"Now, Wind of the Gods!" Bass's voice was low, a warning. "That there ain't our concern."

"That dog has no right talking to her like that," Wind of the Gods hissed, his eyes still fixed on the man. "Besides, she's been sweet as hell to us."

"You might be right, but it still ain't no reason to get involved," Bass insisted, his grip on Wind's arm firm.

Old Moorish saying "If no one stands up, we all fall," his voice now a quiet roar of indignation. He pulled free of Bass's grip and stepped forward. "Mr., that's no way to talk to a lady."

The big man's sneer deepened, a cold, empty look in his eyes. "If you don't mind your business, you won't be talking at all, excepting angels."

The biggest man went to swing, a wild, sloppy haymaker aimed at Wind's of the Gods' head. Wind of the Gods, with a fluid, almost dance-like movement, ducked under the blow, his body moving in a flash of motion. He threw a side kick that landed with a sharp crack against the man's knee, knocking him down. Dick Glass, one of the other men, a lean, wiry Black man mixed with Creek Indian, reached for his gun.

A shot rang out, sharp and sudden, a single, deafening clap in the crowded room. Bass, his gun still smoking, had fired it without even looking. A small hole appeared in the crown of Dick Glass's hat. The bullet had missed his head by a hair's breadth.

"No sense anyone passing on tonight," Bass said, his voice calm, his eyes holding the cold intensity of a man who had seen too much death. "I suggest you boys find another place to drink."

Dick Glass, a man about six feet and one hundred eighty pounds, with a powerful, muscular build, stepped over to his hat, his face an unreadable mask. He picked it up, looked at the small hole, and then looked at Bass.

"Mr., I once killed a man over an ear of corn," he said, his voice low and full of a quiet, menacing authority. "And here you done gone and shot my hat" in disbelief.

Wind of the Gods stepped forward, a wide, defiant smile on his face. "Carry yo ass up outta here before more than that hat get filled with holes."

Dick Glass's lips curled into a smile of his own. "Whoa, the rah in you! Well, that there is some sugar sweet hospitality. That one of these days I'm gonna have too repay."

"Mutha fucka, you threating me?" Wind of the Gods's voice was a low growl.

"Wind of the Gods, no, let 'em go!" Bass said, stepping forward.

"Best listen to your friend, mister," Dick Glass said, a cold, menacing grin on his face. "This shit ain't worth 'passin on' for." He turned and walked out of the saloon, his two companions following behind him, leaving the stunned crowd in their wake.

A laughing Wind of the Gods turned to Bass. "See? Not much trouble at..."

One shot rang out, a sharp, deafening report that drowned out the music and the laughter. Wind of the Gods' chest exploded in a red blossom. He clutched his gushing wound, his eyes wide in disbelief.

"I may have misjudged this one," he whispered, a smile still on his lips as he fell backward, his body hitting the barroom floor with a sickening thud.

Bass was on his knees in an instant, cradling his friend's head in his lap, the warm blood soaking into his trousers. "Wind of the Gods! Wind! No, Wind! No! Just hang on! You're gonna be alright! Someone get a doctor! Hurry up!" he shouted, his voice a frantic plea.

"I don't think so, Bass," Wind of the Gods said, his voice a weak rasp. "This one don't feel so good, and I can see it, Bass."

Tears streamed down Bass's face as he held his friend close. "I'm gonna get that bastard, Wind of the Gods! I promise you that!"

"I know it, my young friend," Wind of the Gods said, his voice growing fainter. "Do me this. This is greater."

"What, Wind of the Gods? Whatever you want!" Bass cried, desperate for a final command.

"Walk as a man should walk. With righteousness and justice in all things. It's glory, Bass, I can see it coming for me. I am not afraid. Be justice, my friend. Be justice."

"Okay, Wind of the Gods. I will. Now you just shut up and hold on, and we will talk about it tomorrow."

Wind of the Gods smiled, a soft, ethereal look on his face. He drew silent, his eyes staring into the unseen.

"Oh, Wind... Wind of the Gods... Fuck, dude, don't die! I need you, Wind! Fight, god-dam it, fight!" Bass shook his friend's lifeless body, a heartbroken sigh escaping his lips.

The barmaid, her face stained with tears, came and knelt beside him. "I'm afraid he's gone, baby," she said softly.

Bass lifted his hands full of blood, his arms stretched out, his face pointing to the heavens, and a desperate plea on his lips. "All I want, Lord, is for you to put him in my sights. My gun is yours to wield. Protect and guide me, Lord, and bring to my feet of that dog. Ameen!"

Outside, in the shanty town, the night was cold and unforgiving. Bass, his body numb and his heart a raw a bleeding wound, walked out of the saloon. The air felt heavy, each breath a struggle. Just as he stepped out, Jennie and her father, Malikai, came running up, their faces a mix of concern and fear.

"Bass, oh Bass, are you okay?" Jennie asked, her voice a soft, worried melody.

"They killed Wind of the Gods, Jennie," Bass said, the words a hollow echo in the night.

Jennie ran into his arms, her embrace a warm, comforting solace that almost broke him. She squeezed him tightly, as if she had almost lost him, too. An older Black man, about five feet nine, with dusty clothes and a livery stable apron, ran in behind Jennie. It was her father, Malikai Johnson, a man with a rugged, bearded face.

"Now, son, I know we ain't met, but my daughter was just telling me about you. She seems to be quite taken by you," Malikai said, his voice a mix of a father's caution and a man's respect.

"Daddy!" Jennie protested, her face turning a deep crimson.

"Girl, if'n you're gonna be courtin' this gentleman, I need to know he ain't no murdering thug," Malikai said, his eyes serious as he looked at Bass.

"Daddy, he is Bass Reeves, a medal of honor nominated soldier who fought for the North at Missionary Ridge. He's a real war hero," Jennie said proudly, her arm still wrapped around Bass.

"Sir, I assure you that I am not a criminal, and I only have the highest regards for your daughter," Bass said, his voice firm, despite his grief.

"I don't think many would raise an eyebrow even if you did kill that murdering mix-breed son-of-a-whore," Malikai said, his eyes softening a little. "I do know, though, revenge can lead a good man or woman wrong."

"My friend was a defender of justice," Bass said, his voice full of resolve. "He was telling me about a Judge Parker, the Hangin' Judge, who is taking on deputies. I'ma hunt down this Dick Glass as an officer of justice. So, I'm heading out to Native Lands. If she would have me, I want to take your daughter as my wife. Set up roots up in Oklahoma."

Jennie looked at her father, her heart pounding. She nodded with a gentle smile, her eyes full of a love that was a balm to Bass's soul.

"Well, sir, knowing my little girl, there would be no stopping her once she is set for it," Malikai said, a hint of a smile touching his lips.

Bass walked over to where Wind of the Gods's body was, now covered up and being carried away. "Old friend, it has been my honor traveling with you. I swear to always place justice first." He turned to Lil 1. "Well, Lil 1, you ready to move on?"

"Well, sir, these people asked me to stay on with them," Lil 1 said, his voice small. "Mr. Johnson & Mrs. Johnson say they can't have kids and always wanted one. Mrs. is a school teacher, and I always wanted to learn to read. Excuse us, please." Lil 1 stepped away, his eyes full of a hopeful sorrow. "These folk seem like good folk, and if I stay with you, I can't never forget what happened. I don't never have to tell them, they never have to know. Maybe one day I'll forget."

The following morning, Bass and Jennie headed out toward Indian country. The sun was a cool, pale orb in the sky, and the air was crisp. As they came into a clearing, they settled in for night before that Texas night breeze cut through you, fully dressed, like you naked. They awoke to the sight of about twenty Comanche scouts. Some were sitting around the embers of a fire, warming their hands, while others admired the horses they had tied to a line between the wagon and a tree.

"Hey, hey, those horses don't belong to you! Step away!" Bass said, his hand slowly descending towards his gun.

Stands Tall, one of the scouts, a man of six feet one hundred ninety pounds with a muscular build, looked at Bass, his face a calm, stoic mask. "We are not raiders, kemo sa bi. We are Tribal police tracking criminals. We thought when we seen they're fire, but it was yours. We see your tracks and theirs crossed at a settlement of your people about one day's ride east."

"Yes, yes, Mr. uhm, these criminals... one of them named Dick Glass?" Bass asked, a surge of adrenaline coursing through him.

"I am Stands Tall of the Comanche Tribal police force. Yes, have you seen him? You, you know him, no?" Stands Tall asked, his eyes sharp and serious.

"Yes, I do know him. He killed my friend," Bass said, his voice tight with emotion.

"I am sorry for the loss of your friend," Stands Tall said, his words a quiet, respectful offering.

"No worries, Mr. Tall, but just how the hell did you sneak up on me like that?" Bass asked, his curiosity overriding his grief for a moment.

Laughter erupted from some of the tribal police officers. Stands Tall turned and looked at the laughing men, speaking to them in their native tongue, ordering them to get back on the trail and get a direction of the fugitive.

"Please, just Stand Tall," he said to Bass. "When hunting a snake, one might crawl."

"Makes a hella lot of sense, Mister," Bass said, shaking his head.

"I have learned that to defeat your enemy you must know his path and his tongue," Stands tall said, his gaze unwavering. "Mr. was learned to be a common title, and I am not common amongst the people of my nation. I am 'Stands Tall'."

Bass looked at the officer next to Stands Tall and said, "Jesus, Mary, and Joseph, is he always like that?"

The officer chuckled. "Ha. Every moon since our paths crossed."

"Mount up, men! We have criminals to catch!" Stands Tall commanded in his native language.

"Thank you, Stands Tall. Travel well, my friend," Bass said.

"Ft. Smith is just beyond the town of Greenwood, two moons' ride Northwest from here," Stands Tall said, his eyes now soft with a quiet wisdom.

"May you travel well, with the Wind of the Gods at your back and success in your path."

As the group rode off, Jennie appeared from under the wagon, dragging a Winchester repeater and smiling. "Well, Mr. Bass Reeves, let's get your average ass packed up and headed Northwest."

Bass charged her, tackling her to the ground, and they rolled back under the wagon, a moment of joy and passion amid the grief.

Coming into a clearing after crossing the Oklahoma state line appeared. The large African American settlement just outside of Fort Towson. Bass and Jennie entered Black Town!

Black Town was a vibrant city, a kaleidoscope of activity and commerce. The streets were filled with the murmur of a thriving community. African Americans, Choctaw, and Cherokees ran the shops, the bank, and pretty much everything in the area, including the whorehouse, which was located upstairs at the Rot Gut Saloon.

As Bass and Jennie passed by, their eyes scanning the lively scene, Jennie's gaze fell upon a woman in a window of the saloon. The woman, a hooker with a knowing smile, was staring Bass down in a way that left no room for interpretation. A sheepish grin spread across Bass's face, a silent enjoyment of the woman's bold appraisal. Jennie's hand clenched around the reins, her knuckles tightening.

"If I ever catch you, mister, I'll cut off all your workin' parts," Jennie said, her voice low and serious. "I swear unto those who gone on before you."

Bass's grin widened, a spark of mischief in his eyes. "Who said you gonna catch me?"

"Uh, hunh, keep thinking I'm playing," Jennie shot back, a warning in her tone.

"Now, you know I only got you in my heart," Bass said, his voice softening, the playful bravado giving way to earnestness. "I plan on being a good man, a man Wind of the Gods would be proud of." My father and Mr. Reeves, but most of all you.

Jennie scoffed, but a faint smile touched her lips. "It ain't your heart that I'm worried about, and stop blaming poor Wind of the Gods for everything."

A genuine, hearty laugh erupted from Bass, echoing in the bustling street. "Ha ha haha!"

The sound of a teenager's voice, a rhythmic chant, cut through the air, drawing the attention of the passersby. "Wanted dead or alive, Robert Burns, for the Robbery and murder of Tom Harding. $1500 dead or alive." The kid, a paper boy for the local gazette, moved quickly up the street. A stack of wanted posters in his hand, distributing them to the townsfolk.

Bass's laughter died down, replaced by a thoughtful silence as he watched the the lil one disappear. His eyes lingered on the poster, the words "dead or alive" and "$1500" seeming to jump out at him. "A man could do a lot with $1500," he mused, more to himself than to Jennie. "I mean, starting a new family and things."

Jennie's gaze remained fixed on the spot where the kid had vanished. "A $1500 a man could die tryin' to do that, too," she said, her voice flat, the playful banter gone.

They continued on in silence, the weight of Jennie's words hanging between them, the casual, easy atmosphere of their journey momentarily lost. They came upon the town center, a small square dominated by a wooden sign with black metal plates. The plates were inscribed with the words "Court House," "Land Patent," "Mayor's Office," and "city and county seat."

Jennie's voice broke the silence, softer this time. "What is our business here, honey?"

Bass's posture straightened, a renewed sense of purpose radiating from him. "Well, a man's gotta work to take care of his Angel." He gestured vaguely toward the sign. "I figure I'll get me one of these cotton suit and tie jobs. Make you a respectable woman of you."

Jennie stopped in her tracks, her hand coming to rest on her hip. A flicker of indignation crossed her face. "Bass, what makes you think I'm not already respectable?"

Bass paused, turning to face her, his hands coming to rest on her shoulders. "I'll be right back, my Queen, and upon my return, I shall adorn you with flowers and scented oils." His smile was wide and sincere, a promise of a future he was determined to build.

Jennie's expression softened, a mixture of exasperation and affection in her eyes. "Just hurry, please, and adorn me with a steak and potatoes," she said, her stomach rumbling audibly, a testament to their long journey.

Bass laughed again, a sound that was both a promise and a reassurance. He turned and walked toward the courthouse, a new resolve in his step, leaving Jennie in the town square, her hunger and her love for him vying for attention.

In the cool shade of the judge's office, Bass stood before a woman he assumed to be in charge. She was Mary, a kind face with sharp, discerning eyes.

"Ma'am, I just arrived here in town and was lookin' for work," Bass began, his voice a smooth baritone. "My friend, Wind of the Gods, said you all were hiring for Deputy Marshalls. I just retired from the Army and was looking for something a little quiet, you know?"

Mary's gaze softened, a hint of a smile playing on her lips. "Well, mister, ain't much of that going on 'round here in the way of jobs. Unlessin you good with a gun." She paused, her smile widening slightly. "Did you say Wind of the Gods?"

"Yes, ma'am, I did say Wind of the Gods," Bass confirmed, a sense of pride in his voice.

Mary turned to a young man standing nearby. "Pete! Go fetch the Judge from the Saloon." She looked back at Bass. "My husband, Judge Isaac Parker, is going to want to talk to you."

Bass hesitated for a moment, the thought of a quiet life still at the forefront of his mind. "Yes, ma'am, and I can shoot a little, but I was really lookin' for something a little more quiet," he reiterated. "Maybe inscribing, accounting, or even translating."

From behind him, a deep laugh boomed, followed by a chorus of chortles. "They could always use a shine over at the Broadway," a voice jeered, "that oughta be mighty quiet for your type of man."

More laughter followed from the two men, their contempt as thick as the dust on the street.

"Don't you pay them boys no never mind," Mary said, a flicker of anger in her eyes. "They call they selves Marshalls, but they're more like bounty hunters. None of the men in their custody ever seems to make it to justice."

One of the men, a slick-looking character named James, tipped his hat with a wide, arrogant smile and placed a toothpick in his mouth. Bass ignored him, turning back to Mary with a determined look.

"Ma'am, where is the land office?" he asked. "I plan to settle here with my wife, who's down in the wagon waiting for me to bring her some good news."

James scoffed, his voice dripping with condescension. "Tommy boy, would you look at the woo in that pudding down there? Now what's a fine bitch like that doing with a soft shoe like him? Hell, I got some good news for her. Tell her James likes her."

Before the words had fully left his mouth, Bass had moved. With a swift outside crescent kick, he dropped James to the floor. The other man, Thomas, went for his gun, but before his hand could close around the hilt, Bass had his Colt 45 revolver out, the working end resting squarely on Thomas's nose, bobbing it back and forth.

"If you wanna keep that, I suggest it mind its own business," Bass said, his voice calm and dangerously low. "How about we take this outside, boys? Address the issue of respect!"

He reached down, taking Thomas's pistol before stepping over to the slowly rising James Fisher and relieving him of his weapon as well. He then walked over to Mary and handed her both of the men's guns, along with two of his own.

"Come on, boys," Bass said, a glint in his eye. Holding up his fist, he says. "Now, boys, these are called the hard lessons."

James, now on his feet, glared at Bass. "Both of us?"

"Well, if that's the hoe that's shaken, let's get her shook," Bass replied.

"Nigga, you 'bout to get yo ass stomped," Thomas snarled, his hand now empty but his knuckles clenched.

The fight spilled out behind the judge's office, Bass bursting through the door with his two would-be assailants chattering behind him, game planning their attack.

"We know you boys bought yo mouth," Bass called out, his voice echoing in the dusty clearing. "Now bring yo ass."

James moved in fast, a quick overhead left. But Bass ducked and pivoted, stepping forward with his right leg and delivering a powerful overhead punch to Thomas's chin, knocking him instantly backward three or four feet. As James attempted a sneak attack from Bass's side, Bass ducked under the right hook, dipping under the punch and planting his shoulder in James's ribcage. He lifted the man and drove him hard into the dusty road.

Rolling over onto James, Bass kicked Thomas in both knees before flipping up and charging him. Stopping a few feet in front of the man, Bass jumped, his right leg extended, his foot landing squarely on Thomas's chin. The man dropped into an immediate snore, a cloud of dust puffing up around him.

As Bass turned, he saw James throwing a vicious right hook. Stepping sideways, he grabbed the extended arm, pulling James close before kneeing him in the ribcage. He twisted and delivered a downward left directly behind the lawman's ear, sprawling the big man out. James also began to snore, contributing to the cloud of dust.

"Well, what do you know, twins!" Bass said, a hint of a smile on his face. He turned and saw Jennie approaching, a shotgun in her hand. "No need for that, honey bugga."

"I see," Jennie said, her expression a mix of awe and exasperation. She disappeared back to the front where the wagon was parked, Bass in tow.

"What the hell was all this about, husband?" Jennie demanded. "I mean, you come to get a job, and end up in a brawl. What in the world is going on with you, Bass Reeves? Should I be reconsidering this marriage?"

"Well, uhm, no, baby, come on, nothing so drastic," Bass stammered, his bravado gone. "This ain't a really big deal. Just boys being boys stuff."

"And all of you are older, professional gentlemen," Jennie said, shaking her head. "Very unflattering."

A deep voice cut through the air, and they turned to see Judge Isaac Parker standing in the doorway of the courthouse. He was a average man in his mid-50s, wearing a black suit with a slim black tie. He wasn't balding and wore glasses.

"Well, that there was a fancy bit of tussling," the Judge said, a faint smile on his face. "My man, Wind of the Gods, used to throw his feet and hands like that, too. Said he learned it from a Qing (Chin) dynasty Chinamen in North Africa. Crazy how small the world is sometimes."

Mary and the Judge cast a smile as Jennie let out a little giggle and sat down on the buckboard.

"Well, your honor, it can get smaller," Bass said, the light returning to his eyes. "Wind of the Gods is dead. He was shot in the back by a hombre named Dick Glass last Spring over in an Arkansas Black Town, west of Lil Rock."

The Judge's smile faded, replaced by a grave expression. "A child, sir? Did he have a child with him?"

Bass shook his head slowly. "No, sir, I am afraid not, and Beetle Bug, correct, sir."

"Yes, yes, that's him," the Judge murmured, a somber note in his voice. "I am sorry, but our friend Lil 1 witnessed his death."

A heavy silence fell over the small group as they processed the news. The Judge cleared his throat, returning to the matter at hand. "I will want to question you about all that officially a little later," he said. "So, you're looking for work, right? Where did you learn how to fight like that?"

Bass looked at his hands, his knuckles still stinging. "Home," he said, the word holding a world of memories. "I learned to fight from a slave and my Dad on the plantation I was born on. We'd leave Arkansas after harvest season and go to Grayson County, Texas, and plant. I grew up shooting, and I won contests at the

County fair for my shooting abilities. I trained in martial arts, and my mother taught me to read. She also taught me how to speak several different languages."

The Judge's eyes widened in surprise and admiration. "Well, the Marshalls office could use a gentleman like yourself. Catching some of these low-life degenerates that seem to plague our beloved Western parts of the country. You say you speak injun?"

Jennie, who had been listening intently, interjected with a playful smirk. "Not only speaks it, but he married it, too. Bass, honey, we've got to be moving along and find us a settling place."

"I'm not gonna let you stay at a hotel, no ma'am," the Judge said, his voice brimming with a newfound generosity. "I got a piece of land in the north hills that must be the most loveliest place on earth. A shade tree covering the back porch, a hop, skip, and a jump from the grandest lake in the county."

Jennie's skepticism was evident in her raised eyebrow. "Being that it's so lovely and all, why isn't someone living there?"

"Excuse my wife, Judge," Bass said, with an amused glance at Jennie. "She ain't never been from home this long."

"You ain't known me long enough to know where I been," Jennie retorted, rising from the buckboard and giving a slight bow to the Judge. "Now, sir, about this home."

The Judge chuckled, finding Jennie's spirited nature charming. "That being the case, I live across the lake, ma'am, in the second home I built for my lovely Mary here. With my own two hands. And it is available to my Deputy Marshall." He paused, his gaze fixed on Bass. "Now, if you'd be so kind as to come out and take a look at it."

"We would be more than honored, sir," Jennie said, her tone softening considerably.

"We would be proud, sir, to look at your property," Bass chimed in, "and then make a decision. If that's okay with you and my world-traveled wife?"

"Well, it's fine with me, Bass!" Jennie exclaimed, her eyes sparkling.

Mary, standing beside her husband, offered a warm smile. "Good then, that's settled. It's about two miles north of town, about 300 yards to your right when you clear the forest. We'll have supper ready for you. You must be powerful hungry after your travels, and we can hear about them travels of yours."

"That's a grand idea, Mary," the Judge said. "And perhaps I can convince our friend Bass here to become more than just a tenant."

"That sounds fine, ma'am, and we would be honored," Bass said, his voice full of gratitude.

"Yes, ma'am, sir, we would be more than honored," Jennie agreed.

Just then, James and Thomas emerged from the courthouse, dusting themselves off and holding their aching faces and bodies. They assisted each other in steadying their balance.

"Whew!" James groaned. "I ain't never had my butt kicked so hard and so fast in all my life."

"Mr., what the hell kinda fighting was that?" Thomas asked, a mix of pain and curiosity in his voice.

"Perhaps, I could teach you boys, but later, okay?" Bass said with a knowing smirk.

Both men began to walk back into the building, murmuring, "Oh, yes, yes, sir, we'd like that, sir."

"We will be seeing you folks around sundown," Bass called out to the Judge and Mary.

"Oh yes, that's fine," the Judge replied.

"That's perfect," Mary added, "at the regular supper time."

"We'll see you lovely folks then," Jennie said with a wave.

Bass smacked the reins on the buttocks of the mules, a sound that sent the team forward. "Hi ho there, hi ho!" he exclaimed.

"Hi ho, there, hi ho," Jennie mocked playfully. "That military stuff. Say giddy up or something."

The wagon rumbled along the dusty road as the sun began its descent, painting the sky in fiery hues of orange and purple. Coming through a break in the forest, a breathtaking sight awaited them. Off in the distance, a homestead lay nestled against the backdrop of the setting sun. A big house and a barn sat about 50 yards apart, a white picket fence running the entire length from the barn to around the house. The setting sun reflected off the water of a grand lake, giving the appearance of two earths, one in the sky and one in the water below.

"Oh, Bass, it's absolutely gorgeous," Jennie whispered, her voice filled with awe.

"I was just thinking the same thing," Bass replied, his heart swelling with pride.

"Hurry, honey, I wanna see the inside," she urged.

As they pulled the wagon up to the house, the door to the lakeside cottage swung open. There stood Mary, the Judge, and a young man no more than 14 years old. Isaac Parker Jr. looked just like his father, a child version with the same serious eyes.

"Isaac, take the wagon and set it next to the barn," the Judge commanded. "Then put a handful of alfalfa down for the beast."

"Yes, sir, Judge!" Isaac replied with a crisp salute.

"Then get yourself cleaned up for dinner," the Judge added.

"Right away, Judge."

"I believe I'll give him a hand," Bass said, stepping down from the wagon. "That drive mule can be a handful sometimes."

"You boys hurry up now," the Judge said with a grin. "I done worked myself up an appetite today, and my Mary is a powerful good cook."

"I knew there was a reason you kept me 'round," Mary said, a playful jab in her tone.

"Yes, ma'am," the Judge replied, his eyes twinkling.

Bass walked next to Isaac as the boy pulled the team toward the stable. "Isaac, how's the fishin' back there in that lake?" Bass asked.

"Shoot, just last week I pulled one outta there big as this here arm," Isaac said, holding his arm up for emphasis. "The Judge made me throw him back in, though. He said he wasn't gonna condemn this one. Heck, weren't gonna eat it anyway, him being allergic and all."

"Isn't the Judge your father? Why do you call him Judge and not Pa or something?" Bass inquired gently.

"Mary calls him Judge, and I think it's fun," Isaac explained. "See, Mary ain't my real Ma. My real Ma was killed when I was a baby. The Judge says traveling out here, some bandits came up on 'em to rob them, and Momma didn't wanna give up her wedding ring. It was a gift from my grandmother and her grand mamma's momma going back a ways. That's when my Pa settled out here and became 'The Hanging Judge,' Isaac Parker." The boy's voice softened with a hint of reverence. "So, Judge just fits, I guess."

"We'd better get on in before the food is all ate up," Bass said, changing the subject with a warm smile. "That Jennie of mine is a little thang, but that gal can put it away."

A moment later, laughter filled the air as they ran up to the door. Isaac Jr. burst through first. "I hope there's something left, Mr. Reeves says that Jennie may be little, but she can sure put it away."

"Kids these days and their imaginations," Bass said, feigning a huff.

"Um, hunh!" Jennie chimed in, a mouthful of something delicious already in her cheeks.

"What you think, darling?" Mary asked.

"Oh, Bass, the back bedroom is huge and open to a back porch with a perfect view of the Lake," Jennie gushed. "And, there's an indoor toilet!"

"An indoor toilet?" Bass asked, his brow furrowed in disbelief.

"Yes, I had that put in after the wife seen one of the New York City home gazette magazines," the Judge explained proudly. "Sent away for the design and had McGregor, the Goat..."

"Judge Parker, don't you say that?" Mary interjected, her eyes narrowing.

"Well, the man is mighty handy with building tools, and has a peculiar fascination with goats," the Judge continued, undeterred. "Came over from Ireland, worked himself out of slavery, came West, and he owns and runs a saloon in town there, too."

"Brothel more like it, Judge," Mary huffed. She turned to Isaac. "You go on ahead, pull up the wagon, we gotta get you home, washed up and ready for bed. You got school first thing."

"Yes, ma'am," Isaac replied.

The Judge turned his attention back to Bass. "Bass, what do you think of the place?"

"Judge, it is a nice piece of land, but I'm not quite sure I can afford it," Bass admitted, his gaze sweeping over the beautiful home and grounds.

"Hmm, well now, I been talking this over with the wife," the Judge said, his voice dropping to a conspiratorial whisper. "How you handled yourself with my two, mind you, two best Marshalls, and the fact that you speak injun - the natives' tongue - a military veteran and all..."

"Oh, dang it, Judge!" Mary interrupted, her patience wearing thin. "Bass, it's yours as long as you take and keep the job as Deputy Marshall. Plus you get all you captures bounties."

Bass looked at Jennie, his expression a mix of surprise and uncertainty. "Well, honey, what you think?"

"Take it, baby!" Jennie said, her eyes shining with excitement.

"I thought the job was too dangerous," Bass said, a small grin on his face.

"The offer didn't have this gorgeous house attached to it then, and I knew you were going to be a lawmen." Jennie said with a mischievous smile. She turned to Mary. "Mary, let's go flush that toilet again!"

Bass chuckled, shaking his head. He looked at the Judge, extending his hand. "It looks like you have yourself a new Marshall."

"Tomorrow, first light, Bass, at the court house, so your new brothers can show you the ropes," the Judge said, shaking his hand firmly.

The Train Robbery

The train was a rhythmic beast of iron and steam, a tireless pulse of life huffing & puffing its way toward Oklahoma. It consisted of a single engine, two passenger cars, and the caboose at the very end. Inside the caboose, four Texas Rangers were on security detail, their presence a silent, but firm, promise of protection. The air was thick with the smell of coal smoke and stale coffee, the low rumble of the wheels on the tracks a constant, hypnotic drone.

One of the Rangers, a lanky man with a wide mustache, stretched and stood from his seat. "I'm going to the front," he announced, his voice muffled by the clatter of the train. "Gonna find the engineer, see our ETA to Ft.

Towson, maybe toss some more coals in the stove and get us moving. I gotta sweet little thing waiting on me when we pull in!"

His companion, a stockier Ranger with a mischievous glint in his eye, chuckled. "You're just trying to get a look at that filly in the second car, 'cause what you got waiting on you ain't sweet, and who's gonna whoop yo' ass when I tell her? You've been googling after that filly up front."

Laughter erupted from the other two Rangers, a brief moment of camaraderie in the confines of the train car. The first Ranger shook his head, a grin on his face, and walked through the caboose door, disappearing into the narrow passage between the cars. The clatter of his boots faded into the background noise, a tiny sound swallowed by the great iron beast.

Meanwhile, on a hill overlooking the tracks, three figures lay low, their heads just peeking over the crest. Dave Cantrell, Dick Glass, and another man known only as Razor watched the train. Cantrell was prone behind a 1874 Sharps rifle, the long barrel pointed at a seemingly insignificant target. A tap on his shoulder was all the signal he needed. The rifle immediately cracked and jumped in his grasp, its report a sharp, violent sound that cut through the still air. Down the tracks, the telegraph wire running alongside the railway on wooden poles snapped, its severed ends limply falling away from the pole. Dick Glass grabbed a small mirror, a glint of reflected sunlight flashing toward a figure about 150 yards in front of the train, a silent command passed across the distance.

Inside the train, the rhythmic rumble was suddenly replaced by a violent, jarring lurch. The passengers were slammed violently forward as the engineer slammed on the brakes. Ahead, a strange, twisted sculpture of train rail shot straight up from the ground. As the dust cleared and the train screeched to a halt just feet from certain derailment, a group of eight horsemen lurched into action from behind the rocks. Four on each side, they began firing heavily into the caboose, their gunfire a deafening roar.

Inside the small caboose, wood splintered and glass shattered all around the three remaining Texas Rangers. They hopelessly reached for their weapons, a futile, desperate gesture. The bullets tore through their bodies, a brutal and unforgiving storm of lead. They slumped into lifeless, sprawled heaps, their final breath a silent gasp in the midst of chaos.

The dust began to settle as Dick Glass, Cantrell, and Razor approached the train on horseback. One of the other bandits, hanging off the back rail of the caboose, held up three fingers, a silent signal. Looking at each other, they nodded, flashing the number three with their own fingers.

Cantrell looked at Dick Glass, a confused frown on his face. "What is the fingers thing?"

"White man, there is supposed to be four Texas Rangers, and only three were in the caboose," Dick Glass said, his voice a low, gravelly rumble. He dismounted, a cruel smile on his face. "Sooo, it looks like my favorite childhood game is in play."

Cantrell dismounted as well, his boots crunching on the gravel. "And what to beat all hell is that?"

"Why, Hide-N-Go Seek, sir," Dick Glass said, the smile widening into a sinister grin. "Ha ha ha."

Inside the passenger car, terror reigned. Women clutched their children, men whispered prayers, and the air was thick with the scent of fear. Razor, a tall, imposing Native American dressed in a surprisingly well-tailored suit with a thin tie, burst through the door, his eyes wide with a cold fury.

"This is a hold up!" he screamed, his voice a raw, animalistic sound. "Don't get in our way, and you'll live.

Shut up bitch, with all that noise!" He fired a shot into the ceiling, the sound deafening in the enclosed space. "Fuck me! I just said don't get in our way, and you will live."

Cantrell stepped into the car, his movements calm and deliberate, a chilling contrast to Razor's frenzy. He scanned the terrified faces until his eyes landed on a man sitting in the third seat from the right. A small, almost imperceptible smirk touched his lips.

"Third seat from the right," he said, his voice a low drawl.

Dick Glass entered, his presence filling the aisle with a menacing aura. He followed Cantrell's gaze. "Yep, good eye for a white man, my friend."

Cantrell didn't break his stare from the man. "What the hell are you anyway? Injun or nig-rah?"

Dick Glass threw his head back and laughed. "Ninjun," he corrected with a theatrical flourish. "Well, hello there, Texas Ranger."

Both men walked slowly down the aisle, pretending not to notice the Texas Ranger. They moved past him, their backs to him, and then, in a smooth, practiced motion, spun around. Dick Glass slowly slid the pistol from his holster and rested the working end under the Texas Ranger's hat.

The Ranger's body was rigid, his eyes wide with a mixture of terror and resignation. "Sir, I have three children," he said, his voice barely a whisper. "Dying was not a part of my deal."

"Boy, you should have been a postman," Cantrell scoffed, a sneer on his face.

Dick Glass's face was devoid of emotion. "Jimmy Jam, take this piece of shit outside." He looked down the aisle, a wicked gleam in his eye. "Now on to what we came here for. Here, Wells Fargo man, here, Wells Fargo man. Olly olly oxen free."

Cantrell took a step forward, his hand resting on his gun. "We know you're on here, boy. Come on, step up, and maybe you go home tonight after this here robbery."

The passengers were silent, their fear a palpable thing. The Wells Fargo man remained hidden, but Dick Glass's voice was like a predator's, coaxing its prey from the shadows.

"Last chance, mister, with the out-east tumbler on," Dick Glass said. "Sitting next to a little girl who I'm sure he doesn't wanna see hurt."

Razor, standing behind Cantrell and Dick Glass, looked confused. "What the hell is a tumbler?"

A voice, defiant and clear, cut through the tense silence. "A hat, you savage!"

The Wells Fargo man emerged from the third seat, his hand already on the butt of a Colt 45 he drew from a side holster. He fired, the bullet piercing a henchman behind Dick Glass. But the Henchman's death was in vain. In a fluid motion, Dick Glass drew his own pistol and fired, hitting the Wells Fargo man dead center in the head. The force of the shot knocked him backward, his lifeless body falling onto a young girl with a ponytail, blonde hair, and icy gray eyes.

The girl screamed, a piercing sound of pure, unadulterated grief. "Daddy, no! Not Daddy!"

Dick Glass didn't even flinch. He walked over to the man's lifeless body, retrieving a small black pouch filled with diamonds. "Bingo, boys!" he exclaimed, holding it up. "These small pieces of glass are worth more than gold."

The girl, her face streaked with tears and a horrifying mixture of her father's blood, looked up at him. Her youthful features twisted in a mask of pure hate. "You nigger sav!" she screamed, the word an ugly, guttural sound.

Before she could finish, before the word could even fully escape her lips, Dick Glass spun and fired. The bullet went through her head, exploding it on the passengers behind her. The train car fell into a stunned, horrified silence.

Cantrell looked at Dick Glass, his face pale with a shock he rarely showed. "What the fuck!"

Dick Glass looked down at the girl's body, his expression one of bored dismissal. "She would've grown up to be a whore anyway without a Daddy," he said, and turned to walk toward the next car. Laughter, cold and high-pitched, erupted from both Razor and Glass as they moved through the silent, terrified passengers. The sound was an alien thing in the enclosed space, a mocking celebration of the bloodshed they had just unleashed.

They left the train car, their boots crunching on the gravel as they rejoined their mounted accomplices. The air was thick with dust and the lingering scent of gunpowder. They didn't look back at the train, a hulking monument of terror left in their wake. Their laughter, now a ragged, joyous thing, echoed across the open land as they spurred their horses on.

Behind them, the sounds of the passengers finally broke free. The car filled with a chorus of screams, wails, and the desperate cries of the injured and the bereaved. Women clutched children, rocking them in their arms as if to shield them from the horror they had just witnessed. A man knelt beside the girl, his shoulders shaking with silent sobs. The air, which moments ago had been filled with a palpable fear, was now choked with grief.

Razor and Glass, oblivious to the chaos and sorrow, rode off over the ridge, their laughter carried on the wind. The sun, a blood-red orb sinking below the horizon, cast long, distorted shadows behind them, making them appear as monstrous figures riding into the twilight. They were gone as quickly as they had arrived, leaving behind a trail of death and a memory that would forever haunt the survivors of the train.

Their laughter, a cruel melody in the vast emptiness of the prairie, was the last thing the passengers heard. It was a sound that told them, with grim certainty, that in this part of the world, justice was a foreign concept, and some men were more beast than human. They were nothing more than a fleeting shadow, and now they were gone, leaving only the wreckage behind.

Justice on the Trail

The late afternoon sun cast long shadows across the dusty ground behind the courthouse, a fitting stage for the quiet drama unfolding between Bass and the two men, James and Thomas. The air was thick with a palpable tension, the kind that precedes a storm, as James's voice, laced with a mix of arrogance and a desperate need to assert dominance, sliced through the stillness.

"Come on down, Bass," he challenged, the words hanging in the air like a gauntlet thrown. "We know you can fight, but can you shoot?"

Bass remained silent, a stillness settling over him that was more intimidating than any show of aggression. His horse, Silver, a magnificent creature of muscle and grace, seemed to sense the shift in his rider's mood. Without dismounting, Bass's hand moved with a fluid, practiced motion. He drew his Remington repeater, the cold steel a familiar weight in his hands. It was an extension of himself, a tool honed by years of use. He didn't need to get off his horse to prove his point. A gentle squeeze of his ribs was all the command Silver needed. The horse darted forward, a powerful surge of energy, and in that fleeting moment, three rounds cracked off from the Remington. The sound was sharp, a punctuation mark in the heavy silence. Silver raised up while three more bursts erupted from the Remington. Just as quickly, Bass squeezed his ribs again, and Silver halted, pulling back to their original position as if they had never moved.

As Bass dismounted, his movements were deliberate and unhurried. He swung a leg over the saddle, the leather creaking softly, and began to walk towards the courthouse's rear entrance. He paused at the threshold, a slow, knowing grin spreading across his face as he turned to look at James and Thomas. "Hope that this satisfies you boys' curiosity," he said, his voice a low rumble.

James, still reeling from the unexpected display, scoffed, his pride bruised and his voice rising in frustration. "The hell you say! This is a professional job, boy. You need to be prepared the proper way, you damn yahoo! You gonna get yourself killed. Get your ass back here!" He couldn't comprehend the effortless precision he had just witnessed.

But Thomas, his eyes wide with a mix of awe and terror, wasn't listening to James's bluster. He grabbed his friend's arm, his voice a frantic, desperate whisper. "James, James! Look!"

James, still focused on his tirade, muttered, "He gotta take this part way more serious."

"JAMES, James, take a look!" Thomas insisted, his voice cracking with urgency as he shoved a pair of long glasses into his hands.

With a look of annoyed impatience, James raised the binoculars to his eyes. His gaze fell upon the two targets, and his world seemed to tilt on its axis. His jaw went slack, the words of bravado dying in his throat. The first target had three perfect holes in the center of its forehead, while at full gallop, a testament to a steady hand. The second target, though, Silver had raised up when he fired. That one was even more impossible. Three holes, all dead center, a feat of marksmanship that defied belief.

"What in the fuck!" James whispered, a mix of disbelief and grudging respect.

"The first one," Thomas said, his voice hushed with reverence. "But the second... He was at full horse in the freakin air whinnying, both hands on the rifle."

"Son of a bitch!" James breathed out, the words a bitter admission of defeat.

As they stood there, dumbstruck by the sheer audacity and skill of the feat, Bass stood in the doorway, his grin a silent, triumphant answer. It was a grin as wide and boundless as the Oklahoma range itself. The moment of quiet victory, however, was shattered by the frantic sound of a galloping horse. Pete, a young man from Black Town, seemed like everybody had one rode up his face, a mask of fear and urgency.

"Dick Glass just robbed the noon train," Pete gasped, his words tumbling over each other in a rush. "And it's bad, boys, it's real bad."

The bravado drained from James's face, replaced by a grim, sobering reality. "Slow down, son," he said, his voice now calm and grave. "Come on in and tell us what happened." The competition was over, but a far more dangerous game had just begun.

The air in the Judge's office was heavy with the silence that followed Pete's breathless report. Dust motes danced in the slivers of sunlight that cut through the tall, crystal clear windows, illuminating the dancing dust particles and the intense look on Judge Parker's face. The boy, Pete, stood trembling before them, his voice raw with the horror he had just described.

"Down at junction springs," Pete repeated, his voice barely a whisper now, the initial frantic energy spent. "Dick Glass and Cantrell robbed the noon train. Killed all the Texas Rangers but one, and two civilians. One of 'em a fourteen-year-old girl. Killed her daddy first, right in front of her, then killed her 'cause she called him a n****r savage."

A cold, heavy weight settled in the room. The Judge, a man who had seen his share of depravity, closed his eyes for a moment, a muscle in his jaw twitching. This was more than just a robbery; it was a testament to a cruelty so profound it defied understanding.

"You boys ride out and take a look," the Judge said, his voice a low, gravelly command. "Get me some witness statements. Something I can use in a Court of Law. Official body count, damage caused to the railway, and said property."

His words were practical, a legal man's response to an unspeakable crime. But Bass Reeves couldn't hear the practicality. He only heard the name that had haunted his dreams, the one that had stolen his friend. His hand, unbidden, moved to the butt of his pistol, a familiar source of comfort and purpose. His gaze, sharp as a hawk's, was fixed on the Judge.

"I want this one, Judge," Bass said, his voice low and dangerous, a coiled rattler ready to spring. "That beast killed my good friend Wind of the Gods."

The air crackled with a new tension. The Judge sighed, the sound a weary rasp. He had known this was coming. He admired Bass's loyalty, but this was a case that required a clear head, not one clouded by vengeance.

"Now, Bass," the Judge began, his tone a careful balance of sympathy and authority. "I'm sorry about your friend, but I want my more experienced marshals on this one. I got a ton of warrants you can start on. Don't get me wrong, these warrants are important, also."

But Bass was not to be placated. He took a step forward, his eyes burning with a personal fire. "I hear ya, Judge, but this is personal for me."

The Judge met his stare, his expression unyielding. "And that's why I'm giving this to James and Thomas."

A smug, satisfied smirk spread across James's face. He clapped Thomas on the back, a gleeful victory in his eyes. "Next time, rookie!" he jeered, unable to resist a final jab. "Come on, Thomas, let's get out there."

As the two men left, the door swinging shut behind them, a heavy quiet settled over the office. Bass's shoulders slumped slightly in defeat, but only for a moment. The Judge watched him, a hint of a smile playing on his lips. He knew Bass was not a man to be defeated, only redirected for a time.

"I got a job for you, Bass, one that needs some skill them boys just ain't got, hear me!" His voice dropped to a conspiratorial whisper. "Nobody knows where the boys go during the day. We've heard that they come home every night after it gets dark to get supper."

A slow, determined grin spread across Bass's face, replacing the earlier frustration. A fire still burned in his eyes, but it was a calculating one now, a hunter's gaze.

"Well, well," Bass mused, his mind already spinning with possibilities. "I think I got a trick for that. Sometimes, to catch a snake, you might need to crawl."

The evening air hung heavy as Bass rode up to Margaret's house. A lone weathered structure silhouetted against the fading light. He dismounted quietly, the familiar creak of saddle leather a stark contrast to the silence of the woods. This was the place. The final piece of the puzzle, Judge Parker had given him.

He took a moment to transform himself. From a leather bag, he pulled out a disguise. A battered hat with holes in the brim, a tattered, worn-out jacket, and a pair of old, scuffed boots. He pulled them on, feeling the rough fabric and worn soles. This wasn't about looking like a marshal; it was about looking like a man down on his luck, a wanderer seeking refuge. He took a deep breath, the persona settling over him like a second skin.

He patted Silver's neck, a silent farewell. "Go on, boy," he whispered, "I'll be fine." Silver, a creature of deep intelligence and loyalty, trotted off into the darkness, leaving Bass alone to face the night.

He approached the front door, the porch groaning softly under his weight. He knocked lightly, a tentative rhythm that was more of a plea than a demand. "Hello! Hello! Anybody there, anybody home?" he called out, his voice slightly hoarse and weary, carefully crafted to convey exhaustion.

A gruff, suspicious voice from within cut through the quiet. "Who the hell is it?"

"Ma'am, can I trouble you for some water and grub?" Bass replied, his tone humble and respectful. "I'm powerful thirsty. I'll pay." He could feel the eyes of an unseen person on him through a crack in the door, studying his every move, his every gesture.

The response came back, colder and more menacing this time. "Mister, I got an eight-gauge loaded with double-aught soaked in skunk piss, and I swear in the name of Jesus. I'll cut you in half if you're playing any games." The threat was not just in the words, but in the low, steady confidence of her tone. It was a voice that had seen a lot and trusted little.

"No, ma'am, no games, in the name of Jesus," Bass assured her, his voice unwavering despite the chilling threat. "I'll pay you for your time."

A tense moment of silence passed, stretching out as if the woman inside were weighing his words against her instincts. Finally, with a slow, deliberate sound, the door began to creak open. First, the dark barrel of a shotgun emerged, a weapon of serious and immediate consequence. It pointed directly at his chest, unwavering. The door opened a little more, revealing a thin sliver of a woman's face. Her eyes were sharp and wary, like a hawk's.

"Unbuckle that there gun belt, and come on in, son," she instructed, her voice softening just enough to imply a reluctant welcome. She hadn't seen through his disguise, and was willing to grant him a chance.

"Yes, ma'am," Bass said, relief flooding him as he slowly unbuckled his gun belt, letting it slide to the ground. He had crossed the threshold. The hunt for the "boys" had officially begun.

Inside, Bass was greeted by Margaret Johnson, a woman whose rugged appearance, a plaid blouse, a long skirt, and a wad of chewing tobacco in her cheek, spoke of a life lived on her own terms. She offered him a plate of buffalo meat and a place to rest.

Bass's answers to her questions were evasive, designed to fuel her suspicions without giving anything away. When she asked if he was on the run from the law, he feigned shock. "I ain't no criminal," he insisted, all while his eyes darted to the doors and windows, the instincts of a lawman kicking in despite his carefully crafted disguise.

His story of a train robbery and fear of the law seemed to resonate with Margaret. She revealed that she had two sons who were on the run from Judge Parker. She revealed he's the man whose "made a career in politics on tryin to hang my boys." She confessed that she helped them evade the law, a mother's loyalty triumphing over any sense of right and wrong.

Bass saw his opportunity and seized it. He spoke of his hatred for Judge Parker, planting a seed of common ground. "What if we just killed that son-of-a-bitch before he gets a chance to get his hands on 'em?" he suggested, a dangerous glint in his eyes.

Margaret's face lit up with approval. "Hell, boy," she said, "I think you and my boys will be a fine group of business partners."

The moment was perfect. Just as she finished her sentence, a loud knock echoed through the house. "It's open, boys! We got company, don't shoot him now, he's a worker."

Two men, Bart and Matthew, stumbled through the door, their clothes torn and their faces smudged with dirt. Their eyes, bleary from exhaustion, landed on Bass. Bart, the older brother, challenged Bass, but Bass, ever the trickster, introduced himself as "Black Mamba." Matthew, confused by the name, scoffed. "Now, why would anybody call a man a Black Momma? That's damn rude."

Bass patiently explained that a mamba was a deadly snake from Africa. The two brothers, unimpressed, were soon put in their place when Bass revealed his true identity. "How 'bout Bass Reeves, U.S. Marshal out of Hanging Judge Isaac Parker's Court?" As he drew two Colt 44 magnums from his back. " You boys are under arrest."

The scene erupted into chaos. Margaret, shocked and betrayed, screamed at Bass, "You son-of-a-bitch! You're a lawman?" Bart and Matthew, equally stunned, were suddenly in handcuffs. Their pleas to leave their mother out of it were met with a firm order from Bass. "Outside, boys!, and ma'am if'n you move on that shotgun. These boys are going to miss your funeral."

As soon as the prisoners stepped onto the porch, Bass let out a sharp, piercing whistle.

From the tree line, a shimmering gray horse galloped out of the woods and up to the house. It was Silver, a beacon of loyalty and a silent accomplice in Bass's deception. He mounted the horse, a determined expression on his face.

The two brothers, Bart and Matthew, were now roped together, their hands tied behind their backs, their faces a mix of confusion and indignation.

Bass, with the two brothers in tow, now has to contend with a combative parent. Who is now following on foot, screaming and cussing every word known and unknown to man or monkey.

Their procession was a chaotic one, punctuated by the relentless screams and curses from Margaret, who followed them every step of the way. She was furious, her voice raw with a mother's fury and a deeper sense of betrayal.

They finally arrived at the jail, dusty and exhausted. Judge Parker stood on the porch, a knowing smile on his face. "I see you got the brothers in tow there," he said, a note of amusement in his voice.

"Yep," Bass replied, the weariness in his voice replaced by a dry wit. "And that sweetheart of a mother they got here, too. She just had to come along."

Bart, ever the hothead, flared up at the slight. "You watch your mouth! That's my mother you're talking about, nigger."

"Well, I guess you told me," Bass said, a lazy grin spreading across his face.

Matthew, who was still trying to wrap his head around the events, piped up. "Black Momma, I still can't believe you're a goddamn lawman."

Bass's patience had worn thin. "Black Mamba! Black Mamba, you dumb bastard!" he snapped, his voice sharp and final.

Margaret, despite her fury at Bass, rose to her son's defense. "He ain't no bastard! That boy has a daddy!"

"Oh, yeah. What's his name?"

The Judge, seeing that the situation was devolving, stepped in. "Whoa, I can see you've been having fun." He motioned for them to continue inside. "Go on, get 'em in jail. Ma'am, visitation is in the evenings. You can come back then and bring them food and clothes. Just don't bake no cakes, Margaret."

Tears streamed down Margaret's face as she watched her sons being led away. "Don't you hang my boys, Judge! Please, Judge, don't you hang my babies!" she pleaded, her voice breaking.

"Now, Margaret, you just go on home," the Judge said, his voice firm but not unkind. "Don't be making a scene. You just as well should be locked up yourself. Now, just go on home." He turned to Bass, his expression now serious. "Bass, what happened during the apprehension?"

"No trouble at all, Isaac," Bass replied, a hint of satisfaction in his voice. "Truth be told."

The Judge nodded, a faint smile on his lips. "See there, Margaret? That weighs favorably on the scales of justice. Now go on home and don't you worry none."

The cold clang of the cell door echoed through the stone halls as the deputy secured the lock on the cell holding the two brothers. The scent of stale air and old wood filled Bass's nostrils as he turned to face Judge Parker.

"How are James and Thomas doing on that Dick Glass hunt?" Bass asked, more than curiosity in his voice. He was aware of the personal mission that drove him, and he knew that somewhere in the vast expanse of the Indian

Territory, his fellow officers were hot on the trail of his friend's killer.

The Judge sighed, the weary sound of a man who had seen too much. "No word as of yet," he said, shaking his head. "Last thing we got was that they were headed into the Indian Territory."

"The Natives," Bass muttered, a deep respect for them in his tone. He knew their way of life, their connection to the land, and their unwavering sense of justice.

"They are the best informants on the plains," the Judge affirmed, his voice growing solemn as he recalled the story he had heard about Dick Glass's cruelty. "Once you've crossed them, you've crossed them forever. The story is he was out in a hunting party with his native family. Came upon some other hunters from Black Town. One in his party asked them to come share their meal and fire. Well, one of the young Black boys made the grave mistake of eating the last piece of corn. Witnesses attest Glass said, 'That's why he doesn't like the n***a side of his self, 'cause they are disrespectful.'"

Bass's face hardened, his jaw clenched in a silent fury. He could almost hear the words, taste the arrogance in them. The Judge continued, his voice a low, pained whisper, "Before the native boy who invited them could tell him the boy had asked, Dick had already drawn and landed a deadly shot mid-forehead."

The story hung in the air, a chilling testament of man with the ability to kill children, evil. Bass felt a surge of rage, a cold fire that ignited in his gut. The need for justice was no longer just a need. It was a desire, the taste for Justice became palatable in every concept of taking the life of Dick Glass.

"I hope James and Thomas wrap this fucker up real soon to present him to your rope, sir," Bass's voice flat and hard.

A grim smile touched the Judge's lips. "With the greatest joy, and a heart full of Justice. I will pronounce the death penalty upon that bastard."

Bass couldn't resist. "He ain't no bastard," Bass quipped, a flash of their shared humor breaking through the tension. "He got a daddy."

The Judge's face broke into a full-throated laugh. "What's his fuckin' name?" he retorted, the words tumbling out in a rush of shared understanding and dark humor.

The laughter filled the room, a brief but needed release from the weight of their duty. It was a reminder that even in the darkest of times, they could find a moment of levity.

"Go get a couple days with Jennie, and I will assign more work for you," the Judge said, his voice now softened with paternal concern. He knew Bass had earned his rest.

"I'm gonna take you up on that, Judge," Bass said, his mind already on his wife and the quiet comfort of his home. "See you soon, sir."

The silence of the house was a welcome balm to Bass, a stark contrast to the endless dust of the trail. He stood in his private sanctuary, a room that served as both a study and an armory. On one wall, an array of weapons hung in a meticulous display, rifles, shotguns, and pistols, each one a testament to the dangers he faced. In the corner, a Wing Chun dummy stood sentinel, its wooden arms and legs worn smooth from countless hours of practice. A sturdy desk occupied another corner, its surface cluttered with bullet-making devices and papers detailing new warrants. This was his space, a reflection of the man he was a warrior, protector, and a family man. Who longed for peace but was forever prepared for war.

Jennie walked in, her presence filling the room with a warmth that the cold wilderness could never provide. The scent of coffee and Coco butter followed her, an aroma that grounded him in her presence. She carried a tray with his favorite bourbon and smoke with rolling papers, and iced tea.

"Hey my love," she said, her voice a melody of affection. She set the tray down on the desk, her eyes sweeping over the scattered papers and weapons. It was a world she had come to accept, though not without a constant, low-level anxiety that lived just beneath her skin. "The babies are enrolled in school up at the fort. It's a good school, a good place for them to be. Mary took me there, and she introduced me to the head Marm, and she is a sweetheart."

Bass's heart swelled with a quiet pride. He had been away so long, the daily rhythms of his family's life a distant, abstract concept. Hearing about his children thriving, about his wife forging a new community for them, was a powerful reassurance. But then, a shadow crossed Jennie's face.

"I need you to talk to Robert," she said, her voice dropping to a low, serious tone. "He's starting to smell himself, and getting a bit mouthy with me."

Bass's shoulders tensed. Robert. His second eldest son, a mirror image of himself in stubbornness and pride. The same fire he had used to forge a path in a lawless world was now burning in his son, but without a clear direction, it was a volatile, dangerous thing.

"Okay, babe," Bass said, a weary sigh escaping his lips. He walked over to her, his arms wrapping around her waist. "But before I get to all this… can I get to some of this?" he whispered, his lips finding the soft skin of her neck.

Jennie laughed, a warm, genuine sound. "Last night wasn't enough for you, huh?" she teased, her hands coming up to caress his face. "Robert won first place at the fair with that Sharps .50 you gave him."

The news brought a genuine smile to Bass's face, his heart swelling with a fierce paternal pride. "Enough of you? Ma'am, there is no such a thing as enough of the prettiest little ol' gal this side of that Mississippi," he said, his voice a low and proud. "First place, huh? Good, good. I'm going to get him a new Henry .44 caliber repeater."

Jennie playfully pushed him away, her eyes twinkling. "I'm need you to eat, get your stamina together. Then get you some rest. There are a lot of chores around here that need to be tended to. Like the barn door and the fence."

"Yes, yes, I got you, baby," Bass said, his voice laced with affection. "But first, let's just do this right here." He pulled her closer, his eyes a testament to a love that had weathered years of separation and danger.

The quiet warmth of their private moment was shattered by the sound of a footstep in the hallway. Robert entered the room, his teenage swagger a flimsy shield for the storm of emotions brewing within him. He was a tall, lanky boy, all sharp angles and restless energy, his face a constant scowl.

"Well, aren't you going to speak to your father?" Jennie asked, a hopeful note in her voice.

Robert's response was a mumbled, reluctant greeting. "Yeah, yeah, how the hell are you, Dad?"

Bass's smile vanished. The casual disrespect in his son's tone was like a physical blow. He straightened up, his stance shifting from a lover to a father, a lawman. The air in the room grew heavy with a familiar, unspoken tension. "I won't have it, son. I won't. Understand me?"

Robert's eyes, a mirror of his father's, flashed with defiance. "You won't have what, Dad? A family? Maybe a group of people who care about you that you don't give a damn about?" The words were a bitter accusation, a verbal lash that stung more than any bullet ever could. The years of loneliness, of watching his mother wait, of hearing the whispers of his father's legend, had festered into a deep, painful resentment. He saw a man who chose the law, chose the chase, chose a life of legend over the simple, daily existence of a father and a husband.

"Boy, have you lost your mind?" Bass asked, his voice low and dangerous. "Why do you think I do what I do? Every day I ride out there, every day I put my life on the line. Why do you think that is?"

"Because you're the Lone Ranger! That's all we hear about. All we see is your back," Robert shot back, his voice rising in frustration. "When are you just gonna be my dad, you know? Did you know I came in…"

"First place at the Grayson County Fair with the .50 cal?" Bass finished for him, his voice softening, the pride bubbling up despite his anger. "Son, I am always your dad. There is nothing that can change that, but I don't want you to live in the same world as I did. You need one where justice stands for something, and it's honored. Most of all, feared. Son, there are some tough, evil men in this world, and some venomous women. If someone doesn't get in their way, they're coming to your front door. I do what I do so you don't have to."

Robert scoffed, the sound a sharp, bitter dismissal of his father's words. "You did alright! I mean, the world you came up in made you the 'Lone Ranger.' I just think you like everything and everyone worshipping you more than you love your family." The words were a venomous parting shot, a final, painful accusation. Robert turned and walked out of the room, leaving a heavy, suffocating silence in his wake.

Jennie came to Bass, her hand on his arm, a gentle anchor. "Bass, Bass, let him go. He'll be back, baby. Now you see what I was talking about. When it comes to that boy of yours, both them babies of yours, well, you and I know who!"

Bass let out a long, weary sigh. "Yeah," he said, the word a whisper of defeat. "He's just twisted a bit, or should I say... we?"

Jennie shook her head, a long-suffering smile on her face. "Oh, Lawd."

"Truth is found, and worth exposed through struggle," Bass mused, his mind turning to the hardships of his own life. The years during the sharecropping with Master Reeves. The unforgiving nature of the land, the constant battle against evil, it had all shaped him, had carved him into the man he was. He had a reputation, a name whispered in saloons and on trails, but it had come at a cost.

"Bass, you ain't spoke much on your momma," Jennie said, her voice soft and thoughtful. "I wonder what she'd think if she knew she raised such a damn fool."

Bass's head snapped up. "Don't start on my momma!" he said, a warning in his voice, though it was softened by a hint of a smile. "Now, you know that woman worked hard to get where she is. Her marriage to my daddy being arranged was probably hard. I believe through her experience, she developed a fine sense of humor."

An idea sparked in Jennie's eyes, a light of pure, unadulterated joy. "We should have a traditional Chupua-style second wedding and invite her to Grayson County. It ain't but a few days' ride away. Our wedding, being one she never got to see. I think it would be as tall as an elephant thing to do for her."

Bass's expression was a mixture of surprise and genuine delight. It was a grand, theatrical gesture, just like Jennie. He considered it for a moment, the logistics of it all, the possibility of getting his mother to travel, the sheer joy of seeing her again. "She's getting up in age now, and I don't know if she would be ready for all that," he said, his voice hesitant, a part of him afraid to hope for such a miracle.

"What do you mean, 'ready'?" Jennie insisted, her eyes shining. "I'm going to write her a letter, and I'll ask her myself. Believe me, I know she was disappointed when she was unable to attend our wedding."

Bass's hesitation melted away, replaced by a surge of excitement. "Yeah, why not? We can send for your father and get them here, too. It'll be great to have all the family here enjoying each other's company. Yeah, baby, let's do it." He pulled her into his arms, his heart swelling with a hope he hadn't felt in years.

Jennie's face was radiant, her smile as wide as the Oklahoma sky. "Really, Bass? Really? You're excited about this?"

He held her close, a genuine, unguarded smile on his face. "Excited might be a stretch," he said, but the affection in his voice contradicted his words.

"That's my man right there!" Jennie said, planting a kiss on his lips. "He always surprises me." With each word, she punctuated her sentence with a kiss on his cheek, his forehead, his neck. "Beautiful... special... strong... and sexy... provider. That can fill me up like no man ever could."

Bass's grin widened, a playful twinkle in his eyes. "What the hell? No other man? How many other men were there trying to fill that there cup up?"

Jennie's laughter was a cascade of pure joy. "That's exactly why!" she said, her arms wrapped tightly around his neck.

"Why what?" he asked, a feigned innocence in his voice, his hands moving to pull her closer.

She pulled back just enough to look him in the eye, a wicked glint in her gaze. "You ain't getting none."

"Whoa, Jennie, baby," Bass said, his voice a low, teasing. "Don't be so quick to judgment now, baby." The air between them was electric, a promise of a future filled with love, laughter, and the quiet comfort of a home he had fought so hard to protect.

The afternoon sun was a relentless fire in the sky, beating down on the vast, unforgiving range. The dust was thick and fine, kicked up by the steady trudge of horses, settling on everything like a second skin. Bass rode with a grim sense of satisfaction, the air of a hunter who has finally cornered his prey. Trailing behind him was Jim Webb, a man whose head was so swollen and bruised it looked as if it had gone a few rounds with a brick wall. His hands, cuffed in front of him, were a stark reminder of his capture, a symbol of the law's long reach.

As they crested a small rise, Bass spotted Stands Tall's camp. It was a simple affair, a small fire crackling merrily despite the heat, a couple of horses tethered to a lone tree. But what caught Bass's eye, what made him rein in Silver and stare in stunned silence, was the sight of Webb's partner. The man was sitting on the ground, his face a mixture of sullen defeat and grudging respect. A long, heavy chain, glinting in the sunlight, connected him to Stands Tall's waist. He was an unwilling accessory, a human leash.

Bass dismounted, his boots crunching on the dry grass, and walked toward the two men, a look of profound disbelief on his face. "How in the hell did you manage that?" he asked, pointing at Webb's partner. The question was a genuine one, laced with a mixture of awe and bewilderment.

Stands Tall didn't even turn his head. He simply looked at Bass, his dark eyes filled with a quiet, knowing pride. "In the same manner in which I sneak upon you." The words were spoken with a quiet confidence that held a universe of meaning. He was a ghost on the plains, a man who could move through the world unseen and unheard, and his abilities were a constant source of surprise to Bass.

"Amazing," Bass muttered, shaking his head. "He's amazing." He said it to Webb, a low, quiet observation. It was a statement of fact, a testament to the man's undeniable skill. There was no need for a lengthy explanation; the evidence was right there, a man chained to another, a physical symbol of a silent and masterful capture.

A Personal Trial

The late morning sun, already high and hot, beat down on the dusty streets of Fort Smith. The wide, well-traveled dirt road leading into the heart of the settlement was baked hard, reflecting the blinding white glare back up at the riders. Bass Reeves rode point, his imposing silhouette framed by the harsh Arkansas sky. He wasn't a man who typically felt unease, not after years of sharecropping Missionary Ridge, and now a Deputy Marshal, but as they rode past the stockade walls and the first cluster of saloons. A subtle, discordant note struck him.

Fort Smith, perched on the border of the Indian Territory, a gateway to chaos and a bastion of U.S. law, was usually a hive of loud, purposeful activity. Today, the noise was exchanged for looks of bewilderment and disbelief. The usual cacophony of wagon wheels, blacksmith hammers, and drunken shouts was replaced by a quick glance. People were moving, as usual, hauling goods, chatting on boardwalks, and such, but they shadowed in doorways quietly whispering among themselves. Something felt distinctly off to Bass.

He steered his horse steadily, keeping his eyes moving, cataloging every reaction. There was a peculiar mixture of sentiment directed their way. A few older men, likely homesteaders who respected the law, offered quick, genuine nods and waves. They saw the badge, the grit, and the danger he represented. But then there were the others. Young men, lounging against posts with hands near holsters. Apparently, plotting their next get-rich-quick scheme. Their eyes lingered on the two bound prisoners, one, a solidly built white man named Webb, and the other, a young Indigenous woman. Who Bass first thought was a man, understood to be Webb's wife or 'squaw', and partner in crime. Then their eyes flicked back to Bass. The imposing Black man riding with the authority of the United States government. The most unsettling behaviors were from the women! Some shook their heads slowly, a gesture that spoke not of anger but disappointment or, perhaps, a resigned belief in the futility of it all. They all knew where Bass was headed: the Federal Court of the Western District of Arkansas, Judge Isaac C. Parker's domain, the notorious "Hanging Judge."

Bass shifted his weight in the saddle, the leather creaking beneath him. His hand instinctively patted the butt of his pistol. This wasn't just a regular run. This was a statement, and half the town hated the statement. He tightened his jaw, pushing the uneasiness down. He had his prisoners, his papers, and his resolve. The law was the law, regardless of the sour faces lining the street. Judging him and whispering and carrying on.

Behind him, riding with a posture of almost regal confidence, was Stands Tall, the bounty hunter who had assisted in the capture. Stands Tall carried himself with a quiet dignity, observing the town's reaction with an almost clinical detachment.

They rode past the last of the businesses, the air growing heavier with the scent of coal smoke and river mud. Finally reaching the stone structure of the Fort Smith jail. A hulking, uninviting building of rough-hewn rock, it looked exactly like the final destination as it was for so many desperadoes.

Bass dismounted first, his boots crunching on the gravel of the yard. The two prisoners were dismounted and pulled toward the entrance.

Inside the jail, the air was thick with the metallic tang of stale musky sour smell and coffee. Even on a bright day, the light struggling to penetrate the barred windows. They were met by Sergeant Fanaghan, a barrel-chested man whose uniform strained over his formidable frame. He wore a perpetual scowl, a testament to the grim nature of his daily work.

Sergeant Fanaghan, feet planted, hands on his hips, let his eyes roam over the trio. The deputy marshal, the unusual accomplice, and the two captives.

"What-a-you have here, boyo," Fanaghan grumbled, the words rumbling in his chest. His gaze settled on the prisoners. "Looks like some common thugs."

Stands Tall stepped forward, his back straight, adopting a formal tone for the official handoff. He saw his role here not as a mere rider, but as a temporary officer of the court, a distinction he took seriously.

"Yes, Sgt. Mister Webb and Mister Webb's squaw."

Bass, who had been holding the lead rope, felt the knot of frustration begin to tighten in his chest. He preferred things simple and by the book. He moved closer, pushing the papers, official warrants, and deposition, into Fanaghan's hand.

"We don't have any paper on the squaw here," Bass stated plainly, his voice low and firm. He was stating a legal fact, an uncomfortable truth that complicated the transfer. In the Indian Territory, a woman might be tied to a man by marriage or custom, but the court's jurisdiction was only for those for whom a Warrant had been issued for, and or the arresting officer wished to file some sort of complaint for a Warrant. The warrant only named Webb, and Bass knew he had nothing but a hunch. During the trip, he had a chance to question the offenders, and she gave up nothing.

Sergeant Fanaghan frowned, peering at the papers, his lips moving as he struggled with the dense, official language. He looked up, his face set in a look of bureaucratic abstinence.

"Then I can not accept her as a guest in our fine establishment." The sergeant's tone was final. No name, no booking. The rules were the rules, however ridiculous.

Bass felt a sigh start in his lungs and immediately swallowed it. He looked at Webb, the primary target, then at the woman who was clearly his partner in crime, but with no proof. Maybe just maybe even, she's a victim in her own right. He had dragged her two hundred miles, through creek beds and thorny thickets, past rattlesnakes and bushwhackers, all to hit this predictable, maddening snag. He knew the risk of simply turning her loose in Fort Smith, a town that showed little hospitality to solitary Indigenous women, but a crooked woman can become a local staple. His whole career was built on following the letter of the law. He must let her go.

"Well, hell," Bass said, the word escaping as a puff of controlled exasperation. He looked around the dim, stale room, taking in the hardened faces of a few nearby jail trustees. "Anybody got anything they wanna say?" He waited a beat. Silence. Webb just stared at the floor; the woman remained impassive. Bass gave a curt nod. "I guess the squaw here free to go. Ma'am, this here is a second chance. Now get!"

He gave the rope a sharp, final flick, freeing the woman. She didn't look at him, didn't thank him, Then why would she? Simply, she turned and walked out of the jail's stifling confines back into the harsh reality of her fate, which was now entirely her own. Bass watched the door close behind her, a small dust cloud at her feet. Justice for Webb would proceed. The other matter was concluded.

He turned back to the Sergeant, pushing the heavy manila envelope with the travel expenses into his hand. "Well, can we get this here bill stamped so I can pay my journeyman?" Bass needed the official sign-off on the expenses so Stands Tall, his temporary deputy, could be paid for his considerable risk and service.

Sergeant Fanaghan took the bill, his attitude immediately shifting from obstructionist to obliging once the prisoner was secured and paperwork was moving. He pulled a heavy rubber stamp from the desk and slammed it down onto the document with a resounding thud.

Stands Tall stepped forward, taking the stamped bill from Bass. He looked down at the paper, then back up at the Deputy Marshal, a genuine warmth in his eyes that transcended their professional relationship. They were men of different backgrounds, bound together by the dangerous, thankless business of bringing order to a new territory.

"Well, my friend," Stands Tall began, his voice taking on a resonant quality, a hint of his ancestral eloquence surfacing. "Again, it has a pleasure to ride with you. Whenever my friend calls on me, I shall arrive as the Wind of the Gods."

Bass Reeves, the pragmatist, simply nodded, a faint, almost imperceptible smile touching his lips. "Get a good meal, Stands Tall. You earned it.

Stands Tall gave a final, formal, slow nod and turned to leave. Bass watched him go, then turned his attention back to the somber business of booking in Webb. The Wind of the Gods, indeed. He knew one thing for certain. In the wild, unforgiving expanse of the Indian Territory, a good partner was worth more than all the stamped papers in the world. He was already thinking about his next warrant. The work, like the hot sun, never truly ended.

The Judge's office smelled of old wood and cigar smoke, a room too heavy with law to ever feel entirely comfortable. Bass Reeves stepped inside, tall as an Elephant, his spurs giving a faint metallic whisper against the polished floorboards. A man like him seemed to carry the outdoors in with him, dust, sunlight, and that grave sense of distance born from long days in the saddle.

Before he could take in much of the room, he saw her, Mary.

"Why, Mary, ma'am," Bass drawled, tipping his hat low and letting the smile creep into his eyes, "if you ain't the prettiest thing a man's seen in months."

Her face broke into a grin, though she turned her head quickly as though ashamed of how much warmth rushed to her cheeks. Mary had that way about her, practical, sharp as a tack, but tender in spite of it all. She put her hands on her hips, mock stern, though the sparkle in her gaze gave her away.

"Well, I missed you too, sir," she said. "But if'n the Judge catches us canoodling and carrying on in his own office, we might both get shot. And that's gospel."

The warning sat halfway between jest and truth. Judge Isaac Parker was not a man known for softness, and Mary knew his temper when it came to lawmen distracted by women.

Before Bass could answer, another voice cut sharp as a knife.

"If'n I don't see you first," Jennie declared from the corner, her tone both playful and deadly serious, "then it's a stabbing."

The three of them burst into laughter, the sound chasing away some of the Judge's heavy air. Jennie had a way of cutting through a moment, reminding Bass of the stakes while also making it all feel lighter. She was no delicate flower; life beside a lawman never allowed her the privilege.

"Bass, baby," Jennie added, her hand resting on her hip now, eyes glittering, "our boy Bennie."

Bass's smile faltered. "Come on now," he said, his voice half-pleading, half-curious. "What is it, Jennie?"

Mary folded her arms, glancing to Jennie as though giving her the floor. "Go ahead, Jennie. Tell him."

The pause stretched a moment too long, long enough that Bass felt his throat tighten. His big hands curled loosely at his sides, waiting, dreading.

Jennie inhaled, then met his eyes square on. "Bass," she said softly, though the words carried enough weight to shake the air in the room, "Bennie done went and killed his wife two nights ago."

The silence that followed was like the ringing of a church bell, vibrating in the bones. Bass stared at her, but she didn't falter. The truth was in her face, plain as the day outside.

"The Judge done issued an arrest warrant," she continued, steady as stone. "It ain't been posted yet, but it's dead or alive, Bass."

For a moment, Bass couldn't breathe. His mind reeled, picturing Bennie, the boy he'd once held up to the sky like a trophy, the child whose first steps he'd steadied, whose laughter had filled their small home. Now that same boy was a murderer, his hands stained with the blood of his own wife.

Jennie's voice had gone quiet now, her anger dulled by sorrow. "Ain't no easy way to tell a father such a thing," she said, almost whispering.

Mary looked at Bass with pity, her eyes shimmering with a grief that wasn't hers but shared nonetheless.

Bass drew in a breath that rattled in his chest. "Where's the Judge?" His voice was low, steady, though the tremor underneath was near breaking.

Jennie's lips pressed thin, but she nodded toward the adjoining door.

The Judge's office loomed just a step away, where justice would be handed down like scripture, unyielding and final.

But on top of it, laid out bitterly the likeness of and the amount of the bounty sought for his son.

The room seemed smaller suddenly, the walls pressing in.

His thoughts scattered, flashes of Bennie as a child, running barefoot in the yard, laughter high as a lark. Bennie chases fireflies at dusk, Jennie fussing over his scraped knees and calling him for supper. That boy had been his joy, the proof that a lawman's life could carry more than gallows and gun smoke.

And yet here he stood, warrant in hand, tasked with bringing that same boy back, dead or alive.

Mary shifted uneasily, watching him with an expression she had come to know well. No sympathy edged with steel, and she knew he would not falter. He never had.

"Bass," she said softly, "you know the Judge won't spare him. The law doesn't bend for blood baby."

Her words only deepened the ache in his chest. He knew she was right, but that truth did nothing to steady his heart.

Jennie finally released the warrant, her hand falling to her side. Her eyes met his, and in them he saw the reflection of every hard choice he'd made before, every outlaw he'd faced down, every bullet he'd fired in the name of justice. But this one was different; this one was family.

The warrant existed between them like a curse. Instead of giving in to the darkness, he lifted his head, tightened his jaw, and exhaled through his nose.

"Where's the Judge?" he repeated, his voice quieter now but heavy with finality.

Jennie pointed toward the office door, her finger trembling though she tried to keep her hand steady. The weight of the gesture seemed to seal his fate.

Bass tipped his hat low again, more out of habit than courtesy, and turned his gaze toward that door. The office beyond it was waiting, along with the Judge who had made a career of pronouncing death. And behind it all, somewhere in the distance, was Bennie, his son, his blood, now an outlaw.

The spurs at his heels gave another faint whisper as he took a step forward. The floor creaked beneath his boots, a sound so ordinary yet in this moment it might as well have been, the tolling of a bell.

The law had spoken. And Bass Reeves, lawman, father, and hunter of men, was bound to answer.

Bass Reeves stood before the Judge's door a long moment before knocking. His broad hand hovered inches from the wood, the edges of his palm roughened by years of gun belts and reins. He'd faced killers, thieves, and desperadoes without hesitation, but never had his hand trembled before lifting to a door. Tonight it did.

The muffled voice inside cut through his hesitation. "Come on in, Bass."

He pushed the door open, the hinges groaning in protest. The Judge's office was larger than the outer chamber, though no less heavy with smoke. The ceiling arched high, bookshelves lining the walls with law books bound in cracked leather. A large desk dominated the center, buried under papers, warrants, and stacks of files that seemed to grow daily. Behind it sat Judge Isaac Parker himself, "the Hanging Judge." His eyes, gray as winter, softened when they landed on Bass.

"Bass," the Judge said slowly, almost kindly, "I'm afraid I have some bad news, my friend."

Bass stepped inside, boots landing firm but slow, the weight of the moment pressing down on him like lead. He closed the door with deliberate care, as though the act itself marked a boundary between past and present.

"I heard, sir," Bass replied, voice low and measured. He removed his hat, holding it in both hands like a shield he dared not lift. "My oldest boy shot and killed his wife."

The Judge leaned back in his chair, the leather creaking. His hands rested on the armrests, long fingers curling slightly as though reluctant to speak. His jaw worked a moment before words came. "I just needed to speak to you, Bass, before I go and condemn your son to the hunters."

The words fell heavy, each syllable weighted with the authority of the law. Bass lowered his gaze, staring at the polished floorboards as though they might open up and swallow him whole. He let the silence stretch long enough for the Judge to shift uncomfortably. Finally, he spoke.

"Sir, you ain't condemn him," Bass said, voice steady though his throat burned. "He condemned himself when he killed his wife."

The Judge studied him, measuring the man against the father. Bass raised his eyes and met that gaze without flinching. "I'm gonna ask you to let me bring the boy in, Judge. No sense nobody else getting in harm's way over my boy."

The Judge exhaled heavily, shoulders sagging under the burden of justice. I'm sorry, Bass. Truly sorry."

"Don't you worry 'bout much," Bass said. His voice had grown quieter, like steel tempered in fire. "This here's my mess. I'll clean it up."

The Judge tilted his head, sorrow etched deep in his features. He'd sent Bass after countless men, but this was the first time he'd seen the lawman stand as both hunter and father.

"Where do you think he went?" the Judge asked, his voice softer now, stripped of courtroom thunder.

Bass put his hat back on, settling it firmly on his head as though it anchored him. He let his eyes drift, not to the Judge, not to the desk, but beyond, seeing in his mind the endless plains, the winding rivers, the open sky of exile.

"Where do they all go?" he said finally, his tone dark with inevitability. "Indian Territory."

The room fell into silence again, the kind that carried no comfort.

Judge Parker sat back, watching the man who had never failed him, who had chased murderers through storms, tracked horse thieves across state lines, who had stared down outlaws twice his number without flinching. Bass Reeves had always been the embodiment of justice in the flesh. Yet here he stood, tasked with bringing in his own son.

"Bass," the Judge said gently, "no man will think less of you if you refuse."

Bass's eyes hardened. "No, sir. A man doesn't choose his duty only when it suits him. Law's the law. My boy made his choice, and I made mine long ago when I dawned this here badge Judge."

The Judge nodded slowly, as though there was nothing left to say. His fingers tapped the desk, restless.

He wanted to offer comfort, but knew in the confines of an Oath. There was no draw nor quarter. The law had no room for comfort, not here, not now.

Bass turned, the spurs at his heels giving their soft whisper once again. The sound seemed to echo longer than usual, filling the office, marking his departure.

At the doorway, he paused. For just a heartbeat, he allowed himself to feel the weight pressing at his chest, the grief clawing at the edges of his resolve. Bennie's face flickered again in his mind, his laughter as a boy, his proud stance as a young man. And now, his name is written cold on a warrant.

He swallowed hard, his throat aching. Then, with a final tip of his hat, Bass Reeves stepped out of the Judge's office.

The corridor beyond stretched long and dim, lantern light flickering along the walls. Jennie and Mary still waited in the outer chamber, their eyes fixed on him, searching for answers he couldn't give. In his coat pocket, the warrant pressed against his chest like a brand.

He didn't speak as he passed them. Words had abandoned him, replaced only with duty. His boots struck the floor with the steady rhythm of a man walking toward a destiny no one would envy.

Outside, the day had grew long. The sun, sitting low, burned over Fort Smith, wagons rattled down the streets, and children played in the dust. The world continued, indifferent to the ruin of one man's family.

Bass Reeves descended the courthouse steps, the brim of his hat shadowing his eyes. Somewhere out there, Bennie was running, westward, toward the wild reaches of Indian Territory.

And Bass would follow.

Because law was law. And even blood could not stand against it.

Fort Smith simmered under a dark sky, lanterns burning in windows like tired eyes. Bass Reeves moved through the streets with purpose, the brim of his hat pulled low, his coat carrying the weight of both the warrant and the grief pressed inside it. Each step carried him closer to the place where answers might spill easier than whiskey.

By the time he pushed through the swinging doors of the saloon, the night air had thickened with smoke and laughter. The room was alive with noise, piano music tinkling above the roar of men's voices, chairs scraping, boots stomping, glasses clinking. The scent of liquor and sweat mingled into something sour, and yet there was life here, a reckless kind of life Bass always found when chasing ghosts and fugitives.

The bartender looked up from polishing a cloudy glass, eyeing Bass with recognition. He was a big man, taller than most in the room, his badge gleaming faintly in the lamplight even when he wasn't trying to show it. Silence spread like a ripple across nearby tables, conversations faltering as eyes turned to watch him.

The bartender, chewing the end of a cigar stub, forced a grin. "What'll I do for you?" he asked, voice half-nervous, half-curious.

Bass stepped up to the counter, slow, steady, his spurs whispering over the floorboards. He laid his palms flat on the wood, eyes steady on the man. "Not a damn thing," he said coolly. "Now sell me some liquor and some information."

The words hung in the air, part demand, part bargain.

Before the bartender could answer, a laugh rang out from the far end of the room. A woman leaned forward from her table, smoke curling from the cigarette in her hand. Her dress was worn but bright, a crimson splash against the brown and gray of the room. Her hair, dark and unkempt, fell in waves over one shoulder, and her eyes, sharp, playful, dangerous, settled on Bass with the certainty of someone who had stories to tell.

"I know you!" she declared, her voice cutting through the saloon noise like a blade. "We know you, and your boy!"

The room stirred at her words. A few men muttered, others turned their heads away, but the woman smiled, teeth flashing as though she enjoyed the attention. She leaned back in her chair, the cigarette smoke drifting up in lazy spirals.

"Yep," she continued, raising her glass as though in toast, "he was through here just last night, runnin' away look like. Had just one drink, and that's something he don't do. Then he bought a bottle and cut out, something else he doesn't do. 'Cause he be here till morning most nights. And so did his wife's boyfriend when he wasn't here."

The words struck Bass like a gunshot. His boy. His Bennie. Running, drinking, desperate. And now this, his wife's boyfriend.

He straightened slowly, his eyes narrowing. His hand twitched near the brim of his hat, adjusting it as though to hide the storm in his face. "Wife's boyfriend," Bass said, the words tasting bitter as he spoke them.

The woman leaned forward again, her lips curling into a sly grin. "Bobby Lee Edwards his name. Buy me a drink, Marshal, and I'll tell you about it."

The room seemed to lean in with her. Men turned their heads, ears straining to catch what might be said next. The piano had faltered, its notes stumbling before picking up again, softer now, like background to a secret being told.

Bass's jaw tightened. He reached into his pocket and pulled out a coin, sliding it across the bar with the steady push of a man who knew money wasn't what mattered here; it was time. Time, and the truth buried beneath all the smoke and whiskey.

The bartender scooped the coin up and set a glass down in front of the woman, filling it with amber liquor that caught the light like fire. She lifted it, swirling the drink lazily, then brought it to her lips.

"Bobby Lee," she began, eyes on Bass as she sipped, "was sweet on her long before she married your boy.

Everybody knew it. He'd come sniffin' round when Bennie was gone, sittin' at her table like he belonged there. Folks whispered it, but no one said it to your boy's face, 'cause your boy, he had your fire in him. And your boy, he'd as soon put a man down as hear tell of such disrespect."

Bass said nothing, only stared at her with the weight of the law in his gaze. She shifted in her chair, enjoying the moment, stretching it out.

"Well," she continued, setting her glass down with a thud, "Night before last, things boiled over. Bobby Lee was in town, drinkin' and struttin' like a rooster. Word came quick that your boy's wife was growin' tired of Bennie's temper, leanin' Bobby's way instead. And next thing folks knew, she was dead. Shot cold in her own house."

The words fell heavy, though the saloon itself seemed to breathe them in, feeding off the story. Men exchanged glances. Some shook their heads. Others smirked, enjoying the scandal.

Bass's face didn't move, but his heart thundered beneath his ribs. His son, his blood, reduced to whispers in saloons, his name carried by women who smoked and men who laughed about murder.

He spoke at last, his voice a low growl. "You see Bobby Lee since?"

The woman smirked, picking up her glass again. "Maybe. Maybe not. Depends on how thirsty I get."

Her meaning was clear: another drink, another piece of the puzzle.

Bass reached into his pocket again, but this time he didn't pull out a coin. He leaned closer, his shadow falling over her table, his voice sharp as the crack of a rifle.

"You'll get your drink," he said, steady as stone. "But you'll tell me where Bobby Lee went first. Then you'll drink. Not the other way around."

The woman's grin faltered, though only slightly. She looked into his eyes and saw no give, no jest. This was the Marshal who had hunted men through storms, who had brought in killers alive when no one else could. She set her glass down slowly.

"All right," she said, her tone cooling. "He lit out after your boy. Indian Territory. Same as him. Looks like both of 'em runnin' toward the same dark patch of earth. One with vengeance, the other with grief."

The words sank deep. Bass straightened, his eyes darkening with resolve. Bennie was out there, torn apart by guilt and rage. And Bobby Lee, fuel to the fire, the rival whose name now stained everything.

Bass tipped his hat slightly, a gesture both of thanks and finality. He left a couple of bits for the drinks and a roll of Silver Dollars. The woman picked up her glass and drank deep, and watching him through the smoke as he turned toward the door.

The saloon seemed to hush as he left, conversations pausing, men staring, the weight of his presence leaving a silence in his wake.

Outside, the night air hit him cool and sharp. The stars glittered faintly above, distant, untroubled. Bass Reeves stood in the dust of the street, his coat heavy, his purpose heavier still.

The warrant pressed against his chest like a heartbeat. His boy's trail was clear now: Liquor, desperation running through Indian Territory. Shadowing him, somewhere ahead, Bobby Lee Edwards.

Bass Reeves stepped into the night, ready to follow.

The morning broke cold and clear, the trail stretching out before Bass Reeves like a ribbon of dust and dew. The rising sun bled soft light across the horizon, painting the land in shades of copper and gold. His horse's hooves crunched softly on the earth, each step measured and steady. The air carried the smell of damp grass and berries, and the remnants of campfires burned low through the night.

Bass had been riding alone since the saloon, his mind restless with thoughts of Bennie and Bobby Lee Edwards. But when the faint crunch of movement broke the morning stillness, he knew at once he wasn't alone.

He turned in the saddle, hand instinctively brushing near his Colt. And there he was, Stands Tall, emerging from the trees as if he had been part of them all along. The man walked silently, as if the earth itself welcomed him and carried him forward.

Bass shook his head, half-amused, half-irritated. "How in the hell do you keep doing that?" he muttered.

Stands Tall offered no answer at first, only the calm half-smile that seemed carved into his face. His braids swayed gently as he approached, his steps unhurried, his gaze steady. When he finally spoke, his voice was soft, deliberate.

"Perhaps one day," Stands Tall said, "I may show you the way of the Spirit walk."

Bass groaned, rolling his eyes. "Oh shh… here we go with that hokey oogy-boogy stuff again." He waved a dismissive hand, though there was no real venom in it.

The corners of Stands Tall's lips twitched into something near a grin. "Or perhaps not," he said simply.

Bass pulled his reins, halting his horse. "Not," he said firmly. "Just start callin' out, or whistling, or something, when you're about to sneak up on a man. Might save me a heart attack."

The two men stood in companionable silence for a moment, the horse shifting its weight and snorting softly. The air between them carried history, years of riding the same trails, of watching each other's backs through gun smoke and storms.

Stands Tall looked out toward the horizon, his eyes narrowing as though he could see beyond what lay visible. "I have alerted my brothers throughout the Five Civilized Tribes," he said at last, his voice carrying a weight that matched the land itself. "They will be on the lookout for your son, Bass. Alive."

The words struck deep. Bass lowered his head slightly, touched by the gesture though unwilling to let it soften his resolve too much.

"I do appreciate that, my brother," Bass said, voice quiet but sincere. "But this one here…" He paused, pressing his lips into a firm line. "This one I gotta do myself. No honor in not."

Stands Tall inclined his head, acknowledging the truth of it. His dark eyes held no judgment, only understanding. He had seen Bass stand against killers without flinching, had seen him drag men back in irons when others would have left them dead in the dirt. But this was different. This was blood.

"May you find him balanced and at peace, not fearful," Stands Tall said, his tone almost like a prayer.

Bass barked a short laugh, though it held no humor. "More than likely I'm gonna find him drunk with a hangover," he muttered. "Ain't neither making me comfortable."

The two men moved forward again, Bass in the saddle, Stands Tall walking with the unhurried pace of a man who carried time differently. The trail wound through low hills and clusters of trees, birds scattering at their approach.

Stands Tall tilted his head back, his gaze lifting toward a pair of owls perched silently in the branches of a dead oak. "The Owl's vision is long," he said, almost to himself. "But it is its wisdom that helps him see best."

Bass followed his gaze, squinting up at the birds, their eyes wide and unblinking. He shivered slightly despite himself. "You and your owl talk," he said, shaking his head. "Always seein' signs and such. I'd rather follow tracks on the ground. At least those don't go flappin' off when the wind blows."

But inwardly, Bass couldn't shake the thought. An owl's vision is long, wisdom guiding it. Wasn't that what he needed now? To see far enough to find his boy before another man did. To see the truth of Bennie's heart, beyond the drunken mistakes and the gun smoke.

The trail stretched onward, but every step Bass took seemed to draw him closer to a reckoning he could neither dodge nor delay.

The ride carried them into deeper country, where the land seemed older, untouched. Streams cut across their path, glinting like silver under the morning sun. Deer bounded at a distance, vanishing into the trees with quick grace. The silence between the two men grew thick, filled with the unspoken weight of what lay ahead.

Bass's mind kept turning back to Bennie, the boy who once followed him with wide eyes, mimicking the way he rode, the way he wore his hat, the way he carried himself like the world couldn't bend him. That same boy is now on the run, drunk, desperate, with blood on his hands.

Stands Tall seemed to sense the storm inside him. "Your son walks in shadows now," he said quietly. "But shadows cannot hide forever from the rising sun."

Bass grunted, not answering. He kept his eyes fixed on the trail, his jaw set. Words, no matter how wise, could lighten the burden he carried.

After a while, Stands Tall slowed his steps and lifted a hand, pointing to the faint impressions in the earth. Hoof prints, leading westward. Fresh enough that the dew had not yet dried inside the indentations.

Bass leaned forward in his saddle, studying the tracks. His eyes narrowed. "Bennie," he whispered under his breath.

The chase had begun in earnest.

And though the lawman in him welcomed the trail, the father in him feared what he would find at its end.

The hotel lobby smelled faintly of kerosene and pine oil, a mixture that clung to the nose and reminded Bass

Reeves of the backwoods cabins where he'd hidden out away from people as a child years ago. The lamps along the wall flickered yellow-orange, casting shadows that stretched long and spindly across the polished wooden floors. Dust motes hovered in the air, stirred by the swing of the heavy lobby doors each time a stranger passed through. The place had a hushed dignity about it, though it was clear the hotel had seen finer days. The wallpaper peeled in places, the floral print fading like old bruises, and the brass fittings at the counter had lost their shine.

Bass leaned against the counter, his hat tilted low, one hand resting easily against his gunbelt, the other tapping idly at the worn leather of his holster. He looked calm, but inside he was coiled tight. His boy was out there, somewhere down the trail, and every stop, every stranger, every whispered word in a dim-lit parlor mattered.

The hotel clerk, a middle-aged woman with hair the color of corn husk and eyes sharp as pins, regarded him with equal parts suspicion and amusement. She was used to drifters, gamblers, outlaws, and the occasional lawman who wandered through, but there was something about Bass Reeves that didn't fit neatly into any one of those categories. His presence filled the room, and the way he spoke, polite, measured, but edged, made even a seasoned frontier clerk sit up straighter.

"Ma'am," Bass drawled, tipping his hat just enough to show the seriousness in his gaze, "where can an hombre such as myself find a strong drink and a sweet gal?"

The woman's lips twitched, almost a smile but not quite. She leaned forward on the counter, folding her hands together as if she were about to tell him a secret. "Yawls saloon's down the hill," she said, her voice a mixture of weariness and warning. "Go right and follow all the hooting and a hollering. Can't miss it. They've been raising Cain & Abel from the dead down there since sundown."

Bass gave a short, deep chuckle. "Well, thank ye kindly."

He turned, but lingered just long enough to glance around the lobby once more. A few weary travelers sat slumped in the high-backed chairs near the fireplace. One was a merchant with a ledger open across his knees, spectacles sliding down his nose. Another was a thin, rail-jawed man in dusty riding clothes who kept one hand hidden beneath his coat, as though protecting something more precious than coin. Both men avoided Bass's gaze when his eyes swept over them, and that told him all he needed. Strangers always noticed him, but guilty men never wanted to be noticed back.

He stepped toward the door, boots echoing softly on the floorboards, but the clerk's voice caught him before he could push into the night.

"Sir," she said, lowering her tone. "If you're headed that way, best keep your wits sharp. The saloon attracts all sorts. Men drink too hard, gamble too heavily, and fight too quickly. A womon or two will try to smile you into forgetting who you are. They say more blood's been spilled in that place than whiskey."

Bass turned slightly, meeting her steady gaze. He studied her for a moment, weighing whether her words were mere gossip or the kind of truth spoken by someone who'd scrubbed too many stains off the floorboards.

"Ma'am," he said quietly, his voice deep as the rumble of distant thunder, "trouble doesn't tend to follow me far. I reckon it knows better."

For a fleeting moment, the clerk's stern face softened into respect. She gave a small nod, and Bass tipped his hat again before pushing out into the cool night air.

The town stretched before him, alive in its own rough-and-tumble way. The saloon was impossible to miss, just as the clerk had promised. Even from the top of the hill, Bass could hear the clatter of glasses, the jangling of a piano played without rhythm, and the rowdy shouts of men who'd lost track of the hour and perhaps their coin purses too. The building's windows glowed warm, spilling light onto the muddy street where horses were tethered in a long, restless line. The sound of their hooves pawing the earth mingled with the laughter and curses that drifted up the hill.

Bass paused for a moment, scanning the shadows. His years as a deputy had taught him never to walk blind into a den of vice. Trouble had a way of gathering in corners, watching, waiting for a lawman to misstep. He drew a slow breath, exhaled, then started down the hill with measured strides, every inch the hunter who knew his quarry was near.

Halfway down, he passed two young boys darting between the shadows, their pockets clinking with stolen coins lifted from the careless drunks inside. They froze when they saw him, wide-eyed, as though they'd been caught stealing bread from the Lord's own table. Bass gave them a look, stern, unblinking, but said nothing. The boys scattered like quail flushed from the brush.

At the saloon's swinging doors, Bass stopped again, tilting his head to catch the sounds within. A high-pitched laugh, almost shrill. A man's angry bark demanding another round. The shuffle of boots as someone lost a bet and shoved the table. And beneath it all, the off-key piano was dragging a ragged tune into the smoky air.

He pressed one palm against the door and paused. In his mind, he could see Bennie, his son, younger by years, sitting at the family table with his head bent low, ashamed after some childish mischief. He remembered Jennie's voice calling the boy stubborn as a mule, but soft-hearted too. That boy was gone now, buried beneath drink and rage, replaced by a man who had killed his wife in cold blood.

Bass's jaw tightened. He wasn't here for whiskey or women. He was here for whispers, for trails that might lead him closer to the truth.

When he finally pushed through the doors, the saloon swallowed him whole. Smoke hung heavy in the air, blurring the lamps into halos of orange. Men crowded the bar, their hats tipped back, faces flushed with liquor. Women in bright dresses leaned over chairs and tables, laughter spilling like cheap perfume. Dice rattled, coins clinked, voices rose, and above it all, the barkeep's shout tried to keep order where none could be kept.

Bass stepped inside his presence, cutting through the din like a blade. Some glanced up, recognized him, and quickly turned back to their drinks. Others stared longer, curiosity painted across their faces. A few, those with the sense to know who he was, shifted uncomfortably in their seats.

He walked toward the bar, boots thudding steadily, his eyes scanning every face, every shadow, every movement. Somewhere in this den of noise and lies, someone had seen Bennie. Someone knew where he had gone.

Beneath the chaos, there were always whispers. A name muttered too loud, a boast made careless in drink, a truth slipping free in the shadows. His boy had passed through here, he knew it in his bones, and this was the kind of place where the trail might pick itself up again.

There, at the far end of the bar, shoulders hunched, hat tipped low, stood his boy. Bennie. Ordering a drink as if the whole world weren't collapsing around him.

Bass froze, breath held tight in his chest. His heart thundered like hoof-beats, not from fear but from the ache of knowing. I knew it. I knew it, I knew it! The words echoed in his mind, bitter as whiskey. I knew he'd bring his ass straight here, and with a bounty on his head too.

The moment stretched, heavy as lead. He could turn away, walk out into the darkness, pretend he hadn't seen. But Bass Reeves wasn't built that way. Duty ran in his bones like marrow.

He pushed through silently, unnoticed by Bennie and half the room besides. The piano clinked a ragged tune, notes stumbling over one another, but the noise gave him cover.

Bass walked straight to the pianist, leaned low, and whispered in his ear. A silver coin slid from his palm to the polished wood of the instrument, gleaming under the lamplight. The music stopped. Silence swelled like thunderclouds.

Straightening, Bass moved with deliberate steps, circling behind his son. He raised his badge high in one hand, Deputy U.S. Marshal, shining with authority, while his other hand lifted his Colt. In a single motion, he fired a shot into the floor.

The blast cracked like lightning. The saloon erupted in screams. Men jumped, women shrieked, chairs clattered to the floor. Every face turned toward the towering lawman who stood behind Bennie Reeves, pistol smoking in his grip.

Scared stiff, Bennie froze at the bar. His back went rigid. Slowly, painfully slow, he turned to face the man he feared most and loved best. His father.

Bass's voice rolled through the room, low and unyielding:

"Everybody out. I am Deputy Marshal Bass Reeves."

The room emptied fast. Boots pounded the floor as drinkers scrambled for the doors. The pianist snatched up his coin and vanished. Only Bennie remained, rooted to the spot, wide-eyed, lips trembling.

"Dad," he stammered, the word breaking like a boy's cry. "I'm sorry! I didn't think, I just shot."

Bass's gaze cut deep, his voice steady as stone.

"Listen, Son. Now listen. What you did you can't take back, but you can't run from it either. What does that say, Son?"

From his coat, he pulled the folded paper, the ink just drying, the Judge's warrant heavy as a death knell. He handed it to Bennie.

Bennie's hands shook as he opened it. His eyes traced the words, lips moving. Finally, he whispered:

"Dead or Alive."

Bass stepped closer, looming, the authority of the badge glinting in his hand.

"What happens when a Marshal other than me comes for you, Son, dead or alive?"

Bennie's face crumpled. His voice cracked.

"What are we going to do, Dad? What are we going to do?"

Bass holstered his pistol, his jaw tightening like a vise.

"We are going to go back to Fort Smith. Where you going to turn yourself in and throw yourself on the mercy of the court?"

Tears welled in Bennie's eyes, his body trembling like a cornered colt. "They're gonna hang me, Daddy."

The words struck Bass like a hammer, but he did not falter. He placed a heavy hand on his boy's shoulder, squeezing with both strength and sorrow.

"Do you still pray, boy?"

Bennie lowered his gaze, shame clouding his face. "No, sir... not in a while."

Bass's eyes burned, but his voice stayed firm, carrying both command and a father's love.

"Well, I think you'd better get back to it."

The silence that followed was thicker than smoke. Father and son stood in the wreckage of the moment, the saloon empty around them, only the echo of that single shot in the roof lingering above like judgment itself.

They pulled out of the little town with the tired clank of wagon wheels and the soft thud of hooves on packed dirt, the horizon a thin ribbon of dust and sky. The road ahead was flanked by scrub and mesquite. The sort of country that made a man feel small, and human and very alone. Bass Reeves rode with his son at his flank, the morning sun cutting hard across the land and catching on the metal rim of the wanted poster folded deep inside Bass's coat. It was when a breeze lifted a loose corner of that paper that something in the inked face caught Bass's eye, and it dawned on him who that poster was, Bob Dozier, the millionaire rancher who'd been bringing them girls and liquor.

Bass's jaw tightened. The road felt narrower all at once, like the map of a life folding in on itself. He glanced at Bennie, young and sullen in the saddle, the man he'd raised now carrying the scent of whiskey and trouble. He cleared his throat, half-smile and half-brooding plan, and said, "Hey, Son, wanna do something with your old man for old time's sake?"

Bennie's face lifted, surprised and then a little pleased. "Really, Dad?"

"Well, if I'm keeping you from meeting your friends out in the Territorial Prison." Bass let the sting sit in the air like a dare.

Bennie barked a laugh that tried for bravado but slid into something thin and brittle. "You know what, the hell."

Bass's eyes narrowed toward the horizon. "Because I saw this guy just North East of Greenwood. This guy is all over the territory, and I think we gotta good chance of catching him by surprise.

Son, I realize what's happening to you now is my fault. I ain't been there for you or your Mom. Hell, Robert Harriett, none of yawl Robert told me straight to my face."

Bennie blinked. "he did, did he?"

"He sure as hell did! I didn't know if I was angry or proud." Bass's voice went low, the confession carrying like a stone dropped in a well, round, solid, and making ripples.

Bennie shrugged, a small, guarded thing. "Yeah, he's been working down in the stables providing for him and that lil boy."

"A boy, you don't say." Bass let the surprise into his face, half-amused and half-stunned by the way life kept accumulating surprises without asking permission.

"You didn't know? nawh, you didn't know! yep youse a grand pappy." Bennie grinned, the first honest smile Bass had seen in a long while. It twitched awkwardly at the corners, piggybacked on the guilt and the hurt, but it was there.

Bass's mouth softened for an instant. "After this one, Ima take a break a real break. We got so much money saved, I never have to work again, Ameen. Get to know you, kids, and my wife. I wasn't there for you either like I should have been, but I ain't going to leave or forget about you, hear me." He pulled up close enough to slide a worn gun belt across Bennie's lap, the leather warm from the sun. It was a gesture as much as a tool, passing weight, passing responsibility, passing a sliver of himself back to the boy who had become a man far too quickly.

Bennie's voice came small and eager. "Yes, sir, daddy yes sir."

They rode on, the land opening into a wide range where the world smelled of grass and hot iron and the rumble of distant herds. By midday, the light had an edge to it, and Bass spied a single set of wagon tracks cutting deep and deliberate into the soft shoulder of the road. He pulled his stallion to a stop and slid from the saddle.

"I got something over here, a single set wagon tracks digging pretty deep, either lost settler or ." His voice was expectant, probing for what the tracks would tell.

Bennie leaned forward, hands on his knees, eyes tracing the grooves. "Or someone selling illegal goodies to the natives."

They examined the earth like men reading a language carved in dirt. The impressions were fresh, barely cooled by the dawn's evaporation. The wagon had gone past and circled back lighter than when it left. It wasn't long before the day folded into night and the range turned gray-blue with a cold that bit at the fingers.

That night, in the dark, Bennie's voice came sharp and small. "Daddy, what in the hell are we going to tell the Judge?"

Bass sighed, the kind that comes from the chest and carries a lifetime. "What do you mean? What are we going to tell him? Like here he goes, my dumb ass Son who killed his cheating wife."

Bennie swallowed hard. "No, yeah, but also how you gave a gun and a badge to a wanted murderer."

Bass's patience and law mingled in that next line, taught as a tight rope. "Alleged murderer, you have yet to be found guilty, so you still have some rights."

Bennie gave a resigned little nod. "Okay, alleged murderer." The word felt strange in his mouth, like a foreign thing he'd been handed cold.

Bass's eyes were on the firelight as he tried to find the right words between a father's love and the law he'd sworn to uphold. "I don't know what you want me to say? Son, look, why did you do it anyway?"

The confession came tumbling out like gravel down a hill: "We were fighting as usual, and she said the baby wasn't mine. I lost it and started packing my things. Then Bobbie Lee shows up, talking that better man won shit. Talking about whooping my ass, and I was a bitch. I spun on him, saw the knife in his hand. I fired. She must of really loved him pop cause she dove in front of his bullet. Shooting her wasn't something I ever wanted too do. I loved her, but she loved someone else."

Bass's anger banked and turned into a softer thing, pity, fierce and plain. "Why did you shoot him, Son? Why not just fight him?"

"He had a knife in his hand." Bennie's answer was small and honest, a child's attempt at reason in the middle of an adult nightmare.

"Don't worry, Son, don't worry, we will get through this too." Bass pulled him into an embrace by the fire, the roughness of his hand like shelter. Bennie leaned into it, the two men shaped by blood and mistakes and the dark world they navigated together.

Later, as the moon rose high and the sky cleared, Bass drew them back to the trail. Dawn to dusk, sign to sign, this was how they'd always gotten along. "You see these tracks here and those there."

Bennie had the instincts; he'd learned quickly in the saddle. "That's the same wagon going this way, and coming back lighter. So this is like their route through Indian Territory away from Rangers and Deputy Marshals."

"So they think you think if we follow these tracks, we can find Dozier?" Bass asked, testing the shape of the plan aloud.

"If not, we will find where he's going to be." Bennie's tone had regained some of the cocky steadiness of youth, hope as armor, truth as edged steel.

They smiled and nodded and continued to ride. The land rolled like a slow sea, cattle ghosts in the distance, and the talk turned, like it always did under the open sky, to small domestic things that tried to stitch them back together.

"How did Momma take the news?" Bennie asked quietly, glancing at Bass like a man afraid to break what he already saw.

"She knows and is broken-hearted, but that's alright. She'll be fine, everything takes time, you know." Bass's voice was a quiet vow, the kind he kept to himself in the dark.

"I guess you're right again, if only I had listened to you, Dad, this stuff wouldn't even have happened." Bennie's regret came wrapped in a fatigue.

Bass's reply was sharp only because he meant to be firm. "We can't do this thinking about that now, boy, you hear me. You got to stay focused on the job at hand. We both need to make it back to Fort Smith."

"Well, this Dozier sounds like the job ole Tommy Willabang was talking about. Some rich rancher was supposed to be out here running all the illegal business in the state. From Larcenist stuff to murder, his hand is supposed to be in the pot." Bennie's words scattered with the way the wind took them, bits of gossip and fact braided together.

"Some Cow Polk slid up on me, and was warning me not to take any Bills with his boss's name on it. Said his name was Bob Dozier. Said if I did, he would kill me. I told that piece of shit to tell him. Not if I see him first." Bass's low growl of a laugh was not a joke, just the kind of promise a man makes when he's pushed.

"Well, Tommy said he was to meet up with him in the Cherokee Nation, but that was some 4-5 weeks ago." Bennie folded his hands over the gunbelt, watching the horizon.

"From looking at these tracks, I would say these people are creatures of habit." Bass's eyes scanned the land, reading what the earth offered like a book.

"Okay, Dad, I see what you're saying, and how you got there, too." "Let's pick up our pace, we might just catch'em off guard." Bass urged, and the horses answered like they knew the work and what was demanded of them. They rode on, two men, father and son, under a wide and indifferent sky, hot on a trail that led to other men's business and, perhaps, karma-tic redemption. The road ahead promised trouble and maybe salvation, and as the sun sloped toward late afternoon, they rode faster, ready to surprise a millionaire if need be, or to pull a weary boy back from the edge of himself.

A Father's Duty

The western sun had long since surrendered to a moonless, star-choked night, its immense quiet broken only by the rhythmic crunch of hooves on loose shale. Bass Reeves, his wide shoulders slightly slumped in the saddle after a long day's ride, led his young companion, Bennie, into the mouth of a deep, jagged ravine. The air here was suddenly cooler, trapped and heavy with the scent of damp earth and dry sagebrush, an isolated, ideal place to make camp.

"We'll water the horses here," Bass muttered, pulling on the reins. "Should be good cover to settle down until the mornin'."

Before the words had fully left his lips, the silence of the night was shattered. The crisp whistle, then a sharp, deafening crack of a rifle, or was it two?, echoed wildly off the canyon walls.

WHIZZZ!

Something struck Bass's head with a violent thwack, not enough to cause pain, but enough to register the terrifying proximity. His iconic, sweat-stained hat, the brim of which had shielded his eyes from a thousand suns and stood as his professional crown, flew off his head and tumbled into the dirt.

Instinct, honed by decades of survival in the roughest territories, took over. There was no thought, only action. Both men went diving for cover off their horses in a single, fluid motion. Bass hit the ground hard behind a thick, sheltering boulder, the shale biting into his knees. Bennie, younger and faster, belly-crawled behind the nearest cluster of low-lying rocks.

The horses, startled and trained for the chaos of a gunfight, whinnied once before trotting a short distance away, knowing better than to stick around the gunfire.

A voice, rough and heavy with self-importance, boomed through the canyon, its sound unnaturally amplified by the narrow space.

"I told you, Bass Reeves!" the voice sneered, dripping with triumph. It was the voice of Bob Dozier, a small-time crook with a large-time reputation for trouble, a man Bass had been tracking for weeks. Dozier sounded close, too close. "I sent my messenger boy. You shoulda have turned back when you had the chance, Deputy. You've done a bit more than you can chew, son."

Bass, breathing shallowly, his pulse drumming a frantic rhythm in his ears, didn't bother to lift his head. He knew responding immediately was an advantage for his attackers. He gathered his thoughts, pulling the familiar weight of his Colt revolver from its holster.

"Now Bob, I think you gotta big head," Bass returned, his voice dangerously level despite the circumstances. He made sure to project it, to let Dozier know the ambush hadn't rattled him one bit. "After all, I ain't lost out chere yet."

He spat a small piece of grit from his mouth. Big head, indeed. Dozier was always more mouth than marshal-killer. Bass needed to figure out how many shooters there were. The first shots had seemed to come from one direction, high up on the ravine's edge.

"What makes you think you can kill me?" Bass finished, adding a slight, derisive laugh to bait the man.

Keeping his voice low, Bass motioned Bennie to flank the pair. He needed Bennie to move right, wide, and low to see if they could get a crossfire angle. Bennie was green but quick and, more importantly, he listened.

Taking a gamble, Bass raised up from behind the boulder, exposing himself for a heartbeat, and fired three shots in the direction of the rounds fired at them, a quick, practiced blam-blam-blam! Aiming not to hit, but to flush them out and confirm their positions.

The response was immediate and terrifyingly accurate. Immediately, from two separate points of fire, return fire is received.

So, two shooters. Dozier and a partner. They were well-placed.

Bass instinctively dropped again, but not fast enough. He felt the sickening whizz of the lead, followed by a sharp, ripping sensation near his chest. His heart momentarily stalled. He looked down. Bass' es button on his shirt flew off from being grazed by a bullet, a dark black disk missing in it's place, with an edge burnt hole. The bullet had torn a clean line through the thick fabric of his coat and shirt, a mere whisper from his ribs. The smell of burnt cordite hung heavy in the air.

Bass felt a sudden, cold wave of rage wash over him, eclipsing the fear. He re-cocked his weapon, his jaw clenched so hard he thought his teeth might crack.

"Yawl missed me, how da hell you gone kill and yawl can't shoot?" he roared, the sheer volume of his voice momentarily shocking the valley into silence. The question was a brutal, professional insult, calculated to make his ambushers rush their next shots.

He then quickly signals Bennie, a sharp whistle, a subtle jerk of his head. Now.

Bennie begins to unload on where the points of fire came from. The young man was a whirlwind of motion, his shots far less precise than Bass's, but his goal was different: suppression. He wasn't trying to hit them; he was trying to make them move. Bullets and dirt whizzing by the two assailants forces them to move from cover and run for it.

The tactic worked flawlessly. Bass watched two dark shapes scramble from the high ground. Dozier was bulky and slow, his partner leaner and quicker, already scrambling down the far side of the ravine toward a path leading out into the open prairie.

Without a second thought, both Bass and Bennie go into pursuit of the fleeing ambushers. Bass didn't wait to grab his horse; his legs were still the fastest thing he owned. He scrambled up the rough terrain toward Dozier, who was already disappearing into the shadows.

"Get his henchmen, Bennie!" Bass yelled, his voice strained from the climb. The henchman was the smaller, faster target, the one who would get away clean if Bennie didn't press him.

Bennie, energized by the chase and the approval, gave a shout of confirmation. "Yep, I'm on him, Daddy!"

Dozier, meanwhile, seemed to have found a momentary patch of thick, stunted cedar trees for cover. Bass, momentarily losing sight of the large man, plunged into the shadowy growth. He wasn't running purely on sight now; he was hiding behind a tree listening for any movement. Every rustle of dry leaf, every shifted pebble, became a vital clue. He held his breath, straining to hear the scrape of a boot or the heavy gasp of his quarry.

Crack-BOOM!

The sound was enormous, far too close. The tree directly next to him explodes with incoming gunfire. Splinters flew into the night, sharp and stinging, and the air was thick with smoke. Dozier, it seemed, had been waiting. Bass felt a rush of heat and the wind of the projectile. The wood saved him by mere inches.

Bass stepped out, his voice calm, yet edged with genuine amusement at his own luck and Dozier's terrible aim. "Missed again, ole friend."

Dozier's return was immediate, raw with frustration. "I ain't your damn friend."

Silence fell again, a taut, straining pause in the fight. Bass could hear Dozier's heavy, wheezing breaths from somewhere just ahead.

Then, Dozier's voice, suddenly hesitant, almost childishly hopeful, cut through the dark. "Bass... hey Bass... you alright... Common now, Bass, don't play with my emotions."

He was talking to the splintered tree, trying to draw Bass out, trying to ascertain if he'd succeeded. The tone shifted to manic, desperate self-congratulation.

"Did I get the Lone Ranger? Do I get to say I shot and killed Deputy Marshall Bass Reeves? I'm am the greatest of all." Dozier was beginning to rave, losing control, convinced that his final, lucky shot had found its mark. He was standing up now, Bass realized, consumed by a need to celebrate his imaginary victory.

This was the opening Bass had been waiting for.

He moved from behind his charred cover, raised his Colt quickly, and fired a flurry of rounds. He didn't stop to aim; he just pointed and fired, letting the pure muscle memory of his training guide his hands.

Dozier let out a gasp, not a scream, but a short, sharp expulsion of air, and stumbled backward. Dozier is hit. He pitched forward, falling into the dirt with a heavy, final thud.

Bass lowered his smoking gun. He felt the grim satisfaction of a dangerous job completed, but none of the elation Dozier had anticipated. He walked slowly toward the fallen man.

"Everything ain't all ways what it seem, huh Dozier?" Bass said, the words quiet, a simple statement of fact. He looked down at the man, who was clutching his chest, breathing hard. The fight was gone from his eyes. "Hey, Dozier, you alright!"

He had to make sure the man was truly disabled, that he wouldn't try one last, desperate grab for a hidden weapon.

The sound of Bennie's scrambling footsteps drew his attention. The young man burst out from the shadows down the hill, breathing hard and defeated.

"He's getting away, Daddy! I missed him!" Bennie wailed, pointing forlornly toward a rising bluff. The second henchman, the fast one, had managed to reach the crest of the hill and was now little more than a silhouette against the barely visible horizon, running for his life.

Bass didn't look angry; he simply looked resolved. His eyes, now entirely focused on the fleeing man, narrowed to slits. He saw the henchman pause at the summit, perhaps glancing back one last time in triumph or curiosity, a fatal mistake.

"Ima a show you how to break a neck, son," Bass said, the words a low promise. It wasn't about revenge; it was about professionalism, about the message it would send to every outlaw who thought they could ambush a U.S. Deputy Marshal and simply walk away.

He quickly turned his attention to his horse, which had wisely retreated to a cluster of nearby bushes, and snatched the rifle that was sheathed in its saddle boot, his imposing .50 caliber Sharps. This was a long-distance weapon, a buffalo gun, used only when a crime was severe and a clear message had to be sent.

He dropped to one knee, ignoring the pain in his joints, and brought the massive rifle to his shoulder. He checked the wind, made an instant, subconscious calculation of the distance, the trajectory, the rise of the land, and the darkness. He lined up the front sight post with the distant, minuscule figure.

Bass takes a deep breath and releases it loudly. The exhale emptied his lungs and cleared the tension from his muscles, turning his body into a tripod of stone. He held the air from his second breath, and then, again on the air release, he squeezed the trigger.

The pop of smoke is seen on top of the hill before the sound of the rifle blast, a deep, booming CRACK! A split second later, the air crackled with the sound of the high-powered round.

The distant silhouette stopped moving. Then the fleeing henchmen's neck explodes. The man's body crumpled instantly, falling out of sight behind the bluff, not a single cry leaving his lips. The sudden, violent finality of the shot was absolute.

Bass rose slowly, blowing the smoke away from the barrel of the Sharps. He never bothered to look at the body. It was done.

"Go on, collect dim boots," Bass told Bennie, a quiet command. The dead man's boots were proof, evidence, and a grim reminder of the cost of tangling with the law.

Bennie, who had been frozen in place, finally let out the breath he'd been holding. He looked from the smoking rifle in Bass's hands to the distant hill, his eyes wide with a profound mixture of shock, awe, and admiration.

"Wow, Daddy, what a shot," he whispered. The rest of the ravine was silent once more, save for the soft, steady breathing of the Deputy Marshal.

Morning After

The rising sun, still low and hazy, spilled a stark, uncompromising light over the scene of the previous night's violence. It softened all of the harsh, cold realities. The ravine was silent now, holding its breath. Bass Reeves, his movements slow and methodical, checked the knots securing Bob Dozier to the saddle. The former outlaw was alive, sullen, and nursing a nasty wound, destined for trial and, most likely, years in the federal penitentiary.

Bennie, his youthful energy subdued by the reality of what was waiting for him, rode his horse alongside Bass. He hadn't slept well. The image of the distant henchman's violent end. His neck was erupting as if a dynamite stick was tied to it, a terrifying specter that hovered just behind his eyelids.

They were now riding out onto the open range, headed east, toward the nearest jurisdiction where Bass could deliver his prisoner. The air was cool, but the sun promised a brutal, arid day.

Bass glanced over at the young man. Bennie was wearing a clean, folded-up shirt that looked fresh-pressed, but his face was drawn, his eyes dark. He hadn't spoken much since they left the camp, occupied with his own turmoil. Last night, Bennie had faltered. He had allowed the second man to get away, relying on Bass to clean up his mess. Bass knew the boy was punishing himself more effectively than any lecture could.

"I see you got your brave face on, Son," Bass observed, his voice calm and low, cutting through the silence of the prairie. It wasn't a question or an accusation, just a simple statement of observation.

Bennie's gaze was fixed on the horse's mane, his grip on the reins tight enough to blanch his knuckles. He wore the expression of a man facing the gallows, not a young rider simply starting his day. The weight of his failure felt like lead in his gut. He hadn't been fast enough. He hadn't been good enough. He had let his father down.

"Like you say, Daddy," Bennie finally managed, his voice thin and dry. He swallowed hard, forcing himself to look up and meet Bass's steady, dark eyes. "I did it. I gotta face it."

He didn't need to elaborate. Bass knew 'it' meant more than just missing the target. It meant losing control under pressure. It meant hesitating, freezing, failing to finish the job he'd signed up for. It meant realizing, in a terrifying flash, that the line between a deputy marshal and a dead man could be measured in the time it took to squeeze a trigger.

Bass let a moment of silence pass, letting Bennie feel the full gravity of his own admission. He guided his horse around a clump of stubborn, dry brush, his thoughts deep. This wasn't just about a gunfight; it was about shaping the next generation of lawmen, about instilling the core value of responsibility.

"That's the difference between a man who enforces the law and a man who breaks it, Bennie," Bass finally said, shifting slightly in the saddle. "When a man does wrong, he can run, he can hide, but he can't deny the truth till the day he dies. But a lawman, son? A lawman must always face the consequences of his actions, whether those consequences are a bullet in the dark or a failure to uphold his duty."

The truth settled heavily on Bennie. The second henchman, the one Bass had vaporized with the Sharps, was a consequence of Bennie's failure. The burden of that death, even justified, felt immense. He was supposed to bring him in alive, to face justice. He'd forced his father to pass the final, lethal sentence.

"You're thinking about the man on the hill," Bass stated, reading his son's mind with effortless precision. "Don't look away. I put a round in his neck to save yours. He was running, yes, but he was running to find a better place to kill us from. That was my choice, made in an instant, to preserve the peace and my own life. That choice is on my ledger, not yours."

Bennie shook his head miserably. "But I let him go, Daddy. You told me to get him. You told me to, "

"I told you to get him, Bennie, not to kill yourself trying," Bass corrected gently, though his tone held the undeniable weight of a Marshal's authority. "But you did hesitate. That's the bitter pill. You let your fear get between you and your duty. And fear, Bennie, is a wildfire in the Territory. It spreads fast, and it kills quickly. It killed that man up on the hill because I couldn't afford to let him kill us, hear!"

They rode in silence again, the sun climbing higher, heating the air. Bass was teaching, not scolding. He was imparting the kind of grim wisdom that couldn't be taught in a book. The law was clear; the execution of it was not.

Bass pulled his horse up slightly, slowing their pace. He reached into his coat pocket and pulled out a small, flat piece of shell, the pearl button that had been torn from his shirt by the bullet the night before. He turned it over and over in his massive palm, the black pearl gleaming softly.

"See this?" he murmured, holding it up for Bennie. "This is how close a man can get to death and still miss. That bullet came from Dozier's man, the one you were chasing. If you had kept your head down, if you had not forced him to run with your barrage. That bullet might have found my heart instead of my shirt."

He flipped the button into the air, and Bennie caught it. "Last night, we were lucky. Luck runs out faster than water in the desert. In this line of work, we don't bet on luck; we bet on resolve. You missed your target, and you missed your opportunity to prove your resolve, but you saved my hide."

Bennie felt the sting, but it was a righteous, clarifying pain. He knew his father was right. He wasn't mad; he was disappointed, and that was far worse. His gratitude, though, eased a lil-bit of hi consciousness

"I won't miss next time," Bennie vowed, his voice gaining a hard, brittle edge.

Bass stopped his horse entirely, turning fully toward his son, his expression stern. "To be so formidable, so resolute, so known for your fairness and your certainty, that men like Dozier choose the easy life over the bloody one."

He fixed Bennie with a meaningful look. "You are going to face your actions, Bennie. You will write your report. You will have to account for every round fired. When you stand before the Judge, you won't lie. You won't hide. You will tell them what happened last night, the good, the bad, and the places where your courage failed."

Bass then offered his final, crucial piece of instruction, the central creed for a lawman caught between the chaos of the frontier and the cold demands of justice. He offered Bennie a path to redemption, not through excuse, but through absolute truth.

"Remember, son, even mercy for the condemned is warranted.

Don't forget to through yourself on the Mercy of the Court."

It was a profound lesson wrapped in a simple phrase. It meant: Take full ownership of the failure. Don't fight the consequences; embrace them. Trust the system you represent. You are the Marshall's spn, not the judge, and certainly nor the jury. If a mistake was made, a moment of hesitation, a lapse in judgment, admit it and ask for clemency. It was the only way to retain the honor from a failed decision.

Bennie stared at him, the meaning of the words sinking in. It wasn't just about his report; it was about the rest of his life as a Marshall of not.

"Mercy of the court," Bennie repeated softly, trying the words out.

Bass nodded, satisfied. He nudged his horse forward, Dozier following grimly in tow. "That's right. That's how you separate yourself from the outlaws, Bennie. They run from the law; a good lawman walks straight into it, even when the law means judgment for himself."

The sun continued its ascent, turning the red dust of the prairie into a shimmering, oppressive heat. They had a long ride ahead of them, a journey that was not just measured in miles but in the slow, difficult education of a young lawman. Bennie rode quieter now, and thoughtful, the weight of his father's lesson heavy on his conscience.

The rumble of the wheels grinding to a stop was the alarm. The moment Bass's wagon pulled into the clearing, the front door of the homestead burst open. Jennie and two small children, their faces taut with confusion and fear, tumbled out. They ran as if chased, their feet kicking up dust on the hard-packed earth toward the man on the wagon.

Bass barely had time to climb down before Jennie & the kids were on him. Her hands clasped his arms with a frantic, desperate strength that threatened to buckle him. Her voice was a choked cry, raw with maternal terror.

"Bass, oh Lord Bass, where's my baby!"

He held her, grounding himself with the solid weight of her in his arms, while the two little ones clung to the folds of his coat, their wide, silent eyes searching his face for answers their mother couldn't speak. He gently loosened her grip, keeping his hands on her shoulders so she had to look him in the eye.

"Down there in Isaacs' jail, baby." Bass's voice was low, a rough-edged monotone of exhaustion and grim certainty. He swallowed, the words tasting like grit and gunpowder. "He ain't harmed, but he did it. He killed his wife." The confession was a heavy stone he had to lay at her feet. "Told me with his own mouth."

Jennie recoiled as if struck. The color drained from her face, leaving her skin the color of bleached muslin. Her hands flew up, not to strike, but to shake her head in a rapid, vehement denial. She stumbled back a step, her whole body vibrating with disbelief.

"No, Bass! No, not my Bennie! He ain't no killer!"

It was a cry from the soul, the automatic, fierce defense of a mother who simply could not, would not, allow this reality to exist.

Bass let her cling to the false hope for one silent, agonizing moment. He understood the need to reject the monstrous truth. But he had to anchor her to reality.

"Well, she was cheating on him with a boy named Bobby Lee." He spoke clearly, laying out the sordid facts without judgment, just weary reporting. "Who came to the house to confront Bennie?"

Jennie's denial fractured. A soft moan escaped her lips as her hands dropped away from her face, her eyes welling up with tears that magnified the grief and shock in her gaze.

"Oh, Lord," she whispered, the words barely audible.

"Yeah, I know, right!" Bass sighed, running a hand over the back of his neck, remembering the rage and confusion of the previous hours. "I wish I could've warned that boy 'bout Bennie's temper." He paused, leaning in, his tone dropping to a confiding whisper that was meant only for her ears, to offer a slight shift in the shade of the crime. "That ain't why he shot her. He wasn't trying to shoot her; he was trying to shoot her boyfriend."

Bass took a breath, the tragic details playing out once more in his mind. "Who showed up with a knife in his hand to chase Bennie away, I guess? Bennie fired, and that girl dove in front of the bullet, saving that boy's life." He shook his head slowly, a profound sorrow for Bennie's mangled soul mixing with the pity for the dead woman. "That's the thing that seems to bother Bennie the most, too."

The news utterly broke Jennie. The specifics didn't lessen the crime, but they shifted the motive from cold-blooded murder to a volatile tragedy of passion, loyalty, and misplaced aim. She crumpled against his chest, her sobs muffled against the rough cloth of his shirt.

"Oh, Bass, I gotta go see my baby!"

He held her tight, his own resolve firming up. He wouldn't let her fall apart. He had to be the rock now.

"You can," he promised, pulling her back gently, his voice firm and steady. "And we will visit him every Sunday."

Jennie pulled back, her tear-streaked face momentarily hardening with cynicism and doubt, the product of a lifetime of hard-won experience with the unreliability of men and the harshness of the world.

"Visit him every Sunday, huh? I will believe it when I see it, never a common man."

Bass stepped closer, closing the small, emotional distance between them. He took her hands, his thumb rubbing soothing circles on her knuckles. His words were a vow, a line drawn in the unforgiving dust of their homestead.

"Well, get used to it, 'cause I ain't going out no more." He looked past her, a sweeping glance that encompassed the house, the porch, the small vegetable patch, their entire life. He was not just talking about the sheriff's work, but the constant, roving nature of a man who always sought the next horizon. That was over. "I ain't gone lose Robert or one more of mine." The memory of Robert, lost to the river and the fevers, was a constant, sharp ache. He was done with grief and wandering. "I am going to be here for you and these kids."

His declaration resonated in the sudden quiet, a profound shift in the fundamental law of their shared life. Jennie looked at him, truly looked at him, and the grief in her eyes was replaced by a staggering wave of recognition and gratitude.

"Oh, honey, you've done more than anyone should ever ask anyone to do." She ran a hand over his cheek, her gaze moving slowly over his face, taking in the lines of fatigue and worry, the stubborn set of his jaw. She saw the husband she had always hoped he would be, fully and finally realized. "Looking like as a husband... I made a fine choice. A fine choice indeed."

A small, grim satisfaction settled over Bass. He didn't want praise, but he accepted her belief, her renewed faith in him. He knew what he had to do next. The tragedy was set, but the fight for Bennie's future was just beginning.

"I gotta save your Bennie now." He squared his shoulders, the exhaustion momentarily forgotten, replaced by the keen focus of the lawman turned defender. "The trial will bring some light to some circumstances that might help." He was already formulating the defense, dissecting the angles. "I'ma talk to Isaac about it, but in the meantime... We can get one of them fancy lawyer types from Little Rock."

Jennie's eyes widened, a flicker of hope, but also a renewed apprehension about the vast moral compromises she knew he faced.

"Are you sure?" she asked softly. "I know how much Justice means to you, and Bennie killed a man."

Bass took her hands again, holding them tight. He thought of his years of chasing bandits, upholding the law, and the clear lines he always drew between right and wrong. They were smudged now, blurred by his own blood and bone. His answer was not just for Bennie, but for himself.

"You know, losing Bennie like this has me thinking different about," he paused, staring out at the hazy western sky, "What is fighting crime? While my own home is in turmoil." The conviction in his voice was absolute. His first duty was here. His first fight was for his. "Bennie gone be alright, hear me. He's gonna be just fine."

He spoke with the authority of a man who had faced down death too many times to be afraid of a jury, or even the rope. He would find a way. He always did.

The office of Judge Isaac Parker, known universally as "The Hanging Judge," was a place of solemn, dusty authority. The room, smelling of old paper, pipe smoke, and the heavy weight of justice. Bass stood before the mahogany desk, a figure of solid, unmoving resolve, yet there was a tremor of uncertainty in the silence he created.

"Good Morning, Isaac," Bass started, clearing his throat. The words he'd practiced on the ride over felt clumsy, insufficient. "Well, I came up here to… Uhm, well, uhm."

Judge Parker, a large man whose eyes missed nothing, set down his pen. The sudden quiet magnified the importance of Bass's presence.

"Bass, are you quitting on me?" The Judge's voice was deep, lacking any surprise, but full of genuine disappointment. He leaned back in his leather chair, the leather protesting softly. "Now, Bass, you know how valuable you are here to us. I know you've made a nice piece of living for yourself and your family. You probably don't need the money anymore, but what about Law and Order, Bass Reeves? That oath you swore to protect and defend?"

The question was a direct challenge to the very essence of Bass's long, storied career. The Marshal felt the weight of that oath, a moral tether that had kept him riding for decades. It was the deepest part of his character, yet he found he was willing to cut it.

"I hear you, Isaac," Bass replied, his gaze steady on the Judge's. "But my children are suffering." He swallowed, the truth of his neglect a bitter pill. "I can't just pay them no attention. I ain't got time to talk to them, be at their events, or nothing." The simple lack of time for simple fatherhood felt like the greatest failure of all his years. "I'm sorry, Isaac, but I gotta be through."

With a decisive motion that belied the turmoil within him, Bass reached into his coat. The badge, a heavy silver star that had been his identity, his shield, and his burden, came free. He flipped it with a practiced wrist, sending the polished metal clattering softly onto the massive expanse of Isaac's desk. It spun once, then settled, catching the morning light like a final star in the morning sky.

Judge Parker didn't reach for it. He stared at the badge, then at Bass, a study in granite silence.

"Bass, I'm going to hold on to this for a while." The Judge's tone softened, moving from challenge to paternal concern. "We will visit this once we get past this thing with Bennie. Fair enough?"

It was a lifeline, a denial of the finality of the act, and Bass nodded, accepting the temporary reprieve. He knew the Judge wasn't ready to lose him, and Bass wasn't ready to let go either. He just needs to handle this Bennie thing.

The Judge pulled out a notepad, the gesture signaling a professional transition. The role of friend and boss receded; the Judge was now ready to hear the Marshal's report, the report on his own kin.

"Isaac, just a report I gotta write," Bass began, his voice shifting into the measured, objective tone of law enforcement. He was building the case for clemency, brick by difficult brick. "It's to say: upon further investigation, I see evidence of self-defense in the accidental death of our victim."

He provided the narrative, stripped bare of emotion, focused only on the facts that mattered in a court of law.

"Bennie had caught his wife cheating, and a domestic altercation began. The deceased wife's boyfriend came to the alleged murderer's home. Armed with a knife in hand to defend his relationship with another man's wife." Bass paused, letting the volatile image sink in. A man with a knife invading another man's home was a different animal than a jealous killer.

"The murderer alleges that seeing the knife caused him to turn and discharge his Winchester. Upon doing so, the wife dove in front of the shot. To save the life of Bobby Lee Edwards." Bass finished with the crucial detail, the evidence that transformed the charge. "Said story confirmed by Mr. Bobby Lee Edwards."

The Judge scribbled a few rapid notes, his expression unreadable as he processed the tragic confluence of adultery, violence, and misplaced heroism. He looked up, his eyes keen.

"You bring me evidence to support the court," the Judge declared. He knew the nature of frontier justice and the mitigating circumstances Bass had presented. "Life, out in ten if he behaves."

Ten years. A lifetime for some, but far better than the noose or a life sentence. Bass pressed the advantage.

"That sounds fair, Your Honor. Can we revisit in five years with exceptional behavior?"

Parker's pen hovered over the paper. He understood the plea, a father desperate for his son's future. The Judge made his terms clear.

"Bring the witness, and it's written in stone, ole boy."

Bass exhaled slowly, the tension draining out of his shoulders. The fight was not over, but the war was winnable.

"I can't wait 'til tell Jennie. It's still going to break her heart, but that's on Bennie to heal."

"I agree with you there, ole buddy," the Judge grumbled, a wry look crossing his face. He leaned forward, tapping the desk. "And goddamn, the back-door man came to the front door!"

Bass shook his head, a mixture of fatigue and philosophical resignation. "These young'uns are different, Judge. Their values are in turmoil."

The Judge snorted, his cynicism for the younger generation fully activated. "I guess turmoil does rhyme with spoiled. They all need ass-whoopin's."

Bass gave a weak, tired smile. The generation gap was real, but his immediate concerns were purely domestic.

"My Robert made me a granddaddy again, and I ain't even seen the baby. That's why I gotta tend to what's important."

The Judge nodded, the professional distance finally dissolving, replaced by genuine empathy for his friend. "I hear you, believe me, I do. But I never thought I would see the day you gave up Law Enforcement. I guess I'm in shock." He picked up the star on his desk, turning it over in his hand. "There's nothing or no one more important than family, Bass. Like I said, I'm holding on to your badge for a few days. Then we will revisit."

Bass nodded once, a final, grateful acknowledgment. The Marshal had left the saddle, but he hadn't completely burned his bridges. The star remained, waiting, but for now, his steps would take him home.

The air inside the homestead felt thick with anticipation, mirroring the late afternoon sun that slanted through the dusty windowpanes on what marked Day 70 of their waiting game.

Jennie leaned forward on the worn sofa, her gaze fixed on Bass, who had just returned from what felt like an eternity at the courthouse. The silence between them stretched thin, punctuated only by the faint chirping of crickets outside.

"How'd things go, Bass?" she finally asked, her voice a low, tight knot of anxiety. She gripped her hands together, a nervous habit she'd developed over the last several weeks. "Was the Judge listening to you, was he... receptive?" She searched his face for any sign, a slump of the shoulders, a furrowed brow, that might betray the outcome. Her heart hammered against her ribs, the rhythm echoing the relentless ticking of the grandfather clock in the hall.

Bass peeled off his ill-fitting tweed jacket, a garment he only wore for court appearances, and tossed it carelessly over the back of a chair. He ran a hand over his close-cropped hair, a small, weary smile playing on his lips.

"Good Lawd, Receptive!" he boomed, a deep chuckle rumbling in his chest, a sound that immediately eased a fraction of Jennie's tension. He seemed... lighter. "You using them Horty Torty words on me now, ain't ya?" He paused, letting the dramatic effect linger, before moving to the table and pouring himself a glass of water from a ceramic pitcher.

He took a long, slow drink, his eyes meeting hers over the rim of the glass. The suspense was almost unbearable, but Jennie knew better than to rush him. Bass liked to savor a good moment.

"I'd say he did," he stated, setting the glass down with a decisive thunk. "He was listening. He was considering."

Jennie let out a small, shaky breath she hadn't realized she was holding.

"But," Bass continued, leaning against the edge of the table, his posture becoming more serious, "there are some things I gotta gather up. Details and documented witness statements. Folks who will speak on his behalf and not run for the hills."

He then delivered the news, the carefully negotiated terms that had cost him days of legal wrangling and nights of agonizing strategy. He didn't soften it, didn't dress it up in legal jargon, preferring to lay the plain, hard truth between them.

"The offer," he said, his voice dropping to a serious, confidential tone, "is life... with a clause. Ten years, provided there's good behavior. And then, if we can show they've seen five years of exceptional behavior, not just staying out of trouble, but truly making a difference, we have a path forward."

It wasn't freedom. Not yet. But in the long, dark tunnel they had been traversing, Bass had just held up a small, steady lamp. It was a lifeline; a sliver of hope carved out of a sentence. It meant that 'life' didn't necessarily mean forever. It meant a chance.

The next morning, Bass was not resting on the small victory of the plea deal. He knew time was their enemy, and the "things I gotta gather up", the corroborating witnesses and favorable evidence, required immediate action. That action led him to a cheap, nondescript hotel on the edge of town. Word around town was Bobby Lee Edwards came back after 4 hours of searching for Bennie.

It was still mid-morning, the sun already glaring off the dusty windows of the establishment. Bass stood in the narrow, stale-smelling hallway, the floral wallpaper peeling at the seams, and hammered his fist against a door near the end of the corridor. This room, he suspected, held a critical piece of the puzzle: Bobby Lee.

"Bass! Bass Reeves!" he called out, his deep voice echoing in the confined space. "Bobby Lee, is that you!"

Silence. Bass knocked again, harder this time, his impatience growing like a sudden fever. He was about to try the handle when a sudden, distinct sound pierced the quiet. It wasn't the door opening; it was the audible shriek of a window being violently thrown up in the room, followed immediately by a panicked, desperate woman screaming: "Run, baby, run!"

Then came the chaotic cacophony of a struggle within: a violent crash, a heavy bang. Bass didn't hesitate. He reared back and delivered a brutal, practiced kick to the lock plate. The thin wood surrounding the bolt shattered, splintering with a sharp crack, and the door flew inward, hitting the wall with a resounding slam.

Bass burst into the room, his hand instinctively hovering near the pistol tucked into his belt. The scene was pure pandemonium. The furniture was overturned, and the open window provided a clear view of an alleyway where a man, presumably Bobby Lee, was already scrambling over, looking for a low spot to jump.

But Bass's path was instantly, and most unexpectedly, blocked.

A figure launched itself at him, a whirlwind of furious limbs and wild panic. It was the woman, and to Bass's stunned surprise, she was entirely naked, having apparently been roused from bed by the commotion. Her eyes were wide with terror and rage, and she was already swinging wildly.

"Get out! Get out, you damn lawman!" she shrieked, driven by a primal need to protect her accomplice, or perhaps herself.

Bass tried to pivot toward the window, but the woman grabbed hold of him with the ferocious, desperate strength of a cornered animal. She clawed, she punched, she grappled, her weight surprisingly effective as she wrestled him away from the open air. Bass was forced to abandon the immediate pursuit of Bobby Lee, now out of sight, and focus on the immediate, bizarre threat before him.

He was a legendary U.S. Marshal, known for his ability to disarm and subdue the most vicious bandits, yet here he was, suffering a bewildering and painful beating he was taking from the naked lady.

"Bitch, if you don't get off me!" Bass roared, trying to maintain some semblance of decorum while fending off her flailing attacks. He tried to grip her shoulders, to push her away without genuinely hurting her, but she was relentless.

She managed to sink her fingernails into his cheek, tearing a small, stinging line of blood. "Yeah! All you lawmen are killers!" she spat, fear and loathing contorting her features.

Bass finally managed to twist free, pinning her wrists just long enough to put some distance between them, breathing heavily as he wiped the trickle of blood from his face. The absurdity of the situation struck him even in the heat of the moment.

"You might be on to something there, but why can't I do right the fuck now?" he grunted, a cynical edge to his voice, his eyes already snapping back to the window. Bobby Lee was gone, and the trail was cold. He'd lost the witness, but he'd gained a fresh scratch and another strange tale for the road.

The dawn of Day 2 found Bass staked out across the alleyway from the rear of the hotel. He was nestled in the shadows of a dilapidated storage shed, his senses keyed to the quiet rhythm of the morning. He hadn't bothered with another tweed jacket; today was about speed, silence, and capture. He wore dark, practical clothing that blended into the gloom.

He waited, not moving, for nearly three hours. The sun began to creep over the rooftops, painting the alley in stripes of sharp reds and yellow light. Then, a movement. Bobby Lee emerged from the back door of the hotel, looking nervous and furtive, his eyes darting quickly around the empty alley. He was clearly operating on the belief that the "slow lawman" was long gone, chasing ghosts in the next county.

Bobby Lee was heading straight for a sturdy roan horse tied loosely to a hitching post near the back wall, its saddle already in place. His plan was clear: mount up and vanish.

Bass saw his opportunity, a moment of overconfidence. He was directly above the man, on the flat, gravel-covered roof of the single-story section of the hotel's storage shed.

With a speed that belied his years, he launched himself off the tar-and-gravel roof. He moved with the quiet grace of a man who had spent his life tracking wanted men across the harsh terrain of the frontier. His feet pounded a silent rhythm on the alleyway's edge.

He saw his prey reaching the animal, his hand already gripping the horn of the saddle, about to swing his leg over. There was no time to hesitate, no time for shouted warnings. Bass took a running leap, launching himself into the open air.

He landed on Bobby Lee with the full, bone-jarring impact of a grown man, tackling him mid-mount. The horse shied violently, whinnying in alarm, snapping the tether. The two men hit the dirt in a cloud of dust and startled grit. The breath was knocked violently out of Bobby Lee's lungs.

Bass was on him instantly, his knees pinning the younger man's arms, the hard muzzle of his own pistol pressed against the side of Bobby Lee's neck. The brief chase was over.

BOBBY LEE sputtered, coughing the dust out of his throat, his eyes wide with shocked disbelief. He'd been cocky, and it had cost him dearly.

"Yeah, old slow man! What the hell !" His bravado evaporated instantly upon realizing the proximity of the cold steel against his skin. His face went ashen, and the arrogance twisted into raw terror. "Come on! Please don't kill! Please don't kill me!" he begged, his voice cracking with desperation, his hands trying futilely to push Bass away.

Bass pressed the gun a fraction deeper, a look of steely resolve fixed on his face.

"Slow, huh? Caught yo' ass, didn't I?" Bass retorted, his tone dry and utterly lacking in sympathy for the man's sudden panic. He holstered the pistol but maintained his dominant position. He wasn't going to shoot him; he needed him alive.

He reached down and hauled Bobby Lee roughly to his feet, dusting him off with a powerful shake. He had to continuously remind himself that this wasn't just a fugitive; he was a potential key to his own son's freedom.

"I'm not going to kill you. What is wrong with you youngsters?" Bass asked, more to himself than to the shivering man. The casual assumption that every lawman was an executioner was a wearisome sign of the times.

Bobby Lee didn't seem to hear the question; he was still reeling from the sudden, violent reversal of fortune. The shock forced a confession out of him, tumbling out in a rush of frantic justification.

"But it's my fault your son is in that trouble," Bobby Lee blurted out, the words laced with guilt and a desperate plea for mercy. "If it wasn't for me, he wouldn't be in jail for murder. I went there to confront him 'cause I was tired of him beatin' on her. She wasn't his anymore."

Bass listened, his expression hardening. He had suspected as much; the violence and the territorial nature of the crime reeked of a love triangle gone fatally wrong. It was a sordid mess, but it offered a path toward proving his son's actions were not premeditated, but rather a reaction to a volatile armed confrontation.

"Oh, and I'm sure she wasn't," Bass responded flatly, his voice devoid of judgment, but not of an ominous weight. He was interested in facts, not morality.

"He wasn't treating her right!" Bobby Lee insisted, grasping for any shred of sympathy. "Smackin' her. She's a pretty girl. She didn't deserve that."

"You might be right about that, but why bring a knife?" Bass's question was a precisely aimed hammer blow, striking at the heart of the legal case. The defense was centered on self-defense, but Bobby Lee's weapon meant that his initial appearance at the scene was an act of aggression, not merely a protective intervention.

Bobby Lee sagged, the energy draining out of him as he realized he'd just admitted to the very thing that made his testimony critical and damaging to himself.

"I wasn't thinking," he whispered, looking down at the ground. "I wanted to scare him, and I didn't know that he ain't somebody you wanna scare. Now someone is dead, you gonna arrest me."

Bass released his grip, stepping back slightly, though he kept his body between Bobby Lee and the runaway horse. He looked at the young man, reckless, desperate, and now terrified, and saw not just a criminal, but a pivotal witness.

"Yes, but you're coming with me now," Bass stated, his tone brooking no argument. He grabbed a set of handcuffs and snapped them onto Bobby Lee's wrists. "To give your statement to one of the notaries. You're going to tell the truth, the whole truth, about how that fight started. Every detail."

The Marshal had his witness. Now, he just had to make sure that the witness didn't hang his own son in the process of saving himself. The legal game was still on.

The morning of Day 3 saw Bass focused entirely on process. He had dragged a subdued and terrified Bobby Lee straight to the County offices, securing a detailed, notarized statement that laid out the timeline of the fateful confrontation. Bobby Lee, faced with the overwhelming authority of a U.S. Marshal and the fear of his own possible arrest for assault with a deadly weapon, had, as expected, talked.

Now, as they stepped out of the heavy wooden door of the Judge's annex, Bass removed the handcuffs. The air was cool and crisp, a welcome change from the stuffy, ink-scented office.

"Well, Bobby, go on home, and thanks for your statement," Bass said, his voice firm but carrying a hint of finality. He had what he needed. "Don't leave town, you hear me!"

Bobby Lee, still pale and shaken, nodded quickly, his eyes wide with relief at his sudden freedom. "I won't, sir, I swear. I never meant for none of this to happen."

"Good, son, good," Bass confirmed, placing a hand briefly on the young man's shoulder. He was a fool, perhaps, but a useful fool. "Now, go on home and stay outta trouble."

Bobby Lee didn't need to be told twice. He turned and practically ran down the steps and across the dusty street, eager to put as much distance as possible between himself and the Marshal.

Bass stood on the landing, taking a deep, restorative breath. The statement was a powerful piece of evidence. It confirmed that the victim had been armed and the aggressor in the encounter that led to Bass's son being jailed. It strengthened the case for self-defense immeasurably, making it even more an accident. He felt the tension that had been locked in his shoulders begin to ease. The path to his son's provisional freedom was clearer now.

But a U.S. Marshal's life never stayed quiet for long.

The relative calm was shattered by a wild, frantic voice. A young runner, a boy named Pete who often carried messages between the Marshal's office and the Judge's chambers, burst out of the office door, nearly colliding with Bass. He was running flat out, hatless, his face slick with sweat, his breath coming in ragged, terrified gasps.

"Bass! Bass!" Pete cried out, his voice a frantic, high-pitched wail. "He done killed 'em both! Both of 'em dead!"

Bass instantly tensed, the easing of his body evaporating. The world of murder and vengeance was never far behind him.

"Who, son? Who got killed? Now, slow down a bit, take a breath," Bass commanded, grabbing the boy's shoulders and forcing him to stop moving. "Now, what happened, and who killed them, and who are they?"

Pete leaned forward, hands on his knees, gulping air, before finally managing to choke out the horrific news.

"James and Thomas, Bass! They're gone!" Pete gasped, his eyes reflecting a deep, primal fear. "Dick Glass killed them both! Sent them... sent them straddling their horses with notes pinned to their backsides!"

Bass's eyes narrowed, instantly dismissing the bizarre insult and focusing on the grim facts. James and Thomas were known to most of the players in the criminal underworld as lawmen.

"They've been scalped," Pete finished, the word hanging lingered in the morning air.

Bass felt a heavy, familiar dread settle in his gut. This wasn't a petty score-settling action. No, this was more of a declaration of war.

"What does the note say, boy? What did the note say?" Bass demanded, his voice low and dangerous. He pulled the boy closer, needing precise details. "Were they dead or alive when they were scalped?" That question was the difference between murder and unspeakable torture.

Pete shook his head frantically, overwhelmed. "I don't know, Bass, I can't tell! And all the note said was 'Hi Bass.' Nothin' more, nothin' less."

The hairs on the back of Bass's neck prickled. It was a personalized message from the demon who murdered Wind of the Gods. It wasn't just a brutal crime; it was a challenge, a taunt aimed directly at him. Dick Glass wasn't just killing; he was sending a grotesque calling card to the most feared lawman in the territory.

"Judge Parker says you ain't gotta bring this one back," Pete managed to relay, finally delivering the most crucial instruction.

Bass understood immediately. Judge Isaac Parker, the "Hanging Judge," had just issued one of his rare, unspoken, but universally understood orders: Bring Dick Glass in dead.

The life of a U.S. Marshal was a constant tug-of-war between duty to the law and personal necessity. One moment, he was a worried father saving his son from the noose; the next, he was the instrument of retribution, tasked with hunting a psychopathic killer who had just targeted him.

He looked down the street, where the dust from Bobby Lee's hurried escape was just settling. He looked at the office door, behind which the notary held the document that could save his son. And then he looked at the terrified boy, whose news had just pulled him violently back onto the bloody trail of the law.

His son's life was secured for the moment, and the territory was watching. The law had been openly mocked. Dick Glass had signed his own death warrant, and Bass Reeves was killer enough to serve it. The Marshal's personal mission was momentarily overshadowed by the overwhelming demands of his badge. He had to hunt.

The stable air was thick with the scent of hay, manure, and the sharp, metallic tang of blood. Bass Reeves and Pete, along with a couple of deputies, entered the dim, cavernous space at the back of the County offices. The sight inside was exactly as brutal as Pete had described, and perhaps worse.

The bodies of James and Thomas were still slumped over their saddles, their hands tied to the rigging, a grotesque mockery of a rider. The notes, scrawled on dirty paper, were indeed pinned to the seat of their pants with long, wicked-looking spikes. The note was brief: "Hi Bass." A personalized challenge.

Bass walked slowly, deliberately, around the horses. He was a Marshal, and he had seen the ugliest face of death countless times, but this specific brand of cruelty, the public display, ignited a cold, slow-burning rage deep in his belly.

He crouched low, examining the wounds and the gruesome state of the victims' heads. The cut lines were ragged, unprofessional, yet undeniably complete. His face was a mask of grim focus. He didn't need a medical examiner. The blood still clung wetly to the lacerations, and the posture of the bodies told a sickening story.

"These boys were alive when they were scalped," Bass stated, his voice flat and hard, cutting through the silence of the stable. It wasn't a question; it was a professional observation delivered with the certainty of a man who knew the language of violence. The manner in which the blood had flowed directly down the head to the trousers, the way their face were distorted from screams of pain. Indicated they had been alive during the scalping.

He stood up, turning to one of the deputies who was frantically covering the gruesome scene.

"Tell Isaac, tell Judge Parker, I'm gonna break ole Dick Glass's neck," Bass vowed, his voice gaining a sudden, powerful resonance that filled the stables. He wasn't just speaking as a Marshall, he was speaking as an avenging force. "For Thomas, for James, and for Wind of the Gods."

The mention of Wind of the Gods, a highly respected friend, and an international lawman who had been brutally ambushed a year prior. A killing widely attributed to Glass's gang elevated this from a job to a vendetta. Dick Glass had gone from an outlaw to a folk hero to a marked man in Bass's personal registry of enemies. The Judge had given the tacit order: bring him in dead. Bass Reeves had just accepted the mission with a personal, spiritual commitment. He would not just catch Glass; he would execute justice in the wilderness.

The emotional weight of the manhunt did not immediately pull Bass from his primary obligation: his family. He spent the next day, Day 4, finalizing the details of the plea deal with the defense team, ensuring that Bobby Lee's statement was properly filed and that the Judge was ready to accept the terms. He ensured the path to his son's eventual freedom was locked down before he allowed the rage against Dick Glass to fully consume him.

On Day 5, Bass returned to the Homestead. He walked into the familiar warmth of his home, the sanctuary he had been desperate to protect. He found Jennie tending to the hearth, but the instant she saw the hard, distant look in his eyes, she knew the fight was not over.

"Thomas and James are dead," he confirmed before she could even ask, his voice devoid of emotion, a controlled instrument trying to mask the fire beneath. He knew the news would have reached her; the murder of two men in such a grisly, public fashion was the only news in the territory.

Jennie's hand flew to her mouth, her eyes widening. But her fear wasn't for the dead; it was for the living, for the man who stood before her, already half-gone to the trail.

"Oh, no, Bass. Oh, no, baby. Oh, my Lord," she whispered, the words trembling with realization. She understood what this meant. A killing this personal, this challenging, meant Bass would have no choice but to ride, no matter the promise he'd made to her two days prior. Dick Glass had essentially thrown down a gauntlet and spat on Bass's badge, and everything law and order stood for.

Bass walked to her, taking her hands in his, his grip firm. He looked deep into her eyes, trying to convey the immense weight of his conflict.

"Jennie, I can't break my promise to you," he insisted, his voice heavy with sincerity. "No matter how bad this is, you and the family are first from now on. I mean it, baby. If you tell me to stay, I'm not moving."

It was the ultimate offering. He was putting his badge, his duty to the territory, and his sworn vengeance against a ruthless killer all secondary to her command.

Jennie looked at his tired, resolute face. She saw the commitment to her, but she also saw the necessary, dangerous duty pulling at him. She saw the rage for his murdered friends and the insult to his authority. She was a woman of the frontier; she knew that when evil threw down a challenge that brazenly, the law must answer, or the whole territory would descend into anarchy. If Bass Reeves didn't ride, not only would Dick Glass be emboldened, but the very law that would eventually free her son would be weakened.

She took a deep breath, steeling herself against the fear that threatened to overwhelm her. The life of a Marshall's wife was a constant lesson in sacrifice.

A faint, almost relieved smile touched her lips, mingled with sorrow. "I'll get you packed and ready!" she declared, her decision made. It wasn't the answer she wanted to give, but the one she had to.

She didn't wait for his response, disappearing into the back of the house with a sudden, purposeful energy. She knew that the quicker he left, the quicker he might return. She needed to focus on the tangible, packing his saddlebags, filling his canteen, checking his rifle, to keep the overwhelming anxiety at bay.

Bass watched her go, a profound sense of love and gratitude washing over him. Her acceptance was both a terrible burden and a huge relief. He was bound by duty, but he was free to follow that duty with her blessing. He turned toward the door, already planning his route, calculating the distance to Dick Glass's last known whereabouts. The hunt had begun.

215

A Hero's Legacy

The oil lamp on the small, scarred pine table cast a sputtering glow against the overwhelming blackness pressing in from the unchinked logs of the homestead cabin. The air was thick and heavy, smelling of desert sage and patchouli. Jennie stood by the table, her back to the single stone hearth where the fire had long since collapsed into a bed of whispering coals. She was a woman who made the Territory bearable and pleasant, her face etched with lines that hadn't been there a decade ago, but her eyes were fixed on the arsenal laid out before her.

"The silver bullets for this demon babe," Bass requested from another room. "The cornbread and jerky," she said, her voice dry, almost clinical, as if reading an inventory list. She pointed a finger, worn smooth from years of mending and milking, at an old-model Colt resting on the cracked tablecloth. The revolver wasn't just old; it looked loved and *used*, the walnut grips dark with oil and sweat. Beside the gun were rations in squares. They were wrapped in cheesecloth. Thin slabs of salt pork & cornbread. There was also peppered jerky. Bass would need a full day's worth of ride before he hit anything resembling civilization, and she had seen to it that he wouldn't starve.

But it wasn't the food or even the gun that held her attention. It was the color of the metal peeking from its cylinder. A soft, dull luster distinct from the blue-black steel of the rest of the weapons.

Bass sat in the single, rickety chair now, by the far wall. The man who seemed not to take up too much space for a small room still seemed imposing even seated. Though he moved with the caution of an old man, he had the coiled tension of a young bull. He was meticulously cleaning his saddle rigging, the rhythmic squeak of leather against worn saddle soap cloth. He paused his work, letting a bridle dangle, before looking up at Jennie. His face was a landscape of deep shadows and lamplight, his eyes dark and unsettlingly serene.

"Well, Jennie," he began, his voice a low, gravelly rumble that could just as easily carry over a canyon as it could fill a small room. He didn't rush, letting the silence draw out until it felt brittle. "I've seen a lot of things out here make a lesser man pea himself."

I don't mean Snakes or Bear or even the casual brutality of a murderous villain. No, nawh baby, there are men who make me wonder if demons can crawl into a man's soul, his being. Where simple bullets won't find him. You need silver, silver kills demons." She knew his reference was to the inhuman element, or what passed for it. Plus, she understood how soft metal leaves big holes in the target. He rose slowly, almost theatrical grace for a man his size, and walked to the table. His shadow enveloped the flickering lamp.

"I have fought some fierce and determined killers," Bass continued, leaning one massive hand on the table, the silver glinting near his elbow. "Fifteen years, I've been wearing this star. Rode through more hail and fire than a man's got a right to. I've stood down gangs of cutthroats that would look a preacher in the eye while emptying his church box. I've dealt with men who carry 12-pound Howitzers in their hearts, and that's how much destruction they got in 'em."

He picked up the revolver, its weight familiar in his hand, and spun the cylinder slowly, the *click-click-click* a morbid percussion in the quiet room.

"But this... this thing I'ma be chasing," he murmured, his voice dropping an octave, becoming a conspiratorial whisper that clawed at Jennie's composure. "Might look like a man, but I'm pretty sure the demon on him has a lust for blood."

He didn't need to describe the quarry. Everyone in the Territory knew about the recent plague of unsolved atrocities. It wasn't the sheer violence that curdled the blood; this land was engulfed in violence. It was the *manner* of it. People have gone from locked rooms. Bodies drained of blood, left behind like discarded sacks. The way the trails simply *stopped* with no sign of a horse, a boot, or even a displaced stone.

"You shoot him, he still gets away," Bass stated, his gaze distant, fixed on a memory she couldn't share. "I've seen men put three rounds of forty-four into his chest, clear as the noon sky, and he just... keeps walking. Walks through the dark like the dark is his home, and then he's gone."

Jennie involuntarily shivered, pulling the shawl tight enough to rub her skin raw. She had heard the whispers, too, down at the General Store when the men thought the women weren't listening, or around the water pump after the sun went down. But hearing Bass, the hardest, most pragmatic man she knew, speak about it with such a profound lack of uncertainty, that was worse than any overheard gossip.

"You hear 'bout him takin' souls of men, women, and children," Bass said, turning the revolver over in his hand again. He wasn't talking about the simple act of murder now. He was talking about something far more ancient and terrifying. The implication was that the body was just the wrapper; the contents were what mattered.

He let out a long, ragged sigh, a sound that seemed to carry the exhaustion of his years and the weight of the endless plains. He rubbed the stubble on his chin, the sound rasping like sandpaper. "Hell, after a while you start wondering is these are really men?"

The question hung there, suspended like a dust mote in the lamplight, heavy with implication. Bass wasn't just wondering if he was chasing a human being. He was wondering if the rules of God and man still applied out here, or if the fight was even fair.

Jennie finally met his gaze, holding it steadily. She knew what he was implying, and she had to draw a line in the unforgiving dust. For her own sanity, she couldn't let the conversation proceed into true darkness. She needed to pull it back. The world had to remain predictable.

"I just wanted to make sure you weren't hunting Vampires," she said, letting the word fall with an almost mocking lightness. It was a word out of dime novels and European fairy tales, not the reality of the American West.

She kept her expression purposefully neutral enough to convey her judgment.

She took a step closer to the table, her hands resting on its edge. "I mean, how would that look on a grown man, a Deputy U.S. Marshal, chasing Vampires?" You'd ride into town, and folks would be saying the pressures of the job done got to him. Old Bass done broke his mind chasing ghosts and fanged devils. They'd take your badge, Bass. They'd say you finally buckled under the sun and the isolation."

The West was vast, but it couldn't tolerate monsters that didn't bleed when you shot them with lead. It demanded explanations, no matter how unbelievable.

Bass stared at her then, a long, searching look that stripped away her forced bravado and left her feeling exposed. A slow, almost imperceptible smile tugged at the corner of his mouth, then an eruption of giggles and laughter between the two lovers.

He put the silver-loaded revolver back on the table, nudging it closer to the jerky and cornbread. The silver caught the lamp's eye once more, a faint, cold beacon in the dark.

"I ain't said I was chasing Vampires," He didn't confirm her fear, but he certainly didn't deny it. He left the answer suspended, forcing her to confront the terrible, expansive, and unpredictable nature of the world they lived in. It wasn't the kind of answer Jennie wanted. It was the kind of answer that meant he might not come back, not because of a common outlaw's bullet, but because he had ridden out past the edge of the map, into a place where the rules of the living no longer applied. She watched him turn back to his saddle, the soft, patient squeak of the leather once again filling the silent space. The wood-handled revolver sat waiting, a deadly relic loaded with a hope colder and brighter than any lead.

Bass spoke to his mount as if Silver were a man who could understand both the bargain and the danger. "Whoa there, Silver. Time to go back out there and rid the world of trash. This time it's a bit personal for me, boy. Look here , you bring me home, and I'll get you that black mare with the big hunches you like so much!" He grinned at the horse, the expression a rough thing that softened whatever hard edge the night could find in him.

Jennie answered from where she stood, hands on hips, the shawl pulled tighter against the cold. "The war wagon this time, huh? Plan on staying awhile. All your supplies are present with the jerky and corn pone. For those fireless nights." Her voice carried a practicality. The kind that kept fear from turning into panic.

Bass laughed, and chased the shadows back a notch. "Shouldn't be no more than a few days, baby! But this type of snake I'm hunting, you never know. I'm gone need all my tricks to keep from getting bit." He lifted a leather strap, slung a cartridge belt across his broad chest, and checked the loops as if counting blessings instead of bullets.

She stepped close enough that her shoulder bumped his, an affectionate nudge forged from years of shared chores and shared dangers. "This one you don't need to bring back. You can take his head and sit wit' 'em till the sun go down," she said, half joke, half prayer.

Bass's smile went crooked and tender. "There's that kind and gentile beast I married," he said, and the irony in his voice made the corner of Jennie's mouth twitch.

"Don't get your crazy ass shot!" she snapped, the warning sharper than the joke, and then she reached up on a sudden impulse and flattened the brim of his hat the way wives do when they want a husband to look like a man they can be proud of.

He took the gesture in stride, nodding to himself as he adjusted his stirrups. Moving back into the armory the lamp guttered as a draft moved through.

Outside, the wind whispered through the long, dry grasses, and somewhere a coyote called , a thin, lonely sound that made the walls of the Territory feel both enormous and very small. Bass paused at the doorway, his silhouette large against the black beyond. He turned back once, and for a moment the stoic marshal was looking for a nod, a wink, any human signal that the world he rode out into had not yet unmade him.

Jennie gave him that, a brief, steady nod that did the work of a dozen long speeches. "Bring back my man Silver" she said simply.

Bass grinned, a flash of teeth in the lamplight. While Silver nodding the universal sign of acceptance. Bass swung up leather groaning under him, and Silver moved like a shadow that had learned to shape itself to a man's will.

The cabin held its breath as Bass road off the door closed eventually. The lamplight sank a little lower; the coals sighed. Jennie stood by the table until she could no longer stand, then fell to her knees in prayer, tear fallen from her eyes.

"Spirits of War my Bass needs you. Dear ancestors to you I pray these words. Bring my Bass back to me whole". She heard nothing and the night whistled gently.

The woods were a canvas of charcoal and indigo, the kind of absolute darkness that felt less like the absence of light and more like a heavy, velvet cloak thrown over the world. A sliver of the moon, stingy with its illumination, struggled to define the contours of the landscape.

Bass was not truly asleep. Sleep, for a man who lived on the raw edge of civilization and frequently had a bounty on his head from outlaws. Sleep was an indulgence he rarely permitted himself. He lay against the rough bark of a thick oak, his rifle cradled like a lover, his senses tuned to the low, humming frequency of the night. He was clad in rough-spun canvas and dense, earth-toned camouflage, a pattern he had adapted from the very environment he patrolled.

The camp was a lie. Three rolled blankets stuffed with deadfall and topped with weathered slouch hats, dummies, lay where a proper camp would be. Bass had positioned himself nearly forty feet away, on the downwind side of the oak, an expert in misdirection.

It was the rustling that brought him fully alert. Not the common tickle of wind through dry leaves, but a calculated displacement of brush, the sound of men who knew how to move in the dark but not how to move past him.

Bass's eyes, the color of wet slate and unnervingly keen, sliced through the gloom. He saw them: two figures, heavily blanketed, moving low to the ground. They carried the unmistakable long, lean silhouette of rifles. They were approaching the decoys with the slow, deliberate focus of hunters who believed their prey was pinned and unaware.

The moment they reached the fire pit, a cold, carefully disguised circle of stones, they stopped. The air hung heavy, pregnant with the silent tension of the ambush. Then, the silence shattered. The two men threw off their blankets and leveled their weapons at the inert forms. A cascade of harsh, rapid commands poured out, not in English, but in the thick, rolling phonetics of the Native Creek language.

"Dick Glass! Your under arrest by the Authority of the Tribal police. Move slow or die!" one of the men, Bass, could only see the shadow of Native 1, screamed, his voice strained with authority and adrenaline.

Bass recognized the tension in the scene, the earnest, righteous anger of the men hunting the same monster he was. But more importantly, his gaze had settled on a familiar, powerful silhouette hanging back in the deeper shadows of the tree line: Stands Tall.

A fierce, relieved, and deeply competitive grin stretched across Bass's face. He knew Stands Tall to be one of the most capable trackers and silent movers in the entire territory, a man who could, and often did, vanish into thin air. He pushed himself smoothly away from the tree, standing tall, his rifle now resting easily in the crook of his arm. His voice boomed through the quiet night, laced with genuine amusement and friendly rivalry.

"Stands Tall, its me, Bass! I guess sneaking up on me won't be so easy anymore, huh? How that feel, Spirit Walker?"

The two Native men who had been shouting at the blankets spun around, rifles jerking up, momentarily blinded by the sheer audacity of the sound.

Stands Tall stepped fully into the weak moonlight, his two companions immediately lowering their weapons, recognizing the powerful, centered presence of their leader. Stands Tall was built like the hickory tree he emerged from, solid, immovable, and weathered. His face, etched with the experience of a hard life lived under the open sky, was completely impassive. He met Bass's triumphant gaze without a flicker of emotion.

"Even a broken clock is right twice a day," Stands Tall delivered the retort, a deep, even rumble that lacked any sting, yet entirely deflated Bass's moment of pride.

Bass scratched his chin, genuinely perplexed by the odd, philosophical jab. "What even does that mean?" he demanded. "I mean, you been sneaking up on me, and now I gotta sneak proof set up you mad?" He gestured to the elaborate decoy camp, a testament to the lengths he had gone to counter Stands Tall's legendary stealth.

"No, my friend, not emotional, not at all," Stands Tall corrected him, stepping closer. The air between them, once charged with playful competition, now settled into a comfortable, familiar truce. The two men, one an officer of the United States Marshall Service, the other a respected tribal police captain. "So who are you hunting, my friend? Dick, Dick Glass?"

The name Dick Glass acted like a lash, snapping away the easy camaraderie. Bass's face tightened, the amusement fading instantly, replaced by the granite hardness of a man possessed by a mission. He began to list Glass's crimes, each word a heavy stone dropped into the quiet pool of the night.

"None other than the notorious Dick Glass. He killed a 14-year-old girl's father right in front of her. Then he killed her." Bass paused, his jaw clenching. He never forgot the names, the faces, the cold details of the violence he pursued. "He killed two of my friends and fellow Marshall's, Thomas and James. And, he took a dear friend of mine. Wind of the Gods."

This last detail hung in the air, heavy with personal loss. Wind of the Gods, a respected member of the community, a friend who straddled the white, black and Native worlds. "He can't have no more of mine. Stands Tall, not nan other one."

Stands Tall listened, his eyes grave. The details of the murders were new, but the name Dick Glass was a dark stain in his own jurisdiction. "He is wanted by the Tribal police for murder of a child and countless illegal trades of the White mans Whisky, and dealing in the slave trade" he confirmed. The illegal trade in liquor was poisoning his people, slowly eroding their strength and their sovereignty. Glass was a parasite feeding on both sides of the divide.

Bass saw the shared objective, a target they both needed dead or captured. The logic was obvious to the practical lawman. "We should team up and rope tie this one with a posse. We'll have this turkey shot in the morning," he proposed. A combined force, Marshall's and Tribal police, would be unstoppable.

But Stands Tall's loyalty was to his own. He glanced briefly at his two companions, who had quietly retreated into the background. "My brothers will not travel with you." He spoke with a quiet finality, acknowledging the bitter, deep-seated distrust that ran between the nations. "You are an agent of the White man's laws, and I don't believe they will bring him back alive." The unspoken truth was that Stands Tall's men were obligated to bring Glass back for tribal justice; Bass's Marshall's were obligated only to stop the violence, an obligation often fulfilled with a bullet.

He offered a compromise, one rooted in their unique, intertwined destinies. "I though will travel with you, our path being who we are." They were two men of power, respected by their respective peoples, yet always operating on the outer boundary, a Spirit Walker and a frontier Marshall.

A wide, sincere smile returned to Bass's face. He knew a genuine offer when he heard one. He reached out a hand, not to shake, but in a gesture of simple, recognized partnership. He struggled for the right words, wanting to honor Stands Tall in his own way. "My friend," he began, before attempting the Native Tongue phrase he'd been practicing, "when you ready to move out. Did I say it right?"

Stands Tall merely tilted his head, dismissing the effort with an easy, almost impatient wave. "Who cares!"

"I don't want to be saying shit all wrong, looking crazy. When I'm trying to tell you something," Bass insisted, genuinely concerned with proper form.

"This you will not avoid," Stands Tall said, a hint of genuine, deep-seated cultural amusement finally breaking his stoicism. He knew Bass would always struggle with the nuances of the language; it was part of his charm.

Bass chuckled, shaking his head. "I can see this is going to be a long lasting friendship." He holstered his pistol and began rolling his blanket with efficient, practiced movements.

Stands Tall ignored the sentiment, refocusing immediately on the task ahead. The time for sentimental declarations was long past. "Friendship or not, we are a half days ride to our prey," he stated. "We have been tracking him for weeks, and all his tracks led to a frequent hideout were the Sun sees himself."

The poetry of Stands Tall's phrasing was often beautiful, but maddeningly vague to Bass. He needed coordinates, not metaphors. He stopped tying his bedroll and stared at Stands Tall, exasperated. "Sun ain't seeing itself, it don't have no eyes. You mean to the East that way," he said, gesturing with his thumb. "All you really gotta say is east, and I will know exactly where your talking about. Stands Tall North South East West."

Bass had spent his entire life mastering the compass points and the grid; Stands Tall relied on the land's own rhythm and poetry.

Stands Tall gave a slight, acknowledging nod. "Indeed, yes, Indeed, Kemo Sobi." He used the old, affectionately insulting name, a nod to the countless stories and tall tales that had grown up around the Marshall. "Perhaps seeing is sometimes better with your ears." He meant listening to the land, listening to the wisdom of the world around him.

Bass was about to protest the 'Kemo Sobi' title, but then the pieces clicked together. He'd heard Stands Tall use the phrase, or similar ones, before. *Where the Sun sees himself...* It meant a place of perfect reflection, a pool of water so still that the sky was inverted upon the earth.

"Oh, paint me green and call me a pickle," Bass exclaimed, a new rush of energy flooding his system. "You're talking about Mirror Lake! That water so damn clear you can see the moon, and the stars clear as looking in the sky."

Mirror Lake. A perfect, bowl-shaped depression fed by cold springs, utterly sheltered and ringed by high bluffs, a perfect, nearly impregnable hideout, and a place only those who truly knew the territory would use for a prolonged stay.

"Two, maybe three hours," Stands Tall corrected Bass's earlier half-day estimate, calculating the distance with the speed of a mind that had mapped every ridge and run. "And we will be staring at that dog face to face. If I let him get that close."

The plan was simple: move fast, arrive before dawn, and pin Glass down. Stands Tall was already planning the deployment, the final, tactical move.

They stood side-by-side, gathering their gear, Bass's leather-bound saddlebags, Stands Tall's meticulously crafted hide pack, when Bass's attention was caught by a movement far off, past the dark line of trees to the west. It wasn't the noise that got him, but the faint visual disturbance.

"Whoa, look there in the distance, a dust cloud," Bass murmured, lowering his voice, the joking gone completely. He squinted hard. "And somebodies ah smokin'!"

A thin, dark plume, barely visible against the predawn sky, rose lazily into the air. It wasn't the slow, steady smoke of a campfire; it was the quick, punctuated puff of a signal.

Stands Tall didn't need to look long. His years of tracking had taught him to read the land as easily as Bass read a warrant. "This is a path to the West," he whispered, recognizing the geography of the distant trail. The dust cloud was moving, meaning riders. The smoke was a signal, a warning, or a summons.

"Wait for my signal," Stands Tall commanded, already dropping into a crouch, his eyes on the distant movement. "And we shall have a bucket full of fish to clean."

Bass sighed, the poetic language grating on his nerves in the moment of high tension. "I thought I was the one suppose to say dumb shit," he muttered. "You mean fish in a barrel?"

"What?" Stands Tall turned back, his brow furrowed with genuine bewilderment. He didn't understand the analogy, the image of the easy target.

"Fish in a barrel," Bass repeated, then shook his head, dismissing the entire linguistic tangent. "Never mind."

Stands Tall turned away again, pulling a small, highly polished piece of mirror from his vest. It was his communication tool, an elegant means of passing messages over long distances using flashes of reflected light. "I will use signal glass!"

Bass felt the sudden surge of adrenaline. The hunt had just escalated, bringing in unknown elements and an immediate need for coordination. The shared mission was no longer a philosophical agreement; it was a tight, desperate necessity.

"Yes, Sir!" Bass affirmed, snapping the words out as he knelt and waited, the vast, silent western frontier opening up before them, two men from different worlds, united by the demand for justice against a single, monstrous outlaw. The sunrise, when it came, would find them already in motion.

The air at the mountain hold up was thin, sharp, and tasted of pulverized granite and dry scrub. The sun, climbing over the sheer, jagged peaks, was already an enemy, beating down with merciless intensity on the narrow trail that wound around the mountain's shoulder. This place was a natural fortress, a craggy, sun-baked nest used by outlaws who preferred altitude and defense over discretion and cover.

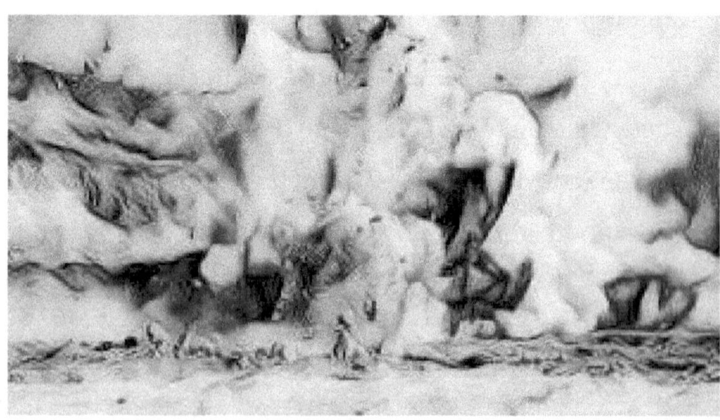

Bass Reeves appeared to be in dire straits.

He stumbled into the fortified clearing, his heavy leather coat dusted white with trail grime, his shoulders slumped. He moved with the slow, staggering gait of a man suffering from acute exposure, his eyes squinted against the harsh light and the feigned delirium of thirst. His throat was a dry, stinging tunnel, but his mind was an icy, calculating machine.

Ahead, behind a hastily erected barricade of loose stone and chopped logs, stood two of Dick Glass's henchmen. They were rough, ill-fed men whose cruelty was etched into the tight, defensive set of their shoulders. Their rifles were aimed casually, yet lethally, at the approaching figure.

Bass played his part with a practiced, desperate intensity.

"Please, mister, some water! I'm a-dying of thirst out here!" Bass rasped, his voice a dry, pleading croak that sounded genuine even to his own ears. He let his body sag, presenting himself as utterly harmless, merely a nuisance of the trail.

Henchman 1, a man with a perpetually greasy face and a nervous trigger finger, spat a dark stream of tobacco juice. He clearly enjoyed the supplicant's misery. "Ain't got no wa-wa, move along or die faster!" he sneered, the words laced with cold contempt. The threat was a casual flick of the wrist; they expected him to melt back into the dust.

Bass took another stumbling step closer, his eyes flicking over the barricade, counting the exposed limbs, judging the distance. He poured every ounce of his performance into his next line. "Please, suh, please!"

The plea was the final straw for the second henchman, a beefier, slower man who found the entire interaction tedious. "Enough of this shit," Henchman 2 growled, raising his rifle barrel slightly preparing to drive the vagrant off with the flat of the stock.

That was the signal. That moment of relaxed readiness, of underestimation.

The transformation in Bass was immediate and total. The slumped shoulders snapped upright; the desperate eyes became sharp, focused points of lethal intent. In a blur of motion too fast for the eye to track, Bass shed the persona of the dying beggar and became the weapon he was.

A series of rapid, brutal movements, not the clumsy grappling of a street brawl, but the devastating, precise strikes of a man trained in the ancient, foreign arts of combat. The techniques, learned years ago from a Chinese man met far out on the frontier, were alien and terrifying to the Western mind.

Bass closed the distance to Henchman 2 in a single, blurring step. A lightning-fast strike to the side of the man's neck, a perfect chop delivered with the rigid edge of his hand, dropped the larger man before he could even register the attack, his breath gushing out in a strangled gasp. Before the body hit the dust, Bass was already pivoting. Henchman 1, stunned and fumbling with his rifle, was met with a brutal kick to the solar plexus. The air left him in a whoosh, and he stumbled backward over the barricade, his rifle discharging harmlessly into the sky as he fell, his limbs suddenly unresponsive to his frantic brain.

The two guards were debilitated, not dead, but neutralized, in less time than it takes to load a cartridge.

Bass stood over the fallen men, his breathing steady, the heavy disguise of desperation completely stripped away. He looked toward the opening of the small, deep cavern that served as the holdout's main entrance, and his voice, no longer a croak but a ringing trumpet of challenge, echoed through the rocks.

"You should've just given me some water." He paused, allowing the words to sink in. "Hey, Dick head! I mean Dick Glass!"

A massive shadow detached itself from the gloom inside the cave entrance. It was Dick Glass, a man who looked exactly like the villain he was, bloated by self-importance and stained by casual cruelty. His eyes, small and piggish, narrowed as he recognized the figure standing in the sunlit clearing.

"Is that you, Bass? The great fucking white law nigger?" Glass's voice was a sneering, guttural sound, dripping with racial venom and contempt for the symbol of authority Bass represented.

Bass, a black man with the full authority of the federal government behind him, never flinched from the epithets. He had worn worse names, and he knew how to use the slur's deployment to judge the exact measure of a man's ugliness. He planted his boots firmly in the dust, the sun catching the brass of his badge.

"Yuuuup," Bass confirmed, drawing the word out slowly. "And the Lord's collector of bad souls. Yours, my boy, has come due." Bass saw himself not merely as a lawman, but as an agent of a higher reckoning, a grim reaper with a badge and a Colt.

Glass's hand twitched toward the pistol holstered on his hip. He was a killer, and a man like Bass Reeves was an affront to his entire existence. "I'm going to kill you, Bass."

"Well, let's see how this plays out, Dick!" Bass retorted, the challenge ringing with mocking confidence.

Glass glowered. "I don't like the way you keep saying my name."

Bass grinned, a flash of white teeth against his dark skin. The game was being played on his terms. "Tell yo Mamma shes the one named you Dick!"

He let the taunt hang for a crucial second before shifting back into the formal, rigid language of the law. He had to offer the chance it was his sworn duty, even to the vilest of men.

"Last chance, Dick! You surrender, you get a fair trial. I promised some folk I was gonna kill yah, but the Law is the law." The law was the one thing that anchored Bass, the single principle he would not compromise, even for the sweet satisfaction of immediate vengeance.

Glass laughed, a harsh, dry sound that scratched the air. "Fuck you, Bass, and your switch ass judge Isaac Parker." He spat toward the ground. "This land don't belong to you, you don't govern me. You're a trespasser and a boot licking Uncle Tom!"

It was the ultimate rejection of the law, of Bass's authority, and of his humanity. Glass was declaring himself outside the bounds of any recognized code.

The words were instantly followed by action. A shot was fired in Bass's direction from the darkness of the cave. It was a warning, a declaration of war. The bullet whined off a rock just beside Bass's head, peppering him with small, sharp fragments of stone.

"Massa Parker don't like that switch pants talk, and fancy boy stuff," Bass called back, his tone deceptively mild, as if chiding a child.

In one smooth, practiced motion, his hand dipped into his coat pocket. He pulled out a dark, wax-wrapped cylinder, a stick of dynamite, already fused and spitting a small tail of burning wick. It was his signature opening move, a way to clear the deck and test the enemy's resolve without wasting precious bullets. He tossed it in a perfect arc, high and deep into the cavern's mouth.

Bass dropped flat behind the makeshift stone barricade. The blast was deafening, a shattering thunderclap that momentarily overwhelmed the senses. Dust, smoke, and debris erupted from the cave entrance, followed by the panicked cries of men.

"Yo, Dick! Hey, Dick, you among the living?" Bass yelled, the ringing in his ears already subsiding.

A voice, ragged with hatred and fear, screamed back. "Die in hell, Bass, just die in hell!"

More gunshots tore toward Bass, wilder now, less aimed, fueled by pure terror and rage.

Bass laughed, a deep, booming sound that was half challenge, half prophecy. "Hey, you're more than welcome to come in. Matter fact, I gots one of them Steam boat Tickets to the Devil's Balls!"

The exchange was devolving into pure chaos. Gun shots rang out everywhere from the cave, blind, desperate volleys. Glass had more men than Bass had initially anticipated.

"Whoa, whoa, whoa! You boys are a bit hostile, ain't ye. Let's cool you off a bit," Bass called, his words barely audible over the din.

He reached into his other pocket. His hand came out with three more sticks of dynamite, fanned out and fused together into a small, deadly bouquet. He lit the wick and lobbed the improvised bomb with brutal accuracy. It sailed deep into the cavern, landing with a soft thud.

The resulting volley of dynamite was catastrophic. It was a much larger charge, designed to collapse supports and create maximum shockwave. The ground shuddered. Screams of men turned into gurgling silence. The shockwave expelled a terrifying torrent: splintered wood, plumes of dark dust, and the limp, broken shapes of men flying through the air, landing lifeless on the rocks below. Bass shielded his face from the raining debris, the smell of burnt gunpowder, and rendered flesh already thick in the air.

When the echo of the blast finally faded, only one voice was left, raw and filled with impotent fury.

"You son-of-a-bitch, you killed them all! You killed them all with dynamite! You fucking coward!" Dick Glass screamed, his words catching on sobs of sheer, overwhelming loss. The dynamite had done the work of a firing squad.

Immediately, another rifle cracked. It was Cantrell, Glass's last remaining man, a loyal, fanatic lieutenant. The shots were a disciplined volley aimed at the entrance, forcing Bass to stay pinned behind the barricade.

"So you still gotta compadre, do yah?" Bass called out, pressing himself flat against the warm stone.

Cantrell, though pinned in a desperate situation, was unwavering. "In a few minutes, you are going to meet your maker, Reeves."

Suddenly, the ridge high above the cavern erupted. The sound was not the wild, panicked fire of the outlaws, but the controlled, measured rhythm of professional rifles. Stands Tall and the Tribal police force, his two companions from the night before, plus several others, had scaled the bluffs and were now firing down from high positions into the cavern. They had used the distraction of Bass's dynamite to flank the entire stronghold.

The rifle fire from above was relentless, aimed at denying Cantrell any cover. A sharp cry of pain signaled the end of Cantrell's stand.

Stands Tall appeared on the ridge, his figure silhouetted against the blinding mid-morning sun. His voice cut through the reverberations of the final shots, calm and absolute.

"There are no more than one. He has no path."

Dick Glass, isolated and exposed in the main cavern chamber, recognized the new voice. His desperate eyes darted up, and a fresh wave of betrayal and hatred washed over him.

"Is that Stands Small? Traitor to his people. Hunter of his own flesh!" Glass shrieked, resorting to the most personal attack he could find.

Stands Tall's reply was delivered with the cutting, casual finality of a knife-thrust. "No, It is Stands Tall who remembers you getting caught Sheep fucker." The memory was obscure, embarrassing, and devastatingly specific.

Bass couldn't help but interject, his humor returning now that the tables were completely turned. "Well, goat fucker!" he yelled toward Glass. "Sounds like you're empty, too!"

Glass's final, desperate attempt at dignity was to correct the record. "Sheep, you bastard, and I didn't fuck any of it!"

"None of that is here nor there, boy, to me," Bass declared, climbing over the barricade and walking slowly toward the cave entrance, his Colt .45 drawn but held low. He was done with the theatrics; the moment of reckoning was at hand. "Who you love ain't my concern. Lay down with a Rattler, I give a damn, but your slithering days are over."

Bass stopped at the threshold of the cave, silhouetted by the sun. "There's a judge named Hang'em High Parker waitin on you."

Dick Glass, standing alone amid the blood and dust of his fallen men, finally looked like what he was: a trapped, cornered dog. His chest heaved, and he stared at Bass with a mixture of terror and resignation.

"Just like I thought. You just gone kill me, huh? No more bullets, hell, no more friends!" Glass's eyes were locked on Bass's holstered revolver, assessing the odds, looking for a fraction of a second to make his move.

Bass smiled, but there was no warmth in it. It was a wolf's smile. "Oh no, pig fucker. I'ma give you six chances. 5 more than I give myself."

Glass paused, confused. The Marshall was offering him something.

Bass gestured toward the loaded Colt Single Action Army he carried. He slowly and deliberately withdrew it, breaking the cylinder. He checked each chamber, making certain they were all full.

"See here, I'm gonna load up this here six-shooter and give it to you fully loaded. Now, how that sound to yah?" Bass said, his voice quiet, measured, and utterly terrifying. "Then I'm gone take my gun, and leave in it one bullet."

This was the core of Bass Reeves's legend, not just his speed, but his absolute confidence in his own righteousness and skill. He was offering the ultimate, final chance: an even, or perhaps slightly superior, fight, dictated by his own twisted, deeply moral code.

Bass tossed the fully loaded pistol in front of Dick Glass's feet. The heavy steel weapon skidded across the stone, stopping just shy of his boots.

A cynical, desperate light sparked in Glass's eyes. He knew Bass's reputation, the fastest gun in the territory, black or white. But he also knew his own speed. A fully loaded gun... six chances.

"There's a fool born every minute, and I know you heard how fast I am, Bass Reeves," Glass boasted, reaching down slowly.

He snatched the gun, the cold weight feeling immediately familiar and potent. He picked up the sliding pistol and quickly, too quickly, slid it into his own holster. He wanted the draw to be seamless, instinctive, an execution rather than a duel.

Bass stood perfectly still, his own Colt resting loose in the oiled leather of his holster, his eyes unblinking.

"You smell that?" Bass asked, his voice low, his tone conversational.

Glass's attention was fixed on the pistol on his hip, mentally rehearsing the draw. "What?"

"The blood on your hands. The blood of children. Innocent men, women raped, tortured, killed over maize." Bass's voice took on a terrible, resonant quality, as if channeling a chorus of the dead. "My friend Wind of the Gods has requested a meeting, and I am your concierge."

Glass shifted his weight, his patience evaporating under the relentless, spiritual assault. "All this God damned talking."

The talking stopped.

Dick went for the Colt on his hip. His hand blurred, grasping the checkered grips of the six-shooter, beginning the draw. He was fast, fueled by adrenaline and a lifetime of ruthless survival.

Next thing he saw was the muzzle flash then smoke coming from the working end of Bass's Colt .45.

Time freezes (Slomo).

For Glass, the world did not just slow; it fractured. He saw the black void of Bass's muzzle, the terrifying blossom of smoke and fire, and the projectile itself, a pure silver slug traveling so fast it seemed to scream as it expanded.

The air around the bullet became a tunnel of unholy psychic energy. As the projectile slammed into Dick Glass's chest, not merely tearing flesh, but tearing the fabric of his reality, a fiery image screamed out of the ground.

It was an inferno of vengeance, a whirlwind composed of the unsettled spirits of his victims. Glass's mind was instantly filled with the faces and terror of those he had murdered.

He saw the face of Wind of the Gods, eyes cold with righteous fury. He saw the 14-year-old girl, her silent accusation a dagger in his soul. He saw the young boy and the countless, unsettled spirits of innocent men and women he had preyed upon. These fiery images, screaming out of the very land he stood on. Dick Glass, tearing at the spiritual energy that bound him.

The psychological impact of the bullet was a spiritual obliteration. As the soft silver ripped flesh through his body into about a 4 inch exit wound. The illusion of his physical strength dissolved. His skin and muscle seemed to melt away in the fiery vision, until his skeleton was revealed, screaming, a silent, visceral roar of absolute agony and terror the pain that repeated itself over and over.

The violent wave of energy rippled the landscape. Stands Tall and his men, watching from the ridge, felt a chill that had nothing to do with the temperature.

For Bass Reeves, the entire event was a single, clean *thwack* of the silver bullet finding its mark, a flash of fire, and the scent of cordite. All he saw, in the cold, clear reality of the clearing, was Dick Glass slowly falling silent and heavily to the ground.

Bass never moved his feet. He broke his stance only to blow the smoke clear from the barrel of his Colt .45, the one silver bullet expended, his promise kept. The collector of bad souls had made his final transaction.

Stands Tall descended from the ridge, walking to stand beside Bass. The silence was immense, broken only by the sound of dust settling back onto the rocks. Bass looked down at the dead man, then glanced toward the ridge where the sun was now fully dominant. Justice, like the midday sun, had finally arrived.

The smoke from the spent cartridge of Bass's Colt .45 drifted lazily on the high mountain wind, a final, sulphurous offering to the silent peaks. Dick Glass lay still on the cave floor, his body a silent monument to his own spectacular failure.

Stands Tall descended from the ridge. His gait was measured, deliberate, the movement of a man who rarely wasted energy or motion. He paused beside Bass, gazing down at the body. The silence between the two men was not empty, but heavy with shared experience, the noise of the dynamite, the rapid fire of the final, lethal showdown, and the profound justice achieved.

The Tribal police officers, Stands Tall's companions, cautiously began moving through the carnage, their faces grim as they surveyed the deadly work done by the dynamite and the bullets. They knew this day meant an immediate, if temporary, lessening of the whiskey trade and the violence it brought.

Bass holstered his revolver, the single, spent shell casing smoking faintly. He reloaded his weapon due this land bore no fools! He looked at Stands Tall, sensing the moment of parting. Their shared path, however briefly aligned, had reached its natural end.

Stands Tall turned from the scene of the death to Bass, his face softening slightly, the deep lines around his eyes easing into a rare expression of deep respect.

"If there is ever a time you call upon Stands Tall," he began, his voice a low, steady promise, "I will find you on the trail. "

It was more than a mere courtesy; it was a commitment etched in the shared dust of the battle.

Stands Tall rarely gave his word, but when he did, it was as solid as the granite mountain they stood upon. It meant Bass had gained an ally whose loyalty transcended the laws of the white man or the boundaries of the territories. It meant Bass was accepted.

Stands Tall's eyes lingered on Bass, a mixture of pride and affection visible in his gaze.

"Kemo Sobi," he continued, using the familiar, once-teasing moniker now imbued with genuine warmth. "I will be honored among my people for riding with the man who healed our open wound."

The "wound" was Dick Glass, not just his presence, but the damage he inflicted on their villagers with his murders and his illicit trade. Bass, the controversial figure, the "white law nigger" to his enemies, had, in this action, become a protector, a bridge-builder, and an agent of healing to the Nation. Stands Tall's acknowledgment was profound, a recognition of Bass Reeves's unique, dual role in the rugged landscape of the frontier.

Stands Tall offered a final farewell, the traditional words a prayer, a wish, and a firm promise for the future.

"Until We Meet Again."

Bass merely nodded, his eyes meeting the Native man's. He watched as Stands Tall turned and ascended the ridge once more, his figure quickly blending into the shadows and rock formations with the practiced ease of a true Spirit Walker. The other Tribal police officers followed, leaving Bass alone in the smoking, silent canyon.

Bass Reeves stood there for a long moment, the sun hot on his neck, the heavy justice of the moment settling around him. He knew the trail was long and the outlaws were many, but he also knew that somewhere in the vast, untamed territory, he had a faithful and powerful ally. He was Kemo Sobi, recognized, honored, and bound by a promise that ran deeper than any printed law. He had collected his soul and, in doing so, had earned the ultimate respect. He turned, retrieved his horse, and boots, leaving the ghosts of the holdout to the wind.

The air in the Federal District for Western Arkansas, despite the late hour of Bass Reeves's arrival, crackled with excitement. Outside the formidable brick courthouse, the operational seat of Judge Isaac Parker, a small, eager crowd had gathered, instantly alerted by the arrival of the legendary Marshall.

It was Pete, one of the courthouse runners, who sounded the alarm, his voice high-pitched with the thrill of being the bearer of momentous news. "It's Bass! Hey, yawl, it's Marshall Reeves!" He practically danced with excitement, reciting the grim roster of the recently departed. "He done killed Cantrell, yuuup, Charlie Three Fingers, and God Almighty! He done killed Dick Glass!"

The collective gasp from the bystanders confirmed the stature of the accomplishment. Dick Glass was a symbol of untouchable savagery; his death meant the cleansing of a vast, bloody stain on the territory.

Inside his chambers, the Judge, a man whose reputation as "Hang'em High Parker" was earned through relentless, cold application of the law, received Bass. The Marshall entered, a figure carved from dust and exhaustion, but with the quiet, settled look of a man who had met his obligations in full.

Parker stood, a rare gesture of respect. "I knew you were the right man for the job, Bass," he stated, his voice heavy with authority and deep satisfaction. "Marshall, you done brought in the one they gone hear about in New York City."

The Judge crossed to the window, gazing not at the dusty street, but at the horizon of history he was trying to shape. "Bass, in Washington D.C., their going to say, 'There is Law in the West.'" He spoke slowly, emphasizing the monumental nature of the Marshall's work. "'There are men who have tame these wild lands, and we owe them a debt that will never be repaid.'" He turned back to his Marshall, his expression solemn. "We will, though, at lease honor them in history."

Bass Reeves, however, dealt in the present tense, in sweat, bullets, and dollars. The grandeur of history was a concept for others.

"Well, Isaac," Bass began, leaning against the door jamb, his stance casual despite the massive reward he was about to claim. He couldn't resist one final, dry reference to the taunt Stands Tall had delivered. "Not countin' Goat Herder of the year, dat's 'bout $23,000 plus expenses." The reward, a life-changing sum, was earned for bringing an end to a half-dozen violent careers.

The Judge merely smiled, a genuine flicker of amusement in his severe eyes. "Come by in the Morning and I'll get you fixed up proper like."

Bass pushed off the jamb. The thought of another day spent filing expense reports and counting money was an anathema. He had a deeper, more necessary appointment.

"I think I'm a-leave the proper fixer up-in' to a sweet little ole thing named Jennie!"

Their shared laugh was a brief, necessary bridge between the savagery of the frontier and the civilization they both sought to build. Bass dipped his head, turned, and walked out, leaving the monumental debt and the pages of history to the Judge. His own ledger was balanced, and the final payment was due.

The two-day ride had been grueling, but every mile was a step closer to the single place in the world where the Marshall was simply Bass. He approached his small, sturdy homestead under a ceiling of indifferent, cold stars. The cabin was a beacon, a low, square shape of peace in the hostile, sprawling wilderness.

He dismounted slowly, the habitual tension of the trail finally releasing its grip. He could feel the accumulated weight of the blood on his hands, the endless vigilance, and the cold purpose that had driven him for weeks. He dropped the reins, the exhaustion profound enough to make his shoulders slump with genuine weariness.

The door opened before he could knock. Jennie, his wife, stood bathed in the warm, mellow light of the oil lamp inside. She was the counterpoint to the wild West, her skin smooth, her eyes deep and steady, filled with a love that demanded nothing but his safe return. She looked at his dusty, worn figure and offered the only true relief he sought.

"Your bath is drawn and food warm," she said, her voice a balm. It was the language of absolute, unconditional comfort. The water would wash away the dirt and the smoke; the food would restore his strength.

Bass stepped toward her, crossing the final, sacred threshold. His Marshal coat, his badge, and the bloody business of Dick Glass all remained outside the frame. He looked at the quiet elegance of her presence, the heat of the hearth spilling out behind her, and saw everything he fought for.

The weariness vanished, replaced by a sudden, intense longing. The exhaustion of the trail was nothing compared to the powerful, life-affirming reality of the woman who waited for him.

"Yeah," he breathed, his voice low and thick with feeling. "But my woman is hot!"

It was a return to their own language, an intimate declaration that sealed the door against the darkness outside. He stepped in, and the door closed softly behind him, shutting out the dead men, the bounties, the Judge, and the history books. All that remained was home.

THE END

About the Author

James Shaffer small town raised kid of average talents and desires. Live my life unhinged by social norms. The outlier the "Rebel" the out of the box thinker. I have dreams and I pursue them with vigor. I wanted to make movies, so I went and got a degree in making film. This book is it!

www.ingramcontent.com/pod-product-compliance
Lightning Source LLC
Chambersburg PA
CBHW060340310726
48976CB00003B/659

Thomas, reassured, nodded and turned, heading down the quaint street. Lisbeth made her way into the hotel, wiping at the tears rapidly falling. She needed to calm down. Lisbeth didn't head to her room, but to the one her brother was residing in, unbeknownst to everyone but her.

She knocked on the door, and Justin opened it. He sighed and began pacing back and forth. "We only have two hours before the ship departs for London. We should be back in ten days. The wedding is expected to be the week after that."

Lisbeth closed her eyes, wanting to rage that she didn't want to wed a duke's son. How could her own brother be so oblivious to her pain? Lisbeth was trading the man she loved for financial stability for her family. Her brother stopped pacing and tapped on a piece of paper on the small desk. "First, you need to finish the letter. You should have done it yesterday."

"Don't rush me," she snapped.

He studied her, frowning. "You have to understand this is the best choice for everyone. Without your marriage, Father and the estate will be destitute."

"I understand that this needs to be done, but don't pretend this is best for me," she exploded. "You are asking me to choose between the man who loves me and saving my family."

Silence hung between them. Contrition, finally, rippled across her brother's face. "I'm sorry."

"Just don't say this is best for everyone. It is best for you, Father, and the rest of our family. It isn't best for Thomas or me. I love him so much. I hope you will never understand what it is like to break the heart of the person that matters most to you."

More tears streamed down her face. Justin strode to her and wiped them from her cheeks. "I'm sorry, Lisbeth. If there were any other way, I would gladly take that path. I've tried everything. The men, whom Father owes money to, roughed him up pretty badly before I left. I don't have any other options."

Lisbeth saw the anger that her brother kept so deeply bottled up within himself. Their father had lost a fortune at the gaming tables and then continued to play, using loans. His debts were all being called in, but the family had nothing to pay them. Well, except for a guarantee of money when Lisbeth married the future Duke of Lusby. A man whom she'd spoken to three times in her whole life. However, they'd been betrothed since she was twelve through a gentleman's agreement between their fathers.

She took a deep breath. As much as she loved Thomas, she couldn't allow her family to lose everything. Lisbeth had been shocked when Justin showed up in Tuscany, insisting he needed to speak with her.

She and her family's housekeeper's son, Thomas Easton, had run off together more than a year ago, hoping to work with famed antiquities explorer Benjamin Calvert. Not only had they found him, but he'd offered them employment. Lisbeth loved her life with Thomas. She loved that they toiled away studying artifacts from the past. Until Justin arrived, she planned to do that forever as husband and wife.

They'd been friends their whole lives, growing up side by side; then, in the Syrian desert, he confessed his love for her. And just like that, it had all clicked into place why he agreed to leave England with her and venture off to faraway lands. For Thomas, she was always his forever lady. She hated that it had taken her longer to figure it out, but now she knew he was her perfect match, actually her only. Thomas had just proposed. She pushed the thoughts away and bit out, "I will do it, but please don't act like this is easy for me."

Justin nodded. "I'm sorry. Would you like me to speak with him? Maybe he would understand—"

"No!" If Thomas knew what she was doing, he would do everything to prevent it. Leaving him a note that she'd returned to England for good was the only way, even though it would devastate him. He would hate her. Maybe that was for the best. She would need to make sure the letter made all her decisions final, or Thomas would come after her. Lisbeth, her heart breaking, sat down at the desk to write the missive—a goodbye letter to the one man who would always have her heart.

Dear Thomas,

I've decided to return to England. While our adventure has been fun, I find I miss my life in London and regret not having a Season. I hope you will understand. Even though I'm returning, I think it is best that you stay and continue your work with Benjamin Calvert and his daughter. I have no doubt you will be like the famous explorers we have always loved to read about. I hope to read about your adventures someday. Please don't come after me. I will not see you if you do. My mind is made up. I release you from our betrothal.

Lady Lisbeth

She placed the letter in the envelope and handed it to Justin. Relief filled his face. "Thank you."

Lisbeth nodded, hating the feeling of loss that coursed through her body. She stood and said, "Never mention Thomas to me again. I will go and do my duty, but I don't want us ever to discuss this."

Justin nodded, sadness hanging to him. It clung to her as well. It wasn't every day a lady abandoned her betrothed. Lisbeth wished she were more selfish because choosing duty over love wasn't what she wanted at all. She wanted to be with the man she loved, Thomas Easton.

Chapter One

January 1851
Syria
Twelve years later

LISBETH STOOD IN the small building in the bustling Syrian port city of Latakia. She waited patiently as Mr. Abbas spoke to the guide who could escort her, Abbas, and her guard, Seth Benson, to the Calverts' excavation site out in the desert. From what she'd been told, it would be another three-day ride.

Mr. Abbas's hands flew in every direction. Lisbeth frowned; once long ago, she'd been able to speak some Arabic, but they were talking much too fast to understand what was being said. Instead, she glanced out the window. The street was alive with street vendors, men and women strolling along, and other lively entertainment.

If she were any other lady, she might be terrified to be in a new country, but the sounds, sights, and smells exhilarated Lisbeth. Partially, she supposed, because this wasn't her first time in this city. However, it had been over ten years.

Abbas turned back to her and sighed, "Your Grace, Mr. Dawoud said Benjamin Calvert, his daughter, and her husband have returned to England."

Lisbeth's eyes widened. "Her husband?"

"Yes, surname Sinclair," their guide, Mr. Dawoud, said.

Abbas frowned at him. "You speak English?"

"Of course I do." Dawoud looked at him, puzzled.

Lisbeth smiled at him. "Did you say Sinclair?"

Dawoud beamed at her. "Yes, they wed in the desert. Miss Calvert's father insisted."

She laughed. It sounded like Benjamin. Joy coursed through her, but then it was replaced with frustration that she'd traveled all this way, and now they would have to return to England.

"Their partner, Thomas Easton, is in the city. Perhaps he can help you?" Dawoud suggested.

This was the one thing she'd feared. Well, not exactly this. She'd never anticipated Rose and Benjamin not being here at all. Yes, Lisbeth had suspected she might have to see Thomas briefly, but nothing more than that. Now, he was the only person who could assist her. She hoped Rose had told him about the map potentially being delivered.

She did her best to shake off her concerns. They didn't matter. What was important was that she had a very old map indicating the location of two ancient cuneiform tablets that her club, The Historical Society for Female Curators, needed to retrieve. The club required them to finish deciphering an ancient epic. In London, they had clay tablets that contained the beginning and middle of the story. The map, if accurate, would lead them to the artifacts that included the ending. It would be a huge success for the club to display one of the oldest completed pieces of literature known to the modern world.

It was an epic that explained one man's quest to win the right to be with the woman he loved. The Historical Society for Female Curators had deciphered and put on display the first half of the story at Seely House in London. It was currently a favorite attraction among the *ton*.

It wasn't often that London society became enthralled by antiquities, but the Historical Society for Female Curators had successfully grabbed their attention. Lisbeth was excited and proud of the club. They'd only been around for a year. Still, the male-only London Society of Antiquaries was doing everything in its power to limit their achievements.

Having a completed ancient epic on display would wow everyone. The club's president hadn't said it out loud, but Lisbeth suspected that Addie and the other board members hoped it would parley them into a chance to showcase artifacts at the Great Exhibition of the Works of Industry of All Nations that the Royals were hosting in a few months.

The global event nicknamed the Great Exhibition promised to be the first of its kind, bringing unique goods, innovations, and items from all over the world for tourists to peruse. The most sought-after architects were building a massive building in Hyde Park to house the event. It was to be known as the Crystal Palace.

Artifacts and historical innovations were only a small part of the exhibits. Still, the Historical Society for Female Curators was determined to be part of the event. To do that, the club needed the tablets containing the epic's ending. Lisbeth pushed away the unease of having to engage with Thomas and asked, "Do you know where we can find Mr. Easton?"

Dawoud nodded. "If you follow the road and pass through two intersections, you will find a small café. He is likely there. I think he is planning to head to another excavation site farther south tomorrow."

Lisbeth ignored the nerves sizzling in her stomach and smiled. "Thank you, Mr. Dawoud."

She glanced at Abbas and Benson. "Shall we?"

They both frowned at her. Abbas suggested, "Perhaps you should wait here."

Annoyance flared in her. "Mr. Abbas, I'm not the first English woman to venture to Latakia. I have spent time here previously.

Both Abbas's and Benson's eyes widened. Mr. Dawoud nodded. "She is safe here. I will escort you all. Follow me"

She departed after him, walking past them and exiting the space. The street was even busier than when they entered the small building owned by Mr. Dawoud. More street vendors had started to fill empty spaces, and locals shopped and socialized. It had been smart to forgo her usual elaborate dresses for practical skirts and blouses. Beyond being sensible, it was bloody hot.

She weaved her way through the crowds with Abbas and Benson scrambling behind her as they followed Dawoud. Memories came flooding back. A man selling dates transported her to a time with Thomas when she was eighteen and he was nineteen—so long ago.

"DON'T EAT THAT, Lizzie," Thomas insisted.

Lisbeth grinned mischievously at him. "You are no fun. We are on an adventure. One that is going well, I might add. We found the famed explorer, Benjamin Calvert, and he is allowing us to work with him and his daughter. We need to try everything."

She bit into the date and closed her eyes, enjoying the sweetness. Lisbeth had expected it to be tart, but it wasn't. Opening her eyes, she found her dearest friend Thomas staring at her lips, transfixed. A moment of something passed between them. She cleared her throat. "Here, try this, Serious Thomas."

He yanked his gaze away from her mouth and glared at her. Thomas hated the nickname she gave him. She laughed and pressed the date to his lips. His eyes widened as he bit into it. When he was done, Thomas said, "It's sweet."

A HAND GRABBED Lisbeth's arms, yanking her out of the decade-old memory. A cart came lumbering by close enough that Lisbeth could touch it. Benson frowned at her. "Be careful, Your Grace."

She glanced around and said, "I think you should call me Lisbeth or Mrs. Lusby."

Abbas nodded. "That is a good idea."

Mr. Dawoud stood farther down the street, motioning to

them. They finally reached the small café, and Lisbeth heard laughter inside, which she suspected was coming from Thomas. How did she know his voice after so many years?

Dawoud said, "Stay here, and I will ask him to join us."

Lisbeth nodded and stood to the side with Benson, her heart pounding.

THOMAS EASTON SMACKED his close friend Desmond Keaton on his back as they broke into laughter. Keaton smirked. "I thought for sure we were goners. Luckily, Rafe found us."

Their Syrian friend, Tarek Al-Rafiq, or as they knew him, Rafe, grunted. "You fools are lucky I found you out in the desert. I sent you a letter to wait for me."

Keaton sighed. "Hawley said it was of great importance."

Thomas snorted. Delivering antiquities across the desert wasn't worth their lives. "I think Hawley is confused about what matters. I care about artifacts as well, but if Rafe hadn't shown up, we would have died from lack of water."

The table fell quiet, but finally, Rafe grinned. "Luckily, I happen to like you two Englishmen. I can't say that about all those that come here."

They all smirked. Keaton looked at Thomas. "What is next? Do you know when Rose and Benjamin will return? I can't believe she is a duchess. I would never have predicted that for her."

Thomas elbowed Keaton in the stomach. His friend grunted. He wouldn't let anyone speak poorly of Rose. He was happy for her. Though he suspected he wouldn't see her in Syria as often as before. Still, the duke was likely her perfect match. He seemed to have no interest in stymying her scholarly pursuits.

He should have returned to England with them. It had been almost a decade since he last saw his mother. She would be happy to see him. Over the last few years, she'd been more pointed about wanting him to return to London, but he couldn't. Lisbeth was there.

Thomas wished his ex-betrothed only the best but had no desire to interact with her. He'd finally made peace with their past. Still, it had taken him a damn long time to do so. "Rose and her husband will be back. She needs to deliver a map that shows the location of the two clay tablets I've been searching for. There are too many corridors and cavities within the cave system down South. Without the drawing of what pathways to take, I'm simply guessing. I suppose they could send someone else. I don't know how long it will take to have a grand society wedding."

Keaton shuddered. "I may pass if you head back to the tunnels. That cave system is so vast, and I hate those tiny spaces."

Thomas grinned. Keaton detested the caves. They spooked him; he often complained about how he hated the tight spaces.

"I've explored them a couple of times and think the best decision is to wait on the map."

Mr. Dawoud stopped at their table. Thomas grinned at the guide, who generally acted as their escort to the permanent excavation site Benjamin Calvert worked at when he was here. "How are you, Dawoud? I don't think I will be going out to the site anytime soon."

Dawoud shook his head. "You have a visitor who wants to speak with you because Benjamin isn't here."

Thomas groaned. Benjamin enjoyed hosting a diverse range of people. He didn't have much going on, but it didn't mean he wanted to take over for his partner. A bit of guilt swirled in him because he knew Thomas would expect him to entertain the visitors. He would do it, but not until the next day. "Can you ask them to meet me at the main hotel tomorrow? We can make plans to head out to the site."

The guide shook his head. "I don't think that will work."

Thomas lifted a brow. "Why?"

Just then, the café went quiet, and he heard rustling behind

Dawoud. His heart nearly leaped out of his throat because Lisbeth, the Duchess of Lusby, joined Dawoud, followed by two other men. His eyes roamed over her uncontrollably. She looked like everything he'd imagined over the years—stunning and untouchable. Why did his hands itch to touch her?

Their eyes connected, and she gulped; he suspected she was nervous to see him. She took a deep breath and said, "Hello, Mr. Easton."

Fury welled in him at her proper tone. They had a past, one that was far too intimate for such formality. Thomas wouldn't allow it. He was a legend in the field of antiquities, possibly the most famous explorer of his time.

He leaned back in his chair and grinned. "Well, hello, Lizzie. I certainly wasn't expecting you. Why am I so lucky to have you grace my presence?"

Fire sparked in her eyes, and she gritted her teeth before saying calmly, "Please call me Mrs. Lusby."

He lifted a brow at her haughtiness. His smile became more of a smirk. The owner motioned for Thomas to use a private room. It wasn't often that women were in this café. He rose and said, "Please follow me, Lizzie."

She stiffened at his second use of her old nickname. He suspected it had been a long time since this duchess had been addressed so informally. She was both the same and so different. He couldn't stop himself from perusing her beautiful face, blonde hair, and slender form. She was dressed far more casually than Thomas believed a duchess would be, but it appeared she'd acquired a regal bearing over the last ten years that gave her an air of importance.

Rafe and Keaton stared at him curiously. Finally, Keaton asked, "Should I join?"

Thomas shook his head and led Lisbeth and her two associates into the private room. What was she doing here?

Chapter Two

LISBETH SAT ACROSS from Thomas. Her heart was pounding frantically. She did her best to stop her eyes from roaming over him. He was certainly no longer the boy she left behind. Gone was the slender, almost gangly young man, and in his place was a man comprised of hard muscle, tanned by countless hours out in the sun.

His mouth tilted into a sardonic smile. She'd read the serials about Thomas Easton, the famous explorer, and his roguish charm. She'd never really believed the description was accurate, but now, sitting across from him, it was apparent that it was she who was wrong. Still, he was both familiar and different. His perceptive green eyes remained the same.

The air was charged with emotions that Lisbeth never thought she would feel again. Benson and Abbas stood behind her, but that didn't dissipate the tension that swirled between her and Thomas. He stretched, causing Lisbeth's eyes to dart to his broad chest. She wasn't sure if she was ogling him because he lived up to every physical description the serials and gossip sheets wrote, or because he was so different from the boy she left.

"What are you doing here, Serious Lizzie?"

She bristled at the nickname. "That was never my name. I called *you* that."

His eyes flicked down her, and he became somber for a moment, but then he shrugged. "You appear to be awfully serious now. I hear you are a duchess. Is that true?"

Lisbeth had no doubt Thomas knew about her title, but she didn't want to quarrel with him. "Yes, it is."

"Then the nickname suits you perfectly."

Quietly, she said, "You used to be Serious Thomas, though I don't think that would describe you now."

He leaned forward, placing his elbows on the table, and grinned rakishly at her. "What do you mean?"

Lisbeth studied him. She wished a piece of the practical, rule-following boy she used to know still existed. Was he still in there? The longer she stared, the more intense his perusal of her became. Benson cleared his throat, breaking her stare off with Thomas.

Lisbeth said, "I'm here to deliver the map that shows the location of the last two cuneiform tablets for the ancient epic my club has on display in London."

Excitement flared in Thomas's eyes. "I've been looking for those tablets for months now."

She nodded, feeding off his enthusiasm. "The Historical Society for Female Curators is thrilled that we may find them. Once put on display with the other tablets, our exhibit will be the first of its kind."

While some scholars had translated ancient cuneiform texts, Rose Calvert was the first to decipher a large piece of literature. It was even more exciting that she was doing it for the Historical Society of Female Curators. The ancient writing was from the civilization of Mesopotamia. Thomas smiled at her, a real one this time, and the once forgotten connection of friendship zinged between them. They'd always both loved artifacts.

I cannot get too close to this man, she reminded herself. It wouldn't be good for her life. Lisbeth added, "I can provide the map to you tomorrow if you will call upon me at my hotel. I will return to England and let my club and Rose know that you have it. How long do you think it will take to acquire the tablets with the map?"

He was quiet for a moment, and Lisbeth waited for him to say anything. She glanced back at Abbas and Benson, who were both waiting for his response as well. Finally, he shook his head. "There was a time when you would have demanded to join me on the search."

"I have responsibilities," Lisbeth huffed.

A gleam of amusement flashed in his eyes. "You have really turned into Serious Lizzie. Don't you miss the excitement of the search? Digging around in hopes of finding something the world has never seen?"

She didn't say anything. Thomas sighed, "Perhaps time has changed you too much. I imagine you are used to others doing work for you now."

Anger flared in her, and she scowled at him. "How long do you think it will take?"

He shrugged. "I'm familiar with the caves. They are extensive, but if the map is as detailed as the village elders have told me, it should only be days."

She could stay for a little longer. The idea of joining the search with Thomas should make her want to run back to London, but something stirred in her. It was the thrill of discovering something never seen before. Lisbeth suspected Thomas knew she was considering it. Even though they'd been apart for a decade and were very different people, he still seemed to be able to read her so well.

"One last adventure, Lizzie, and then you can go back to being a duchess," he said quietly.

Abbas leaned forward, "I would be happy to join you."

Why did Lisbeth want to join Thomas? She'd chosen a different life for herself. Yet, the desire to be out in the world, exploring, thrilled her.

She glanced at Benson. He said, "I'm here no matter what you choose."

Lisbeth nodded and told Thomas, "I will join you for the next few weeks. If we don't find them by then, I need to return to England. I have—"

"Responsibilities," her ex-lover finished for her, almost tauntingly.

She rose and insisted, "Yes. I do, unlike you, who now seems to make decisions without any serious thought. Please call upon me tomorrow at noon."

Thomas chuckled. "I wish Rose and Benjamin were here. It would be like old times."

The words he spoke weren't true. They were both drastically different people. And, of course, all the feelings they felt for each other were long gone; ten years had passed since they'd been near each other. Yet, their eyes connected, and something stirred between them. She scolded herself. Lisbeth had no interest in this version of Thomas, or any other for that matter.

"Tomorrow," she said, ignoring his remark, and heading to the door.

THOMAS SAT IN the empty private room of the café, his heart pounding. He'd been shocked to see Lisbeth, but the full force was hitting him now that she was gone. She'd been so different from the young woman who'd abandoned him for England all those years ago, but also, in some ways, strangely familiar.

It was evident she'd been shocked by his drastically different appearance. When Lisbeth had left, she'd been twenty, and he'd been twenty-one. Christ, he'd barely been a man, and a scrawny one at that. Hard work had transformed his body, and if he was being honest, at least to the ladies, for the better. Neither the changes in his body nor becoming a famed explorer had been something he planned. Thomas, growing up, had always been a bookish and introverted person.

A few years after Lisbeth broke off their betrothal, a man

expressed interest in writing about him. Intrigued, Thomas agreed to let him travel with him for a year. People had devoured the serials he published. Connor Anderson was the author. The man was back in London now, wealthy and retired, but he made Thomas promise that if he ever wanted to write more serials, he'd contact him first.

Rafe and Keaton slinked into the room, curious. Thomas didn't say anything as they settled in the chairs across from him. Rafe twirled a glass in his hand and finally said, "So that is your duchess?"

He scowled. "She isn't my anything."

Rafe looked at him skeptically. "Did you know she planned to travel to Syria?"

Thomas shook his head, shocked that Rose hadn't even mentioned the possibility. Had she known? "I invited her to join me to find the tablets."

Rafe's brows shot up. "Did she say yes?"

"I may have goaded her into it."

"Was that wise?" Keaton asked. "The tension between the two of you was evident."

Thomas wasn't sure why he'd behaved so abominably, taunting her. Something about her regal composure annoyed him— she certainly wasn't the girl he once knew. He'd wanted to draw the old Lizzie out. Yet he realized that keeping Lisbeth around probably wasn't a good idea. "I will speak with her tomorrow and let her know she isn't needed."

Keaton and Rafe chuckled, and he glared at them. "What?"

"I'm not sure anyone would like to be told that," Keaton said.

"It will be fine. She will likely come to that conclusion on her own before we meet. Will you both be joining me?"

Keaton sighed. "Not me. I have other work, but I wish I was. The trip sounds entertaining."

Rafe grinned. "I will let you know."

Thomas frowned. "She isn't going."

The next day, Thomas waited in the small sitting area of

Rose's hotel lodging. She was staying at the only real hotel in Latakia, and he suspected the nicest room. He shouldn't be surprised; she was a duchess after all.

Her guard and Mr. Abbas sat with him as they waited. Finally, she entered the room, smiling stiffly and carrying something in a cloth bag. "I'm sorry I took so long."

Thomas shook his head. "It's fine."

She nodded and placed the bag on a table in the sitting area. Thomas studied her as she delicately opened it. She was so different from the Lisbeth who left him. Her hair was perfectly done up, and she moved with a grace that he didn't remember from their younger years. He watched her hands as they pulled a fragile antique map out. They were slender, and his mind flashed to a moment in their past.

⇶⇷

EIGHTEEN-YEAR-OLD LIZZIE GRINNED and swirled her finger down his bare chest as they lazily lay naked on pallet bedding in her tent in the desert. "You are stuck with me now, Thomas Easton. You've compromised me."

He laughed. "Does that make me a rogue?"

She snorted, her blue eyes sparkling with mischief. "You are the last boy I would ever suspect of being one."

Thomas leaned forward and kissed her lips. "Not a boy, a man."

She lifted a brow. "A man?"

"I seduced you, didn't I?"

Lizzie giggled. "I was the seducer."

"You are the daughter of an earl. This shouldn't be happening. I was trying to be respectful."

She kissed his chest, causing his body to hum. "Yet, you ran off with me to seek adventure."

Her mouth drifted further down. He couldn't fight the words any longer. "I don't care about adventure. I'm here because I love you, Lizzie."

Her head jerked up, and she looked at him. "Don't say those words unless you mean them."

Thomas flipped her on her back and looked down at her. "I've always loved you. My whole life, and I always will."

She beamed a smile so beautiful that Thomas knew he'd never forget it.

⟫⟫⟫⟪⟪⟪

"THOMAS?" LISBETH ASKED, snapping him out of his memories.

Why was he thinking about the past? He shook his head. "Sorry."

She frowned at him, and he smirked at her, knowing it would rile her up. Lisbeth took a deep breath. "As I was saying, the map is old, and we need to be careful with it. Still, it is quite detailed and hopefully should help us find the tablets."

He leaned forward and looked at the old document. The person who drew the picture took great care to ensure it accurately reflected the actual cave system. Thomas had spent enough time there that he identified some of the corridors he'd explored. Yet there were spaces he'd never seen. One cavern on the map had various objects painted in it.

"Is this the location?"

Lisbeth nodded. "That is what Rose and the club suspect."

Lisbeth placed her finger, showing three corridors that led to the place of interest. He frowned. "I've never seen some of these areas. The entrance to them must be obscured somehow."

She bit her lip and asked, "Do you think one of the corridors is still traversable?"

He grinned at her. "Anything is possible?"

She seemed startled by his optimism. Thomas lifted a brow, and a small, amused expression filled her face. "You certainly are no longer Serious Thomas."

"That boy disappeared long ago."

The past hung between them. Thomas cleared his throat; he

needed her to leave. All of this was too much. "I wanted to suggest that you return to England. I give you my word that this will be my main priority, and once I find the tablets, they will be shipped to England."

She frowned and then turned to Benson and Abbas. "Could you give us a moment to speak privately?"

The men rose and departed the room. Lisbeth said, "Why are you suggesting I leave after you all but taunted me to go with you?"

He sighed. "It has been years since you did this type of work. I don't want to have to keep an eye on you."

Lisbeth bristled. The tiny display of emotion flared feelings in Thomas that he thought were long gone. When they'd been together and much younger, Thomas had always been the reasonable one, with Lisbeth more emotional and dramatic. Over the last ten years, she'd learned to master that. He was a cad because he enjoyed riling her up.

"I don't need a sitter or keeper. I'm the one who introduced you to antiquities all those years ago."

He snorted. "Lizzie, I've traveled the world since then."

She rolled her eyes. "Yes, the famed explorer, Thomas Easton, has done everything. I'm aware that you've discovered never-before-seen ancient libraries, Assyrian and Mesopotamian historical sites, and Roman buildings across the continent."

His lips twitched at her lack of awe for his fame. She tilted her chin up. "I'm going, Thomas. When do we leave?"

Thomas had tried. *Not very hard*, his rational side taunted. Ignoring reason, he answered, "The day after tomorrow."

He stood and headed for the door.

Lisbeth said, "Thomas."

Stopping, he turned back. She smirked and looked down at her dress. "Can you help me acquire more practical clothing?"

The duchess before him was breathtaking, but for some reason, the idea of Lizzie, dressed ready to explore, might bring him to his knees, Thomas thought. *She left you*, he reminded himself.

Still, he nodded. "I'm sure Rose has something at the building where we store all our items in Latakia. I will make sure clothes are delivered to the hotel."

Chapter Three

LISBETH COULDN'T BELIEVE she was going with Thomas on this trip. They wouldn't be alone, as Benson, Abbas, and Thomas's associate would be traveling with them. Still, she hadn't envisioned doing more than delivering the map to Syria. Yet, now, she was on her way to assist in the search.

She glanced down at the clothing Thomas had sent her the previous day. The items belonged to Rose and were designed primarily for convenience. It was a blend of Bedouin culture in Syria and what one would imagine a man would wear for adventuring.

The shirt that covered her from her collarbone to her calves was a garment called a thawb, and it was paired with a pair of light men's English breeches. The ensemble was finished with a belt and a hat. No ball gowns for her. She smiled, freer than she'd felt in a long time.

Lisbeth left her room and joined Benson and Abbas in the lobby. The hotel agreed to hold their luggage while they were gone. They would be taking a much smaller portion of their belongings on the trip. Abbas smiled at her. "You look very comfortable today. Much more than yesterday."

She nodded. "Yes, I am."

Benson, her guard, who'd been with her for years, looked at her amused. She lifted a brow, and he grinned. "I'm pretty sure if your daughter ever saw you like this, you'd never be able to tell her she can't wear trousers again."

Her daughter Alice idolized Rose Calvert, including her love of wearing pants when at home. Lisbeth laughed. "These are Rose's clothes."

Benson snickered. "Of course they are."

Thomas entered the lobby, and his gaze roamed over her before he seemed to realize what he was doing. He briskly asked, "Are you ready?"

Lisbeth nodded, and she, Benson, and Abbas followed him out. A striking man stood by a group of horses. Their eyes connected, and he smiled. Whoever he was, if he ever visited London, the city would be in love with him.

"The pretty face over there is my friend Tarek Al-Rafiq. Rafe, for short," Thomas bit out.

"What an unfriendly introduction, Easton," Rafe said, and then he turned to Lisbeth. "It may not seem like it based on his gruffness, but I happen to be a close friend of this famous explorer."

Next, he introduced himself to Benson and Abbas, then turned back to Thomas. He pulled a stack of letters from a bag and shoved them playfully at Lisbeth's ex-lover. "You can carry your worship mail."

Lisbeth studied the missives. Several of them were floral and smelled like perfume. She leaned forward, curious. "Are those love letters?"

Rafe smirked. "Easton has many admirers from London. He is famous there. I wouldn't believe him if I weren't always delivering love notes."

A flush covered Thomas's face, and he scowled at his friend before shoving the missives into a bag on the side of his horse. "They aren't love letters."

Rafe snorted. "He is very famous. All the ladies speak about him in a grandiose fashion."

Benson nodded. "I've heard the stories in London."

Abbas looked at them all as if he were missing some joke. Rafe tapped Thomas jokingly on his cheek. "You are a handsome fool. Not as attractive as me, but still, the ladies love you."

The amusement continued to course through her, but deep in her heart, Lisbeth felt a flare of jealousy. She pushed it away. Thomas was allowed to spend time with whomever he liked. She imagined he had plenty of lovers because Rafe was right; he was an attractive, strapping man. He wore ruggedness in a way that most men could never pull off.

He sighed and held out his hand to assist her onto a grey horse. She stepped towards him, and he lifted her up and made sure she was settled safely and comfortably on the animal's back. Thomas handed her the reins. "This is Asta. She will be your horse for the trip."

She nodded. "Thank you, Thomas."

He grunted in response, and he and the rest of their group climbed onto their horses. "This is an all-day ride, but we will keep it nice and slow."

Hours later, Rafe joined Lisbeth. He grinned. "I think I've upset Easton by flirting with you."

Lisbeth suspected it didn't matter if a lady was young or old; Rafe could easily charm them. She assumed he was well aware of the effect his handsome face had on others. Lisbeth wouldn't encourage him. She lifted a brow. "Were you flirting? I hadn't noticed."

He laughed loudly, causing Thomas to glance their way before turning forward, his jaw clenched. Rafe smiled. "So you are Thomas's lost love."

She blushed. "No…I wouldn't call it that…it is complicated."

Another bark of laughter erupted from him, and the man smiled slyly at her. "It was just a guess, but now I suspect, based on your response and my friend's fierce scowl, that there is a grand story there."

She shook her head. "It was a long time ago. We were young, really just children."

"Love happens at all ages."

Lisbeth frowned at Rafe. "Why do I sense you are a trouble-maker?"

He looked at her, his gaze turning serious. "I have the same question about you? I've seen Easton charm many ladies, but he's never glowered at me over one. Don't hurt him, Your Grace. He is a good man."

Anger sparked in Lisbeth that he was lecturing her. "I've no intention of doing anything but obtaining the tablets."

"Rafe, I need you up here," Thomas barked.

The man sighed and galloped up to him. He laughed and insisted, "I wasn't flirting."

Annoyance coursed through Lisbeth. Who was he to warn her against hurting Thomas? She wasn't the known rake. No, that was the famed explorer, and he had the letters to show it. She glanced to the left of her, and Benson asked, "Anything amiss, Your Grace?"

She shook her head. Lisbeth had no intentions of doing any-thing with or to Thomas. All of that died between them a long time ago. He glanced back, and their eyes met. A spark of something flared between them. *No*, she told herself. Thomas Easton had a whole world of ladies to tup, and she wouldn't be on his list of conquests.

⟫⟪

THOMAS RODE BESIDE Rafe, and his friend smirked at him. "Why don't you go speak with her?"

"What do you mean?" he asked, feigning ignorance.

"She is your Layla."

He snorted at his friend's quiet declaration. He was compar-ing him and Lisbeth to a forbidden Arabic love story. The Majnun loved Layla, but she married another, and he went mad, roaming the desert for years. "I'm not a madman."

Rafe lifted a brow. "Madness comes in different forms. You take risks other men wouldn't, bed numerous women but don't take the time to know them and refuse to put down roots anywhere. I think that could be considered a form of insanity."

Thomas rolled his eyes at his friend. "You are no better—a man who won't claim his heritage, flirts but won't touch any woman, and spends time with a madman. What does that make you?"

Rafe chuckled. "An imbecile."

They both laughed, and it momentarily eased the tension in Thomas's chest. Rafe jerked his head. "Go talk to her. She may be with us for weeks. Forgiveness is the best gift you can give or receive."

The problem was that he wasn't sure if he had forgiven Lisbeth. A part of him carried a bit of hatred for her everywhere he went. It propelled him into so many rash but successful decisions. In truth, part of his success as an explorer came from not wanting to be Serious Thomas, the young man she'd decided she couldn't wed.

With every one of his achievements, he'd become more boisterous and confident, not because it came naturally to him but because deep down he'd always believed the practical, quiet young man he once was hadn't been enough for her.

"Go," Rafe said.

"You better hope we never run into the woman you are behaving like a saint for."

Sadness fluttered across his friend's face. "Only fate can bring us together."

Thomas lifted a brow. "It isn't like you to be this dramatic."

Rafe shrugged. "I've never known you to be angry when I flirt with a woman. She is special."

Thomas glanced back at Lisbeth, who was talking with Abbas. "She is my past."

"Then let her go so you can be free from the weight of your feelings."

He sighed but slowed his horse until he was next to Lisbeth. Abbas said, "I think I will join Rafe."

Thomas nodded, and Lisbeth gulped, seemingly nervous. Their horses moved at a leisurely pace. Finally, he said, "I'm still shocked you are going with us on this little exploration."

"Honestly, so am I."

"I feel in some ways I goaded you into it," he confessed.

Her blue eyes flicked towards him, and her mouth tilted up. "You did, but I don't blame you entirely. I'm not some young girl; I shouldn't be so easily incited."

Thomas chuckled. "You seem much calmer as a duchess."

His mention of her title cast a heaviness between them. Her lips trembled, and Thomas had the shocking urge to comfort her—to provide her forgiveness for the choices of the past. Perhaps Rafe was a wise man. Being this close to her, the fury didn't fester in him like he thought it would. Thomas found himself wanting to forgive her so they both could move on from the past.

"I want you to know that I don't hate you or hold any grudges for the decisions you made."

Her eyes widened, and she pressed her lips together.

He added, "We were so young."

Lisbeth nodded, gratefulness reflecting in her eyes. "Thank you, Thomas. There are many things I wish I could have done differently. I'm sorry for any pain I caused you."

While Thomas appreciated her apology, what he really wanted was to know why. Yet, she didn't provide any details on why she broke their betrothal and returned to England. He didn't push her. Maybe the past was best forgotten. Attempting to lighten the conversation, he said, "I can't be too upset. I'm a famous explorer. Not once did I ever predict that."

Her mouth tilted up in a smirk. "Apparently, with several admirers. Do you read all the letters?"

He shrugged. "There is a good deal of downtime at the excavation sites. Sometimes, I will respond if they leave their address.

A few of the letters are a bit unhinged. I've had more than a few proposals."

She giggled. "You truly embody what every London lady envisions when they think of a dashing explorer."

Her eyes flicked over him, and Thomas's body became alert. They'd both changed so much. "I'm not the slender, bookish man you once knew."

"No, you aren't," she said quietly, a blush tinging her cheeks.

"Thomas," Rafe called from up front.

He grinned and said, "I'd best go see what he wants."

"Thank you for your reassurance that you don't hold any resentment towards me," she replied. "I don't think we need to rehash the past any further but know that there was nothing ever wrong with the bookish boy you once were. My choice wasn't about you or us."

Thomas could tell by the tone of her words that she wouldn't share more, and he didn't push it. What was the point? Peace and forgiveness between them would need to be enough. He nodded and joined his friend.

Chapter Four

LISBETH WATCHED AS Thomas joked with a man in perfect Arabic. They'd just arrived in the small village of Al-Wāḥa. Mr. Abbas was speaking with the village elders in one of the houses with a courtyard, hoping to obtain their support in finding the tablets. From what Lisbeth saw, she suspected it wouldn't be a problem. Thomas seemed to know everyone well.

Rafe explained, "Thomas has been working with them for the last few months, exploring various caves, but having Abbas here will put them at ease even more. The elders of Al-Wāḥa highly respect his mother's village."

Rose nodded. "Good. My club can't wait to have the tablets, but I want to make sure we are working in a way that is respectful to the area and those who live here."

"This time of year, there is a good deal of flooding. They can assist us in understanding when rain will be a problem and escape options if the caves and tunnels flood."

She shivered, remembering that while this was all exciting, there was a danger to it. Rafe smiled. "Thomas will not let any harm come to you."

"Thank you for the reassurance. I must admit I'd assumed my adventuring days were far behind me."

Rafe explained, "The serials' author likes to write Thomas as this cavalier explorer, but he is quite deliberate and thoughtful about how he handles excavations. He respects the artifacts too much to do it any other way."

She smiled. "So deep down, he is still Serious Thomas?"

He raised a brow. "Is that what you call him?"

"I was always jumping into things when we were children, and he made sure we were considering the repercussions, so I bestowed that nickname on him."

Amusement filled Rafe's face. "Serious Thomas is still in there. He is no saint, but when it matters, he comes out."

She laughed, and Thomas glanced their way, frowning. They both grinned at him. Rafe said, "Excuse me."

Lisbeth nodded and watched Rafe join the conversation. She tried to make sense of what they were saying, but it had been too long. Thomas had always been better with languages. Her mind drifted back to when they'd been in Syria for almost a year.

➤➤➤◄◄◄

"YOU HAVE TO learn. It is disrespectful not to try," Thomas insisted as they sat on the pallet in his tent in the middle of the night.

Annoyance flashed in Lisbeth. "I'm trying. I'm sorry I'm rot at languages, unlike you and Rose. Perhaps the two of you can become dear friends."

"Rose is my friend, and she is yours," he insisted.

A scowl marred Lisbeth's face, and Thomas, leaning on his side and staring down at her, wiped his thumb across her lower lip. "Don't be jealous of her. I didn't travel thousands of miles for her."

Lisbeth glanced away and gulped, but Thomas grasped her chin, turning her back. "What is wrong?"

"You and she have so much in common. Rose is serious and studious like you. This world of antiquities suits you."

He kissed her lips before releasing her chin. "It suits us. I wouldn't be in this country without you. Never in a million years would I have boarded a ship for a place we've only read about and sought the famed Benjamin Calvert. We are lucky he hired us."

She smiled at his reassurance. "I'm being petty about Rose. I should be nicer."

He rolled his eyes. "You should. She is only sixteen."

"I'm only eighteen, and you are only nineteen."

Thomas laughed. "I feel much older than that. Regardless, I like the Calverts and hope we can stay with them for a long time."

"I do, too."

He kissed her nose. "Good. Now, back to practicing."

She groaned.

He stated, "Antī jamīlah jiddan."

Liseth shook her head. "I don't know."

He leaned down and kissed her neck. "I said you are beautiful."

Happiness flared in her as Thomas's lips trailed up her throat to her mouth. She smiled against his lips. "I think I will remember that."

"Good," he groaned.

⟫⟪

LISBETH SHOOK THE thought away as warmth flared in her body. She glanced at Thomas, who was staring back at her. She knew he couldn't know her thoughts, but a sizzle of emotion sparked between them. She gulped and yanked her gaze away.

Abbas, just then, stepped outside, grinning. She, Thomas, and Rafe made their way to him. He said, "The elders seemed to adore you, Easton. I'm not sure I was really needed, but they are willing to help us while we are in the cave system. They are excited that the map is back in Syria and have no problem with it eventually being stored in my mother's village. They plan to provide two or three guides to help us watch for the rain and explore the caves."

Thomas nodded. "Do they suspect rain will be a problem?"

Abbas shrugged. "It is the time of year for it, but they think they can assist so any potential flooding doesn't catch us off guard."

"Perfect," Lisbeth said.

Thomas suggested, "Perhaps you should stay at the village while we explore the caves."

She frowned. "Why?"

"I merely want to ensure your safety," Thomas emphasized.

Abbas said, "The elders have assured me that they can make sure we are safe."

Thomas scowled at him, and he went instantly quiet. Benson, who'd been sitting in the shade, joined them. "Your Grace, if it is unsafe at all, I must insist you stay here."

An exasperated sigh escaped Lisbeth. "I'm not trying to put myself in danger. I want to help."

Benson looked at Thomas. "Is she safe?"

Thomas's eyes connected with hers. Lisbeth didn't realize how badly she wanted to assist with the search until it was on the cusp of being taken from her. Thomas seemed to sense it as well because he begrudgingly said, "We should be fine as long as we listen to the guides."

"Good," Lisbeth said, excitement coursing through her.

Abbas nodded to the women, bringing out a plethora of food. "The village elders want to celebrate the finding of the map."

Rafe grinned. "An excellent idea."

⟫⟫⟪⟪

THOMAS STUFFED HIMSELF with the food the villagers had laid out. He was so full that he felt as if he wouldn't need to eat for days. One of the village elders, Omar Al-Sayed, sat next to him, and, in Arabic, he asked, "Who is she?"

"She is a titled lady from England," he responded in the same language.

The man smirked at him. He shook his head. "Who is she to you?"

"We've known each other almost our whole lives."

"Tarek says she is your Layla."

Thomas sighed. Rafe was such a bloody gossip. He glanced at her. She was beaming and attempting to speak with one of the women in the village. "She is someone I care about, but not my Layla. She hasn't turned me into a madman."

The man chuckled as if he didn't believe him, but didn't say anything more. Rafe joined them, and the village elder left, going to speak with Abbas. He skewered his friend with a glare. "I would appreciate it if you didn't spread gossip about me."

Rafe sighed. "He is an elder. Did you want me to lie to him? He asked me about Lisbeth. He is curious because you've never brought a lady down here besides Rose."

"Why would I?"

His friend shrugged. "Lisbeth is a beautiful woman."

Thomas scowled. "When did you start addressing her so informally?"

"Benson said she is a widow. Why not pursue her?"

He looked at him in shock. "We have nothing in common and took very different paths. That is a preposterous idea."

"Why? You are alone, and she is as well. What is in the way?"

He didn't say anything but glanced at the woman he'd once thought would be his wife. Maybe Thomas had lied to Lisbeth. The hurt should be long gone after a decade, but it flared within him. "Today, I decided I can forgive her and hold no grudges about the past, but I don't think I can ever open my heart to Lisbeth again."

Rafe didn't argue with him. "Did she tell you why she left?"

"She didn't want to discuss the past in detail."

His friend glanced at her. "I think it would benefit both of you to talk through it. You may not want to love her, but there is something between the two of you."

Thomas snorted, not wanting to believe anything existed between him and Lisbeth.

Rafe gave him a knowing glance. "Or you can continue to be the madman."

"I'm not the Majnun."

"And I'm not the imbecile."

A chuckle escaped Thomas. "I may disagree. Who is the woman you haven't moved on from?"

While Thomas had slept his way across the globe, Rafe had flirted but abstained as far as he knew. Rafe sighed. "It doesn't matter."

"Perhaps you should take your own advice."

Rafe grinned and smacked him on the back. "We are a bunch of melancholy fools. Enough of this. What do we really have to complain about?"

Thomas grinned. "Nothing."

They both stayed silent. He watched Lisbeth. She laughed at something the woman she was speaking with said. His chest felt tight. Why did she leave Tuscany all those years ago? Had she decided she missed London so much? For years, Thomas had done his best to put it out of his mind, but now he felt as if he had to know.

Rafe wasn't always right about everything, but he was correct in this instance. Why did she leave? They'd loved each other, and that hadn't been enough for her to stay. Thomas needed those answers from her. Beyond that, he wasn't sure if anything else could exist between him and Lisbeth. Still, having the truth about what happened in Tuscany would at least allow closure.

Thomas would never admit it, but he still dreamed about Lisbeth almost every night—her touch, mouth, and moans. Now, she was here. Not a dream, but the real Lisbeth. He clenched his fist to control the urge to go to her and pull her against him. *Christ!* Why did Rose not bring the damn map?

Chapter Five

LISBETH FOLLOWED THOMAS, Benson, Rafe, Abbas, and the guides to the entrance of a cave. Truthfully, it looked like a small opening. No one would assume it was the start of a massive cave system. Thomas had drawn a copy of the map so the original wouldn't get damaged while they were in the tunnels and caverns.

She glanced up and frowned. The sky was overcast, but the clouds weren't dark. Hopefully, that meant the rain would hold off. She sighed, and her eyes connected with Thomas's. He had a concerned look on his face. "You can wait here."

Lisbeth frowned at him and then asked Abbas, "Did the guides say they were worried about the rain?"

Abbas shook his head, and she turned back to Thomas. "I will be fine."

His jaw clenched, and fury flared in Lisbeth. Thomas had no right to tell her what to do, especially if she was in no real danger. He laid the paper that contained the replicated map on a rock. Everyone joined him, perusing the drawing. The cave system was miles and miles of tunnels. In the far back was a cavity that had two, potentially three, tunnels leading to it. In the small open space was an X.

On the original map, it contained a more elaborate drawing with various items from the time period, but she supposed

Thomas wasn't an artist. The paths of two tunnels leading to the X were long and winding. The other one followed a more well-known corridor, according to Thomas, but then veered off onto a smaller tunnel leading to the X.

Thomas traced his finger along the paths. "I think it is best if we split into two groups and cover the longer routes first. The map is thousands of years old. We will likely need to dig our way through some areas, or the tunnel system might not exist any longer."

He then turned to the guides and spoke to them in Arabic. Both men nodded. He looked back at Lisbeth and Benson. "You two will join me and our guide, Farid. Rafe, Abbas, and the other guide, Badr, will take the second path. The last guide will wait outside to alert us to any potential rain or flooding."

Everyone nodded. Thomas stuffed ropes and other supplies in a bag and handed a lantern to Benson before grabbing another one for himself. Lisbeth said, "I can carry something."

"Trust me. We will all need to help. Who carries our gear is irrelevant."

She nodded, and he frowned. "I'm in charge there. Do you understand?"

Lisbeth flushed. "I'm not some young girl looking to cause trouble."

He lifted a brow as if he didn't quite believe her. She bristled. Truthfully, at nineteen, Lisbeth probably wouldn't have taken the situation seriously, but she wasn't that girl anymore. She rolled her eyes. "Understood. What happened to the fun, dashing explorer? I see you've pivoted back to Serious Thomas."

Rafe chuckled, and Thomas glared at him before turning back to her. "I don't want to see you hurt."

She sighed. "Thank you."

Thomas, Benson, Rafe, Fadir, and Badr lit their lanterns, and they all moved to the entrance of the cave. Stepping in, it felt small. There was only one tunnel before them, and it was necessary, due to the narrow width, for them to move in a single-file line. The glow of the lanterns off the cave tunnel walls added an eerie feel to the space, making Lisbeth shiver. She glanced at Thomas to see that he held a piece of chalk, which he ran along the side of the corridor.

She imagined it was in case they became turned around. Lisbeth had just started to wonder if that was even possible when they burst out into a large area. The space had exits to eight separate tunnels. Fadir spoke to Thomas in Arabic, and he nodded before turning to everyone. "Fadir wants me to explain that if we get trapped in the tunnels by water, there are two options to survive the flooding."

Nerves flared in Lisbeth's stomach. His words made her realize that this wasn't some game. This was a serious situation. Thomas pointed to a ledge above them. "You can hoist yourself up to the ledge. If you look at the markings on the wall, the water never reaches that high."

Benson muttered. "Christ."

Lisbeth shot him an apologetic look. He'd been in her employ for many years, but this was likely the craziest situation she'd ever placed them in. Thomas then drew a circle above one of the tunnels. "If you can't reach the ledge, this tunnel forces water out into the river. You will need to hold your breath for a minute and allow the water to take you."

Abbas tugged at his collar, his nerves on edge. Thomas looked around, and Rafe said, "Can you be any more ominous?"

Badr spoke in Arabic, and relief seemed to fill Abbas's face. "Fadir said that no rain is expected today. It is merely a precautionary measure."

While the explanation was frightening, in some ways, Lisbeth felt relieved to have options. Thomas, Rafe, Badr, and Fadir studied the map. She, Benson, and Abbas waited. Thomas drew a triangle over one tunnel opening and a square over another. "My team will take the triangle tunnel. Rafe's team will take the square."

Everyone nodded, and Thomas glanced at her. "Ready for this?"

"Yes."

THOMAS SAT ON a rock, exhausted. They'd finally reached the end of the long, meandering tunnel. There, they'd found a sliver of an opening that led hopefully to the cavernous space where the tablets were supposed to be located. Unfortunately, it required shimmying through a narrow corridor to reach it. Benson looked reluctant to go any further. Thomas had measured the width of the slender space; they would all fit, though it would be tight.

"We need to travel in pairs," he explained. Thomas had a friend become stuck in a cave a few years ago and almost died, so he always had specific rules when traversing any underground system—working in pairs or trios was one of them.

"I can go," Lisbeth said.

Her guard, Benson, frowned so deeply that Thomas had to refrain from laughing. Lisbeth sighed, "I'm the smallest. It would make sense for me to go. Thomas will be with me. I will be fine, Benson."

Her guard sighed, unsure. "Your Grace, this makes me nervous."

Lisbeth stepped into the opening and pointed at the space between her and the wall. "Look how much room there is."

Thomas slapped him on his shoulder. "How about Lisbeth and I go see if this leads anywhere. If it doesn't, we can come back and try the next tunnel tomorrow. If we are lucky and it leads to the opening on the map, everyone can push their way through."

Fadir nodded, seemingly at ease. The man had been traversing the tunnels probably his whole life, so Thomas wasn't surprised. Benson finally sighed and sat down on a rock. "Fine. I know you want to find the tablets, but I hope I don't have to push my way through that opening."

Thomas chuckled. He turned back to Lisbeth and moved her out of the opening. "I will go first."

She looked as if she wanted to argue, but he shook his head.

"You are smaller than me. If I fit, we know you will."

Lisbeth nodded, and he handed her the lantern. She smirked. "At least I've become responsible enough to carry our light."

He gave her a pointed look.

She shrugged. "Just a jest."

Thomas shook his head but then focused on the opening. He slid in sideways. He wasn't truly the biggest fan of exploring caves, and this was precisely why—the damn tight spots. His back slid against the tunnel's cool surface, but the further he moved in, sometimes his front was pushed against the wall he was facing, and in other places, he had more than enough room.

He could tell Lisbeth was by his side because of the light. In most spots, there wasn't enough room for him to turn his head. "How are you doing?"

A gasp escaped Lisbeth, but there was amusement laced in her voice. "I don't think cave exploration will be something I continue to pursue, but I'm fine."

He grinned. "You wanted to do this."

She nudged him in the side with her elbow. A familiarity flowed between them. It was an emotion he'd felt his whole life with Lisbeth growing up, and when they'd run away together. His thoughts were distracted as he stepped further and found himself in a large cavern. He stopped Lisbeth with his hand. "Hand me the lantern."

She did as he asked, and he held it up. The space was breathtaking. They were on a large ledge, but further out was a drop and then a large basin of the clearest water Thomas had ever seen. Lisbeth joined him and gasped. "It is beautiful."

He sighed. It was, but unfortunately, the opening to the cavity they were looking for was underwater. That meant, at some point, it had been permanently sealed, likely from a tunnel collapse, Thomas guessed.

"This path won't get us to the cavern we are looking for."

He pulled instruments from his bag and took measurements to ensure he was correct. Lisbeth looked around at the sizable space. "How do you know?"

Thomas explained, "Based on the dimensions of this cavern and the map, the opening would be underwater if it still existed."

Lisbeth frowned, and Thomas began to step back into the narrow corridor from which they had just emerged. Lisbeth looked at him, shocked. "You won't take a moment to enjoy this?"

Thomas turned back to her. Even in the lantern light, she was quite a messy sight. Part of her braid had unraveled, and her long shirt and pants were smudged with dirt. She had a bit on her cheek as well. "You are a mess."

She beamed at him and held her arms out. "I do not care, Thomas Easton."

Thomas shook his head, but he was mesmerized. She was a vision. Lisbeth smiled at him. "We will go back in a minute. Sit on the edge with me and look at the water."

He looked at the edge of the rock ledge dubiously. "It could crumble."

She sighed. "We will be careful."

Thomas followed her as she tentatively tapped the ground with every step. Once they reached the ledge, they sat. He placed the lantern next to him, and it reflected off the cavern walls and water. It was a stunning space. The rock and stone had been shaped by moving water, giving it a completely unique look.

Lisbeth swung her legs back and forth, making him queasy. She glanced at him and said, "I promise I will scoot back before I stand up."

"Please do."

She giggled. "You still are Serious Thomas."

A bark of laughter escaped him. "I never said I wasn't, Lizzie."

She turned to look at him. "You are the only person who has ever called me that."

Why did that statement thrill him? Damn it, and why was she still so beautiful? Her blonde hair was a mess, but in a way that made him want to unbind it. Her blue eyes sparkled with excitement. For a moment, he wondered what adventures with Lisbeth would have been like over the last ten years. Instinctively, he leaned over and gently rubbed away the smudge on her cheek.

The air around them changed; it became charged with something that Thomas knew was not appropriate. His gaze flicked down to her lips, and her mouth parted. A memory of kissing her flashed in his mind. All the desire he'd been holding back for Lisbeth roared to life.

He didn't want to crave this woman still, but he did. She bit her lip and leaned towards him. Thomas wanted to kiss her. Christ, he craved to push her down in this beautiful space and get lost in her body, if he was being honest.

Their bodies bent towards each other, and his lips hovered over hers. He heard her breath hitch. Would one taste destroy him? Did he care? His hands slid up the back of her neck into her hair. She whimpered. His mouth touched hers in a whisper of a kiss.

"Did you find it?" Benson bellowed from the other side of the small tunnel they'd just traveled through.

Lisbeth pulled back, scooting herself away from the ledge, and jumped to her feet. She hollered through the opening. "We don't think so. We are coming back now."

She looked at Thomas nervously. "We shouldn't have done that. We have both moved on, and it should remain that way. We are different people. Those feelings are long gone."

They weren't, though, and the way she rocked on her feet skittishly, Thomas suspected she was lying to both of them. He grabbed the lantern and joined her by the opening. She glanced at him and said, "It was nothing, right?"

He could lie to her, but instead, he placed the lantern on a small natural shelf. She gulped, and before she could deny that the brief touching of their lips was nothing, again, Thomas pulled her to him. He smashed his mouth down on hers. No, this was certainly not nothing. This was everything.

The softness of her lips molded against his. He ran his tongue along the seam, and she parted her mouth. He delved in and brushed against her tongue, taking and enticing. His cock, already hard, strained against his trousers. He threaded his hands in her hair, deepening the kiss as she pushed herself against his form.

Thomas wanted to slide his hands down her body and find the heat between her thighs, yet he stepped back. She looked at him wide-eyed and touched her lips.

Benson yelled, "Should we follow you in?"

Thomas hollered back, "No. We are on our way."

He grabbed the lantern and stepped back so she could go first. Lisbeth watched him. Thomas quietly said, "I don't think it's nothing."

She slid sideways into the opening, fleeing as fast as one could in a small space.

Chapter Six

LISBETH GLANCED AT Thomas as she ate her food. They were back in the village. Rafe's team hadn't found anything either. There was only one other path. She hoped that it would lead to the cavernous area where the tablets were supposedly located.

She frowned, puzzled. By the time they'd popped out of the other side of the narrow tunnel after their kiss, Thomas had acted as if their moment had never occurred. *It wasn't nothing*. What did he mean by that?

Placing her fingers to her mouth, Lisbeth's mind flashed to their kiss in the cavern, specifically her yearning and desire for him. Before departing on this trip, she'd convinced herself that what she and Thomas shared was young love and she'd feel nothing now that she was older.

Lisbeth was a fool because all the emotions that she expected to stay gone came roaring back the moment he kissed her. She still wanted him. A frown marred her face. Nothing further could happen with Thomas. Their past was too complicated and filled with too much hurt.

There were things that if Thomas knew, he'd never forgive her. She didn't want to think about it. Lisbeth had made her choices all those years ago and swore she wouldn't spend her life filled with regret. It didn't benefit anyone. He'd moved on, and so had she, eventually forming a loving bond with her husband until his passing.

Yes, the moment with Thomas was nothing; it had to be. Her stomach clenched at the lie she was telling herself. Thomas glanced at her, and at first, his expression seemed perfectly normal, but then something flared in his eyes. Desire swirled between them, and not just the physical kind but an all-consuming need that made her tremble.

"I'm disappointed that I didn't get to see the grotto you and Easton saw," Abbas said, sitting down next to her.

She tore her gaze away from Thomas, gulping. *Dratted kiss!* Turning to Abbas, she did her best to push away the swirl of emotion still lingering and said, "It was beautiful. What was your area like?"

"Badr believes that our tunnel must have collapsed at some point because it simply ends without breaking into a larger room. We were out much sooner than your group."

Lisbeth suggested, "You can ask Fadir to take you down the tunnel we took."

Abbas shivered. "While it would be nice to see, I will decline. I've already told Easton I will sit out tomorrow's exploration. I didn't enjoy some of the areas of the corridor my group was in. At one point, I feared we'd get stuck. Badr told me I was being dramatic."

She laughed. "I wish I could convince Benson to do the same, but he is adamant that he will go."

"I'm grateful that you all will explore the last corridor on the map. I still have hope that the tablets will be recovered."

Yes, Lisbeth wanted that more than anything, as well. If they had the completed deciphered epic, she suspected the Historical Society for Female Curators would be given a space at the Great Exhibition at Hyde Park.

"Me too. I want to believe we didn't travel all this way for nothing."

Abbas frowned and looked at Thomas. "Why do you think he has never returned to London? He is famous, and most would want to bask in all that."

Lisbeth suspected it was because Thomas hadn't wanted to see her. She glanced at him. The man was strikingly handsome, and jealousy unfurled in her, thinking about all the ladies who would flock around him if he ever returned to the city.

Why was she thinking about him returning? She had no right to be jealous if he found a lady to be in his life. She'd given him up long ago.

"Maybe he doesn't want people fawning over him," Abbas added.

Just then, two women placed food in front of him, and he beamed at them, delighted to be taken care of. Both Lisbeth and Abbas laughed. He said, "Maybe something else then."

"I think so. Perhaps an explorer like him finds London boring."

Abbas nodded, but Lisbeth didn't believe her own words. No, she'd hurt Thomas Easton, and he'd fashioned himself into a completely different person, one that wanted nothing to do with England. It wasn't hubris that made her believe that. She had endured her own profound loss and devastation when she walked away from him. That was how she knew.

Still, Lisbeth didn't want to hurt him again, so she needed to ensure that he knew they couldn't repeat what happened in the cavern. She would make sure he understood it was a one-time thing.

LATER THAT EVENING, Thomas found Lisbeth sitting in the courtyard of the house they were staying in. She seemed lost in thought. He owed her an apology. Thomas shouldn't have kissed her. He'd forgotten himself, and if he was being truthful, their history made anything else impossible.

He leaned against a stone wall, studying her. She'd cleaned up from their adventure earlier. His mouth quirked up in amusement at how much enthusiasm she had for venturing into different parts of the cave system. She may have the regal bearing of a duchess, but the thrill-seeker Lizzie was still in there as well.

She leaned back and stared up at the stars, twirling her blonde braid. She sighed. "You can come sit with me. We don't have to avoid each other."

He chuckled. "I wasn't."

She glanced at him. Her blue eyes filled with disbelief. He joined her where she sat on an oversized rock. Thomas cleared his throat, unsure how to start, but eventually, he said, "I'm sorry for kissing you today."

Lisbeth let out a puff of air. "I'm not sorry. I just don't think it should happen again. We have different lives."

Her lack of regret should thrill him, but it didn't. She was right. They didn't suit—too much had changed in the last ten years. Still, he believed they had loved each other long ago. Yet, she'd abandoned him. He asked, "Why did you leave me in Tuscany?"

Pain slashed across her face. He didn't want to hurt her, but couldn't let her leave without understanding why she'd chosen to return to England. She gulped. "Does it matter?"

"I would like to know," he said quietly.

Lisbeth frowned. "Justin found me in Tuscany. He explained that the family was ruined, and my father was facing debtor's prison. The only thing that could fix everything was my planned marriage to my eventual husband. If I married, my family would have enough money to make the earldom solvent again. Without it, both my father and brother were doomed to spend years locked away. So, I did what was needed."

Fury and pain barreled through him. He'd suspected she'd left because of something to do with money, but back then her note had simply explained she wanted to return to England. She'd likely known Thomas would have gone after her if he suspected she still loved him. Lisbeth left him because of her duty to her family. Their eyes connected, both watery. He grasped her hand and said, "Thank you for telling me the truth."

She nodded. "My husband, Nicholas, was a good man. We grew to care for each other, but he came into the marriage just as reluctant. Still, over time, we developed an unexpected friendship."

"I'm glad you found happiness," Thomas said and truly meant it.

He wanted to be furious, but what good would it do? She took a deep breath and faced him. "What we had, Thomas, was special. You were my best friend and my first love, but too much has changed for this...us...to become anything."

Irrationally, he wanted to argue that she was wrong, but the words didn't come. She was a duchess with children, and he was a man who hadn't been to England in a decade. He nodded and pressed his forehead against hers. They sat there quietly, and finally, he pulled away. "I wish I had been in a different place so that I could have helped."

She smiled sadly at him. "Neither of us had anything. We were happy, though."

"If I ever see your brother again, I will give him the thrashing of his life."

Lisbeth shook her head. "It wasn't his fault. He was desperate."

Thomas wasn't sure he agreed with her. Saving her family should never have been put on Lisbeth's shoulders, but he remained silent. She'd always been close to Justin. She smiled and added, "It didn't turn out too badly. You are richer than most of the lords in London, I imagine, and a famous explorer."

He wanted to scream that he would have given it all up to have her, but didn't. Instead, he forced himself to smile. "I guess it was the right decision to run off with a hoyden to seek out adventure all those years ago."

A huff escaped her. "I wasn't hoyden."

"You were, and I would have followed you anywhere."

She gave him a half-smile but then grew serious. "I'm telling you all this because I want you to know the truth, but nothing more can happen between us. We've grown too much in opposite directions from each other. I can pretend that the Lisbeth in Syria is me, but it simply isn't. You are more likely to find me attending a lady's tea or helping my children with their studies."

He didn't want to imagine Lisbeth with her children. Thomas had no doubt she was a good mother, but the thought was too painful and so far removed from his life now. No one he knew had children. He supposed if Rose did someday, she'd be the first.

"I agree. Still, I'm glad we had our time together."

She threaded her fingers through his. "Me too, and I'm also happy we were able to see each other again. I needed this."

"I agree," he said, releasing her hand and standing. "I think I will go inside."

"I want to stay out here a little longer."

Thomas nodded and walked away. He didn't go inside but instead exited the courtyard. He took a deep breath and stared up at the sky. A tear ran down his cheek, and he wiped it away. He couldn't remember the last time he cried. Lisbeth had given him the gift of closure, he told himself. Thomas should be happy with that, but all he felt was profound sadness.

Chapter Seven

LISBETH STOOD WITH Rafe, Thomas, Benson, and the three guides outside the cave entrance. Fadir frowned at the sky, shaking his head. Lisbeth wondered if that meant they wouldn't be able to enter. Badr shrugged, and then they argued back and forth. Finally, they seemed to come to some sort of conclusion.

She was the only one who didn't speak Arabic, and it frustrated her. Thomas turned to her and said, "Fadir thinks it may rain, but Badr doesn't believe it will until later. Fadir will travel with us, Badr will be further back in the cave system, and another guide will stay outside to alert us about any potential weather. We all need to stay close to one another."

Lisbeth nodded, hoping that the weather would hold. This path had to lead them to the tablets. She followed Rafe, Thomas, and Fadir into the cave, carrying one of the lanterns. They walked until they reached the cavity, containing the eight tunnels leading in opposite directions. Thomas drew a circle over the tunnel that would lead out to the river and a triangle over the pathway that may potentially lead to the tablets.

She closed her eyes, silently pleading they would be found. Lisbeth needed them to be there. As they walked, Thomas trailed the chalk along the wall. A thrill coursed through her as they went deeper into the cave system. There was something exhilarating about being back out in the world, searching for antiquities. In truth, it didn't even have to be the tablets.

Most excavation work was far more boring than those reading about it in London would imagine. Days consisted of repetitive tasks that focused on caring for artifacts. While searching for something new could be exciting, even that might become mundane to those who weren't enthusiasts of the field. It often took months or years to discover something from the past. They were lucky to have the map, or they might never have found the last two tablets containing the epic.

She smiled. Still, the search was rather exciting. Liseth had forgotten how much she enjoyed this part of the antiquities field. She was glad to participate but knew that if they didn't find anything in the next two weeks, she would have to return home. Her children, Alice and Jeremy, were her entire world, and after this little adventure, she couldn't imagine leaving England for the foreseeable future.

The heaviness and sadness from her talk with Thomas the previous night still hung on her. The conversation had been needed. She was glad that they'd reached some level of comfort with the past. *Tell him*, her guilty conscience whispered. Lisbeth had revealed everything but one crucial detail. Her chest tightened thinking about her omission. She pushed the thought away. She would not dwell on the decisions she'd made so long ago. It helped no one. She and Thomas had closure.

This tunnel appeared to be well-traveled, and she remembered Thomas saying yesterday that there would be another corridor they needed to traverse. Benson glanced back at her, checking if she was still there. She smiled at him. Her guard nodded, and Lisbeth decided silently that the man deserved a raise when they returned. She didn't imagine that this was what he expected when she'd explained she needed to travel to Syria.

They stopped, and Thomas handed Badr one of the lanterns.

He turned to Rafe. "Will you stay with him so we are all traveling in twos?"

His friend nodded, and the rest of the group continued on. A smile filled her face. The man everyone saw as the famous easygoing explorer was still very much Serious Thomas. She wondered how much exaggeration the author of the Thomas Easton serials used when writing them.

They walked for another half an hour, and then Thomas and Fadir stopped. They were using measurements to determine their location. The tunnel had widened. On both sides, there were rocks of varying sizes. Fadir said something in Arabic, and then Thomas turned to Lisbeth and Benson, pointing at the wall of stones. "Fadir believes the tunnel is behind here. We are going to see if any of these rocks are movable. If so, we can attempt to travel to the cavern where the tablets and other artifacts are located.

Fadir pulled a metal rod from a bag and pieced it together. Once done, he motioned for Thomas and Benson to join him. The first few rocks they attempted to pry out wouldn't move. Sweat was pouring down the men. Lisbeth offered to help, but Thomas said, "Not yet."

They all sat, sharing water. Lisbeth stared at the rocks. Some of them, over time, had become one. She hoped that the tunnel beyond the pieces of stone hadn't caved in. "Can we use black powder?"

Fadir frowned, and Thomas shook his head. "These tunnels are sacred. While Al-Wāḥa villagers are willing to assist us in obtaining the tablets, they won't allow that."

Lisbeth glanced at Fadir and nodded. "I'm sorry for the suggestion. I understand."

Thomas translated for her, and the man smiled in return. She studied the rock formation on the wall and then asked Thomas, "Can I see your water pouch?"

He handed her the leather pouch that was still half full. She poured a little along the wall. Fadir nodded excitedly, knowing what she was doing. The water traveled along the areas of the rock formation, puddling on the ground.

Thomas leaned over her, and she did it again. This time,

some of the water puddled on the floor, while some of it disappeared between two rocks. Liseth looked at them excitedly. "These are not permanently fused."

Fadir placed the metal rod between the rocks and wiggled it. The stone barely moved, but it did a little bit. Benson and Thomas joined him, using their weight to push the rock aside. The first couple of times they tried, it only moved an inch or two at most. Then they tried again, and the rock slid to the side. It wasn't a large space, but it was big enough to slide the lantern in.

Thomas leaned down and looked. "It is a tunnel."

Fadir looked at the other rocks, but Lisbeth wasn't optimistic that they could get them to move any more than they had. Thomas tried to wiggle his way into the opening but couldn't. Excitement flared in Lisbeth because she thought she could fit. Thomas stood up and sighed, unhappy.

"I can go," Lisbeth declared.

Immediately, both Thomas and Benson said, "No."

She frowned at both of them. "This tunnel to the cavern isn't that long. If it hasn't been traversed, the tablets and whatever else is there may be undisturbed. Remember that tomb we found in Tuscany, Thomas. Besides the dust, it was as if everyone had just walked away. Items were sitting in the open, unchanged by time."

"It could be caved in."

"I think I should at least go look," Lisbeth insisted.

"Your Grace, this isn't wise," Benson said, not happy about her idea at all.

Lisbeth bent down and wiggled through the opening. She was momentarily terrified as she'd blocked out all the light.

"Lisbeth," Thomas hissed. "We travel in pairs."

The light from the lantern filtered in, calming her. She took a deep breath. "Thomas, let me just see what is at the end. It will only be a few minutes. You can call me back if there is a problem."

Fadir said something in Arabic, and Benson said, "She

shouldn't be in there."

Rolling her eyes, she exasperatedly said, "But I already am. Don't treat me like I'm fragile."

Thomas slid on the ground and looked at her through the hole. "You are a duchess, which makes you so."

Annoyance surged in her. "They could be at the end of the tunnel. The map showed the corridor I'm in connecting to the cavern. We could be minutes away from discovering the tablets and other important artifacts."

Thomas scowled but slid the lantern her way. "Promise you will go to the end and return right away."

"I promise."

He grabbed her hand. "I mean it, Lisbeth."

She nodded. "I will not linger."

Lisbeth rose and stood, peering down the large tunnel. Excitement surged in her, and if she was being honest, fear as well.

THOMAS, BENSON, AND Fadir sat in silence in the darkness. It had been too long. Where the fuck was she? He heard pacing and suspected it was Benson. He imagined Lisbeth's guard was furious. The move to climb into the hole without asking had been so typical of the Lisbeth he knew when they were younger. He suspected back in England, she didn't make such rash decisions.

"Where is she?" Benson snapped.

Thomas slid down on his stomach. "Lisbeth!"

Fadir, in Arabic, said, "She has only been gone a short amount of time."

"No, it has been too long," Thomas insisted.

In the dark, Fadir squeezed his shoulder. "You are nervous."

Thomas took a deep breath, knowing he was right. He rose to his feet and was startled to see the tunnel lighting up. Rafe and Badr walked towards them.

Fear clawed at him because there was only one reason they were down here. Rafe confirmed it when he said, "We have to go. The rain is here. We don't have a lot of time, but we should be more than fine if we leave now."

"Her Grace is in the fucking tunnel alone," Benson snapped.

Damn it! Why did he let Lisbeth go? He dropped to his knees to yell into the hole again, but was greeted by her grinning face. She pushed two pieces of stone through the hole in a cloth. "I found them. You will never believe what else is in—"

"We have to go. It is raining," Thomas said, relief flowing through him.

She pushed the lantern through next, and then he yanked her out. He grasped her shoulders. "Are you hurt?"

Lisbeth grinned, clueless to how much fear she'd caused him. "Did you hear me? I found the tablets and there are more objects to study."

"We have to go now," Rafe reiterated, starting to look nervous.

He grabbed Lisbeth, guiding her down the tunnel, but she pulled away. "We have to reseal the opening we created. There are priceless artifacts in the cavern. They are protected by the rocks that are preventing water from getting in."

Rafe translated her words to the guides. The men nodded. Thomas, concerned for her, said, "We don't have time. We were barely able to move the rock previously."

"If we all help, we can," Lisbeth insisted.

Thomas and Rafe looked at each other. They could now hear the sound of water. Lisbeth joined Fadir and Badr, along with Benson. Thomas said, "Fuck!"

Still, he and Rafe joined them. They slowly wedged the rock back over the opening. It slid back into place, settling as if it had never been moved. Lisbeth beamed at him. He handed the tablets to Rafe and the lantern to her. "Go."

He raced behind her. A small amount of water was starting to weave its way down the corridor. They needed to reach the initial cavity with all the tunnels before it filled. If they made it, they could climb on the ledge and be safe. They hadn't encountered rushing water yet, so that was good.

Thomas breathed a sigh of relief as they reached the cavern. The water was ankle-deep, but there was no rushing water yet. He pushed Lisbeth up the ledge, then Benson, and then Rafe. The sound of water was getting louder. Lisbeth peered over with the lantern. "Give Rafe your hand. It sounds like it is coming."

He and Fadir hoisted up Badr. The roaring sound of water was now reverberating through the cave system. They weren't going to make it up the ledge. Lisbeth saw the moment he and Badr stepped towards the opening that kicked out to the river. He didn't have time to reassure Lisbeth because, seconds later, the water swept him away.

Thomas held his breath, remembering to keep as straight as possible and not hold onto anything. The water was moving so fast. In spots, it didn't fill the whole tunnel, and he was able to get more air. Still, the blackness terrified him. Fadir had said it would be sixty seconds; he closed his eyes and embraced that he had no control. He began to count to sixty.

Chapter Eight

LISBETH SAT ON the ledge with Benson, Rafe, and Badr, shivering, unsure if it was from the cold or the shock of watching Thomas be swept away. She held back the tears threatening to burst from her eyes. Benson pulled the lantern from her clenched hand.

The water, while it swirled beneath, was still at least six feet away from reaching the ledge. Thomas and Fadir had been right below, and then they were gone. Her body shook; he couldn't be dead. Rafe sat beside Lisbeth and frowned at her, concerned. "He made it out."

Her eyes watered. "How do you know? You have no idea. Anything could have happened to him."

"Thomas and I have been friends for a long time. While some of the stories written about him are exaggerations, the man has survived more frightening situations than anyone I know. He has survived stampedes, civil wars, other weather-related problems, and being attacked by thieves."

His words did provide her some comfort, but Lisbeth couldn't stop imagining him trapped in the tunnel. Rafe squeezed her shoulder, and their eyes connected. "Now is not the time to despair. Badr believes they will be fine. It isn't the first time someone has been swept away."

She took a deep breath. He was right. Hope was the emotion

she needed to focus on right now. Still, the guilt that lodged in her chest expanded. "Do you think if we hadn't resealed the opening, we would have made it in time?"

Rafe shook his head and frowned. "Don't do that. We have no idea."

Benson joined her on the other side. "He will be fine, Your Grace."

She smiled, grateful for his reassurance. "I'm sorry you ended up becoming part of this."

He laughed and ran a hand through his hair. "I must make sure you are safe. I take that seriously."

"Thank you, Benson."

Badr spoke to Rafe in Arabic. Rafe then said, "He wants to know what else you saw in the cavern?"

A small smile flitted across Lisbeth's face. It had been like the tomb she and Thomas stumbled across in Tuscany years ago. The tablets rested on the ground, along with other artifacts, untouched by humans or the passage of time. "Someone from the village should go back in there. I suspect there are important items they will want. I saw some small statues, scrolls, and pottery."

Rafe translated for him, and then he told her, "Badr says thank you for telling them to seal the tunnel. That may have been destroyed without your guidance."

She nodded, but still, the fear and guilt wouldn't go away that she might have cost Thomas and Fadir their lives. Her eyes connected with Badr, and he said, "Toka al-khayr. Hum eaeshon."

"Have hope. They live," Rafe translated.

She smiled at Badr, grateful for his assuring words. Lisbeth pulled her knees to her chest, hoping that everyone was right. The thought of Thomas not being alive was something she couldn't even bear to fathom. It left her breathless and in pain.

It was absurd because she hadn't seen Thomas for years. Still, Lisbeth had always been comforted by the thought that Thomas was out living his life. Her eyes watered again, but she brushed the tear that hit her cheeks across her knee, not wanting anyone to see how upset she was.

"When the water drains, we can depart," Rafe explained.

She nodded and glanced at the cloth in which the stone tablets were wrapped. Lisbeth should feel euphoric that she had them, but right now, all she felt was fear. Thomas Easton better be alive because if he weren't, Lisbeth may fall apart. She hated the feeling of looming death. Lisbeth knew the emotion well because she'd felt something similar when Nicholas passed away.

As if sensing her thoughts, Rafe said quietly, "Remember, have hope."

THOMAS PACED BACK and forth in the village. It had been five hours since the rain started. It was beginning to slow but hadn't completely stopped. Fadir had been correct. The tunnel pushed them and the water into the river. He'd made his way to the riverbank and lay there, grateful to be alive.

The guide found him not long after. Sore from being knocked around, they walked slowly to the village. The village elders had already gathered to discuss the rain and that they were trapped in the cave system. Thomas wanted to return to the opening immediately, but the elders insisted he wait in the village. It was too dangerous because the entrance was situated on low ground and was likely still taking in water.

Restless energy surged through him. Fadir assured him that Lisbeth and everyone were fine—the water never reached the ledge. Still, there was a first time for everything, and it was that thought that made him unable to sit.

Fadir approached him. "Omar Al-Sayed wants you to join him for food."

Thomas responded in Arabic. "I don't have time for a meal."

"He suspected you may say that and told me to remind you that all you have is time right now."

He scowled at Fadir, who shrugged. It wasn't the guide's fault. If it were remotely possible for them to reach everyone, Fadir would be one of the first people there. He was behaving like an ass because he felt powerless. Sighing, he motioned for the guide to lead the way.

Thomas entered the building and found Omar Al-Sayed seated on the floor with food laid out in front of him. He motioned for him to sit. Thomas did as he was asked. The village elder smiled at him. "She is your Layla, and you are the madman."

He'd spent enough time with Omar Al-Sayed that he respected him and considered him a friend. Still, annoyance filled him at the older man's insistence that he and Lisbeth were like the lead characters in the old Arabic tale.

Rafe was the cause of all of this. He gulped, thinking about the fact that it wasn't just Lisbeth in the cave system but one of his closest friends. "When can we go to the entrance?"

The village elder pointed to the roof of the building, and they both listened for a moment to the rain hitting the surface. He sighed. "I should never have let her join me. It was too dangerous."

Omar laughed. "Do you believe you have control over her?"

That made Thomas smile. "No, I've known the lady for a long time. She has never been one to listen to me."

"How do you know each other?"

"We almost were married years ago," he provided, unsure why he was sharing this with the man, except it helped keep his mind off the flooded cave system.

"And is she married now?"

Thomas shook his head. "Her husband passed away."

The older man lifted a brow. Thomas flushed. "We've changed too much. What we once had has faded."

The man chuckled, shaking his head. He sighed and was about to explain why they didn't suit when the elder pointed to the ceiling. "No rain."

Thomas listened for a moment and realized he was right. He jumped to his feet. "Can we go now?"

Omar nodded.

He raced out of the building to find Fadir and other men already preparing to head back to the caves. Thomas joined them. Fadir said, "They will be fine."

Thomas wanted to believe that and nodded. As they reached the cave, he was surprised to see that most of the water had subsided. If someone hadn't been in the tunnels, they would never have guessed how fast the water moved or how high it reached. They entered the cave system. While there was water on the ground, it now reached only as high as his ankles. He glanced at the tunnel to see that it had been fully filled. Water dripped from everywhere.

He reminded himself that the ledge he had left Lisbeth and the others on was much higher than the top of the tunnel. They moved closer to the cavern with all the corridors, and Fadir stopped. He smiled and motioned to listen. Voices, including Lisbeth's, echoed down the tunnel. Thomas rushed past the guide, rushing towards the sound. He stumbled to a stop as he saw Lisbeth, Badr, Rafe, and Benson walking towards them.

Rafe spotted him first and grinned. "I'm so happy to see that cocky smile of yours."

He laughed, and then his eyes connected with Lisbeth's. A strong emotion crackled between them. She was unharmed. Thomas stopped himself from falling to his knees and thanking anyone who would listen. Perhaps he was truly like the Majnun, the madman, because he wanted to wrap her in his arms and never let her go. A primal need coursed through him to claim Lisbeth—to tell the world she was his.

When Lisbeth, Rafe, Benson, and Badr finally reached him, he hugged Rafe. "You scared the hell out of me."

He laughed and whispered, "Relax, she is fine."

Thomas didn't argue with him but simply nodded. Rafe

moved aside, and Lisbeth stood in front of him. They studied one another. She seemed suddenly nervous and blurted out, "We have the tablets."

Not thinking about the others around them, Thomas pulled her to him, kissing the top of her head. "I was so worried. No more cave exploring with you for a while."

She looked up at him, her eyes watering. "You were worried? We watched as you were swept away. Don't you ever do something that crazy again, Thomas."

He smiled at her. "It wasn't on purpose."

"Let's go, you two. The villagers have promised that a feast awaits us."

Chapter Nine

LISBETH LISTENED TO the music surrounding her. The village was euphoric that the tablets had been discovered, but more importantly, that everyone had survived the flooding. She studied a man playing a stringed instrument. It had been so many years since she'd heard the distinct sound of the rebab that was often coupled with the poetic singing of the region.

She closed her eyes, enjoying the song, and was startled when Rafe joined her. Lisbeth jumped, and he grinned. "I didn't mean to scare you."

A chuckle escaped her. "It has been a long time since I've heard this type of music. I wish my understanding of the words was better."

"It is a song about the madman who loved Layla."

"That forbidden love story seems to be a popular one," Lisbeth said, excited that she remembered something.

Rafe nodded. "It is one of the most beloved Arabic tales."

They quietly listened to the song. Even without understanding the words, she grasped that they were intended to evoke longing and regret. She glanced at Rafe and smirked. "It sounds like a very sad tale."

"The madman grew up with Layla and loved her his whole life, but she ended up with another. Afterward, he wandered the region creating poetry about his lost love."

Lisbeth nodded. "I remember now."

Sadness filled her. It was one of the stories Thomas had enjoyed when they first moved to this area. She gulped because he'd always told her they were like the story, but happier. Rafe wandered away, summoned by one of the village elders. Lisbeth let her mind drift to memories from the past.

LISBETH LEANED FORWARD and kissed Thomas as they sat outside under the stars. Recently, they'd revealed to each other their true feelings.

Being out in the world had emboldened Thomas to declare he loved her, and Lisbeth couldn't be happier. He'd professed that he always had. The words had made her feel guilty because she'd not realized her feelings for him until recently.

She looked around, shaking her head. They were sitting inside an ancient, unused stone courtyard with a lit fire to keep them warm. They'd only been working with the Calverts for a few months now, but it felt right. "Are you happy?"

Thomas grinned at her. "I'm the happiest man in the world. We did it. We are working with the famed Benjamin Calvert and on our way to being famous explorers ourselves."

She giggled. "I'm not sure about that."

He pulled her to him, wrapping his arms around her form. "We are like the Majnun and Layla. Destined to be together."

Lisbeth frowned. "Doesn't that story end in heartache?"

He sighed. "I'm trying to be romantic. How about we are like them, but instead of the Majnun roaming the desert alone, he roams it with his true love?"

Warmth coursed through her, and she snuggled deeper into his chest. "I like that much better."

"WHAT ARE YOU frowning about? You should be happy; we have

your tablets and are alive," Thomas said, beaming down at her.

Lisbeth pushed the memories away and forced herself to smile, but it wasn't lost on her that their happily ever after had turned out just like the Arabic love story. At her lack of response, he sat next to her. "You can talk to me, Lizzie?"

She forced herself to smile. "I'm fine. Rafe mentioned this was a song about the Majnun and Layla. It brought back some memories I had forgotten."

He nodded. "I understand why you left. I don't like it, but knowing the truth provides a sense of closure that I haven't had until now."

Lisbeth smiled, truly happy that she was able to give him that. "I don't think you turned out like the Majnun."

He laughed. "Well, I didn't roam the world reciting poetry. I would be atrocious at that."

A gasp of amusement escaped her. "No, I can't imagine Serious Thomas writing or reciting flowery words."

"I'm not that boy anymore either."

She glanced at him. "I think there is still some of him in you."

He tilted her chin up and looked down at her. "Possibly, but if that is the case, I suspect the old Lizzie I used to know is still part of you. Your duchess traits haven't fully replaced her."

Their old camaraderie flared between them, mingling with something much more dangerous—a primal need for one another. The all-consuming emotion crackled and hissed, tempting them both. Lisbeth had no doubt Thomas felt it, too. He dropped his hand from her chin and cleared his throat. "I think tomorrow we can return to Latakia so you can arrange a trip back to England."

She nodded, desperately trying not to concentrate on the feelings swirling around them. "I think that is best."

Thomas nodded and stood. He looked around and then turned back to her. "I was worried today, Lizzie. I'm glad it all turned out fine."

"Me too,' she responded, shivering as she remembered the

fear that had overwhelmed her, thinking Thomas was gone.

So many unsaid things seemed to hang between them. It was strange because yesterday, she'd felt they'd found closure and shut the door on their relationship, but now it felt different. When she saw Thomas in the tunnel, she wanted to wrap her arms around him—to get lost in him. All things she should not want.

Thomas wandered away, and Lisbeth let out a breath she didn't realize she'd been holding. It was good that she was leaving soon.

THOMAS STRETCHED HIS back; it ached from the events of the last few days. They were only a few hours away from Latakia. The plan was to stay at the main hotel there, and Abbas would secure passage for him, Lisbeth, and Benson back to England. His time with Lisbeth was almost over.

Rafe glanced at him, and Thomas scowled. "Don't bring up the madman to me now. I suspect you are the one who told the men to play those songs last night."

His friend feigned a look of innocence. "Why would I do that?"

He shot him a disgruntled look. Rafe shook his head and sighed. "It has certainly been a crazy few days. I can't believe we found the tablets."

Yes, Thomas was happy about that. He didn't know much about the Historical Society for Female Curators beyond the letters that Rose Calvert sent him. Still, it seemed like they were holding their own against the London Society of Antiquaries.

Both Thomas and Benjamin had received invitations to join the latter society, but in a show of support for Rose, they declined. The stodgy group didn't allow women, regardless of the value of their work. It was a shame because the group was missing out on many capable club members. For over a hundred years, the club had been the most prestigious and unchallenged establishment for all things related to antiquities. The Historical Society for Brazen Curators was changing that.

Thomas rolled his shoulders again and grimaced. "I'm getting too old for exploring."

Rafe snorted. "You are only thirty-two. But maybe you should consider going to England and settling down? You could convince that author to work with you to publish more serials."

"I'm not returning to England."

His friend glanced at Lisbeth and then back at him. "You are going to let the lady go? Why?"

He studied Lisbeth. She was still wearing the trousers and long shirt that Rose liked to wear, but soon, she'd be back in her regal dress. While he knew this woman, the one she would transform into in Latakia was a stranger to him.

"We decided we've both changed too much."

Rafe snorted. "That doesn't mean you aren't compatible or the love you once had has disappeared."

Thomas sighed. "She is a duchess. What do we have in common?"

"You are now a famed explorer, but I imagine some of the old you still remains. What did she used to call you?"

He didn't respond, and Rafe, already knowing, added, "Serious Thomas. You are still that person. Trouble seems to find you, but you are far more cautious than you lead most to believe. You could go to London and be with her."

His gaze once again drifted back to his old love. The tiniest amount of hope flared in him. To date, he'd not allowed himself to consider it. But he suspected that if he returned to England, the *ton* would welcome him with open arms. Although he may have been the son of a housekeeper, he was now quite wealthy. His mother would be delighted if he were to return. She'd never flat-out asked him to settle back in London, but he sensed it from her letters.

Lisbeth laughed at something Abbas said, and Rafe added, "You could at least visit Rose, Benjamin, and your mother."

"I will think about going to London but not to re-establish anything with Lisbeth," he insisted. "We are too different."

Rafe shook his head. "Daft man."

Thomas lifted a brow and said, "You are not pursuing the lady that you never speak of."

His face turned serious. "She isn't unattached."

Thomas did his best not to appear surprised. That was the most Rafe had ever shared about his heartache. He sighed. "Perhaps we both are a little bit like the Majnun."

Chapter Ten

ABBAS SUCCEEDED IN booking passage on a ship for him, Lisbeth, and Benson. They would be departing the day after tomorrow. Lisbeth had been surprised that he'd found a ship returning to England so soon. She supposed she shouldn't be that shocked. Ship travel seemed to be rapidly evolving all over the world. She sipped her wine while she, Abbas, and Benson enjoyed a last meal with Thomas and Rafe.

Conflicting emotions swirled within her. She missed Jeremy and Alice, but she'd also rediscovered a part of herself in Syria— one she delighted in. Her life in England, aside from her involvement with the Historical Society for Female Curators and her children, was one marked by tedious appointments and events. Perhaps she needed to do less of them and more things she enjoyed.

Her gaze flitted to Thomas. She was happy to have reached a truce or resolution with him. Lisbeth reflected on the emotions she felt when he'd been swept away. She never wanted to feel that again. While she and Thomas were different people, imagining a world where he didn't exist any longer seemed devastating.

Over the last ten years, she'd often imagined what his life was like and hoped it was exciting. When the serials came out about him, she'd been equally jealous of his pursuits but also happy that he'd been so successful. She'd not enjoyed all the talk about the women, but studying him now, she suspected it was all true. Serious Thomas had become a broad-shouldered man with an easy smile.

His eyes connected with hers, and he held up his wine glass. She raised hers in return—her stomach flip-flopped. Lisbeth's eyes flicked down to his large hand, and for a mad moment, she wondered what it would feel like to have it run along her skin. A flush heated her cheeks, and he tilted his head as if trying to decipher what she was thinking.

Abbas interrupted the moment by tapping on his glass. "I would like to propose a toast. Thank you to Easton and Rafe for assisting us in locating the tablets, and thank you to Her Grace for not only bringing the map to Syria but also for squeezing into the small hole in the cave tunnel to retrieve the artifacts. I don't think I would have done the same. I don't think I realized the duchess was such an adventuress until traveling with her."

Lisbeth laughed. Anyone who knew her in London would never believe all she'd done in the last week. She held her glass up. "To you, Mr. Abbas, for helping the Historical Society for Female Curators negotiate a deal with your mother's village and the village of Al-Wāḥa to display the amazing artifacts that contain the complete epic."

Rafe added, "And to Benson, who I don't think wanted to do any of this but made it through."

Everyone laughed, and Benson shrugged but didn't deny it. Her guard would, without a doubt, be happy to be back on English soil. They all drank, and Rafe said, "Tell me about this Historical Society for Female Curators."

Lisbeth nodded. "About a year ago, Viscountess Hawley stood the club up as a place for women to study history as well as educate the public on antiquities. The tablets that Rose previously deciphered are our main exhibit. Still, they only contained half the epic. We are hoping that when Rose translates the remaining tablets, it will complete the story and allow us to obtain a spot in the Great Exhibition of the Works of Industry of All Nations."

"What is that?" Thomas asked.

She looked at him in disbelief that he'd never heard of the historic exhibition. "It is a world event that Prince Albert is organizing. The primary focus is to showcase innovation worldwide. The field of antiquities will only be a small part of everything that is expected to be displayed. They believe hundreds of thousands of people will attend."

Rafe frowned. "Why wouldn't the portion of the deciphered epic be enough? Rose Calvert's work is the first of its kind."

He was right. Lisbeth sighed. "It should be, but our club is still in the beginning stages. We are a mixture of scholars, ladies, and eccentrics. It hasn't endeared us to many."

Thomas muttered, "Fools."

She smiled at him. "Thank you."

"Perhaps I will return to London and give my support to you and Rose's club. I don't like to brag—"

Rafe snorted, and Thomas rolled his eyes but continued, "But I am well-known in the field."

Dread filled Lisbeth's stomach that he would return to England. She didn't want him in her world or her space. *That is because you are still keeping a secret*, her conscience whispered. She didn't want to think about it now. Lisbeth needed to keep her time here and her real life separate.

She shook her head. "There is no need. We are an intrepid group of women. I'm confident we will have a spot at the Great Exhibition."

He smiled at her, but it didn't reach his eyes. Lisbeth wasn't trying to hurt him, but he couldn't return to England. He just couldn't.

THOMAS SHOULDN'T BE standing outside Lisbeth's door. He and

Rafe had plans to leave the next day and had said their goodbyes to Lisbeth and her group at dinner. Yet, the longer he sat in his room, the more he thought about her face when he said he would go to England. Fear had crossed it. Why?

Was he fooling himself right now? Was this an excuse to see her alone one last time? Thomas wasn't sure if he cared. He knocked on the door quietly, wondering if she would answer. He waited a moment and considered knocking a little louder or leaving. Then the door opened, and Lisbeth stared back at him wide-eyed.

Fuck. This was a bad idea. Her blonde hair was hanging down around her shoulders, and she was only in a nightgown and a wrap. She tilted her head, frowning. "What are you doing here?"

"I thought we could talk before you left."

She bit her lip, and, attempting to be funny, he added, "I promise not to ravish you."

It only heightened the tension. She frowned. "I didn't assume you would."

He sighed. "I was trying to be charming."

Lisbeth rolled her eyes but stepped aside, allowing him entry. His gaze bounced around the room. Dresses and other items hung over a chair, a book was face down on a table, and the bed was rumpled as if she'd been lying there. He gulped, envisioning them tangled in the bedding. *Stop it*, he told himself.

She sat in one of the wingback chairs by the fire, and he joined her. His ex-lover seemed nervous. "What do you want to discuss?"

"You appeared apprehensive when I said I may return to London."

She sighed. "In all honesty, seeing you has been overwhelming—helpful, but still not without some awkwardness and sadness."

He nodded, understanding her sentiments. "Even though it didn't end up the way I imagined as a young man, I'm grateful that we left together all those years ago. I wouldn't have this life without your determination to seek out Benjamin Calvert. Everything I am is because of you."

Lisbeth frowned, shaking her head. "You are successful in your own right. I had nothing to do with that."

Thomas was unsure if that was true. With every discovery, she was always in the back of his mind. It was her that he wondered about when someone said an artifact or find would be talked about in London. She'd always been what drove him.

"Was it hard to give up your interest in antiquities?"

She smiled. "I wouldn't say I gave it up. Nicholas was always so encouraging of my hobbies, but it became a smaller focus. The family estate was always filled with antiquities, but now they are more global."

A warmth emanated from her when she talked about her husband. He'd met him a few times in passing when they were younger. The Duke of Lusby had been the Earl of Montclair at the time. Lisbeth had been betrothed to him since she was a child, even though he was twenty years her senior. Still, the engagement had been nothing more than a business arrangement between families. "Was he good to you?"

She nodded. "He was. Nicholas, like me, didn't come into the marriage with any false ideas about love. Over time, we developed a fondness for each other. At first, he was a very stiff and closed-off man. I don't blame him. His father was the same way. He probably would have continued to be formal with me, but days after we married, I confessed everything I'd given up to wed him and secure my family's safety; of course, I promptly burst into tears then. It was quite a day."

Thomas wanted to hate the man, but wasn't sure he could. "It sounds like he was understanding."

"It made us open up to each other. Nicholas explained that he didn't know how to show emotion and didn't want his children to grow up the same way. We made a pact—to focus on raising them in a loving environment," she said, and then gulped. "When he passed, I was adrift for quite some time. It was very sudden. I made sure the children were happy, but when I was alone, I missed him terribly."

"I'm sorry," Thomas said, hating the loss she endured and surprisingly finding himself no longer able to hate the duke he'd spent much of his life loathing.

Lisbeth took a deep breath. "The Historical Society for Female Curators eased some of my loneliness."

They sat in silence and, unsure if he was overstaying his welcome, stood. She followed him as he walked to the door. Thomas turned to her. "I guess this is goodbye for the second time in our lives."

Her eyes watered, and her lips trembled. "I only wish you the best, Thomas. I'm so proud of all that you have accomplished."

He wanted to tell her he'd done all of it for her, but suspected it would cause more harm than good. Thomas huskily said, "I wish you only the best in London."

She nodded, and they stared at each other silently. Finally, he turned and opened the door, but instead of walking out, he paused and closed it, still inside. Then, he made a very unwise choice. Thomas turned around and swept Lisbeth into his arms. If this were the last time he would ever see her, he needed to kiss her. Their lips mashed together hungrily. His hands slid over her back as her arms wrapped around him. They moaned as their mouths continued to press against one another.

Since their kiss in the cave, he'd hungered to do it again. His mouth broke away from hers, and he kissed her jaw, throat, and then the sensitive skin at her collarbone. Lisbeth moaned but then stumbled backward. They studied each other ravenously. Quietly, he said, "One night, Lisbeth. It is all I've dreamed of for the past ten years."

Chapter Eleven

LISBETH STARED AT Thomas, her heart still pounding from their kiss. She'd dreamed about being in this man's arms one more time since she'd left him in Tuscany. Rationally, Lisbeth should say no, but every part of her being prevented her from doing so.

"Only one night," she reiterated.

His eyes glowed with desire, and he brushed his lips across hers. "One moment to say goodbye, and then you can go back to being a duchess, and I can continue with my life as is."

The words were both a blow and a tempting offer. Deep down, Lisbeth had no desire to say goodbye to this man, but knew she had to. His hand trailed down her shoulder, arm, and then along the curve of her lower back. He leaned closer, and his lips brushed against her ear. "Let me love you tonight, Lizzie."

She nodded, unable to deny his request. He was her Serious Thomas, and she was his Lizzie—at least while they were in this room.

His mouth made its way back to hers, making the desire spike within her. She wanted this man desperately. Thomas's tongue dipped into her mouth and sparred with her tongue, tempting and enticing her. Lisbeth folded her body into his, needing to feel his warmth against her. Her core clenched as his shaft pressed against her belly.

He untied her wrap, and it fell to the ground. He palmed one of her breasts through the thin fabric of her nightgown. Thomas groaned, "You are so responsive to my touch."

Thomas pinched and teased the tip as she whimpered, arching into him. The front of the gown contained dozens of buttons, and too impatient, he grasped the fabric and pulled. Buttons flew everywhere. One side of her gown fell off her shoulder, revealing her from the waist up.

Her gaze returned to Thomas's face, and she studied him as his eyes hungrily perused her form. An amorous sigh escaped him as he dipped his head down, bringing one of her nipples between his lips. Thomas walked them backward towards the bed, stopping only to allow the nightgown to fall completely off her.

She flushed, finding herself suddenly shy to be naked in front of him. Her bottom bumped the edge of the bed, and any reservations about being bare before him quickly disappeared. His face was filled with such a deep longing that it made her tremble. She felt emboldened that he desired her so much.

He stepped back and removed his jacket and shoes. His eyes didn't leave her. "Christ, Lisbeth, how are you still so beautiful?"

She flushed. "Older, still."

He pulled his shirt from his head and stepped towards her. "Only more beautiful with time."

His lips sprinkled kisses along her shoulder and down her arm until he reached her fingertips. Lisbeth clenched her legs together, wanting much more from him. Gently, he placed his hand on her chest and pushed her back onto the bed. She looked up at him, and he ran a thumb across her lips. "You tempt me like no one else ever has."

The words were too much for one night, but she didn't care. Lisbeth wanted them to feel everything in this moment—not to hold anything back. His fingers ran down her breasts and stomach, causing her to whimper. He stepped back and removed the rest of his clothes, then returned to staring down at her.

His broad chest and taut stomach had been bronzed by the

sun. Absurdly, she wondered where he spent so much time shirtless outdoors. Her body ached for him. His hand palmed one of her breasts again before trailing down her stomach, stopping right before he reached her quim.

Her legs fell open, and she rocked her hips. Thomas ran his tongue along his lower lip. The fingers on her stomach moved further down and dipped into her most feminine place. She groaned and closed her eyes, enjoying the sensation of Thomas's touch.

"Open your eyes," he said gruffly.

They fluttered open. She looked at him through a haze of desire. His mouth turned up at the corners. "You have no idea how beautiful you look. This right here will be seared to my memory for the rest of my life."

A flash of pain passed between them, and Lisbeth didn't want to feel it. She murmured, "Thomas, kiss me."

His slight smile turned to a cocky smirk. He pressed a finger to her mouth and then her quim. "Where do you want my mouth?"

She rocked her hips, hoping he would catch on. Huskily, Thomas added, "Show me with your hands."

Lisbeth, wanting to drive him mad, ran a finger over her mouth, her tongue darting out. He stroked his cock. Then she ran her hands down the path his own took before she touched herself, feeling how wet she was for him. "Here."

He slid her further up on the bed. "There is nothing I would like more."

Thomas kissed her hip, then the roundness of her belly that never disappeared after her last pregnancy, before his mouth found the spot she wanted him so badly. Lisbeth dug her heels into the bed, arching up. His large hands grasped her bottom as he lapped at her.

Lisbeth threaded her fingers through his hair, savoring every kiss, scrape, and lick. Her body bucked against his mouth. The ache in her became heightened, and she whimpered, "Thomas."

He briefly looked up, the taste of her glistening on his mouth. "I want you to explode, Lizzie. Do that for me."

Her body throbbed for her release, needing it. His mouth teased her most sensitive nub, and her hip movements became more frantic until the ache exploded in her. She crashed against the bed, moaning. Her climax pulsated through her body.

Lisbeth threw an arm over her eyes, gasping with delight. He slid up next to her, pulling her body against his chest, spooning her. His cock pressed against her bottom, but they lay there. His hand roamed over her leisurely. As her breathing slowed, Thomas kissed her neck and then her shoulder.

She pushed against him, playing the part of a temptress. He groaned and grabbed her hips, pulling her more firmly against him. "Do you see how much I need you?" he hissed.

The ache flared up again in her lower body. She nodded and ground against him more. His shaft pushed against the opening of her quim. She shivered in anticipation, wanting more than anything to have Thomas deep inside her. "Please."

His tongue ran along her neck, and he quietly said, "I only want to please you."

He slid a little further into her, and she attempted to push him even deeper, but he grasped her hips, stopping her. "If I'm going to have one night with you, I'm going to slowly savor the first time my cock slides into you."

She nodded, and he slid further in and moaned before running kisses along her shoulder. Lisbeth thought she would combust. She wanted him to bury himself in her. She wiggled but tried to stay still. He chuckled darkly. "Do you want me deeper? Is that what has my minx all frustrated?"

Lisbeth didn't deny it. "Yes."

He arched into her, pushing his shaft as deeply as he could. Both he and Lisbeth gasped. The fullness of having him in her was perfection. Why did this man feel so right? He slid out of her and then back in. She rocked into him backward—the closeness was not enough, but she doubted it would ever be.

The ache in her intensified; her body screamed for another climax, demanding it. He chuckled as he continued to pump into her. He slid one hand to the front of her, stroking her mound as he took her from behind. "Is that what you want?"

She gasped, nodding, his fingers tormenting her in the best way. And then a sob tore from her lips, her body exploding for the second time. He kissed her neck. "Good girl."

One of his hands gripped her hip tighter, and his own movement became quicker and harder. He was driving towards his release. She pushed back into him continuously, knowing he was so close. His lips grazed her neck, and he moaned, "Lizzie."

Thomas's hand moved to one of her breasts, caressing and exploring as his thrusts continued. The way his body wrapped around her was perfection. How did they fit so right, even after all these years? With his other hand, he dug even more deeply into the skin at her hip as if he didn't want to ever let go.

The rocking of their bodies became more frantic, and then suddenly, he withdrew, spending. They were both gasping for air. He rose briefly and cleaned them up. Afterward, they said nothing, their breathing mingling together.

⇥⟫⟩⟨⟨⇤

LISBETH ROLLED AWAY from Thomas, lying on her stomach. He wanted to pull her back into the curve of his body, missing the feel of her, but refrained from doing so. She turned her head to look at him, where he still lay on his side. Her eyes were wistful.

He brushed a blonde strand out of her face. "What is it?"

"I'd convinced myself that I imagined how special this was between us."

Thomas leaned forward and brushed his mouth across hers. "You weren't wrong."

She blushed. "I'm sure you've had a dozen lovers, or at least that is what the serials indicate."

He grimaced. "Wildly exaggerated."

"You do receive plenty of mail from admirers."

Thomas stroked her cheek. "You can try to change the subject all you want, Lizzie, but this is special."

Her eyes watered. "I know. It makes me think this was a bad idea."

"I could come to London."

Real fear flashed in her eyes. Why didn't Lisbeth want him to visit London? He didn't understand it. "Are you concerned about what people will think if you associate with a commoner?"

Her eyes sparked with outrage. "Of course not. I would be proud to be your friend."

Yet, he expected she didn't want any more than that. Thomas supposed he couldn't blame her. They were practically strangers, well, not in this bed but in real life. His hand slid along the curve of her back, swirling over her bottom. Desire flared in her eyes.

They'd promised each other just this night. He wouldn't push it. Lisbeth was a duchess and lived a completely different life from him. Perhaps the next few hours could resolve all the anger of the past and allow them to move on. She reached for his hand, kissing his knuckles.

He rolled to his back, pulling her on top of him astride. Lisbeth gasped. Thomas grinned at her, even though his heart was aching, and said, "We still have a few more hours left of this night."

⇛⤜

DAYS LATER, THOMAS paced back and forth as he watched other people board a ship. He glanced at Rafe, who chuckled at him.

"Is this a crazy idea?" he asked his friend.

Rafe shrugged. "Who cares if it is? If you don't go to London, you will always wonder about what could have been between you and Lisbeth."

He and Rafe had departed Latakia before Lisbeth, Benson, and Abbas's ship. The further Thomas was away from the city, the more he started to realize that he shouldn't have ever kissed Lisbeth goodbye. His need for her was too strong. He didn't want to go decades without seeing her again.

Why couldn't he live in London? Rose had moved there, and she was happy. Still, there had been no confessions of love or promises of a future. In all honesty, they'd departed like they would never see each other again.

"I'm chasing the woman who abandoned me once," he explained to his friend.

"You, yourself, said she didn't have much of a choice. Why not go back to London and woo her?"

Thomas hated to admit it, but he was nervous to return to the city. He'd been barely a man when he left, and the son of a housekeeper.

Rafe grasped his shoulders. "Do you love her?"

He did. It didn't matter that a decade had gone by. Thomas loved her with every part of his being. "She has always been the one."

"Then go and fight for her."

Thomas hugged Rafe. "Will you come visit?"

"Eventually, but you've inspired me. I might return home first and see where things stand. If I don't, I will always wonder."

"Good luck, my friend. You are always welcome at my home in England."

Rafe grinned. "On the ship, you go. Tell Lisbeth I said hello."

Thomas stepped onto the gangplank, ready to change his entire life if Lisbeth would have him. In three weeks, he'd be in London.

Chapter Twelve

Late February 1851

LISBETH SMILED AS she watched Jeremy and Alice race around the gardens of the ducal townhouse. It was good to be home. Their governess, Miss Ashby, insisted they'd not grown much since her departure, but she wasn't sure she believed her.

Alice skipped around the fountain. She was eleven years old. Time flew. Soon, she would have her first season. Lisbeth frowned at her thoughts. She and Nicholas had discussed at great length that they would make Alice wait longer than other ladies to find a husband.

They'd even talked about taking her on a grand tour first. Lisbeth gulped, sadness flowing through her that Nicholas wouldn't be part of that. She studied her daughter, who, according to all of London, bore a striking resemblance to her father. Lisbeth was grateful the world believed that.

Her mind flashed to Thomas, and guilt intermingled with the sadness flowing through her. She'd desperately wanted to confess the truth while she was in Syria, but knew it wouldn't do any good. Now, though, she was filled with regret that she'd omitted something so important from him. Alice was Thomas's child. She'd been pregnant when she returned, not that she knew until after she and Nicholas had married.

She hadn't lied when she told Thomas that she revealed everything to Nicholas. Lisbeth, greatly distressed, had blurted it out to her husband of only a week. She'd expected him to cast her out, but he hadn't. Instead, he explained that he'd lost someone he loved, too. She was his mistress, Margaret, of fifteen years, and had died of a fever only a few months before.

In that one night, they formed a friendship that strengthened over time. He'd vowed to accept Alice as his own, and they'd agreed to try for an heir shortly after. Their lovemaking was more about fulfilling their duty than passion. Still, Lisbeth had grown to adore Nicholas.

They'd both promised that their children would never be forced to be with someone they didn't choose. Nicholas had loved his Margaret until the very end. A sad memory sparked her mind.

LISBETH SMILED AT Nicholas as she entered his study at the Lusby Country Estate. "Are you ready for our daily walk, husband?"

He groaned. "I was hoping it would rain."

She laughed. "No such luck. You will have to explore the fields with me."

Over the last few years, they'd begun to search the grounds for any artifacts from the past. They'd found a few things here and there. Lisbeth had a whole room filled with antiquities from around the world. One section was a case with only items they'd discovered on the grounds of the ducal estate.

"We will have to see what we can add to your collection," he mused.

Nicholas stood and walked towards her but stopped midway. He grasped his chest. Recently, their doctor had been to see him frequently because of fainting spells. They suspected it was his heart but hadn't been overly concerned. Alarm filled her that they'd been wrong. "Nicholas, what is the matter?"

He shook his head and collapsed. Lisbeth rushed to him, rolling him onto his back. His eyes were unfocused, and she hollered, "Send for the doctor."

His state filled her with fear, but shocking her, he smiled and reached up to stroke her cheek. "Be happy."

Tears dripped down her cheeks. "Please don't leave us."

Nicholas closed his eyes, smiling slightly, and murmured, "Margaret, my love."

Lisbeth screamed for the doctor again.

SHE WIPED AT her watery eyes, hating that she was remembering such a tragic time. It gave her peace to know that his last thought was one of happiness and his lost love. Nicholas had once suggested that she write to Thomas and tell him the truth, but she'd been terrified at the thought. Thomas would hate her. She knew it. Did that make her a coward? Thomas's mother knew, and that secret also hung over her head.

Lisbeth had run into Louise Easton during an outing once, and the woman had taken one look at Alice and instantly recognized her familial connection to her and Thomas. She'd called on Lisbeth, asking to know her granddaughter. Lisbeth had been apprehensive to agree. It was Nicholas who encouraged it. Over time, Louise became a close family friend who doted on both Alice and Jeremy.

She shook her head, regretful that she hadn't told Thomas the whole truth. She'd been a coward. Lisbeth wondered if she should write to him. She would speak with Louise about it. Lisbeth was yanked from her thoughts when Rose Calvert rushed down her terrace steps into the garden.

She appeared worried and also very duchess-like. She wore an elegant emerald gown, and a lady's maid had somehow secured her unruly hair into a sleek bun. Thomas had told the truth. Rose had married the Duke of Sinclair in Syria only a week before Lisbeth's arrival.

Grinning, she stood and curtsied, loving that it would annoy her friend. Rose sighed. "Don't do that. I am being curtsied to death. How do you tolerate so much bowing? I detest it."

Lisbeth laughed and hugged her friend. "It is good to see you, and congratulations to you and Sinclair. You are perfectly suited."

Rose snorted. "We love each other. Still, mismatched, but we've both decided we don't care as long as we have each other."

Seeing her friend in such a blissful state was an incredible sight. However, Rose frowned at her intently. It seemed as if she was examining her for something. Lisbeth lifted a brow.

"How was it with Thomas? He wasn't too difficult, was he? I honestly didn't believe Lord Harston would provide us with the map so soon."

It was heaven and heartbreak all over again, Lisbeth thought, but she only smiled reassuringly at Rose. "It was fine. There were some uncomfortable parts, but I think we both found closure."

Rose seemed skeptical, but Lisbeth squeezed one of her hands. "Truly."

"Your missive said you have the tablets," Rose said, her voice filled with excitement.

Lisbeth nodded. "They'd been delivered to the research room at Seely House."

Her friend clasped her hands together. "I can't believe we have the entire epic."

"I think this should cement our place at the Great Exhibition."

"Agreed," Rose said, and they both grinned at each other.

It was nice to distract herself from what her next steps with Thomas should be. She had the urge to confess her secrets to Rose, but held back. Thomas was also one of Rose's closest friends. She didn't want her in the middle. She would eventually need to decide whether to tell Thomas about Alice. No, she would tell him, she decided. She just needed to find the right words.

"Rose!" Alice said, excited to see her. Lisbeth's daughter adored her scholarly friend.

THOMAS SAT IN one of the saloons of the SS Dipper. The ocean, luckily, had been relatively calm during the trip. The ship's previous stop had been at Malaga. They'd spent two days there so the captain could resupply.

This wasn't the nicest vessel Thomas had been on, but it wasn't the worst. All ships seemed to be undergoing changes of late, marketing to those wanting to take a grand tour. It was a booming business. Benjamin had even proposed to Rose's club that they might offer to host a few ladies at their excavation site.

Both Benjamin and Rose would be surprised to see him in London. He'd sworn he would never visit the blasted city, but he was days away from doing so. It was all for Lisbeth.

"Are you playing?" Jacob Matthison questioned.

He shook his head. Thomas was playing cards with the man to ease the boredom. Matthison was an engineer of some type. He was returning to work on a building for the Great Exhibition after spending three years in Syria working on wells.

The engineer sighed and tossed his cards down on the table. "We've played three days in a row. I can tell when the game isn't holding your interest. I think we can pass for today."

Thomas took a sip of his brandy and smiled. "We could sit here and talk."

Matthison leaned back in his chair. "Are you ready to be in London? I imagine your admirers will be seeking you out."

He snorted, not believing him. Matthison's eyes widened. "I don't think you understand how famous you are."

"I receive letters, but I doubt it is at the level you are suggesting."

His card partner chuckled. "I both envy and feel sorry for you. Ladies will throw themselves at you, but you may not be able to escape them. I imagine some of them may be intense."

His mind flashed to the letters he received. Most were polite, some flowery, but there were a few that made him uncomfortable. Written by ladies who thought they had some type of ownership of him. It didn't frighten him. They were, after all, young women who wrote to him from afar, but a few he'd found peculiar.

A chuckle escaped Matthison. "I think you are regretting your choice to return to London."

He shook his head. "Not at all, but I'm not interested in getting to know my admirers."

"Ah…there is a woman."

Thomas didn't deny it. He was returning to London for Lisbeth. He didn't know what would happen or what that meant, but he was tired of being the Majnun. It was time to go home and claim what was his. A vision of Lisbeth kissing him in Latakia flashed in his mind.

Matthison sighed. "I think I will go enjoy a cigar. You are not your normal talkative self."

Thomas laughed and stood. "Shall we play tomorrow?"

"Of course."

He strolled back to his room and pulled out the last stack of letters he had received from his admirers before departing Syria. Would it really be a big deal to London society that he was returning? It seemed so far-fetched. He pulled an envelope with hand-drawn flowers from the pile. It emanated the same distinctive floral scent that was only associated with one admirer. Thomas wrinkled his nose, wondering how much perfume the woman put on her envelopes that the scent always lingered after its journey from England.

He unfolded the letter and read, the hairs standing up on the back of his arms.

Dear Thomas,

I read about your recent find in northern Syria. I can't wait until it is exhibited somewhere in London. Even though it wasn't mentioned in the newspaper, I suspect it was a gift for me. Am I correct?

While I love all your thoughtful mementos, I yearn for your return so we can be together. I can't wait to read in the papers that Thomas Easton has returned to London, because then we can get married.

I know you're a man and have needs, but I hate hearing about your conquests. That will have to end when you return, or I shall end it for you. You belong to me.

Your ever-patient love,
C

Thomas shook his head and tore the letter up. C was the only admirer who caused alarm. Some writers were more suggestive or romantic, but this author seemed to imply that they were together. He didn't always read her letters, but whenever he did, they filled him with concern.

He sighed, hoping that Matthison was wrong and his return wouldn't be a big deal. He had no interest in his admirers, especially C.

Chapter Thirteen

LISBETH SAT WITH the rest of the board members of the Historical Society for Female Curators. They were drinking tea in the sitting area of their office at Seely House. Rose had just finished explaining what one of the two tablets Lisbeth had brought back to England revealed. She was a renowned philologist who had developed a key to decipher the ancient cuneiform texts.

Sarah Martin sighed, "So our hero makes it back to the princess."

Rose grinned. "Finally. I suspect that the last tablet is the battle between our hero and the king."

Lady Esme shook her head in disbelief. "I can't believe we have the entire epic. The London Society of Antiquaries will be so envious."

Addie, wife of Lord Hawley and member of said club, giggled loudly. Her laugh was infamous throughout society. It tended to carry and had a distinct sound. Lisbeth couldn't stop the chuckle that escaped her.

Sighing, Addie said, "And what a story it is. First, the hero falls in love with the princess, and the king discovers their secret. He then sends our hero on a quest for the golden fruit. After enduring all that, he makes his way back to fight the king and win the princess and the kingdom."

"Well, I haven't deciphered the last tablet," Rose pointed out. "It could end horribly."

Diana Devons, previously Lady Hensley, sighed. "No, it will end happily. I know it."

Addie giggled. "You are newly married. All you see is love."

Diana grinned sheepishly. "I can't deny it."

"So is Rose," Lisbeth said.

Rose blushed. "Married and will be married again in some grand church."

"Most ladies would love that," Lady Esme pointed out.

Rose scrunched up her nose, and all the ladies giggled.

Addie's butler, Harrison, entered the room. Lisbeth wasn't sure if he was truly her butler or more a man of affairs. He seemed always to be not far from her.

"My lady, a special cut of the newspaper has arrived. I know you like to be apprised of events that London society is following."

Addie smiled and took the paper. Harrison didn't linger. She glanced down and gasped. Her hand covered her mouth. Lisbeth frowned. "What is it?"

"A telegraph was sent that Thomas Easton will be arriving in London in two days," she said, turning the paper to show them.

The Famed Explorer Returns was written across the top in bold letters. Lisbeth's heart hammered. Thomas was returning to London. She should have told him about Alice. He would quickly discover the truth. She blinked rapidly, overwhelmed by a mix of emotions—it was a combination of terror and excitement.

Rose leaned over and grabbed the paper, reading the words. When she was done, she glanced up. "It doesn't say why he is returning."

Their night together flashed in her mind. Her heart pounded, and her stomach fluttered at the memory. He wasn't returning for her, Lisbeth told herself. That would be ridiculous. Yet, she, herself, had lain in bed every night thinking of him and wishing he were by her side.

Addie shook her head. "The *ton* is going to be in a tizzy. Imagine all the ladies that will be throwing themselves at him—widows, debutantes, and married ladies."

Her chest felt tight. It didn't matter that he was coming to London. Maybe they wouldn't see each other. That was possible. Her eyes connected with Rose's, who was looking at her with concern. "Did he mention coming back?" she asked.

Lisbeth answered, "No. Last I spoke with him, he and his associate Rafe were headed somewhere else in Syria."

"Do you think he will do a talk for the Historical Society for Female Curators?" Esme asked.

Sarah Martin groaned. "I hope he doesn't join the London Society of Antiquaries."

Rose scowled. "He would never do that."

Lisbeth only partially listened to the chatter around her. Thomas would be here soon. She had to see his mother before he reached London. Why didn't she tell him the whole truth in Syria? *Because he will hate you*, she reminded herself.

Regret flared in her, and she bit her lip, knowing the truth would end any reconciliation between them. Reconciliation? She'd left Thomas in Syria, planning to see him never again. Hadn't she? She needed to think and be alone.

Lisbeth rose to her feet, startling everyone. She forced herself to smile. "I must go. I have an appointment that I just remembered."

Addie asked, "Will you return?"

"I don't think so, but I will be back tomorrow."

She headed to the door, hoping she wasn't causing a scene. Lisbeth reached the bottom of the grand staircase when Rose said, "Lisbeth."

Turning back, she saw that her friend's face was filled with concern. Rose rushed down the stairs, stopping in front of her. Lisbeth waited.

"Do you know why he is returning?"

Lisbeth shook her head. "I don't know."

"You seem upset."

She was, but also, a hum of need coursed through her. It was as if her body refused to allow her to keep Thomas in the past. Or was it her heart?

"Lisbeth?" Rose said, concern flaring in her eyes.

She shook her head. "I'm fine. I've too much to do, is all."

"If you need anything, will you let me know?"

Lisbeth forced herself to calm down. "I will. Truly, I'm fine."

Rose looked as if she wanted to say something else, but Addie called her from the office. Lisbeth squeezed her hand. "I'm fine. Go, Rose."

Her friend frowned at her but went. Lisbeth walked towards the door. She took a deep breath. Thomas would be in London in a few days. She needed to tell him the truth as soon as possible. He deserved that. Pain pierced her heart because she suspected Thomas could forgive many things, but not this.

⁂

THOMAS SAT IN the small pub in Guernsey. The small island was their last stop before they arrived back in England. Word had traveled quickly that he was on the ship. Women and men both greeted him everywhere he went. The serials couldn't truly be that successful, were they?

A server with her bosom on full display sashayed towards him. He looked down, not wanting to give her a hint of encouragement.

"Mr. Easton, is there anything you need?"

He lifted his head and had to admit she was quite beautiful. Still, she wasn't Lisbeth. No, this woman was stunning in her own way with her hourglass figure, brown curly hair, and heart-shaped face. Yet, he felt nothing. He shook his head. "No, I'm fine."

Disappointment flashed on her face, and she walked away.

Matthison hollered, "I could use another pint."

She didn't look back. His friend laughed. "Imagine how insane it will be in London. Guernsey is a small island. Is your lady worth your attention? You could pick any woman you want or multiple."

Lisbeth was the only woman he wanted. He would show her that loving and choosing each other after all these years was the right thing to do. They'd taken different paths for reasons out of their control, but now they could do as they liked.

"She is worth it. I love her."

Matthison choked on his drink. "Well, I wasn't expecting that."

"We grew up together, and then she married another in England."

His friend nodded. "And you became the famous explorer Thomas Easton."

He shrugged. "Something like that."

"Have you ever heard of the Arabic tale about the Majnun and—"

Thomas groaned. "Yes, I've heard the story."

Matthison grinned and held up his hands. "Ignore me. I didn't know it was a sensitive subject."

"You are not the first to bring it up to me," he complained.

"Will you go see her right away?"

Thomas wasn't sure what he would do. Part of him thought it was better to enter Lisbeth's life slowly, but he also wanted to arrive at her doorstep and confess all his feelings. They were mature adults, both being in their early thirties. Dramatics may not be the best course of action. Still, wasn't one supposed to put on a big show when they found love? He wasn't sure about anything, to be honest. "I don't know."

"You need a grand gesture," Matthison said.

He smirked. "Are you a love expert now? You've not mentioned that at all on our voyage."

"Hell no. I'm good without the affliction you are suffering

from."

Thomas laughed. A man approached their table clutching a serial. It was the fifth one since they'd entered the pub. "Mr. Easton, would you sign this for me?"

Chapter Fourteen

LISBETH STEPPED OUT of the carriage and took a deep breath. She'd been to this townhouse so many times over the last decade, and suddenly, she felt nervous. Did Louise know? She would be ecstatic that Thomas was returning. Lisbeth didn't fault her. A part of her was as well, but the rest was terrified.

She walked to the entrance, and the housekeeper opened the door at the same time. Mrs. Donnelly gasped and curtsied. "Your Grace, you gave me a fright."

"I'm sorry. I decided to call upon Louise today. Is she in?"

Mrs. Donnelly nodded. "I will lead you to her."

Lisbeth shook her head, glancing at the basket in the housekeeper's hand. "It isn't necessary. You seem busy."

The woman smiled at her gratefully. "She is in the drawing room."

"Thank you," Lisbeth said and stepped back, allowing Mrs. Donnelly to pass.

The housekeeper smiled, and she saw herself in. Her stomach clenched, but she wandered down the hallway. It wasn't lost on her how comfortable she was in this place. Louise looked up as she entered the drawing room. A smile split across her face. "I had a feeling I would see you."

Lisbeth plopped down into a wingback chair. Formality didn't exist between them. They'd become friends so long ago. Louise,

Nicholas, and her brother, Justin, were the only ones who knew her secret.

"I should have told him," Lisbeth confessed.

Thomas's mother sighed. "I agree, but I understand why you didn't. He will be upset with you and me."

Lisbeth twisted at her skirts, and Louise rose, moving to the sideboard and pouring them both a brandy. "You were forced to make a difficult choice, and it only became more complicated by your pregnancy with Alice."

Lisbeth took a sip, enjoying the burn of the liquid flowing down her throat. Louise settled back in her seat. She silently sipped her drink but eventually said, "Maybe this is an opportunity for you to start anew."

Her heart pounded at the thought. She looked away, sensing that Louise could read the emotions flashing across her face. She wouldn't dare to believe it. Lisbeth had kept too many secrets from Thomas.

Louise insisted, "Look at me."

She did, and the older woman said, "You aren't a man, Lisbeth, and because of that, there were very few choices you had. You made the only one you could. My son will be hurt, but he will understand. He knows what it is like to be born into a certain lot in life."

"I haven't even told Alice yet. Nicholas and I both agreed someday we would tell her, but I thought it would be when she was much older."

Louise insisted, "Tell Thomas right away."

She wished she'd told him before she departed Latakia. Lisbeth bit her lip, pondering her next steps, and then she glanced at Louise. "I'm sorry you will become mixed up in this. Thomas will be furious with you as well. I know it."

Louise nodded and took a sip of her drink. "He has every right to be mad, and I will accept his fury. Still, I plan to explain that you had no other choice, and he wouldn't be the acclaimed Thomas Easton without your encouragement."

She flushed, unsure if she felt comfortable with accepting any part in Thomas's success. He'd done that mostly on his own. "He did that. Also, please don't fight with your son because of my choices. You should enjoy his return, not worry about defending me."

Louise snorted. "I love Thomas, but he was never naturally adventurous. Before the two of you ran off, he'd accepted that he was to be a servant in a household. It was you who encouraged him to seek something greater. He is a practical type. What did you use to call him?"

"Serious Thomas," she provided. "We complemented each other. He kept us out of trouble, and I ensured we tried new things."

The older woman nodded, agreeing with her. "Exactly. Thomas would be a butler right now without you. Not that there is anything wrong with that field, but I suspect, based on the allowance he gives me without any thought, he is richer than most lords in London."

"I don't think he understands how famous he is or how popular the serials about him are."

"Well, he is about to find out," Louise drawled.

What Louise said made sense, but she couldn't imagine Thomas not being devastated about being kept from his daughter. She needed to tell him as soon as possible. The paper indicated he would return in the next few days.

"I imagine he will come here first; will you send word when he arrives? I want to speak with him as soon as possible."

Louise nodded. "I think that would be best."

Lisbeth shook her head. "I feel both relieved to tell him and terrified."

"Do you still love him?"

The question startled her. She'd buried all her feelings for Thomas so deep that she'd not dared think about them. Louise watched her intently. Guilt coursed through her again that she'd roped Thomas's mother into all of this. "Louise, I don't want you to get your hopes up. Thomas and I are not the same people as when we were young. I kept his child from him; he will hate me when he finds out."

Louise smiled softly. "He may be angry at first, but the two of you were always a team. I suspect you both still love one another."

Lisbeth wouldn't allow herself to hope for a future with Thomas. So much had happened. "I don't want you to be optimistic."

The older woman shrugged. "We'll see."

❧»»»⟩⟨⟨⟨«««

THOMAS HAD FINALLY arrived in London. He'd been startled to be greeted by so many people when he stepped off the ship. How had so many reporters discovered he was in England? He sat in the carriage, trying to decide where he should go. When he'd been trying to escape the crowds, he'd told the hack driver to take him out of the area.

Now, he had to determine his next stop. The carriage raced down the cobblestone street as Thomas glanced out the window to see the London Docks drifting out of sight. He'd earlier bid Matthison goodbye. They planned to meet up in the next few weeks.

Thomas was intrigued to learn about Matthison's new position. It involved building the Crystal Palace, the main area that would house the Great Exhibition's displays.

The carriage came to a halt, and then the driver opened the door. "Where should I take you, Mr. Easton?"

Rationally, he should head to his mother's, but the desire to see Lisbeth surged through him. He could at least stop there and see if she was in. Was that rash? Likely, but he found himself fixated on seeing her.

"Can you take me to Mayfair and locate where the Duchess

of Lusby resides?"

The driver nodded. "Of course, I have associates in the area."

Thomas nodded. "Thank you."

He sat back as the carriage drove on. Was it reckless to go to her immediately? Perhaps, but Thomas had to see her. She'd always haunted every aspect of his life, but now that he'd seen her, touched her, he couldn't fathom waiting to see her again. He leaned his head against the back of the seat, hoping he wasn't being reckless.

Almost an hour later, the carriage halted. They'd stopped before so the driver could obtain Lisbeth's address, but this seemed as if they'd arrived somewhere. He pulled back the window curtain. He was correct. They were outside of an elegant townhouse in the heart of London's most prestigious neighborhood, Mayfair.

His stomach clenched, feeling like he didn't belong in the area where he grew up. In truth, some might say that was correct. His mother was a housekeeper in Mayfair, and as a child, he shared a room with her in the attic of the Earl of Adnin's home. It wasn't a bad life, but now, being away for so long, he was aware it wasn't wrong to aspire for more.

Still, this wasn't the Earl of Adnin's home, and in truth, he could buy multiple of these posh townhouses. His gaze fixated on the front door. His chest burned. This is where Lisbeth lived with her children. It was where her day began every day.

The driver opened the carriage, and Thomas handed him some money. "Please park farther down and wait."

The man nodded. Thomas stepped out of the carriage and felt frozen in place. He was about to declare his love for the woman who'd abandoned him years ago. Was he a fool? He smiled likely, but he found that he didn't care. It was the only option he had. Thomas loved Lisbeth, and he wasn't sure anything would ever change that. The carriage rumbled away.

Before he could cross the road and approach Lisbeth's home, a woman opened the front door with two children in tow. He suspected they were Lisbeth's. It was a girl and a boy. The girl appeared to be older. She turned towards him, smiling, and he gasped. Her green eyes darted around the street, perusing what was taking place. He didn't seem to warrant any interest as her perusal moved quickly past him.

Yet, she held all his. His gaze roamed over her dark brown hair with reddish highlights, but what had him shocked was her green eyes. They were so much like his own. No. He shook his head, stumbling backward. Lisbeth had broken his heart all those years ago, but she would never do something so cruel.

The girl smirked, and Thomas realized that he was wrong. Lisbeth had been keeping a cruel, devastating secret from him. He spun away from Lisbeth's home, deciding he couldn't go there. Hurt and fury coursed through him. Was he making an incorrect assumption? He hoped so, but then the girl's smirk flashed in his mind so much like his own.

He approached the carriage, and the driver's brows shot up in surprise. "That was a fast trip, Mr. Easton."

Thomas nodded and pulled an envelope from his jacket. "Please take me to the address on this paper."

He stepped into the carriage and shut the door. Fury boiled in him. He had a daughter. One that had been alive for the last ten years. Rage made him want to scream and holler. Had he known she existed, he would have come to London sooner.

Lisbeth had kept this from him. All of the emotions he felt for her turned hard and cold. Plans swirled in his mind, none of them soft and tender, but fixated on making sure he had all that he wanted and deserved. Thomas never believed he could hate Lisbeth, but today, he discovered he was wrong. She would pay for her actions.

Chapter Fifteen

LISBETH PACED BACK and forth, waiting for Justin. Her brother had been meeting with business associates when she arrived at his townhouse unplanned. The butler had shown her to the drawing room to wait. It was strange to be in this building as a guest. This was where she'd grown up with Thomas. His mother had been the housekeeper here.

Justin would be upset if she ever said she was a guest aloud, as he insisted that this place would always be her home. A petty part of her whispered, *it should be; she'd given up enough for it.* She sighed, pushing the thoughts away. Lisbeth had made peace with her decision to leave Thomas in Tuscany. She wouldn't dwell on it.

Yet, it was the cause of all that was happening now. The door opened, and Justin strode in. Her brother epitomized what an earl should be. His bearing and dedication could never be questioned. Their father had passed a few years ago, and her mother spent most of her time, by choice, in the country.

Lisbeth wondered when he would marry. Justin seemed to have no interest. He spent most of his time involved in business deals to increase the earldom's financial portfolio. She sometimes suspected that he felt working hard was his penance for having begged her to leave Thomas and marry Nicholas. Desperation had forced him to collect her in Tuscany. She suspected he never wanted to feel that way again.

The family had been so broke, and the only way they could fix it was by sticking to the arrangement their father had made with the Lusby family. Usually, ladies came with dowries, but Nicholas's family had agreed to pay her father a large sum of money once she married their son. Lisbeth wasn't aware that her family had been on the verge of losing everything when she ran off with Thomas.

"Has he arrived?" Justin asked, taking her away from her thoughts.

She shook her head. Lisbeth hadn't spoken with Justin since before she departed on her trip to retrieve the tablets. She'd not wanted to endure any of his questions about Thomas. Justin blamed him for their running away. It didn't matter that she'd explained it was her decision. He always insisted that Thomas should have felt obligated to make sure they were doing the right thing.

"Do you think he is here to see you?"

"I don't know."

Justin stalked to a side table and poured himself a drink. He held a glass up to her, but she shook her head. Sighing, he said, "The best we can hope for is he gets wrapped up in his admirers, and you are forgotten."

She flinched at his words, and he frowned. "I'm sorry, Lisbeth. I didn't mean to be so harsh."

Lisbeth shrugged. "I know why you are saying that. I think if he sees Alice, he will quickly deduce that she is his."

"Damn it," Thomas muttered.

"I plan to tell him about Alice as soon as he arrives."

Justin's eyes flared with alarm. "What good would that do?"

"Thomas deserves to know the truth."

He took a sip of his drink. "He should not have been gallivanting across the world with a young lady."

A sigh escaped her. "Justin, I've told you repeatedly that I was the one who planned everything. I wanted to find Benjamin

Calvert and work with him. It wasn't Thomas's idea."

"Would you have gone without him?"

She didn't respond. Justin's lips twisted in a smirk. "No, you wouldn't have. You two were always bad for each other."

Annoyance flared in her. "We were not. Neither of us expected Father to be broke. Excuse me for not factoring that into my dreams when I was eighteen."

They were both silent, but eventually, Justin sighed. "I'm sorry for being abominable. I hate that you are in this situation, and my request all those years ago is the cause of it."

"I will take that drink now," Lisbeth said. "You didn't have any other options. We both know that."

He handed her a glass of wine. She took a sip, her stomach filled with worry. She had to tell Thomas. It was the only option. "I asked his mother to send me a missive when he arrives."

"I want to be there with you when you tell him."

Lisbeth's eyes widened. "I'm not sure that is needed or helpful."

He scowled. "I promise not to give him the thrashing he deserves."

Any interaction between Thomas and Justin wasn't a good idea. Justin loathed him. He hadn't before she found out she was pregnant. No, he'd felt sympathy for Thomas. Yet, the moment she'd confessed she was carrying Thomas's child, he'd begun to rage about him. Lisbeth suspected it helped him deal with his own guilt about the awful decision she had to make in Tuscany. "I think it would be better if I spoke to him alone."

Her brother clenched his jaw in annoyance. She walked to him and placed her hand on his. "This is something I need privacy to explain. I know you are concerned, but this isn't something you can do for me."

Justin nodded jerkily. "If he hurts you, I will destroy him, no matter how famous he is."

THOMAS STOOD IN front of his mother's townhouse. His heart ached because he suspected that she already knew the truth about Lisbeth's oldest child. This would be the first time he'd visit his mother in ten years, and it was likely to end poorly.

Hell, he'd never even been to this house before. His mother had purchased it seven years ago. She'd retired from housekeeping once he began to do well. Initially, he'd sent her money every month, but after a while, she wrote to him to stop, stating it was too much and that she had more than enough.

Her home wasn't in the posh area of Mayfair, but it was a beautiful location. Baker Street had become fashionable in the last few years, and Thomas couldn't help but feel pride that he'd contributed to his mother being able to afford this place. Her townhouse was not the most elaborate, but he didn't expect that. It wasn't in his mother's nature.

The door was thrown open, and his mother stood there with tears in her eyes. "My housekeeper said a man was standing out front, staring at the townhouse. I suspected it might be you. All of London is gossiping about your return."

They would fight inside, but all he wanted right now was his mother's embrace. He held out his arms, and she rushed to him. "My boy is finally home."

He stepped back, and tears streamed down her face. She reached up and grasped his cheeks. "Who knew you would grow into such a large man. You left here such a slender boy. I understand now everything the serials wrote about you."

A bark of laughter escaped him. He'd only felt anger of late, so the sound felt foreign to him. "I finished growing later than expected."

She smiled and stroked his cheek. "Come inside. We have much to discuss."

Briefly, he'd forgotten Lisbeth's treachery, but it all came roaring back. He followed his mother in. She guided them to a drawing room decorated in subdued colors, and he spotted the hand-sewn curtains that could only be her own. "This place suits you."

She squeezed his hand. "I couldn't have purchased it without your support. All the money you've provided me, I invested wisely."

He nodded, and she asked her housekeeper to fetch them tea. Thomas couldn't prevent the corners of his mouth from tilting upwards. The housekeeper now had one of her own. She sat and noticed his smile. "Yes, it was strange at first, but now I've grown accustomed to Mrs. Donnelly."

Thomas nodded, unsure how to begin. She said, "I'm assuming you've come back for Lisbeth."

Fury and anger welled in him. He had. What a foolish man he'd been! "It doesn't matter why I came back. She—"

They were interrupted by Mrs. Donnelly re-entering the room. She laid out the tea and some small sweets before departing. His mother lifted a brow. "She?"

"I have a child," he bit out.

She didn't deny it or express surprise, and Thomas's heart shattered. His mother had known. She frowned. "Thomas, what happened when you and Lisbeth were young was so complicated."

He scowled. "You are on a first-name basis with a duchess."

"She planned to tell you."

"I just spent weeks with her, and trust me, revelations of truth were no part of our time spent together," he snarled.

His mother took a sip of her tea, and he stood, pacing back and forth. "She had very few options."

Thomas stopped and glared at his mother. "She had the option to let me raise my child."

His mother sighed. "With what money? The two of you ran off but, at the time, had nothing."

He closed his eyes, hating that his mother was justifying

Lisbeth's awful choice. "Have you met her?"

His mother bit her lip as if trying to formulate her words. It was like someone had taken a knife and stabbed it into his chest. Had Thomas known he had a child, he would have returned to London immediately. He would have insisted that Lisbeth marry him. Finally, she said, "I've spent time with Alice since she was three years old. I ran into them out and about. I knew immediately."

Thomas shook his head, the anger hissing and snapping within him. His mother rose and walked to him. "This is an opportunity to start anew. You have both always loved each other."

He looked at her incredulously. Whatever he felt for the lying duchess was gone. It had shriveled up and died the moment he saw his child. Thomas stepped away from his mother. "I have no desire to start fresh with her. She will abide by my choices regarding our child. That is her only option."

His mother frowned at him. "Thomas, do not let hurt and anger destroy the potential of the life you've always wanted."

He scoffed. "I've lived a spectacular life."

"You have loved Lisbeth since I started working at the Earl of Adnin's townhouse. The moment you saw her as a six-year-old boy, and she was five."

Thomas refused to allow her words to dull his anger. "That was a long time ago, Mother. We are both very different people."

She frowned. "What do you mean to do?"

He didn't answer. "I have to leave."

She grasped his arm. "Thomas, I'm sorry, but you have to understand there was no other choice."

"Yes, because she wanted to be a duchess."

His mother shook her head. "You know it isn't that simple."

"I have to leave. I can't believe you have known this whole time." He shook her hand off.

Thomas stalked out of the townhouse. It hurt that his mother kept Lisbeth's secret from him. He couldn't believe he had a daughter. Lisbeth wouldn't get away with this. No, he alone would determine what would happen next, and she would have to go along with his plans.

Any warmth he felt for his ex-love vanished. She'd betrayed him in a way that was unforgivable. Pain pierced his heart as he thought of his mother's role in the entire sordid fiasco. Hopefully, over time, they could mend their relationship.

Chapter Sixteen

March 1851

LISBETH STEPPED INTO the hotel, nervous. Thomas had sent her a missive requesting her presence. She glanced at the letter clutched in her hand. Lisbeth wasn't sure why she was holding it. Somehow, it helped ease her nerves.

She found it peculiar that he hadn't called on her but had instead asked her to come to his room. It felt salacious, but perhaps Lisbeth was paranoid. Discreetly, she took the stairs to the second floor of the Delmont Hotel. It was one of the most lavish establishments in all of London. Lisbeth was shocked that Thomas had managed to obtain a room. It was often rumored to be fully booked.

She reached the door with twenty-six scrawled in gold across the front. Quietly, Lisbeth knocked, feeling fortunate that no one was in the hallway. A bit of annoyance flared in her that Thomas was putting her in this position. She was well-known, and if anyone spotted her here, gossip would explode in the newspapers.

The door opened, and he stood there in only his shirt and trousers. She found herself blushing at his casual state. He smiled sardonically. "Duchess, you've received my missive."

Her gaze jerked to his eyes, perplexed by the new nickname he'd given her. She forced a smile on her face. Lisbeth reminded herself that it was good that she was here. She would tell him the truth. Thomas stepped aside, allowing her entry.

She walked in and examined the room. It was a beautifully designed sitting area. She glanced at two doors and suspected that one was his sleeping area and the other was a bathing room. When this hotel opened, a key marketing point was that all rooms on the second and third floors featured private bathing spaces.

Nerves fluttered in Lisbeth's stomach, but she forced herself to smile. "This is beautiful lodging. I can't believe you secured a room."

He strode to a side table and poured them both wine. "Apparently, the owner wanted to be able to say the famous explorer Thomas Easton was staying here."

She frowned at his words. From their time in Syria, he'd never struck her as a braggart. Thomas motioned for her to sit on the sofa. She did, and he joined her, his leg pressed up against hers. She frowned as he handed her one of the glasses of wine.

Thomas took a sip of the drink, "So tell me, Lizzie—no, I'm sorry, duchess, how have you been?"

Annoyance surged in her. Thomas wasn't acting like himself. Still, she was glad she was here. Taking a deep breath, Lisbeth said, "I'm glad you sent me a note. There is something I must tell you."

He ignored her words and said, "May I kiss you, duchess?"

She frowned at him. "Please stop calling me that."

"Isn't that what you are?"

His fingers stroked one of her arms, and a jolt of desire shot through her. It infuriated her because she was doing her best to tell him the truth. She needed him to know about Alice before he discovered it himself. His hand grasped her chin, and his thumb stroked her lower lip. "Why have you tempted me my entire life?"

His words should have been romantic, but they seemed to be laced more with frustration. Thomas sighed. "I've slept with dozens of women to forget you, and you are still the one I dream of."

She yanked out of his grasp, standing. Lisbeth took a sip of her drink, trying to gather her thoughts and also unsure why he was behaving so strangely. "Thomas—"

He stood and said, "Come here, Lizzie."

The use of her childhood nickname on his lips soothed some of her annoyance, but she still studied him apprehensively. She started again, "Thomas, I need—"

Thomas shook his head. "Before we discuss anything, kiss me one more time."

She gave him a pointed look, and he added, "Let me just feel your mouth against mine. I traveled here to see you."

Lisbeth placed her glass on a table, worried. His eyes flared with desire, and warmth shot through her. Suddenly, she found herself wanting to kiss him before everything was known. There would be so much turmoil afterward. One kiss, and then Lisbeth would reveal it all.

She stepped towards him, her lower region flaring with want. She'd always been attracted to Thomas, but at thirty-two, he had a rugged appeal with his scruffy face, tan skin, and broad shoulders that was so much different from the boy she fell in love with.

The desire in his eyes sparked more, and he ran his tongue over his lower lip. Her core clenched; memories of him tasting her in Syria flashed in her mind. She reached him and placed a hand on his hard chest. His heart pounded underneath her hand.

One of his hands grasped her hip, and she felt herself leaning into him. Lisbeth wanted to feel his body against hers. His head dipped down, and he kissed her gently, but then it deepened. The touching of their mouths became one of dominance and hunger. It should frighten Lisbeth, but instead, her body screamed for more.

She clung to him, and then, in one swift motion, Thomas had her pushed up against the wall with her legs wrapped around his waist. He broke his savage kiss and ran his mouth down her throat. Thomas started to release one of her breasts from her dress when her rational side broke free from the fog of desire that had ignited.

Lisbeth pushed at his chest. "Please put me down."

He tried to claim her mouth again, but she shook her head. Thomas released her and strode to the other side of the room, facing away from her, taking deep breaths.

"Thomas, I didn't come for this. There is something I need to tell you."

He didn't say anything at first, and she added, "Please turn around. I need to speak with you. I've done something—"

Thomas turned, and his eyes glittered with hatred. "I know what you've done, duchess. I've already decided what will happen next. You will marry me tomorrow."

Horror filled her face. "No."

He glared at her, and Lisbeth felt all the animosity she'd expected. Still, they couldn't marry. Lisbeth shook her head as if somehow, she could make this all disappear but deep down she knew that was impossible.

"You don't have a choice. I will be in our daughter's life."

THOMAS STUDIED HER as the realization that he already knew sank in. The color drained from her face. She grabbed her wine glass and took two large gulps. Finally, she said, "I know you are upset, but marriage tomorrow is an impossibility. We would need a license."

He grinned bitterly. "Fortunately for us, being famous helps you procure one faster. I've already obtained a special license."

Her eyes widened. Thomas smirked at her. "I explained to the church that we'd fallen madly in love while you visited Syria. They found it rather romantic."

She bit her lip as if trying to deduce what to say next. His rage crackled within him. He wanted her to beg for his forgiveness or even cry, but instead, she stood staring at him, unblinking.

"Nothing to say for yourself?"

"I'm sorry I didn't tell you, but I can't marry you."

He laughed darkly. "Do you truly believe you have a choice, Liz—duchess?"

"Why are you calling me that?"

Thomas stalked to her, but she didn't flinch or fall apart. He hated this woman, but shockingly, desire still swarmed in him for her. Marrying her would be madness, but he didn't give a damn. His daughter and this woman would then be permanently a part of his life. No one could take that away from him.

He asked, "What else should I call you? You aren't the sweet Lizzie I once knew. That girl died a long time ago."

She jerked back as if his words had struck her. "I won't marry you, but I do want you to meet Alice."

He stepped away, frustration burning in his chest. "As a family friend? Someone who comes over for dinners once a week?"

"Thomas, please let me explain."

Shaking his head, "I don't care why you did it. You will marry me tomorrow, and we will raise our child together. We won't tell her the truth right away, but eventually I want her to know.

Her eyes flashed with anger. "And if I refuse?"

He shrugged. Thomas would get everything he wanted, and he didn't care if he had to dirty his hands to obtain it. Lisbeth could hate him. The feeling would be a mutual thing between them.

"If you don't, I will tell the newspapers that she is mine and that before you wed your husband, you ran off with your housekeeper's son."

Her face turned red with anger. "You would destroy my life and my children's lives."

Thomas stalked to her and grabbed her chin. "Your children's lives can only be destroyed if you refuse to make the right decision. It's in your hands, not mine. My daughter will grow up with me in her life, no matter what. Regarding ruining your life, I don't care how you feel. Again, my only focus is the child you kept from me."

He was so furious. Thomas found he wanted to hurt this woman as deeply as she'd devastated him. Shockingly, as they stared at each other, the hum of desire intensified between them. His attraction for her had never subsided; not even a tiny bit. The realization only heightened his anger. Still, it wasn't just him. He saw the same need and want in her eyes.

Thomas jerked his gaze away, hating their feelings for each other now that all Lisbeth's secrets had been revealed. He'd been a damn fool thinking he'd follow her back to London and they'd live happily ever after. She continued to stare at him in shock and alarm—the unhinged need to see her as undone as he felt surged in him. "Don't worry, it will be a marriage in name only. I have plenty of women willing to share my bed and comfort me—"

Lisbeth slapped him. His head snapped back. Fury glittered in her eyes. "I will not wed you, and don't worry, my desire to share your bed is gone completely."

A nibble of guilt flared in him. Thomas had taunted her with the other woman to hurt her, and it had worked. *No.* Thomas would not feel bad for this woman who denied him his child for over a decade. "You don't understand Lisbeth. You have no choice. We will wed tomorrow. I will arrange for witnesses."

She was quiet, weighing his words. Eventually, resignation filled her face. "What will I tell my children?"

"Tell them while in Syria, you fell in love with the famous explorer Thomas Easton," he bit out.

"You aren't the man I thought you were. I don't care for this cocky explorer persona you are embracing."

"Don't!" he snapped. "You kept her from me. You and my mother schemed to keep my child a secret. Was it to be forever?"

"Thomas, you don't understand," she whispered. "It isn't that simple."

"I don't care," he snapped and stomped over to the desk, grabbing a paper. He handed it to her. "You will meet me here tomorrow."

She looked at him pleadingly. He wouldn't feel bad. "We will wed, and I will move in with you and your family. I don't care what you tell society. Tell them we have fallen in love, or tell them you are marrying me for my money. Whatever makes you feel better."

"Please give me time."

He would not yield, no matter what. "Tomorrow, Lisbeth."

She shook her head in frustration before stomping out of the room. His heart pounded, and his stomach clenched. Thomas knew he was behaving like a monster, but he was determined to be in his child's life every day.

In another lifetime, he'd wanted to wed Lisbeth because he loved her so desperately, but this union wasn't about that. It was about righting a wrong caused by the temptress. He didn't foresee sharing a bed with her or touching her. *Liar*, his mind mocked.

It frustrated him that, despite his dislike for her, Thomas still found himself drawn to her. The moment he saw Lisbeth, he wanted to kiss her. Even with all the fury bubbling in him, he'd wanted to taste her lips one more time before all was revealed. Christ, he'd almost taken her against the wall. A chaste kiss had never been enough with her.

Lisbeth would hate him for a long time. Thomas told himself it didn't matter. This marriage wasn't about them but about his daughter.

Chapter Seventeen

LISBETH ENTERED THE tiny church hidden by larger buildings in the London area of Piccadilly. She'd been quite surprised to see the older structure in an area where so much new development was occurring. The walls were made of ancient stone. She ran her hands along one side of it, suspecting this place dated back to the Roman period.

"It is a beautiful space, Your Grace," the bishop said, entering from a side door.

She smiled. "It's lovely. I was wondering if it dates back to Roman times."

The older man nodded. "It does. Dozens of buildings have been built around the church, but luckily, no one has tried to remove it."

"I'm glad," she said. The uniqueness of this building had taken away the melancholy of her impending wedding.

The bishop frowned at her. "Are you sure you wish to wed, Your Grace?"

Her eyes flew to his face, and he added, "My leadership indicated this was a rushed request, and your future husband had asked for a discreet location."

She wanted to confess that she didn't want to marry, but didn't think it mattered. The determination and anger in Thomas's eyes yesterday left no room for debate. She swallowed the lump forming in her throat, wishing that all of this could have happened differently. Lisbeth should have told Thomas about Alice in Syria.

Yesterday, she sat down with Alice and Jeremy, telling them that she was to be married. Jeremy had been intrigued, and her daughter furious. Her chest ached because Alice had always been close to Nicholas. Her revelation about her imminent marriage to Thomas hadn't gone over well. Lisbeth suspected that more difficult roads lay ahead in establishing a relationship between Thomas and Alice.

"My betrothed likes ancient things. That is why I picked this church," Thomas said from the entryway of the building.

Her stomach dipped because even though he looked messy and disreputable, the man was still breathtaking. She wondered if he'd slept at all last night. Another man bumped into him. He laughed. Stepping aside, the other man, also looking rumpled, stepped in, followed by a more studious-looking person.

"Here are my two witnesses, Father. Mr. Matthison and my solicitor, Mr. Green."

The bishop's lips pinched in disapproval. Lisbeth suspected they were thinking the same thing. These men had spent the evening enjoying vice a little too much. Her heart clenched, wondering if women were involved. She pushed the thoughts from her mind. It didn't matter. They weren't marrying because they cared about each other. *He'd loved you once*, her heart whispered to her.

Still, that wasn't why they were here. Lisbeth was marrying Thomas because of his threat. Anger coursed through her that it had all come to this. The man who was in London wasn't the boy she left in Tuscany all those years ago, nor the man she said goodbye to in Syria. He was angry and hurt, and Lisbeth didn't know how to fix it, but doubted their wedding would improve anything.

Thomas and Matthison laughed about something, and the bishop skewered them with a glare. They immediately quieted.

The bishop leaned closer to Lisbeth. "Are you sure, Your Grace?"

She glanced at Thomas, who watched her intently. Even after she'd married Nicholas, she'd fantasized about being his wife and raising their children together. None of those fantasies had ever come close to this debacle, but she didn't have a choice. Maybe they would find a way to be happy again. Skepticism filled her. Yet, she suspected without this marriage, there was no healing. Still, it pained her that this wasn't one forged on love but hatred. It would be the second marriage foisted upon her.

She forced herself to smile. "Yes, Father, it is my choice."

Thomas made his way to the front of the church. He smelled of smoke and liquor. Her soon-to-be husband had been out getting foxed while she laid in bed a bundle of nerves. Frustration flared in Lisbeth, but she kept it tamped down.

"Shall we begin, or do we want to have you leave and come back in?" the bishop asked Lisbeth.

She shook her head. "I think we can simply start."

The bishop began the farce of a ceremony that Lisbeth was still struggling to believe was hers. In all honesty and fortunately, it passed in a blur until the bishop said, "You may bestow a kiss on your bride."

Lisbeth's gaze flicked to his. A coldness emanated from him, and she suspected he would hate her forever. Thomas's friend, Matthison, whistled, "Kiss her, Easton."

The bishop cringed at his obnoxiousness. Thomas quickly brushed his lips across hers. It was the briefest of touches, and it broke Lisbeth's heart. Any fantasy she'd had about marrying Thomas had always ended in a spectacular kiss. *This is reality*, she reminded herself, *not a dream*.

Thomas turned to his friend and solicitor. "Thank you for your assistance today. We will be on our way."

He held his hand out to her, and she took it, but no warmth existed between them. They both thanked the bishop and walked out of the church directly to a carriage. Once inside, Lisbeth asked, "Where shall we go now?"

"Home."

He meant her townhouse. Nerves filled her. "I told the children yesterday that we were getting married. Alice didn't take it well. Perhaps you could gradually move in."

"No, you've denied me my child long enough."

There was so much pain etched on his face. She'd been the cause of that. "I'm sorry, Thomas. Truly, I am, but I think if you heard me out, you would see that I didn't—"

"I don't want to hear any of it," he said harshly. "You made your choice, and I have made mine."

Lisbeth didn't want to argue. "I told the children we'd be arriving today. Jeremy reads your serials and is excited to meet you. Alice has a love of history, and I think, eventually, she will come around. Please treat their feelings gently. Their father has only been gone for three years."

He scowled at the mention of Nicholas. They needed to have an open and honest conversation. "I think we need to talk."

Thomas shook his head. "I'm not interested, duchess."

She flinched at his new nickname for her and remained silent. Sadness and guilt coursed through her, but fury at his behavior was starting to build. This man sitting across from her wasn't the Thomas she knew. He was being an ass.

THOMAS STEPPED INTO the foyer of Lisbeth's townhouse. The staff had curtsied and fawned over her as they entered. The entryway was extravagant but not gaudy. It very much suited the lady. She took a deep breath and nodded as the butler whispered something to her.

Turning to him, she said, "The children are in the drawing room. I think it is best if we do an introduction now."

His heart hammered. Thomas would meet his daughter. He couldn't form any words and simply nodded jerkily. She said,

"Follow me, please."

They walked down the wide hallway before stepping into a room. A girl of eleven and a younger boy sat on a sofa and a chair, reading. The boy looked up and smiled, "You are home."

Lisbeth smiled. "Yes, I wanted to do introductions. Alice and Jeremy, this is Thomas Easton, my new husband."

The girl slammed her book shut and glowered at him. His heart broke slightly because the fiery eyes were so much like his. He was looking at a reflection of himself—well, his younger self anyway.

He smiled. "Hello, Alice and Jeremy."

The boy slid off the sofa. "I'm reading a serial about when you discovered a statue on the island of Sardinia."

"I remember that. We had to deal with an awful storm while we were there. It was quite the adventure."

Alice snorted. "Everyone knows those serials are an exaggeration."

"Alice," Lisbeth warned.

Thomas knew this would take time, and for the first time, he rationally comprehended how his demand that they marry might not have been wise. Still, it was too late now. "I would love to share the real details of my adventures with both of you."

Jeremy nodded excitedly, but Alice shrugged. Still, she hadn't said no. Lisbeth explained, "Both the children love history and artifacts."

"We have a room here of antiquities from across the world and a room at our country estate of ones found on the grounds there. Would you like to see the room?" Jeremy asked excitedly.

Thomas nodded. Alice jumped up. "I think I will go to my room."

She stomped out, slamming the door behind her. Lisbeth frowned and rose. He shook his head; he didn't want Lisbeth to scold her. Jeremy bounced on the balls of his feet excitedly.

"Lead the way, Jeremy."

Most of Lisbeth's house contained antiquities, but when

Jeremy opened the door to the space that he wanted him to see, Thomas was shocked. The room was twice the height of most rooms and featured a second-floor walkway that overlooked the first floor. Shelves lined all the walls, and they were filled with a variety of relics.

He glanced at Lisbeth, surprised. Thomas figured she'd given up her love of all things old, but no, she'd become a collector. He suspected that her private collections surpassed those of most museums and clubs. "This is quite stunning."

"Mother acquired all these. Father said she was obsessed."

Lisbeth flushed. "My husband—Nicholas, was very supportive of my hobby."

"I see that," Thomas murmured. Envy flared in him, imagining the conversations they had. Being in this townhouse suddenly felt like all too much. It was late afternoon. He needed to settle up with the hotel and attend to some other matters. In truth, he just needed some air from this space and the past. "I have an appointment, so I must depart."

Jeremy nodded. "Maybe when you return or tomorrow, we can talk about Sardinia."

Thomas forced himself to smile. "I promise."

He practically fled from the room and quickly headed to the door. Footsteps followed him, and he looked back to see Lisbeth coming towards him. Harshly, he asked, "What is it?"

"Where are you going? Will you return?"

He felt smothered here. "That isn't your concern."

She bristled. "I'm your wife."

Thomas leaned forward so only she could hear him, "Only because it allows me to be near my child."

She wore a pained expression. "I will have the bedchamber connected to mine prepared for you."

"Was that the duke's?"

Lisbeth nodded, and he shook his head. "Prepare a guest chamber for me."

"Thomas, can we please talk?"

He didn't let her say anything else but yanked the door open, escaping her and everything that he'd lost because of choices that were made outside of his control. Thomas would never allow that to happen again.

Chapter Eighteen

LISBETH, AN HOUR ago, had heard one of the servants escort Thomas to the guest chamber. She needed to speak with him. Even if it was an argument, they needed to discuss in detail how all this would unfold. It wasn't good for the children to be around so much animosity.

She walked to the guest chamber, feeling as if she was sneaking around even though Thomas was now her husband. Lisbeth opened the door and found him asleep, not in the bed, but in a wingback chair. A glass of brandy rested in his hand, sitting on one of his knees.

Tonight, apparently, would not be the time for their discussion. She gently pulled the glass from his hand and retrieved a soft blanket from the foot of the bed to cover him with. When Lisbeth turned back, she was surprised to see his green eyes staring back at her.

"I'm sorry if I woke you," she murmured.

He smiled softly at her, and it was filled with warmth that startled her. Since their encounter at the hotel, he'd not looked at her in that way. She shook out the blanket, but he pulled it away, dropping it on the floor. "Come here, Lizzie."

The endearment from his lips made her body hum. She frowned at him but stepped closer. "Have you been drinking?"

He laughed. "I've drank, stopped, and now I'm here."

"You are home," she said.

Thomas grimaced. "I'm not sure that is what this place is."

"It could be. May we talk?"

He pulled her towards him so his legs were between hers, hiking her nightdress up slightly. "This place is like a museum containing all the things I could have had but were denied to me."

She stroked his cheek. "It doesn't have to be. We can start anew."

His hand stroked the outside of her leg, sending warmth through her body. Lisbeth should step away, but for once, he wasn't staring at her with so much hatred. It may be desire, but she would take it over animosity.

Thomas's hand drifted up, reaching her stomach, her hip, and then sliding down her lower back and bottom. "Thomas, we shouldn't—"

"Kiss me, Lizzie—just one time. Let's pretend that none of this exists for a moment," he said gruffly.

There was nothing wise about appeasing him, but she found herself unable to resist. She dipped her head down and placed her lips to his. Thomas's warm hands pulled her closer until she stumbled onto his lap astride.

The soft kiss deepened. They explored each other with a yearning that Lisbeth felt so deeply her eyes began to water. His hands threaded through her hair. Thomas broke the kiss and whispered, "I used to dream about wrapping this thick blonde hair in my hand."

Lisbeth kissed his jaw and his throat. Her core clenched as his shaft pulsated against her most feminine spot, only his trousers separating them. He pulled her mouth back to his. The kiss turned hungrier and needier. He arched his hips upward, and Lisbeth threw her head back, moaning. He ran his fingers down her throat and tugged at the top of her nightgown. It remained in place.

Thomas leaned forward and took the tip of one of her breasts through the fabric in his mouth, sucking and teasing her. Her body was inflamed, and their rocking against each other became more frantic. One of his hands dipped down between her thighs, and she moaned. He released her nipple. "You are so wet. I need to be inside you, Lizzie. Please."

She nodded and shifted upwards while he removed his shaft from his pants. He bunched her nightgown up so she was bare from the waist down. Lisbeth lowered herself onto him, and he watched intently until he was fully buried in her. She wanted this every day of her life. Lisbeth wanted him.

The ache for him thrummed through her, and she began to ride him. Each meeting of their bodies was hard and deep. It was as if all the emotions that had been buried within each of them were coming out with every thrust. Their movements shifted between tenderness and frustration.

The throbbing in her was building. She was close to her climax. Her body was thirsty for it, and she rode him harder, needing it. Thomas seemed to be racing towards his finish as well, as he bucked underneath her. She whimpered when he wrapped her hair in his fist and held her so they were looking at each other.

"Why are you such a fucking temptation, Lizzie? I shouldn't want you or this."

His words hurt, but also inflamed her. The anger Lisbeth felt at his unwillingness to talk surged within her. She rocked harder, hating his words. "Do you think I want to desire you? A man who has forced me to wed him for life, even though he hates me."

He growled and pulled her head down for a punishing kiss. The ache in her core spiked to a level that left her breathless. She was so close. He grasped her hips frantically. They pounded into each other, and gone was any tenderness. In its place for both of them was desire, a need to be sated, and anger.

Her eyes connected with his fiery ones just as the ache in her lower body exploded. Thomas groaned at the same time, spilling his seed deep into her. She fell against him as he slowly rocked his hips. Eventually, she pulled back and looked down at him. A look of devastation covered Thomas's face.

Lisbeth pulled herself from his lap. He stood and handed her a cloth to clean up before taking care of himself and closing his trousers. Thomas didn't make eye contact with her. Finally, Lisbeth said, "Thomas, look at me."

He shook his head. "I have to go."

She grasped his arm. "Stop running."

Yanking his arm free, he said, "This was a mistake. I could have gotten you with child."

Frustration and anger welled in her. "Is that so wrong? You are my husband. I love you."

"Don't say that," he bit out.

Lisbeth did. She always would. "Tell me you don't love me. I want to hear the lie on your lips."

He remained quiet, but there was no mistaking his anger. Yet, he didn't say the words aloud. Why did that make her hopeful?

"I'm so sorry for everything, but we have a chance to be together and happy, Thomas. Why would we deny ourselves that?"

"I can't help wanting you. Damn it, I've tried for years," he ground out.

Lisbeth silently pleaded for him to let some of the anger go. She knew if she asked him aloud right now, it would fall on deaf ears.

His glare turned darker. "Love is no longer what I feel for you, duchess. That is gone and will never return."

Her heart shattered. She'd thought he wouldn't be able to say such a thing to her.

She shook her head. "I don't believe you."

"We are only married so that I can be near my child. So she can know me, and I can be a part of her life. You and I, duchess, will likely end up fucking again, but don't be a fool and think it is love. We need to be better at making sure I don't get you with child."

She closed her eyes, fury welling in her at his hurtful words.

She grabbed a glass and threw it at him. It shattered against the wall. He looked away, stunned. In truth, Lisbeth was also shocked by her actions.

"Mother," Jeremy yelled from down the hallway.

Lisbeth was shaking and took a deep breath to calm her nerves. She turned to walk away, and Thomas grabbed her arm. She yanked away from him. "Leave at least until you can learn to speak with me. I will not have my children grow up with this animosity between us."

He nodded and rushed from the room. She wiped at the tears, hating him so much.

"Mother," Jeremy called again.

She hurried to his room. The governess was already there. He was crying. "I had a bad dream, and then I heard a loud noise."

Lisbeth waved Miss Ashby away and sat on the edge of his bed, stroking his hair. "I dropped a glass. Go back to sleep, little one."

He did as she asked, drifting off. Lisbeth shook her head, horrified by both her and Thomas's behavior. She wouldn't live with him if they could not get along. It was too much for Alice and Jeremy. They would have to figure something out. Perhaps she would take the children to the country until things settled down.

The Historical Society for Female Curators was planning an event to reveal the end of the epic. She would miss that. Still, it didn't matter. If she stayed, she and Thomas were likely to destroy each other.

THOMAS SAT AT the Den in one of the quieter rooms. He needed a moment to himself. In his anger, he'd tipped the newspapers off about his wedding to Lisbeth; now, it was everywhere. The minute he'd walked into the club tonight, men had wanted to congratulate him.

He sipped his brandy, hating all the poor choices he'd made of late. Thomas had truly turned into a madman, not like the one in the Arabic tale, but an actual lunatic. He'd forced Lisbeth to marry him. Still, anger shot through him whenever he thought of his daughter being raised by another.

When he met her yesterday, she looked at him with pure hatred. Thomas suspected that suddenly having a new father figure would make any child feel that way. Jeremy, Lisbeth's other child, seemed to deal with it better, but it was a disaster.

He took a sip of his drink. His mind flashed to last night. He'd wanted her so badly, and then she'd shown up in his bedchamber. It was like his dream had come true. For a moment, he didn't want to think about all the bad stuff between them. He'd simply wanted to feel Lizzie's body against his.

Then, in the middle of it, his brain couldn't stop thinking about the townhouse he was in and the life she'd lived without him. Any tenderness he felt for her evaporated instantly. The end of their coupling had been one filled with anger and selfishness. The sad part was that afterward, he still wanted her even though he despised Lisbeth now.

Devons sat down across from him. "I hear congratulations are in order."

Thomas scowled and said nothing.

"Why are you here if you are newly married?"

He sighed. "Didn't you just marry recently?"

The club owner smirked. "I did, but this is also my business. I've also been married for a few weeks now. If gossip is correct, you've just gotten married yesterday."

He forced himself to smile. "I'm just getting away for a few hours."

"I know we haven't seen each other since Latakia, but if you ever need anything, let me know. It is very easy to become wrapped up in all your admirers. If you need a real friend, I'm here."

Some of Thomas's anger subsided. He did appreciate Devons.

Since his arrival, people seemed to fawn over him. In truth, it was overwhelming and something he wasn't enjoying all that much. Well, except that, at times, it helped him keep his mind off his debacle with Lisbeth. He was in so much pain right now, but he cringed every time he remembered his words to her yesterday evening.

"Do you think if two people have hurt each other deeply, they can overcome that?" he asked.

Devon's eyes widened. "I'm not sure. I believe it depends on what they've done and if they love each other more than they hate each other."

Thomas nodded, unsure how he felt. Their conversation was interrupted when Lord Jude stumbled into the room. "Mr. Easton, join us for drinks out here. We want to hear about your adventures and congratulate you on your wedding."

He forced himself to smile. "I will be there momentarily."

Jude stumbled back out of the room. Evidently, he'd already been celebrating a great deal.

"A word of caution: Lord Jude is a notorious gossip. It isn't wise to reveal anything to him because all of London will know about it," Devons explained.

"I appreciate you letting me know."

Devons added, "Go home. Spend time with your bride."

Thomas couldn't go back to the duke's residence. He took a sip of his drink and stood. "I think I will join the revelry in the main hall for a bit."

"It won't help with whatever you're upset about," Devons stated.

He finished his drink and forced himself to smile. "I'm fine."

Thomas walked out into the main hall, and a large group of men applauded him. Yes, this was what Thomas wanted. He needed to get lost in the noise. He hoped that would help him forget about everything else.

He smiled at a server and loudly said, "Bring all these men another drink. I have a story to tell them."

Everyone cheered.

Chapter Nineteen

LISBETH SAT IN the drawing room, exhausted. She hadn't slept well after Thomas left her in the guest chamber the previous evening. Now, night was approaching, and she hadn't heard from him at all. A sigh escaped her. The day had been awful. She'd planned to spend most of it at Seely House, meeting with the other board members of the Historical Society of Female Curators, but couldn't.

Her marriage was all over the papers, as well as the fact that Thomas was out celebrating his celebrity status and their union. She felt foolish. Alice wouldn't speak to her, and Jeremy wouldn't stop asking when he would return. Lisbeth had no idea. She felt so alone.

A knock on the door jerked her from her melancholy thoughts. Her butler, Morrison, opened the door. Perhaps it was Thomas, still not comfortable just walking in, but it wasn't. Rose, now the Duchess of Sinclair, asked Morrison, "Where is she?"

Lisbeth tilted her head back against her wingback chair. Tears burst from her. Rose barged into the room, frowning. "I'm going to murder Thomas Easton."

She stared at her once frenemy, who always liked Thomas more. Her eyes continued to water, and her chin trembled. "I've made my own mess of things."

Rose sat down. "Tell me. He loves you, but somehow, I

suspect this marriage isn't what you anticipated or wanted."

Lisbeth rose and shut the drawing room door. Rose pulled a flask from her reticule and uncapped it, handing it to her. The absurdity of Rose carrying it around caused her to giggle even though she was so upset. Her friend grinned. "I wanted to come prepared."

"I have wine, brandy, and champagne."

Rose grinned at her cheekily. "This is more fun."

Lisbeth took a sip and handed it back to her. Her friend took a large gulp. Another giggle escaped Lisbeth. Rose smiled. "I'm glad to hear that sound from you."

It felt good, but the drama of the last day hit her with full force again. "There are so many things I wish I had done differently, but I truly never felt I had a choice."

"Start at the beginning."

Lisbeth stood and paced back and forth. She'd never shared this with anyone but Nicholas, Justin, and Thomas's mother. Still, the need to let it out flowed through her. "When Thomas proposed to me in Tuscany, my brother Justin showed up a few days later. My father was destitute. He'd just been beaten badly by a creditor and was close to debtor's prison. There was no money. It was all gone. Justin had used the last bit of it to find me."

"Why?"

Bitterness filled her. She smiled sadly. "My father and my husband's family arranged a marriage between us. Nicholas, at the time, hadn't wanted to marry and refused to put in any effort, so his father offered an exorbitant sum to mine."

Understanding flashed across Rose's face. "You left to save your family."

Lisbeth grabbed Rose's flask again, drinking it. "I left because I had no other options. While you and your father were success-ful, Thomas and I were still barely surviving. None of us were wealthy at the time."

"Thomas would understand that," Rose insisted.

"He did," Lisbeth said with a sigh and sat down. "But he saw Alice and instantly realized she was his."

Rose's eyes widened. "I suspected, but then I saw portraits of your husband. They all have similar traits."

Lisbeth wiped at another tear. "I didn't know until shortly after I wed Nicholas that I was with child. I told him the truth right away. Shocking me, he dealt with it more compassionately than I believe most husbands would. Likely because he also loved another, but she'd passed away, which is why he'd agreed to the marriage. I spent years wondering if I should write and tell Thomas the truth. His mother has always known. I just didn't want to cause more pain. It is awful."

"It is," Rose said, never one to mince words. "But I don't know what other option you had. What did his mother think?"

"She worried about what he would do if he knew, especially since I was married, and Nicholas had claimed Alice."

"What a bloody mess," Rose muttered.

It was. There was no fixing it. "I should have told him in Syria, but selfishly, I enjoyed having a few moments with him where the past wasn't so heavily hanging over us."

"Still, as a young lady, had you returned to London and told everyone, you would have been ruined. I can't believe your husband stood by you," Rose pointed out.

Lisbeth smiled sadly. "Nicholas was a good man. I didn't hold his heart, but we grew to be dear friends."

Rose sighed. "How did you and Thomas end up married?"

She shook her head. "He is so angry. He acquired a special license. I don't think he cares about me. He detests me but wants to be in Alice's life."

A snort escaped Rose. "I can't imagine Alice wants anything to do with him. She is protective of you."

Lisbeth sniffled. "It makes it even more awful. Alice is so angry, and he enthralls Jeremy."

"He should have wooed you properly."

She shook her head at her friend. "Did you hear what I said?

He hates me."

"Thomas Easton loves you. Everything he has ever accomplished is to prove he is worthy of you."

He had always been worthy of her. It was she who wasn't worthy of him. "The wedding was a disaster. There is no love left, trust me."

"Can you annul it?"

Lisbeth flushed and fidgeted uncomfortably. "It has been consummated."

Rose shot her a pointed look. "But the love is gone?"

Lisbeth had no words to convey how much anger existed in Thomas's eyes every time they spoke. Rose squeezed her hand. "Give it time."

"You don't understand. Too much hurt and lies have occurred. Some things can't be fixed, and this can't. We will live separate lives. I plan to take Alice and Jeremy to the country for the time being at the end of the week. I need to get out of the city."

Rose sighed and took a drink from her flask before handing it back to Lisbeth.

THOMAS SAT AT the Den; it was his third night there. Devons reluctantly offered to let him stay at one of the cottages on the grounds that bachelors frequented when they were visiting London. Of course, he first explained to him why he should go back to his wife. The woman would not stop tormenting his thoughts.

He'd played cards and drank, and a few of the lords had tried to entice him into visiting some ladies with them, but the thought left him disgusted. Lisbeth was his wife, and as much as he despised her, now that he'd made the vow, Thomas couldn't break it. She was his. When he was completely in his cups, sometimes he wondered if he'd forced the marriage so he could have her or because of his daughter.

The daughter, who hated him. Thomas suspected only time would fix that. Guilt coursed through him that he hadn't been back since the night he'd made love to Lisbeth and she'd thrown a glass at him. In truth, he deserved it. He took a sip of his drink.

The whole situation was a sordid mess. Thomas shouldn't have forced Lisbeth to wed him, no matter how angry he was. He cringed, remembering the horror he'd seen on Alice's face when Lisbeth explained they were wed. What the fuck was he doing? Thomas considered leaving England altogether, but something held him back.

"Easton, you've been a bore tonight," Lord Braxton moaned.

Matthison, his friend from his voyage to England, nodded in agreement. Before he could respond, both men's eyes widened, and gasps echoed through the great hall. He wasn't facing the entrance, so he turned in his chair to see. A furious Rose was stalking towards him, with her husband following behind her as if a duchess charging into a gentlemen's club was perfectly normal.

"Bloody hell," he muttered, standing.

She reached him and glared. "I would like to speak with you, Mr. Easton."

"What are you doing here? You are in the middle of a gentlemen's club," he whispered to her, and then glanced at her husband, who shrugged. He sighed. Rose was lucky she married a duke; gossip could only affect the hoyden so much.

Devons approached and nodded to a room. "That is a private space if you need to use it."

Sinclair nodded before following Rose to the room. Thomas sighed and joined them. Once inside, the duke shut the door. Rose hissed, "Did you force Lisbeth to marry you?"

"You have no idea what she's done."

"Alice is yours."

It was like another stab to his heart. Rose and her father were like family to him. "You knew?"

Rose rolled her eyes. "No, I went to see Lisbeth, and she told me."

"I had to make sure I could see my child," he bit out, somewhat relieved that she hadn't known all along. "How can you side with her?"

"I don't, and I told her she should have revealed the truth when she went to Syria, but honestly, what choice did she have?"

Thomas glared at the woman who was like a sister to him. "She could have annulled her marriage."

Rose glanced at her husband. "Augustus, would you give us a moment?"

He nodded. "I will join Devons for a drink."

She smiled at him, and a look of adoration passed between them. Thomas was so envious, but he kept it tamped down because it had nothing to do with Rose. The woman he loved had lied to him for over a decade.

"Rose, I don't want to talk about this."

"What do you think would happen to an unmarried pregnant woman whose family is destitute? What would happen if that woman married a duke and then revealed to society that she needed an annulment?"

He would not feel bad for Lisbeth. "I would have supported her."

Rose snorted. "With what? While we've become wildly successful in the last ten years, we had nowhere close to the money Lisbeth would have needed."

He didn't want Rose to make him understand. "She and my mother kept my daughter from me."

"And that is wrong. But I'm asking you, as the man who loved her, to try to understand that she had no other option as a woman."

"My mother knew."

"Thomas, you were a mess after Lisbeth left. Your mother was probably terrified of what you would do. You would have returned to England and destroyed your life. The famous explorer

Thomas Easton wouldn't exist."

"I don't give a damn."

Rose squeezed his hand. "That is a lie. Would you have picked a life with Lisbeth and your child ten years ago? Of course. Still, life doesn't always give us what we want. You've enjoyed traveling the world, sometimes too much. Now, you have a chance to love Lisbeth openly and to raise your daughter. I've spent time with both Alice and Jeremy. If you let yourself, you'd love them both."

Thomas found himself unable to speak.

His friend added, "There are so many wrongs between you and Lisbeth that can't be changed. But I remember the love the two of you had. I used to think how lucky you both were. What are you doing in this club? If you want to be her husband, you both have a great deal of work to do to mend the hurt and trust between you."

Hoarsely, he confessed, "I do still love her."

She smacked him on the arm. "I know. Go figure it out. Right now, you look like the pompous, famous explorer from the serials. That isn't you, no matter how hard you are trying to behave that way. You will regret all of this."

Thomas sighed. "I'm so angry."

"You deserve to be angry, but you have Lisbeth now. It is up to you how real your marriage and your relationship with your daughter are," Rose said, and then she glanced around. "At least leave this club. The gossip you are creating by staying here after your sudden marriage is atrocious."

The back of his neck went hot. Thomas nodded. "Thank you for coming to see me and being honest. Do you think you and your duke could drop me off at my mother's?"

She beamed at him. "Of course."

Thomas was still angry, but Rose had pierced through some of it, and now the desire to stay and celebrate left him empty. What was he going to do about his marriage?

Chapter Twenty

LISBETH SAT WITH Jeremy and Alice, wishing that this wasn't all so difficult. Her daughter sulked. "Why do we have to go to the country? I want to stay in London. You said I could attend the next event at Seely House. I want to be there when Rose reveals the end of the epic. You should want to as well. You helped find the tablets."

Alice's older-than-her-years words did make Lisbeth smile. "I know you want to go, but I think we have had so much change; we should leave for a bit."

"Is he going with us?" her daughter asked, folding her arms.

"Thomas Easton will stay with us in the country!" her son said, excited.

Her eleven-year-old rolled her eyes at her younger brother. "He is married to Mother."

"I'm not sure what he will do."

Alice looked at her weirdly. Her daughter was becoming far too perceptive. Lisbeth sighed. "I have to visit Seely House today for a few hours, but I promise tonight I will read your favorite story."

Lisbeth kissed them both and smiled at their governess on her way to the foyer. Before she could leave, Morrison stopped her, carrying a bundle of mail. Her eyes widened. "Are those for me?"

He shook his head. "They are for Mr. Easton."

They must be letters from his admirers. Jealousy flared in her. One of the gossip sheets had insinuated that Thomas might have married too early and didn't realize how many admirers he had. She pushed the thought from her mind. "Please bring them to the guest chamber."

Morrison nodded. Lisbeth pushed away all the emotions bubbling in her. She needed to go to Seely House. The place and the club had become her refuge over the last year.

A few hours later, she sat in the office alone. Lisbeth was somewhat relieved. The papers were printing outrageous stories about Thomas, and Lisbeth had no way to explain it. She glanced at the ledger she was working on. She'd taken charge of the club's finances and enjoyed it. They weren't making a great deal of money, but more than breaking even.

She had hoped Rose would be here. One of the guards had told her she had finished the ancient epic. The hero lives happily ever after with the princess. Why did the epic seem so less complicated than real life? Feeling restless, she rose and walked to the research room. The two tablets were held in a glass case there. They would join the three other tablets in the exhibit room and be revealed at their next event in a month.

Lisbeth ran her hand across the glass; pride thrummed through her that she'd found them. Traveling to Syria was nothing like her current life, but she'd enjoyed it. She'd played a part in finding the first-ever ancient cuneiform story.

Motion at the door made her glance up; Addie peered at her. "Hello."

She smiled at her. "Hello, friend."

"Diana, Esme, and I just arrived and thought we'd have some tea. Would you like to join?"

Lisbeth wasn't sure she wanted to do that. She didn't want to answer any questions. As if reading her mind, Addie held out her hand. "Only share what you want."

She placed her hand in Addie's, and they walked to the office. Sarah and Rose were now in there as well. Lisbeth said, "Everyone is here."

"We're here for you. We want you to know that you aren't alone," Sarah provided.

She felt grateful for these women. "It is too complicated even to begin to explain."

Esme ushered her over to the sitting area, and Diana asked, "Do you love him? He's been at the Den, looking pretty miserable, my husband has told me."

"We were so in love once. He felt like a part of me, and I felt like a part of him. Still, there have been so many changes in the last ten years. Marrying may have been foolish. No, not may, but was."

"He loves you, Lisbeth," Rose said, her voice filled with certainty.

"I believe he does, but it may not be enough."

"He is behaving like a fool," Esme tutted.

She shrugged. "He isn't the only one at fault."

Addie squeezed her hand. "What can we do?"

She smiled softly. "Just being here like this makes it better. Tell me something that doesn't have to do with what is in the gossip sheets."

Rose smiled. "I finished the epic."

"The guard told me that,"

Her friend grinned, "Belit and Sibri end up together. He fights with the king but doesn't kill him. The king agrees to let him and the princess be together, and then they eventually rule."

"I love it," Lisbeth said. She glanced at the other ladies. "Do we think that will gain us a spot in the Great Exhibition?"

Addie's eyes sparkled. "I didn't want to share too much, but I received a letter from the Royal Commission for the Great Exhibition, which is sending someone to our next event. I think we are close."

The Great Exhibition would primarily showcase industrial technology from around the world, with a small area of the event dedicated to highlighting clubs and work being done in the field of antiquities. Of course, the London Society of Antiquaries would have a space there, but they were so close to obtaining one as well. Excitement fluttered in Lisbeth's stomach.

Addie said, "Rose mentioned you may leave before our event."

"So much is going on."

Sarah frowned. "You are part of the success of the Historical Society for Female Curators. You should attend."

"I will think about it, but don't plan on me being there."

The ladies looked disappointed. Rose stated, "We are here for you."

She knew they were and was grateful.

THOMAS SAT IN the drawing room with his mother. He'd spent the night, but she'd given him space, not pushing to talk. That was always his mother's way. Eventually, he asked, "Why didn't you tell me?"

His mother sighed. "I didn't know until Alice was about three. I ran into Lisbeth, and we both knew I deduced that she was your child."

"I still don't understand why you didn't write to me."

A sigh escaped his mother. "Your letters after Lisbeth returned were so angry. I could feel the hostility and buried deep down the sadness, but around the same time I found out about Alice, your letters changed. You'd just had your first famous discovery in Syria. It was the ruins of an ancient library. You were so excited and even happy. I feared if I told you, you'd run back here and make yourself miserable."

"She was my daughter," he bit out.

His mother reached over and squeezed his hand, "I know, and it ate at me every day, but I also didn't want you to destroy your life. Lisbeth has always been the one thing you wanted more than anything else. If you came back, you still couldn't have her. And Alice would be another person you were denied."

"I'm still so angry at both of you."

"I'm sorry, Thomas."

He couldn't hate his mother forever. Thomas nodded. Relief seemed to fill her face, but then she frowned. "Why did you marry Lisbeth?"

Thomas groaned. "Because I was angry."

His mother frowned at him. "You married her because you love her and want a life with her and her children."

He didn't deny it but said, "I've made a mess of things."

She nodded. "You have, but you can still fix it. Do you love her? If so, admit it to yourself. Once you do, you can figure out what needs to be done next."

Thomas sighed. "Of course, I still love her, but I fear it isn't enough. We've both behaved poorly."

"If you don't try, you'll never know."

He loved Lisbeth and wanted to try. Over the last few hours, he'd come to that realization. Still, Thomas wasn't sure how it would end. He wasn't optimistic. "I want to work things out with her."

She beamed at him. "Before you leave, I wanted to provide you with some letters you received."

Thomas watched as she walked to a table where a large bundle of mail was. She brought it back and shrugged. "They are admirers, I'm assuming. Except for this one. Try to be rational, no matter what it says."

Intrigued, he looked at the letter on top of the pile. It was from the Earl of Adnin, Lisbeth's brother. He opened it and read.

Easton,

I expect you to call upon me right away.

Adnin

He scoffed, sensing the man's condescending tone. Thomas

rose. "Thank you. If you will excuse me."

"Thomas, don't do anything reckless."

He was already stalking out the door.

Less than an hour later, his hack driver stopped in front of the Earl of Adnin's townhouse, the place he'd grown up in with Lisbeth. Fury roared within him. This was the man who'd made Lisbeth leave him in Tuscany. He paid the driver and knocked on the front door.

He didn't let the butler speak, but walked in. "Please let Adnin know Thomas Easton is here to see him."

The butler was not the man Thomas had grown up with, but someone younger. "Mr. Easton, I'm not sure he is in."

He walked to the drawing room, which he was so familiar with. "I will wait."

Standing in the room, a dozen memories flashed in his mind. The previous Earl and Countess of Adnin had allowed him to spend time with Lisbeth, he suspected, to keep her occupied. They'd formed an instant connection. It was not normal for the child of a housekeeper to have so much freedom, but no matter how rot the previous earl was with money, he had been kind.

Adnin stalked in, his eyes glittering with anger. "I wasn't sure you would show your face here."

Thomas glared back at him. "How could you allow your sister to make such a sacrifice?"

"How could you compromise her?"

He must know everything, Thomas realized. Adnin bit out, "I don't know how you convinced her to marry you, but I will get it annulled."

Dark laughter from him. "You don't have that power. I could buy you ten times over."

Adnin charged at him, throwing a punch and hitting him in the jaw. Thomas responded, striking him in the eye, causing his head to snap back. Adnin grabbed him, and they crashed into a cart before tumbling to the ground and tussling.

"You ass," Thomas hissed.

"You disreputable—"

The rest of the sentence was silenced by water being thrown at them. Thomas looked up to see an angry Lisbeth and a shocked Benson. He and Adnin froze. She glowered at them. "What is wrong with the two of you? You are grown men."

"Lisbeth—" Adnin started, still clutching the front of Thomas's shirt.

She shook her head. "No. I don't need this."

Thomas smirked, and then she glared at him. "And you, if you planned to enjoy all the vices of London, you should not have married me."

With that, she spun around, her skirts swirling around her. Her footsteps thundered down the foyer and out the front door. Benson shook his head and hurried after her. Thomas and Adnin released each other, both moving to sitting positions on the floor.

"End the marriage," Adnin demanded.

Thomas sat there, the last bit of his apprehension of trying with Lisbeth disappearing. He'd been acting like a fool. What was he doing? "I love her."

Adnin's eyes widened. "You haven't been behaving that way."

"I was upset about Alice, but I want to make things right."

The man, whom he didn't want as his brother-in-law, said, "She didn't have a choice."

Thomas nodded. Adnin added, "If you hurt her, I will give you another thrashing."

He scowled. "I gave you a thrashing."

Adnin snorted.

Chapter Twenty-One

LISBETH LOOKED AROUND her small study, trying to decide if there was anything else she needed to do before she left for the country. Thomas still hadn't returned, but she couldn't wait any longer. She needed space. Alice was upset with her that they were missing the event on the epic, but she didn't want to face all of society when she didn't even know where her husband was.

The newspapers certainly did. They'd been giddily sharing his whereabouts and antics for the last few days. She stood, stretching. It was later than she realized. Lisbeth stepped out into the hallway and frowned. Light was coming from the drawing room. She walked to the doorway, and her brows shot up in surprise to find Thomas sitting there, frowning at the fire.

Her dress must have made a rustling sound because Thomas's gaze flicked to her. Their eyes connected, and they studied each other silently. As if remembering himself, he stood. "I thought you were already asleep, or I would have come to find you."

Thomas had a dark purple bruise on his jaw. She grimaced. It was likely a result of his scuffle with Justin. She pursed her lips and then said, "I'm leaving tomorrow and taking Alice and Jeremy with me."

He frowned. Her eyes sparked with anger. "You can't think I would stay while you make a fool of yourself, me, and the children."

Thomas ran his hands through his hair. He looked rumpled and scruffy. Her heart clenched, wondering if she stepped closer, if he would smell like perfume. Some of the gossip sheets had hinted at him carousing. It didn't matter; their union made a mockery of the institution of marriage.

"Can we sit and talk?" he asked.

What was he up to? Reluctantly, she nodded. Lisbeth sat on the sofa, and Thomas took a seat in a wingback chair. "I've behaved abominably."

Lisbeth snorted. "You wed me and then left to spend your days embroiled in vice. You have made me look like a fool."

"Most of the men I spent time with think I'm simply enjoying my celebrity status."

Did he really think that? She leaned forward. "Have you not read any of the papers? People are betting about why you married and then abandoned me."

A stricken look filled his face. "Lisbeth, I'm sorry. I've been so angry."

"We need to get an annulment or live a separate life."

Lisbeth meant the words, but she'd be lying if they didn't cause her pain. Yes, she'd hurt him, but he'd made her pay for it. No more. Thomas quietly said, "I don't want that, Lizzie."

"Don't call me that," she hissed. "Be reasonable. The last few days have been a debacle."

"They have. I was angry, but I want you, Alice, and your son in my life."

Lisbeth shook her head. "You don't even know them."

He joined her on the sofa, and she stiffened, not wanting to be close to the man who'd hurt her so much. "Lisbeth, can we start anew?"

Her eyes widened. "You can't be serious. I'm leaving for the country tomorrow."

"Doesn't your club have an event for the tablets we found?"

"In a month," Lisbeth provided.

Thomas stood and paced. "Don't leave."

Lisbeth looked up at him, confused. "I can't stay here."

"I will stop with all the revelry and craziness."

Lisbeth threw her hands up in the air. "Why? What does it matter?"

He was quiet for a moment. He ran his hands through his dark brown-red hair. Thomas turned back to her, his eyes serious. "I love you, Lizzie. I think we would be making a mistake if we don't try."

She stood and faced him, her anger evident. "You told me you hate me, Thomas. That you want other women to frequent your bed. I understand why, but I can't stay or keep my children around this chaos. We will find a way for you to be in Alice's life."

"There is no one else I want but you. I don't want you and the children to leave. I want a life with you. It is all I've ever wanted."

Deep sadness coursed through her because she understood his feelings. They'd been denied so much. Even though she was angry, Lisbeth couldn't stop herself from pressing her hand to his cheek. "There's been too much hurt. Sometimes, no matter how much you love someone, it isn't enough."

"Allow me one month to convince you otherwise," he said quietly.

"It isn't a good idea. The anger you have for me is still there, and again, I don't blame you."

He grabbed her hand and held it. "Rose and my mother have allowed me to think of it differently. I'm still angry, but I understand why you did it."

Lisbeth could still remember how hopeless she felt when she left him in Tuscany and then found out she was pregnant. "I didn't have many options."

"I know, and I hate that I couldn't fix that for you."

She looked at him. "We were so young and full of big dreams. My decision wasn't a choice; it was a necessity."

He ran his hand along her back, comforting her. Lisbeth wanted to lean into him. She was so tired.

"Give me a chance."

She straightened and stepped away. "You've barely been here."

"We deserve a real opportunity to make our marriage work. I can't change that I forced you to wed me. I'm ashamed that I did that, especially because of what happened with your first marriage. I've been sitting here thinking about that. I've done the same thing that your father and Justin asked of you."

Guilt covered his face. He had. They'd both hurt each other so much. She just didn't see them coming back from it.

"Give me a month. You can stay for your club's event, and if you decide after that we won't still work, then we can figure out how to separate."

She bit her lip, and he added, "There is a love so deep between us, and maybe you are right that it doesn't mean we should be together, but shouldn't we at least try?"

Lisbeth did love Thomas. She always had. Eventually, she said, "A month, and that is it."

He smiled. "A month to learn about you, Alice, and Jeremy."

"Also, a month to see if you can truly forgive me for not telling you about our daughter."

Pain slashed across his face. He didn't debate the point with her but said, "Agreed. I think I will get some rest so I can start fresh tomorrow."

She nodded. "I will stay down here for a little longer."

Lisbeth watched him leave and then sat down on the sofa again. Could they weather all of this? She was scared to have hope, but it was trying desperately to flare within her.

THOMAS SAT IN the garden with Lisbeth. He was nervous. She

wanted them to tell Alice and Jeremy, together, that they were staying in London. The children burst out of the terrace doors, and the governess closed them, waiting inside. Lisbeth had asked Miss Ashby to give them some privacy.

Jeremy's face lit up when he saw Thomas. Alice stumbled to a stop and glared at him. Thomas wondered if one's heart could truly shatter. He reminded himself that they all needed time. Still, he'd missed so much of his daughter's life. Jeremy skipped towards him. "Hello, Mr. Easton."

He smiled. "Please call me Thomas."

Alice slowly made her way to them. Thomas studied her. While she had his hair coloring and eyes, he saw so much of Lisbeth's personality in her. Lisbeth was defiant and rambunctious as a child. He often speculated that he'd been allowed to play with her because her parents hoped it would tire her out.

Lisbeth pointed to the seats for Alice and Jeremy to join them. "I have great news. We are staying at least until after the Historical Society for Female Curators event on the epic."

Jeremy grinned and continued to stare adoringly at Thomas. He liked the boy. Actually, he liked both the children, even if Alice wasn't sure of him.

"Aren't you excited, Alice?" Lisbeth asked.

She shrugged. Thomas said, "I would like to learn more about both of you. Your mother explained you both have an interest in history."

Jeremy nodded. "I want to be an explorer like you."

He smiled. "Perhaps someday we can go on an adventure together."

Alice glared at him. "You will never be my father."

Thomas had rationally understood that this would be painful, but not how much. He gulped, as if he couldn't speak.

Lisbeth warned, "Alice."

"It's fine," Thomas was finally able to say.

Alice grabbed Jeremy's hand. "I want to play."

Jeremy seemed uninterested, and Lisbeth said, "Both of you

go and play. We will have a treat in a little bit."

They rushed off farther into the garden, chasing each other. He glanced at Lisbeth's devastated face. It was precisely how he felt.

"I'm sorry, Thomas."

He wanted this. "What we need is time to become acquainted with each other. We will be fine."

She nodded but was uncertain. Lisbeth said, "Alice was very close with Nicholas. I don't want to hurt you, so please tell me if you don't want to know certain things."

"I want to know everything about her," he said, determined.

"He died when Alice was eight, and it was tough for her. Nicholas doted on her and was affectionate with both children. He'd grown up in a very cold household. He didn't want that for Alice or Jeremy. Most of his free time was spent teaching and playing with them."

"While I want to hate him, your husband seemed like a good man."

Lisbeth nodded. "We became close friends, but there was always a sadness that hung over him. He'd lost his true love, Margaret, and I'm not sure he ever recovered."

"The *ton* can certainly make a mess of life," Thomas muttered.

She nodded in agreement. His wife looked beautiful today. He perused her form, unable to stop himself. Lisbeth was dressed in a green gown, and it accentuated her slender waist and firm, small breasts. A surge of lust coursed through him. He imagined his hands sliding along her body.

Her face heated as if she could sense his thoughts. They were trying to salvage their relationship, and he couldn't stop thinking about touching her. Unable to stop himself, he said, "You look lovely today, Lisbeth."

A hum of attraction surged between them. Her eyes connected with his. "I don't think we should be intimate until we figure out what we are doing."

Thomas wanted Lisbeth, but would not rush her. "When you are ready, I will be."

She nodded, her gaze momentarily flicking to his mouth before going back to his eyes. He smiled softly. "I want you as much as I did when I was a boy. I think I will always crave you."

Lisbeth gulped, seemingly flustered. He grabbed her hand and kissed the top of it. "But I can wait until you are ready. I forced you into this marriage; I won't force you into my bed. I want you to come willingly."

She flushed. "We've already done that."

"Next time you are in my arms, I don't want it to be because we are both angry."

They stared at one another, and then Thomas broke his gaze and looked at Alice and Jeremy. He wanted Lisbeth physically, but more importantly, he wanted everything. Thomas wanted her heart, her friendship, and a life with her, Alice, and Jeremy.

Chapter Twenty-Two

LISBETH STOOD IN the library, enjoying a brandy and flipping through the pages of a book. It was far too late to be awake, but she couldn't sleep. Maybe another story would help. She stood and walked to one of the bookshelves, hoping to find something that would keep her interest or help her fall asleep.

"You have the same idea as me," Thomas said.

He was in trousers and a hastily buttoned-up shirt. Lisbeth gasped at the sight he made. She still couldn't get over how different he was from the boy she left all those years ago. He was all hard muscle and temptation, she thought. Warmth flowed through her.

Thomas smiled at her. "You are ogling me, duchess."

She flushed. "I hate it when you call me that."

He winced. "Noted. I will refrain from doing so. Why, though?"

Lisbeth gave him a pointed look. "You only call me that when you are angry with me."

He frowned, and she insisted. "It's true."

A sigh escaped him. "I can't call you Lizzie or duchess?"

She loved that he called her Lizzie, probably too much. It did something to her heart. "I don't mind the first one."

"You will always be my Lizzie."

He stepped closer to her, running his knuckles up and down

her arm. She shivered, something delicious coursing through her. Flustered, she moved back. "You are too much and so large."

He laughed. "You don't like how I've changed."

She shook her head. "I didn't say that. I just never envisioned you'd fill out so much."

A smirk flashed across his face. It gave him a rakish appearance. She sighed. "You were always so bookish and slender."

Thomas nodded. "It wasn't intentional, but I think it came with the work I was doing."

"I can't believe you're so famous."

"It was not my grand plan," he explained.

Lisbeth, unable to control her tongue, said, "You've certainly been enjoying your success recently."

He was quiet for a moment. "Everything I've ever accomplished, it was you who was always on my mind. I would wonder what it would be like if you were with me or what you thought, and if it ever made you regret leaving me."

Antiquities had been their dream together, and he'd accomplished far more than she ever imagined on his own. "I did follow your escapades, and when I was alone sometimes, I would wonder what it would have been like to be with you."

He hoarsely said, "I'm glad I wasn't alone with my torturous thoughts."

They stood there awkwardly, and then finally Thomas asked, "Are you tired?"

Lisbeth shook her head. He smiled and sat in a wingback chair. "Sit and talk with me."

Hesitation filled her. She wasn't sure why—probably because so much had happened in the last week.

"How am I supposed to show you we are meant to be if we don't talk?"

"You need to decide if you can forgive me. We can't tell Alice until she is older," she said, but sat.

Thomas nodded, and sadness seemed to settle on his shoulder. She frowned. "I wish things could have been—"

He shook his head. "We need to move past wishing things were different. They weren't. We won't survive if we keep dwelling on what could have been."

Since the first moment Lisbeth had seen Thomas in Syria, she'd been lost in what-ifs. It was easier said than done. Thomas squeezed her hand. "Tell me about Alice and Jeremy. Would you like a glass of wine?"

Lisbeth nodded, and he rose, heading to a small table with a wine decanter and glasses. An odd sensation pricked her skin. This all felt oddly normal. She kept the thought to herself and took a wine glass from Thomas before he settled back into his chair.

She smiled. "Alice is eleven. She is rebellious and curious. A dangerous combination, but I wouldn't want it any other way. She loves history. She is fascinated by the finds that are being discovered close to the Amazon River."

He took a sip of his drink and smiled. "I've never been there before."

Her eyes widened. She'd assumed he had. Thomas added, "I've been to Africa, America, Asia, and the Arabian Peninsula, but never there. I wish I had. It could have been my way to win her over."

"You will eventually," Lisbeth assured him and then added, "She probably doesn't want to betray Nicholas."

Thomas took a large drink of wine. She said, "I'm sorry."

He frowned at her. "Stop saying that."

She was, though, even if she couldn't have done anything different. He sighed and said, "What about Jeremy?"

"He is such a sweet boy and a rule follower. Alice is always trying to get him in trouble, but he normally resists. He loves history as well, but he is more fascinated by modern inventions. He is very excited about the Great Exhibition coming to London soon."

"I'm interested in attending as well. Do you think that your club will have a display?"

Lisbeth thought they deserved a spot, but she wasn't sure what would happen. "Someone from the Royal Commission for the Great Exhibition will be at the event for the epic. I'm hoping we will be granted our place then."

Thomas frowned. "Why were you going to leave London if the event on the epic was so important?"

She flushed, and Thomas shook his head. "I'm sorry my behavior has been so atrocious, and I forced us to wed. I wasn't myself. I would take it all back if I could."

It comforted her that he was apologetic, and she said, "We are starting anew, correct?"

He nodded. "I want only to spend time with you and the children. I want to show you and them that we can be a family."

She still wasn't sure, but the hope that she thought was dead was growing.

⋙✳⋘

THOMAS SAT IN the townhouse study, reviewing what he would need to do to settle in London. Rose's father, Benjamin, was away from the city but still in England. He'd need to make final plans with him. He wouldn't be traveling for the foreseeable future. Thomas suspected Benjamin would return to Syria.

Lisbeth had mentioned that the Historical Society for Female Curators hoped to partner with Benjamin. They wanted a lady studying history to spend time at Benjamin's main excavation site in Syria. One of their board members, Lady Esme, who studied ancient civilizations, would be the first lady to try out the idea.

He smiled. Benjamin would be able to teach another group of young adults all about antiquities. Thomas also needed to write to Rafe and Keaton and let his friends know he was staying in London. He wasn't sure where Rafe was, but Keaton should be in Latakia.

The real question, though, was what he would do now that

he was settling in London. Thomas supposed he could reach out to Anderson, and they could create some new serials. He wasn't sure that was what he wanted. It would certainly make money, but he didn't enjoy the fame that went with it.

Thomas, Benjamin, and Rose were all relatively wealthy, so he had time to decide, but he was never one to be idle. He frowned, wondering if he was getting ahead of himself. He hoped not. He glanced at the doorway and spied Alice peeking in on him. She quickly hid behind the wall.

"I know you are there," he said, somewhat amused and also excited that she was interested in what he was doing.

An annoyed sigh filtered into the room, followed by her entering. She said, "This is my father's study."

Her words felt like a punch to his chest, but he didn't let it show. "It is a wonderful space to work."

She nodded and pointed to a wingback chair. "I used to sit here and read. On the bottom shelf behind you are multiple books on ancient tales. I would read one while he worked."

Thomas asked, "Would you like one now?"

Alice looked conflicted, and he said, "Sometimes it is nice to do something familiar and think of the person you lost."

She nodded jerkily. "The second book is about the Hanging Gardens of Babylon. Can you hand me that one, please?"

This was a positive step for their relationship. Thomas grabbed the book. "Do you know that it is suspected to be in Mesopotamia, which is governed by the—"

"The Ottoman Empire," Alice interjected.

He smiled. "Yes."

She grinned at him, and a kinship passed between them. Alice settled into the chair, and he did his best to focus on his plans, when all he wanted to do was ask the child dozens of questions. "Where is your brother?"

Alice laughed. "Our governess made him stay and study his math longer."

"I hated math too."

"It isn't that hard," she said, rolling her eyes.

She sounded so much like a young Lisbeth. He stared at her, and she shifted uncomfortably in her chair. Thomas, not wanting to frighten her, remarked, "You sounded just like your mother."

"You grew up together?"

He nodded. She went back to her reading. Thomas looked down at his plans again, but didn't make any further progress because his mother entered the room. "Thomas—"

She'd stopped mid-sentence, staring back and forth between him and Alice, speechless. Her eyes started to water, and Thomas hoped she wouldn't cry. Alice would be confused.

The girl jumped up and she ran to his mother, hugging her. "Mrs. Louise, I didn't know you were visiting."

Now it was Thomas's turn to be speechless. Generations of his family stood before him. His mother kissed Alice's head. "It was a surprise. I needed to bring Thomas something."

Alice frowned. "How do you know him?"

Thomas answered, "She is my mother."

"You are, Mrs. Louise?" the girl said as if she didn't believe him.

"Yes, I am."

Alice looked at him as if that had changed something. His mother carried a small bag, and she pulled letters from it. He groaned silently, suspecting it was more messages from admirers. "Alice, would you go retrieve Jeremy for me? I have some sweets for both of you."

The girl darted from the room, and his mother burst into tears. Thomas rose and folded her into his arms. She sniffled. "I shouldn't be so overcome with emotion. I don't think I ever fathomed the two of you in the same room. I'm sorry I didn't tell you until now. I should have."

Thomas appreciated her words and squeezed her tighter. "Lisbeth and I agreed to not dwell on the what-ifs. I think that would be good for us as well."

She cried some more but finally took a deep breath. "I need

to stop before Alice and Jeremy return."

He gruffly said, "You do."

She pulled back from him and wiped her eyes. "Enough of that. I brought all this ridiculous mail you've been receiving at my home, but there is one that I'm concerned about that I wanted to point out."

Thomas frowned, taken aback by her words. "What do you mean?"

She pulled a letter from the pile and put the rest on the desk. "This one is addressed from your wife."

He blinked. "From Lizzie?"

"Is it Lizzie now? I hope that means your relationship is improving?" his mother said with a raised brow.

Thomas flushed. "It was a slip, but we agreed to work on it over the next month and go from there."

"I'm glad," she said and then handed him the letter.

He frowned and glanced down at it. It was from C. He could tell from the floral drawings and the scented perfume. It was addressed to him, but stated it was from his wife. He opened the letter and read.

Thomas,

You are returning to me. When will I see you? I knew if I were patient, we would be together.

Yours,
C

He handed it to his mother, and she glanced at him, alarmed. "Have you heard from this woman before? Do you get these types of letters often? I'm concerned for Lisbeth."

He shook his head. "This person sends me letters that are the most intense, but I've never met her, and I don't even know her name."

She frowned, "Be careful."

Thomas hadn't worried about any of the strange letters he

received, but now his mind went to Lisbeth, Alice, Jeremy, and his mother. "If I receive any more, I will have someone look into it."

She kissed his cheek. "Thank you. I don't want to worry."

Alice and Jeremy burst through the doorway. The young boy grinned. "Mrs. Louise, Alice said you brought us something."

His mother laughed, and Thomas had to take a breath to control his emotions. This moment felt so right, even with every bad thing that had happened in the last few weeks. A genuine smile spread across his face as he watched his mother talk with Alice and Jeremy, pulling treats from her bag.

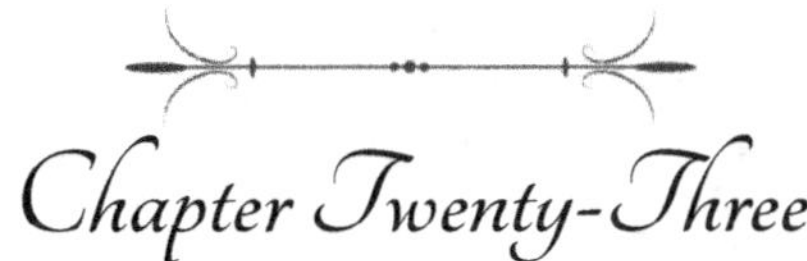

Chapter Twenty-Three

LISBETH WALKED INTO the research room of Seely House. Rose was hunched over an ancient clay tablet. "I thought you deciphered the tablets already."

Rose glanced up. "I did, but I don't have Lord Hawley to review my work before the event, so I'm double-checking with the key he provided me."

Her eyes widened. "Hawley gave you his key?"

She smiled. "He is out of the country working on some project for the London Society of Antiquaries, so he entrusted me with his work."

"I find that shocking."

Rose frowned. "I don't think Lord Hawley dislikes our club as much as his other associates."

She smiled. "Perhaps."

Her friend studied her. "How are things?"

"Thomas has returned. We are going to try to spend time together over the next thirty days and decide after that."

Rose beamed, swinging her legs excitedly. Lisbeth rolled her eyes. "I find a loved-up Rose Calvert a bit much."

The lady in question grinned impishly. "Is it strange how happy I am to be married to Augustus?"

It wasn't. The Duke of Sinclair loved antiquities as much as Rose. It was clear he was prepared to adjust his life so that his wife could continue to pursue her work in deciphering ancient texts. Lisbeth wasn't surprised; he had the means to do so.

"When is the wedding?" Lisbeth asked.

Rose groaned and dramatically threw her arms and head down on the table. Lisbeth giggled.

"Not soon enough. I adore Augustus's mother, but the second and official wedding won't be for a few more months, and it will be a grand affair."

"I suspected so. He is the wealthiest duke in all of England. I'm not surprised."

Rose sat back up and stretched. "I spoke with Thomas a few days ago."

Lisbeth smiled affectionately at her. "He told me."

Her friend continued, "I told him that he was behaving abominably and tried to make him understand that as a woman, you didn't have a choice."

"It was still wrong," Lisbeth said quietly.

"It was also wrong that you had no other choices all those years ago."

Lisbeth smiled at her friend, grateful for her support. "Thomas has said that we can't dwell on the what-ifs. We need to move forward."

Rose nodded. "I agree, but don't shy away from the hard questions or keep it bottled up."

"You are so wise," Lisbeth said.

Her friend laughed. "Please be sure to tell Augustus that."

Sarah popped her head into the room. "Are we ready to discuss the event on the epic? We are all in the office."

Both she and Rose made their way to the room. Rose looped her arm through hers while they walked. "I think all will turn out well."

Lisbeth swallowed the lump in her throat. Trying her best to keep the conversation light, she asked, "Who is this Rose Calvert, full of such optimism?"

They both laughed. The other Historical Society for Female

Curators board members were chatting in the sitting area. They looked up, and all smiled at her. Esme said, "I'm so glad you are staying for the event."

Lisbeth said, "Me too."

Addie's eyes sparkled with excitement. "I've heard through a friend that the Royal Commission for the Great Exhibition is quite excited about the epic."

"I can't believe we've done something no other antiquities club has managed."

Diana glanced at Rose, beaming. "Well, it was mostly you."

She shook her head. "No, we've all accomplished this."

Addie turned serious. "We can't get comfortable. We need more artifacts to display."

Diana laid a list of potential exhibits and partnerships on the table between the ladies. "You will see there are a good number of options from Asia, everything from China to Syria."

"It is such a large area."

Diana then pointed to a man in northern England. "I've been corresponding with Sir William Halethorpe. He is an avid collector of artifacts from the Iron Age. He plans to allow us to show pieces at Seely House. I believe that will make for a nice, smaller exhibit."

Lisbeth studied the artifacts from Syria. There was a large statue, more maps, and more minor artifacts. She wondered if they could work with Benjamin on what remained in the cave system. She was confident that they'd sealed it enough.

"The tunnels also house other relics."

Esme's eyes brightened. "Mr. Calvert said that we would work there during my stay."

Lisbeth smiled at Esme. She was the youngest of all of them but had somehow convinced her parents that she should be allowed to study abroad in Syria. Of course, she'd be traveling with a chaperone—not that Benjamin would allow anything to happen to her.

"Be careful. Thomas and I had quite a scare due to the flash flooding that occurred in the area. The opening to the cavity where the artifacts are is rather small."

"Can the opening be widened with black powder?" Addie asked.

Sarah Martin looked at her, horrified. Addie sighed. "What have I said now?"

Addie and Diana were vital to their club, but they had the least experience with excavation sites and artifact care. Sarah explained, "It could damage the cave system and the artifacts."

Lisbeth added. "The villagers do not want anyone using black powder in the caves. They are considered sacred to them."

Addie nodded, not arguing. Unlike other clubs, they'd implemented a policy to abide by local beliefs at excavation sites. It was part of their plan to partner with owners of antiquities instead of outright purchasing all artifacts.

"Is everything going according to plan for your trip?" Lisbeth asked Esme.

She grinned. "My family has asked me multiple times if I still want to go, but yes. I'm very excited."

Addie stated, "And Sarah will be going on our first grand tour cruise. Instead of stopping in Tuscany for two weeks. They will stop in Sardinia for three weeks and work with Count De Messina, an associate of Diana's, on cataloging artifacts there and bringing some back to England."

"Messina has been wonderful. He is in England for business and will also return on the *SS Lark* with Sarah," Diana added.

Addie's eyes filled with excitement. "Have you met him, Sarah? I spoke with him at a ball. He is rather swoony."

A prim and pinched expression crossed Sarah's face. "I don't care if he is round or handsome. My interest lies with the cruise for ladies and cataloging of the artifacts."

They all smiled at her. Sarah was entirely devoted to the study of artifacts and never deviated from the topic. It benefited their club.

"I imagine he will be at the ball Augustus's mother is hosting," Rose pointed out.

"Perfect. I don't believe our group of ladies will need much from him during the voyage or our stay in Sardinia. Still, I should at least introduce myself as the lead of our trip," Sarah said.

Addie giggled. "He is very attractive."

Sarah looked at her, perplexed. "It matters not to me."

Lisbeth shook her head. "Let's discuss the plans for the epic."

THOMAS SAT IN Lisbeth's study. He called it that because it disconcerted him to call it the duke's, but that was what it was. Lisbeth wasn't entirely wrong when she stated he needed to think about what it meant to have a life with her. Her deceased husband's title surrounded them.

It unsettled him at times, and he needed to figure out a way to work through his feelings. This home was Lisbeth, Alice, and Jeremy's space. Thomas couldn't ask them to leave it. Hell, someday, this study, along with the whole house, would be handed off to Jeremy. He was the duke now, even if he was a child.

Thomas had been pondering the idea of building a country estate, a place where Lisbeth, Jeremy, and Alice could escape to. He wanted something that he could give them. Not that Lisbeth or the children needed anything. He frowned. How did he fit into this life?

Morrison stepped into the study. "Mr. Easton, you have a visitor."

He lifted a brow. "Are you sure I do? It isn't for Her Grace?"

The butler appeared slightly offended to be questioned. Thomas supposed he shouldn't have asked. It was, after all, the man's job to know who was needed. "Sir, it is Lord Harston and Mr. Martin."

He frowned, confused. It was the president and vice president of the London Society of Antiquaries. "Please escort them to the drawing room. I will meet them in there."

Morrison nodded and departed. He wondered what the men wanted. From time to time, he associated with Lord Hawley and provided artifacts to the club. Still, because they'd refused Rose entry, he'd never joined them. Now, he certainly wouldn't. His wife was part of their competing club.

He took his time making his way to the drawing room. The men who'd given Lisbeth and Rose's club problems could wait for a bit. Thomas smirked, amused and impressed, thinking that the London Society of Antiquaries must be very worried about their club if they were visiting him.

Eventually, Thomas entered the room, and Mr. Martin and Lord Harston turned to face him.

"It is so nice to meet you in person, Mr. Easton," Martin said, smiling.

He nodded. "Thank you. Yes, I think until now, our communication has only been through letters."

Harston didn't seem nearly as happy to meet with him. He stood with his legs wide and his arms folded. "I'm Lord Harston."

Thomas didn't bother to bow. He already didn't like this man for various reasons he'd heard from Lisbeth and Rose. This was the man who had attempted to hold the ancient map hostage so Rose couldn't finish deciphering the club's cuneiform epic.

Harston turned a blotchy red, offended by his lack of deference. Thomas motioned to the wingback chairs and sofa. "Can I get you both something to drink?"

They shook their heads but sat. Thomas joined them, sitting in an elegant navy wingback chair. Martin seemed nervous. Lisbeth had mentioned that his daughter was part of the Historical Society for Female Curators, but Martin had never attended any of their events. Apparently, Harston went to every one of them to be a nuisance.

"Now that you are settling in London, Mr. Easton, we'd like to offer you a permanent lecture position at the London Society of Antiquaries," Martin said.

Thomas should have been shocked, but he knew that even though Harston was looking at him with contempt, if he accepted a position with this men's club, it would be mainly to their benefit.

"Would there be a conflict because my wife is part of the Historical Society for Female Curators?"

Harston's mouth twisted in distaste. "We'd assumed you'd ask her to step down from her position at her club."

Ahh…that was their game. They wanted to use him in hopes Lisbeth would leave her role at her club. Thomas looked at Martin. "Isn't your daughter part of the Historical Society for Female Curators?"

"Yes, but she isn't a duchess," Harston snapped.

Even Martin flinched at the condescending man's tone. Martin cleared his throat. "My daughter has long ago decided her sole focus in life would be the study of artifacts. She is particularly interested in Roman and Renaissance art. She doesn't frequent societal events or cause gossip."

"What your daughter and the other ladies have achieved to date is quite remarkable. I would think, as the president of an antiquities club, you'd be interested in their work."

The man shifted uncomfortably, but Harston changed the subject, oblivious to the awkwardness swirling around them. "It wouldn't look right if she stayed on with the Historical Society for Female Curators. I mean, it is already questionable that she is marrying a commoner—"

Thomas glared at the man, and the rest of his words died. Harston flushed and pulled a handkerchief from a pocket, dabbing at his forehead. Martin stood. "Please consider it, Mr. Easton."

Harston joined him. Thomas shook his head. "I have to decline respectfully. I would never ask my wife to resign from her club."

Harston's mouth became pinched. Mr. Martin didn't seem as concerned but said, "I would love to meet you for a drink."

Thomas could like Martin. Not Harston, he was an ass. He nodded, "Send me a missive. Good day, gentleman."

He sat and snorted. Harston was the wrong person to convince him to join the men-only club. He wouldn't participate because of their comments about Lisbeth. Still, he shuddered because even if there were no Lisbeth, Rose would be furious if he joined.

Thomas wondered why Martin didn't visit his daughter's club. It seemed strange. He imagined all families had their problems. Deciding not to work with the London Society of Antiquaries was no issue for Thomas. He was content with that decision. Still, he needed to find something to do with his time.

Jeremy burst through the doorway. "Thomas, will you go out in the garden with us? We are free from our studies. The governess said we can spend the rest of the afternoon outside."

Alice stood behind her brother, not nearly as excited, but she was there. It was a start. He smiled. "I would like nothing more. Did you know that most of this area sits on top of Roman ruins?"

The young boy jumped excitedly. "I didn't. Did you, Alice?"

The girl shook her head. Thomas leaned close to both of them. "Maybe we can find signs of the Romans."

Jeremy's eyes grew round, and Alice scoffed. He headed toward the door. "Let's explore."

Chapter Twenty-Four

LISBETH STEPPED THROUGH the doors onto the terrace and discovered Thomas, Alice, and Jeremy on their knees studying the stone wall and a few pieces of rock. Jeremy's eyes went wide. "Did we just make a discovery?"

Alice snorted. "It is make-believe."

"But it could be real. Thomas said that the whole neighborhood of Mayfair was built on Roman ruins."

Lisbeth smiled. "It is true."

All three of them turned to look at her, still on their knees. Jeremy looked at Alice triumphantly. "See."

Thomas chuckled. "We won't ever know, but how exciting is it to speculate?"

Alice smiled at him, and Lisbeth's heart equally ached and overflowed with love. She walked towards them. Both Alice's and Jeremy's faces were flushed. She giggled. "How long have you been exploring?"

Thomas shrugged, "Probably a couple of hours.

"He told us all about how you and he used to explore Mayfair searching for artifacts. Thomas said your first find was an ancient spear."

"Don't you have a spear on your vanity? Is it that one?" Alice asked.

Her eyes flew to Thomas, and she flushed. It was true,

Lisbeth did keep the keepsake in her room. While she'd parted with some of the treasures she and Thomas found as children, she'd never been able to give that one up. It was special.

A brief memory flashed in her mind.

EIGHT-YEAR-OLD LISBETH HELD the book open while Thomas brushed at the item. "Rinse it with water."

Thomas shook his head. "The artifact preservation book explains how to brush off the dirt gently. Hand me the brush."

Lisbeth rolled her eyes. "Here you go, Serious Thomas."

He scowled, jutting his ten-year-old chin out. They both grew quiet as he gently removed the debris. Dirt fell off to reveal a pointy object. Lisbeth quickly flipped to the pages at the back of the book, which contained pictures of artifacts. There was a whole section on weapons. They both looked on as she flicked one page at a time until they both gasped.

It was right there, a Roman spear. Their eyes grew round, and they jumped up from their spot on the ground before spinning each other in circles. Lisbeth smiled widely. "Our first find."

Thomas snorted. "Probably our last."

She shook her head. "No, our first of many. Thomas and Lisbeth, the next famous explorers!"

He smiled at her. "I like the sound of that."

Lisbeth grabbed the spear and shoved it in her skirt pocket, racing away. Thomas chased after her. "You have to store it in a safe spot, not in your pocket, Lizzie."

"MOTHER?" ALICE PRODDED.

She smiled. "It is the one we found. It was mine and Thomas's first discovery."

It was one of her favorite memories of them. Lisbeth sensed

he'd been remembering the exact moment, too. They smiled softly at each other. Jeremy gasped, his eyes going wide. "Did you find it at Uncle Justin's home? Can we go there?"

Thomas grimaced. Lisbeth suspected it was because the bruise on his jaw was starting to fade. Lisbeth glanced up at the blue sky before turning back. "Why don't we take a walk in Hyde Park? Maybe we can explore there."

Both Alice and Jeremy bounced on their heels, excited. Lisbeth laughed. "Go ask your governess if she wants to join."

They raced off, and Thomas joined her. "You kept our spearhead, Lizzie."

She smiled at him. "Our first find."

Thomas brushed a loose curl off her cheek, and his innocent touch made warmth flare within her. She didn't step away. His gaze drifted to her lips, and she ran her tongue along the bottom one. His eyes flared with desire. "Are you trying to tempt me?"

She wasn't sure, but it felt so lovely to be standing next to him and gazing at him this way. Thomas leaned closer to her, and he nuzzled her neck. She lifted her hand and almost grabbed his jacket, but remembered herself, stepping back. She smiled tentatively. "We should wait in the foyer."

Lisbeth headed towards the terrace doors. He called out, "Lizzie."

She turned. His eyes still glowed with want. "I'm here when you are ready. You are the only woman I want. The only one since the moment you walked into the café in Latakia."

"I just need a little more time."

She made her way through the terrace doors and into the foyer. A floral letter rested on a plate where mail was kept. Lisbeth picked it up and wrinkled her nose. It smelled of too much perfume. Tearing the top, Lisbeth pulled a paper out, and another one tumbled to the floor. She picked it up.

Her eyes widened, and she gasped. It was a caricature of her and Thomas from a gossip sheet after their wedding was announced. Her face was blacked out, and large cross-out marks were scribbled over her body.

Thomas joined her, concerned. "What is it?"

She handed it to him and opened the letter.

Your Grace,

Leave my husband alone. Thomas Easton is mine.

C

He cursed, and she turned to him, lifting a brow. "Do you have a wife I don't know about?"

He shot her an incredulous look. "No, it is one of my admirers."

"Do you know their name?"

Thomas shook his head. "I only know who it is because it always has the same floral drawing and has an overwhelming sense of perfume."

An uneasiness filled Lisbeth. "Should I be alarmed?"

He frowned. "I will see if Devons can help me hire some investigators. Hopefully, it is some young girl who doesn't know any better."

She nodded, but concern still emanated from both of them.

Alice and Jeremy appeared at the bottom of the stairs. "Miss Ashby doesn't feel well, but we are ready."

Lisbeth smiled. The letters were probably nothing, she told herself. She glanced at Thomas. "Ready?"

"I was going to see Devons."

She looped her arm through his. "You can do that later. I'm sure you are correct, and it is some young fan."

LATER THAT NIGHT, Thomas sat with Lisbeth enjoying an after-dinner drink. He frowned, thinking about the letter she'd received. It seemed like an escalation of the other ones sent to him.

"Why have you turned so serious?" Lisbeth asked.

"I'm worried about the letter. The author, while I was in Syria, sent me multiple missives, always explaining that when I returned to London, we'd marry. I never thought much of it because I never planned on setting foot in the country again."

She took a sip of her wine. "I can't imagine it is more than a young woman who is upset."

"I hope so. I plan to make it a priority though."

"Thank you," Lisbeth said and then added, "You never explained why you came back?"

Thomas looked at his beautiful Lizzie, lifting a brow. "Isn't it obvious?"

A blush streaked across her cheeks.

"I came for you. After we spent that night together, I told myself that was all the closure I needed, but the further I was from you and Latakia, the more I realized one night wasn't enough."

"I'm glad you came back," she admitted.

He glanced at her, skeptical, but she nodded. "I am. Even though the revelation of all these secrets has been difficult, it was for the best."

"Is Alice why you didn't want me to come to London?"

Pain flashed across her face. "I'd already hurt you so much, I was terrified to do it again. The moment I returned, I regretted not telling you. I planned to write you a letter explaining everything."

"Then I showed up."

She nodded. "And now we are married."

He frowned. "I hate the way it all happened. I've wanted you as my wife since I was a boy."

Lisbeth laughed. "I doubt you've wanted me since we were children."

It was true, though. "Almost from the moment we found the spear, I knew I wanted you to be my wife. It felt as if our lives would be full of excitement. At that time, I hadn't grasped that the daughter of an earl couldn't marry the son of a housekeeper."

"But we would have if everything with my father's debt hadn't happened," Lisbeth said, her voice filled with sadness.

Their eyes connected, and Thomas said, "Come here, Lizzie. Let me hold you for a moment. Nothing more than that, I promise."

He was hungry to wrap his arms around her, to feel her head rest along his chest. Thomas held his breath, wondering what she would do. Shocking him, she rose, and he pulled her onto his lap. She laid her head on his chest. They sat there quietly for a moment. Eventually, she said, "It is fine to be angry about everything."

He wasn't. His mind whispered, *liar.* Still, he pushed it away. More than anything, he wanted to be with this woman. She lifted her head and looked at him. "If you keep it all bottled in, it won't help."

"You had no choice," he said before brushing a gentle kiss across her lips. It wasn't one meant to ignite passion, but rather to offer comfort.

She frowned but went back to lying her head on his chest. He stroked her back. Thomas would endure any internal pain to have nights like this. "Mr. Martin and Lord Harston visited me today."

Lisbeth didn't lift her head, but an annoyed sigh escaped her. "What did they want?"

"To offer me a lecture position at the London Society of Antiquaries."

"Is that something you want?" Lisbeth asked.

He didn't want to do it for the London Society of Antiquaries, but it wasn't a bad idea. "I like the idea about teaching regular people about antiquities and excavations. Maybe even children. How excited would we have been if we attended a lecture by an explorer?"

Lisbeth bolted up and began to pace. Excitement seemed to emanate from her. "You could do it for the Historical Society of Female Curators?"

"It is only an idea right now."

She frowned. "We couldn't pay you much."

He smiled at her. "I don't need much or any."

"We'd have to pay you something. I will talk to the board members. Should I?"

He loved this excited Lisbeth. It reminded him of how she was as a girl. Thomas nodded. "Now come back here and sit with me."

Lisbeth rejoined him, and still curious, he asked, "Does Sarah Martin's father support your club?"

"That is a difficult question. He doesn't prevent Sarah from being part of us but also isn't an advocate for her work or the club."

"Why?" Thomas asked.

"I suspect because most of those in higher-up positions at the London Society of Antiquaries are lords or quite wealthy. Mr. Martin is a scholar. I think he worries about us causing trouble."

Thomas snorted. "He should be worried about that."

She playfully smacked his arm, and he laughed.

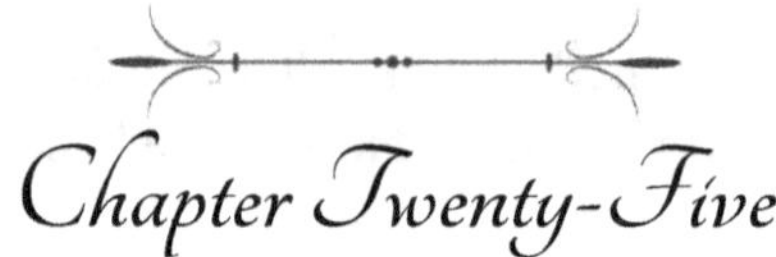

Chapter Twenty-Five

LISBETH TRIED TO ignore the heightened chatter as she stepped into the Duke of Sinclair's theater box with Thomas. It appeared as if the entire place was watching them. Thomas held his hand out to help her step down into the space. He grinned at her, and her heart fluttered. Based on the gasps around her, she suspected it wasn't only her heart.

They'd agreed to attend the theater tonight to help show society that whatever happened at the beginning of their marriage was over. Lisbeth assumed everyone believed her husband was out having a bit of fun to celebrate his status as a famous explorer. The truth was so different.

It amused her in some ways that Thomas seemed so perplexed by his popularity, but it also made her nervous. A young lady in the box next to theirs coyly batted her eyes at him. Instinctively, she looped her arm through his. He glanced down at where they were touching and smiled. The swirl of attraction between them seemed to be intensifying with every day that went by.

"How are you enjoying London, Easton?" Sinclair asked him.

Thomas laughed. "It is not the city I left."

No, he was right about that. So much innovation had occurred. Buildings were being built taller and faster, trains were more common than taking a stagecoach, and London's population had doubled.

"Will you stay in the country?" Sinclair asked him.

They'd not talked about traveling, and she wasn't sure that was possible. Worry filled her, but Thomas seemed to understand. He said, "I think we will be firmly settled in London. Perhaps down the road we will travel somewhere, but for now, making the city my home is my focus."

Warmth filled her that Thomas seemed perfectly fine with staying in London.

"Will you stay in England?" Lisbeth asked Rose.

Sinclair and her friend looked at each other. Rose said, "We aren't sure. I'd like to visit when Esme is in Syria, but I will see how things are after our official wedding."

Easton grinned. "Your first wedding was the best."

Sinclair nodded. "Agreed."

Rose laughed. "Still, Augustus's mother is so excited about the exchange of proper vows."

Bells began to chime, signaling the beginning of the opera. Lisbeth and Thomas settled into seats in the front row of the box. The curtain opened, and she became enthralled with the story. It was about a boy and a girl who grew up together, but then the girl marries another. The man goes mad. Lisbeth leaned towards him. "This reminds me of the Majnun and Layla. I suppose that story plot is in every culture."

"Agree," he said, before grasping one of her hands and threading their fingers together. "Maybe it will end happily."

He brought her hand to his lips, and Lisbeth swore she could hear all the women in the theater sigh. She whispered, "I think people are more interested in watching us than the show."

Thomas smiled. "I don't care as long as I'm with you."

"Still, it would be nice to have a day or night out without so much attention."

He leaned closer, his mouth brushing her ear. "Are you saying you want to be alone with me?"

Her heart started to beat faster. She did want that. "Yes. A day for just us would be lovely."

Thomas turned to stare at her face, studying her intently. The underlying desire that always existed between them raged. Eventually, he said, "Consider it done. I have some ideas."

A few hours later, they sat in the carriage. Lisbeth was exhausted and looking forward to sleep. Thomas had pulled her over onto his lap when the carriage started moving. They'd fallen into this pattern over the last couple of days—gentle kissing and caressing. She felt his shaft push against her bottom, and her core clenched.

Her need for him, which she was doing her best to keep subdued, threatened to bubble over. His hand grasped her hip, and he pushed against her bottom. Again, it was only gentle kisses and touches. Lisbeth looked down into his eyes and she said, "Thomas, will you really kiss me?"

His brows drew together in confusion. "What do you mean?"

"Without restraint."

He groaned and pulled her head down, pressing his lips to hers. She gasped but kissed him back with just as much yearning. Their tongues sparred and pressed against one another. His hand slid up and grasped one of her breasts. She whimpered. "Thomas, please."

He started to slide her skirt up, but then just as suddenly, he deposited her back on the bench on the other side.

Frustration coursed through her. She ached for him. "What are you doing?"

"We've not been intimate since we decided to try again. Our first time won't be in this carriage."

She rolled her eyes, squeezing her legs together, desire still throbbing through her. "This isn't our first time."

He shook his head. "Our next intimate moment won't be in this carriage or tonight."

Lisbeth frowned at him, but Thomas turned serious. "I forced you to marry me. I want our next time not to be rushed and special."

Her ache for him still pulsated through her, but she nodded. He winked at Lisbeth, making her heart flutter, and the throbbing in her body intensified. She sighed. "Fine, but don't make me wait too long."

Thomas grinned at her wickedly. "I won't."

THOMAS SAT IN one of the private rooms of the Den. He leaned his head against the back of the wingback chair. He couldn't believe he'd refused the opportunity to bury himself inside Lisbeth last night. When they were in the carriage, he'd wanted her desperately. Hell, he always wanted her, but they'd been through so much.

Thomas was a fool, but the next time he was able to touch Lisbeth, he didn't want to be rushed. He wanted them to get lost in each other's bodies and not worry about anything else. It was such an odd thought, but now that he had Lisbeth, he didn't want any part of their rediscovery of each other to fly by. He wanted to revel in it.

"I hope your return to my club doesn't mean that there are issues with your wife," Devons said, carrying two full glasses of brandy.

Thomas nodded his thanks, taking one. "No, it is nothing like that. I have a request."

Devons frowned and lifted a brow. Thomas pulled a stack of letters from inside his coat. "I need to hire an investigator to track the authors of these down."

Devons looked at the floral envelopes before sneezing from the overwhelming smell of perfume. "Why?"

Thomas pulled the top three from the top. "Read these."

One was the one addressed to Lisbeth, the other he received from his mother, and a strange one he received in Syria.

The club owner asked, "Do you know who C is?"

He shook his head. "I never worried about it because I didn't plan on moving to London. I'm hoping that it is some young lady with a crush, but the letter Lisbeth received has me alarmed."

"I would be concerned as well. I have a regular investigator. May I keep these messages? Hopefully, he will be able to find out who it is."

Relief coursed through Thomas. Once he had a name associated with the letters, he'd feel much better. "Thank you, Devons."

"Not a problem. How is everything else going?"

He smiled. "I think Lisbeth and I are going to be okay."

"Good."

Yes, he was still struggling with some of his feelings internally, but no matter what, he wanted a life with Lisbeth, Alice, and Jeremy. "Mr. Martin and Lord Harston visited me today. They asked if I would become a permanent lecturer for the London Society of Antiquaries."

Devons choked on his drink. "The ladies would be furious."

He grinned. "I think Lisbeth and I came up with an idea for me to lecture at Seely House. I would like to do something for adults, but also for children."

His friend chuckled. "It certainly sounds like you are becoming settled."

Thomas stated, "I'd hoped to see Lord Hawley soon. We've communicated through mail for years, but he doesn't seem to be around."

He nodded. "Yes, he's out of the country. That man is always up to something."

Thomas smiled. "My friend Rafe likes to call him the man of mystery because he always seems to be in the mix of things."

Devons laughed. "I would have never suspected that until recently.

"Perhaps the man is different abroad than at home."

The club owner held up his drink. "A toast to your new life here in London."

Thomas felt optimistic. Everything seemed to be moving in the right direction. Happiness filled him.

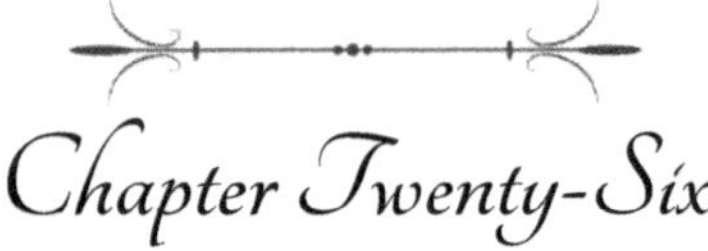

Chapter Twenty-Six

LISBETH WALKED WITH Addie, Rose, Diana, and Sarah through the grand exhibit room at Seely House. The last two clay tablets had been placed in the exhibit that stood in the middle of the room.

She couldn't believe it. They had a fully deciphered epic. The display divided the large room, allowing people to view the tablets and deciphered text on either side. Addie had proposed employing an artist to render drawings of the world contained in each tablet. Those sat on small tables on each side of the display.

"I still can't believe we have the whole story," Diana said.

Addie hugged Rose. "And it is because of this lady's talents that we know what it means."

Rose shrugged. "I'm glad I was able to join the Historical Society of Female Curators."

She'd officially become a board member in the last week. Sarah and Esme would be traveling for the club, and Rose would step in to fill some of their duties. The door was opened by one of the guards, and Lisbeth turned to see Abbas walking in. She hadn't seen him since their adventure in Syria.

He gasped as he walked through the room. "This is amazing. I'm delighted that my mother's culture is being highlighted here."

Lisbeth nodded. "We have Arabic translations and copies of the art for when you travel back to your mother's village. We thought the Al-Wāḥa villagers and your mother would like to have them."

Abbas beamed. "They would."

Addie stated, "We are grateful to have the tablets on loan."

Lisbeth and Rose had worked with Abbas to create an agreement where they would display the tablets on loan from the villages. The villagers would receive a portion of the proceeds, and within three years, the artifacts would be returned to Syria.

Lisbeth walked to the last tablet, which showed Belit and Sibri as much older in their roles as king and queen. Her mind went back to her moment with Thomas in the carriage. She'd wanted him desperately last night, but he'd held her off. Desire coursed through her as she thought about his promise that he wanted them not to be rushed.

Things were going well, but Lisbeth worried that he'd moved on past her deceit too quickly. She feared that he was keeping it bottled up, and it would eventually burst. The worrisome thoughts made her fearful that they could truly move on.

Lisbeth wanted Thomas in her life and as her husband. His relationship with Alice and Jeremy was progressing. While Jeremy had been immediately smitten with him, Alice had warmed up to him as well. Still, she was worried.

She frowned, wondering why she was looking for something to be concerned about.

"Lisbeth, are you joining us for tea in the office?" Sarah asked.

Benjamin Calvert, returned from his travels up north, was in the office discussing plans with Esme.

"Of course. I was just lost in thought."

"Daydreaming about your famous husband," Addie said, snickering.

Lisbeth rolled her eyes. She fibbed and said, "Certainly not."

All the ladies smiled. Abbas joined her while they walked upstairs to the office. "Congratulations, Your Grace. I suspected there was something between you and Mr. Easton while we were on her trip."

"Thank you, Mr. Abbas. It was a whirlwind."

"You seem well-suited."

Her eyes widened. He shrugged. "You do. It is as if the story of the Majnun and Layla has a happy ending."

Laughter burst from her. "We have been compared to them."

He grinned. "I know."

They entered the office to see Esme and Benjamin reviewing a map in the sitting area. Lisbeth was excited for Esme, but somewhat surprised her family was allowing her to travel to Syria. Yes, she was considered a spinster, but still unwed. A family friend, Mrs. Stanton, would be traveling with her.

They all joined them. Rose frowned, looking at the map. "I thought you were traveling to our main excavation site."

Her father grinned. "Lady Esme here said she'd be open to exploring some other areas. We are considering the cave system Lisbeth and Thomas were just at, or this other location further south with Rafe and Keaton."

Rose grimaced and said to Esme. "Keaton and Rafe will flirt outrageously with you."

Esme's face took on a red hue, and Benjamin added, "They are shameless flirts, but I promise between your chaperone and me, your reputation will remain intact while abroad."

Lisbeth hoped her chaperone would be diligent, as Benjamin tended to be clueless about flirtations and liaisons occurring around him. Rose assured, "Rafe and Keaton are only flirts. You will have no real concerns from them."

"I'm sure it will be fine," Esme demurred.

Many exciting events were happening for the Historical Society of Female Curators. Lisbeth was proud of all they'd accomplished. Benjamin stood and beamed at her. "Are we ready to meet with your husband?"

Benjamin had asked to visit with Lisbeth and Thomas at her home. Thomas was like a son to him. She smiled. "Of course."

He grinned. "I still can't believe the two of you are married after all these years apart."

⋙⋘

THOMAS STEPPED INTO the Lusby Townhouse, expecting to hear Lisbeth and Benjamin or Alice and Jeremy, but not the hum of several female voices chatting away excitedly. Was Lisbeth hosting the Historical Society for Female Curators here? He didn't think so; they'd made plans to spend the rest of the day with Benjamin.

He was excited to see the man. He'd been in northern England since Thomas arrived in the country. Morrison hurriedly rushed down the foyer to him, looking frazzled. "Mr. Easton, there are ladies in the drawing room, and they are insisting on meeting with you before they depart."

He frowned. "Who are they?"

Morrison whispered. "I believe they are fans."

"How many are there?"

"Eight."

Thomas blanched. "You let eight young ladies in."

Morrison flushed. "They more or less pushed their way in, insisting they stay."

Perhaps one of them would be C, Thomas considered. He nodded. "Thank you, Morrison. I will see to it."

"I'm sorry I couldn't convince them to leave."

Thomas grinned. "I imagine eight ladies are an overwhelming force to deal with."

Morrison shuddered. "Sir, I can't fathom how you handle it all."

It was starting to wear on Thomas lately. He wouldn't lie to himself. The first few days of people fawning over him had been flattering, but recently, he'd just wanted peace. Sighing, he headed to the drawing room. Once he reached it, he took a deep breath and entered.

In unison, seven very young women screeched excitedly. There was one comparably older lady, whom he suspected was a chaperone, who grimaced at the noise. They stood and excitedly started talking. A lady who seemed to be leading the craziness whistled. "He can't hear any of us."

The older woman shook her head, appearing horrified. The leader of the group said, "I'm Lady Chloe, and we are fans of your serials. We meet every week to discuss your adventures."

Her name began with a C. Another lady said, "I'm Lady Chelsea, and I have reread your serials more than ten times."

Christ, another C name. Thomas smiled and said, "How about each of you introduce yourself?"

They did one by one, and of course, there was another C name. He stopped in front of the woman, who was closer to his age. She smiled and mouthed, "Sorry."

He smiled back. Louder, she said, "Miss Georgina Sanders. I'm Lady Chloe's companion and chaperone. I apologize that we have descended on your home."

Thomas nodded and addressed all the young women. "I would ask, ladies, that next time you schedule something. I do have a prior engagement, but don't fret, I plan to host bi-weekly lectures at my wife's club, the Historical Society for Female Curators."

More squeals erupted, and Thomas winced. He wasn't sure any of these ladies were truly C. Hoping to weed out if someone could be, he asked, "Have any of you ever sent me a letter abroad?"

Lady Chloe's eyes flared with excitement. "We could have done that?"

More chatter increased. No, he suspected none of these ladies were C. From the text of the missives, that lady seemed far more serious than any of these young women.

Miss Sanders addressed the girls. "We should leave as Mr. Easton has another engagement."

A young lady said, "Would you at least sign my serial?"

He'd received dozens of these requests since returning to England, but it always startled him that someone would want his signature. "I will sign whatever you have brought, and then I must send you on your way."

All seven ladies waited while he signed something for each one. It was four serials, a handkerchief, a card with flowers, and a piece of paper. Thomas and Morrison began to usher them out into the foyer when Lisbeth and Benjamin entered. Lisbeth looked around at all the ladies in shock. Benjamin's eyes met his, and he started to chortle. The blasted man delighted in the mess. Still, Thomas couldn't stop the smile from filling his face. He'd missed him.

As the ladies filed past Lisbeth and Benjamin, only Miss Sanders stopped before her and provided a small curtsy. "Sorry, Your Grace, for the chaos. They wanted to visit the famed Thomas Easton."

Lisbeth politely nodded. Once the door was shut, she turned back to Thomas and Morrison. The butler said, "Your Grace— Mrs. Easton, I mean, they descended on us."

Thomas shook his head. "Morrison, it isn't your fault. I will speak with my wife."

Morrison looked at Lisbeth, who nodded in agreement. The butler rushed off. Lisbeth lifted a brow. "Should I expect ladies to call upon you daily?"

Benjamin snickered and said, "I will join the two of you in the drawing room. I know where you keep the brandy, Lisbeth."

They waited for him to leave the foyer, and Thomas peered at her. He'd expected her to laugh at the chaos, but the emotions emitting from her seemed darker. His eyes widened. "You can't be jealous of those ladies, Lizzie. I'm not sure if they are even out for the season."

"I'm sure not all your fans are so young."

He strode to her, grasping her chin. "You are the only lady I want."

She wrinkled her nose. "Are you sure? It appears you could have a lady for every day of the week."

Thomas, unable to stop himself, brushed a light kiss over her lips. "It is only you that torments my thoughts."

Desire flared between them, and unable to stop himself, Thomas said, "I've arranged something for us tomorrow. A date for you and me to be completely alone."

She gulped, and his eyes flicked down, lingering on her throat, wishing he could run his lips down it.

"Are you ever going to join me?" Benjamin hollered from the drawing room, breaking their stare off.

They both stepped back from each other, and Thomas said, "Until tomorrow, wife."

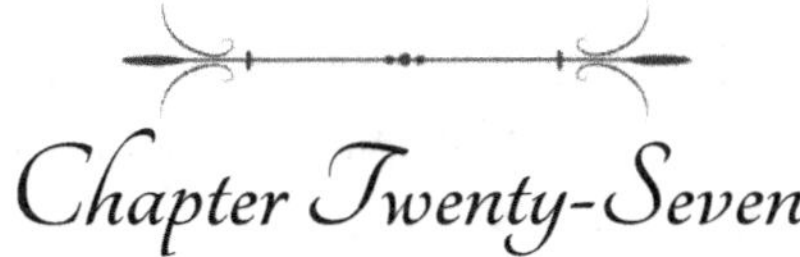

Chapter Twenty-Seven

THE NEXT DAY, Lisbeth sat with Thomas in a small stone cottage on a beautiful property outside of London. Benson, her guard, had dropped them off there with two horses and would return later in the evening.

The land was adorned with a gorgeous lake, fields of flowers, spectacular manor ruins, and plants just starting to bloom. Lisbeth had been shocked when they arrived at the stone cottage that already had a roaring fire and food laid out for them.

She glanced around and smiled. "Did you have Morrison and Benson help you out with this?"

Thomas grinned. "I did. You said you wanted to be alone, so here we are."

Nerves flared in Lisbeth's stomach. She wasn't sure why; they'd been intimate before. Thomas laid out bedding, creating a makeshift bed in front of the fireplace. He removed his jacket, cravat, and shoes. Warmth shot through Lisbeth.

He sat and held out his hand. "Join me, Lizzie."

She blushed and removed her shoes before sitting. He wrapped her in his arms and pulled her against his chest. Lisbeth snuggled into him. Thomas kissed the top of her head and asked, "Two weeks together. How do we think it is going?"

She smiled impishly. "Fine, besides your many admirers."

"It makes me wish I hadn't agreed to work with Anderson all

those years ago."

Lisbeth shook her head. "Don't. It made you wealthy and also sparked people's curiosity about antiquities. There are dozens of boys and girls out there who want to be the next Thomas Easton."

He slid her off his chest, so she was lying on her back, and he was staring down at her. Thomas frowned. "Still, I'm worried about that letter you received."

Lisbeth sighed. "You can't control the actions of someone else. I'm sure it was an angry young fan. They will move on."

One of his hands glided down her front, and Lisbeth sucked in a breath. Their eyes connected, and desire crackled between them. "Did you bring me here to seduce me, Mr. Easton?"

She hoped so. He smirked. "And if I did, Mrs. Easton?"

Her heart pounded, and a rightness coursed through her. Lisbeth teasingly said, "Well, you denied me in the carriage. Perhaps I'm not interested now."

Disbelief flicked across his face. "I could never deny you anything. We both wanted to wait. Had you pushed me on it, I would have gladly hiked your skirts up and filled you with my cock."

Her core clenched. Thomas frowned. "The last time we were together, we were so angry, but saying I didn't enjoy it would be a lie. Still, I wanted our next time to be more than that. I wanted it to be an opportunity for us to discover each other with love and care.

Lisbeth blinked back tears. His words reverberated with sincerity. A million hurts existed between her and Thomas, and he still loved her. She could see it on his face. He leaned down and ran kisses up her neck, and as if to lighten the mood, he murmured, "Now, going forward, I promise to tup you in the carriage anytime you request."

She giggled. "I may demand it quite often."

He grinned wickedly at her. "I would like nothing more."

Lisbeth was done with all the games and the coyness of when

they would be intimate. She grabbed his hand and raised it to her lips. "Thomas, make love to me, please."

He groaned and shot to his feet, startling her, before holding out his hand. She smiled. "What are you doing?"

"Benson won't be back to pick us up for hours. I need to see you out of all those clothes. A man could suffocate in all the clothing women have to wear in the West."

She laughed loudly and took his hand. He pulled her up and spun her around so her back was facing him. His fingers made quick work of the buttons of her dress, petticoats, chemise, and drawers. He turned her to face him, and Lisbeth lifted a brow. "How did I end up completely bare, but you are still dressed?"

Thomas didn't respond but let his eyes roam over her form. Lisbeth blushed, feeling suddenly shy even though he'd seen her this way in Syria. "You are so beautiful. It dazes me every time I look upon you."

"I'm not as young—"

He interrupted her. "No, don't say it. Every curve of your body is a work of perfection. It causes a hunger in me that leaves me breathless."

Thomas pulled her to him, lifting her slightly off the ground. He kissed her as her body slid down his. She whimpered as his hard shaft slid against her feminine folds before pressing against her belly. His lips pressed against hers, as his tongue demanded entry into her mouth. She didn't fight him, wanting to spar with him. Their tongues pushed and stroked against one another until they both pulled away breathless.

Lisbeth began to unbutton his shirt as he pulled the fabric from his pants. It fell to the floor, and she ran a hand along his firm, broad chest. Her hand drifted down to his flat stomach, tense from her touch. She unclasped his pants, and they fell around his ankles before he stepped out of them.

His large shaft stood at attention, demanding to be touched. She ran one finger down its length, and Thomas hissed. "Do you know how empowering it is to know how much you desire me,

Thomas?"

"There is nothing I want more," he moaned as her hand stroked him. His hips began to rock.

Lisbeth squeezed her thighs together in anticipation of having him buried so deep in her. "What do you want, Thomas?"

He groaned. She leaned up and kissed his jaw and then his lips. "I want to please you."

Her hand swirled over his taut stomach. "Do you want me on my knees?"

Thomas looked down at her ravenously. Lisbeth bit her lip, drawing his eyes to her mouth. Finally, he hoarsely muttered, "Christ, I think I may combust, but yes."

Lisbeth dropped to her knees and slid the length of him into her mouth. She delighted in the taste of him at the tip. He wrapped his fingers in her hair. Pins went flying everywhere as her hair tumbled about her shoulders. She looked up at him, and their eyes connected. The ache in her core intensified as she took him in and out of her mouth. With every thrust, he groaned or whimpered. His pace increased, and Lisbeth could tell he was close.

The hold on her hair tightened, and with one last thrust, he spent in her mouth. He moaned as she drank him down. She pulled back, sitting on her heels and smirked up at him. Thomas leaned down and rubbed his thumb across her lips. "My temptress. My Layla. My everything."

He joined Lisbeth on the bedding. She rolled onto her back and wantonly splayed her legs. He lay on his side, looking down at her form. Minutes passed as they enjoyed the comfortable silence between them. It had always been like this with them, comfortable and easy.

Thomas's hand slid down her body until he reached her quim. She tilted her head back and moaned, needing his touch. He teasingly stroked her at first, but it wasn't enough. Lisbeth wanted his fingers in her. She needed to ride them. His fingers penetrated her, and she gasped. He slid them in and out of her as she bucked and moaned. His eyes grew hungry, and he brushed a kiss across her mouth.

Thomas positioned his hard shaft at her entrance. Her eyes flew to his face, and he said, "Once will never be enough with you."

Lisbeth pulled him to her, and he thrusted into her deeply. She let out a whimper, reveling in how he stretched her. He slid in and out of her, taking his time. The movements were driving her mad. She wanted more of him and deeper.

She urged him on by wrapping her legs around him and demanding more. He chuckled darkly. "My ravenous temptress. Tell me what you want?"

Lisbeth demanded, "Harder and deeper, Thomas."

He kissed her neck. "As you wish."

His next thrust was exactly as she requested, and so was the one after that. She moaned. Lisbeth took all he offered, needing him more with every joining of their bodies. He slid into her again and then this time swiveled his hips as he was buried in her. Her feminine nub throbbed, and she let out a strangled moan.

As his movements continued, he murmured in her ear, "Is that what my Lizzie likes? A good pounding?"

She moaned. He pulled out and thrust again, rotating his hips. The ache in her core was so intense that she could barely utter a comprehensible word.

"Does my cock please you, love?" he asked, the breath of his words against her skin sending shivers down her body.

"Yes," she finally gasped out.

He thrusted and swiveled over and over again until the ache in her lower body exploded. She whimpered, and he cupped her bottom, pounding into her, chasing his own release. Thomas continued with his relentless thrusting. She clung to him, and then he plunged into her one more time before sliding out and spending onto a cloth. He fell down on the bedding next to her, breathing heavily.

Their hands found each other, and they intertwined their

fingers, both staring at the ceiling. He'd pulled out. Lisbeth whined, "You didn't finish in me."

Thomas rolled to his side and looked down at her. "I didn't want to presume anything."

She smiled at him. "Why are you such a decent man, Thomas Easton?"

He leaned down and kissed her. "That doesn't mean I'm not going to slide myself between those lovely thighs of yours a few more times before Benson appears."

Lisbeth wrapped her arms around his neck and kissed him back. "I would hope not."

THOMAS AND LISBETH grinned at each other as the carriage door shut. Benson and the driver had returned to retrieve them, though Thomas now wished they'd spent the night. He had a surprise for Lisbeth and was nervous about how she would take it.

Still, she'd seemed to love their alone time today. "I have a surprise for you."

Lisbeth lifted a brow. Thomas had the urge to kiss her again. She still had the look of a flushed, sated lover. He continued, "I bought the land I showed you today. I was hoping that we could build a house and live there when we don't have events in London. It is only a half-hour train ride or a one-hour carriage ride from the townhouse in Mayfair."

He had hoped for excitement, but she looked back at him, blinking and stunned. Hurt flared in Thomas. "I'm sensing you are not as excited as I thought you would be."

"It is very thoughtful, but we have a townhouse in London and a country estate," she explained calmly.

"The dukedom does," he said, trying to reason with her.

"I don't want to add stress to Alice and Jeremy's lives."

"Change is good sometimes," he said. It didn't escape him that the anger he thought he'd buried deep enough never to flare was bubbling and demanding to erupt.

Lisbeth bit her lip as if she wasn't sure what to say. He was choosing to step into another man's life. A life that should have been Thomas's to begin with. The anger erupted. "Will I be denied everything? First you, then my child, and now I can't build anything for our family. It all should have been mine. You should never have left Tuscany."

The moment he said the words, he knew he shouldn't have. The color drained from Lisbeth's face. "I'm sorry. Blame me. It is all my fault."

"I blame the expectations of society, I blame your father and brother, and yes, I blame both of us for thinking it was wise for the daughter of an earl and a housekeeper's son to fall in love."

Thomas needed to calm down. He was being irrational. Somehow, this conversation had morphed from discussing whether to buy an estate to addressing all their problems. Her eyes watered. "It was a foolish decision to fall in love, but one I couldn't have stopped, nor do I regret it."

He gulped and looked away. She leaned forward and placed her hand on his. "I knew these feelings still lingered and I don't blame you, but we must be honest with each other for this to work. My only concern about your purchase of the estate is Alice and Jeremy."

"I want this life with you, Alice, and Jeremy, but I can't only exist in the duke's spaces. I need a place that is just ours."

She smiled sadly at him. "Let's take some time to think about this. This has become too heated. I just need you to understand that a new estate won't make the past disappear."

Lisbeth was likely right about needing time. The anger snapping and sparking in him would not soften. "It seems we both have plenty to think about. I don't think it is too much to ask for you to build something with me."

She remained silent.

The next day, Thomas watched as Alice and Jeremy played in the garden with Miss Ashby. They were comfortable in this space, and it was because they'd grown up here. This was their home. He was still hurt that Lisbeth wouldn't consider the estate at all. Thomas had thought the nearby property was a perfect compromise.

Still, she'd been right. He was the only one who could decide whether he could live in London with them. Hell, right now he was staying in a guest chamber of this house because he couldn't fathom sleeping in Lisbeth's deceased husband's bed. Fuck. Everything was a bloody mess.

Yet, he knew with all certainty that he loved Lisbeth. He glanced at Alice and Jeremy, and his heart ached even at the thought of leaving them. He never wanted to blow up on Lisbeth again. She'd been hurt and shocked.

He would make this work, he told himself. What other option did he have? To live the rest of his life incomplete? Without Lisbeth and the children, that is what it would be. Thomas walked down the terrace stairs, and Alice and Jeremy smiled at him. This was his family, and he wouldn't give it up.

Chapter Twenty-Eight

LISBETH SAT AT Seely House, reviewing the club's finances. In truth, she was hiding. Her fight with Thomas the previous day had been atrocious. He'd been so angry, and the feelings he'd been keeping bottled up exploded. Her heart ached as she remembered him saying that he blamed them for foolishly falling in love.

She scoffed quietly as if they had any say in that. Lisbeth gulped, wondering if they could be together without making each other miserable. There were so many hurtful things between them. Still, she wasn't completely faultless. Why had she said no right away about the country estate? The request wasn't that unreasonable.

Her thoughts had been focused only on Alice and Jeremy. She didn't want them to go through more change after enduring Nicholas's death and her and Thomas's shocking wedding. Still, it was a lovely property. Had she reacted without really considering it as an option? Jeremy would love the small lake, and Alice would adore the Manor ruins. She sighed.

"What's wrong?" Rose said from the door.

She shook her head. "Thomas and I had an awful quarrel yesterday."

Her eyes started to water, and Rose rushed into the room. "It couldn't have been that bad."

"He bought some land outside of London as a surprise. It is beautiful, but then he suggested we could split our time between there and the townhouse. I told him no, and it went downhill from there."

"Why did you say no?"

Lisbeth sighed. "I was thinking of Alice and Jeremy. I was worried about how it would affect them if we were to move. Truthfully, my response and reaction were not well thought out."

"It sounds like a valid point," Rose said.

"I wish we had discussed it more. Instead, I refused to consider it, and he became angry. It wasn't a good moment for either of us."

"Talk with him. All lovers fight."

Lisbeth added, "I've feared that he was keeping all his emotions bottled up. Our fight confirmed all my worries."

"It isn't good for him to do that," Rose said, concerned.

Tears started to run down Lisbeth's cheeks. "In minutes, we went from discussing the land he'd acquired to everything he'd lost or been denied. Thomas isn't wrong. He was cheated out of so much, and I wish I could make it right, but I can't. I worry he will never be able to let go of his resentment."

Rose squeezed her hand. "I care for both of you. Thomas can be a bit of an ass, but truthfully, he needs to admit that he is still grieving and angry. The only way the two of you move on is if you talk to each other."

Lisbeth wiped away her tears. "How did you become so wise?"

Her friend grinned. "It is a new thing. Remember, I tried to set up my husband with another woman because I assumed she would be a better fit for him. He traveled all the way to Syria to retrieve me."

A giggle escaped Lisbeth. "It was rather romantic."

Rose grinned. "I agree."

Addie walked into the room and stared intently at Lisbeth. She frowned at her in return. "Is something amiss?"

A guard entered the room. Addie asked, "Did Benson travel with you today?"

Lisbeth nodded. "Thomas has been receiving some strange letters, so he asked Benson to escort me whenever I leave the house."

Addie and the guard looked at each other. Rose frowned. "What is it?"

Addie pulled a letter from an envelope decorated with hand-drawn flowers, and Lisbeth's stomach dropped.

"This was addressed to me," her friend said, handing her the paper.

Lisbeth unfolded the message and read.

Lady Hawley,

You have a strumpet on your board. The Duchess of Lusby is fornicating with my husband. I insist she stop, or I will have to fix this situation myself. Perhaps the threat of losing her position there will be a motivator. I insist that you offer an ultimatum—either she leaves my husband alone, or she will be removed from the board of the Historical Society of Female Curators.

C

Lisbeth blushed at the horrible letter. "Thomas has hired someone through Sebastian Devons to find the lady. We suspect it might be some young woman with an overzealous but innocent crush."

"It doesn't seem innocent but threatening," Rose remarked.

"I will make sure Thomas gives this to the investigator."

"Please do. I don't want anything to happen to you. The whole kidnapping debacle with Rose was more than enough."

"It all ended fine," Rose insisted.

Lisbeth supposed. The situation had been frightening, with Rose being kidnapped by thieves seeking to make a quick profit. It also had strange ties to the British Secret Service. She shivered.

Not once had she thought the letters could be as serious as Rose's kidnapping. Lisbeth needed to talk with Thomas about this.

She stood. "I'm going to depart for the day. I need to prepare for Rose and Sinclair's ball."

Rose shook her head. "We can all be honest. It isn't my event. I adore Augustus's mother, but the ball is her masterpiece, not mine.

All the ladies laughed.

THOMAS WALKED INTO his mother's drawing room, happy to see her. She was sewing the hem of a dress. He frowned. "Can't you hire someone to do that for you?"

She looked up and smiled. "I could, but I can also do it myself, and I enjoy sewing. It is one of the few tasks I miss about being a housekeeper."

He sat in the wingback chair across from his mother, who was seated on the sofa. "What else do you miss?"

She smiled softly. "Taking care of a family. The Adnins were good to us. Even after you and Lisbeth left, they made sure I had a good reference."

Thomas often wondered how his and Lisbeth's choice to run off when they were young impacted his mother. He knew she'd found new employment. "They fired you?"

His mother shrugged. "My son ran off with the Earl's daughter. I didn't find it unreasonable."

"It wasn't your fault."

She shrugged. "Sometimes we have no control over what happens to us. Life and other people's choices make it that way. We can only make the best of those situations."

Guilt coursed through him. His mother loved her job at the Earl of Adnin's townhouse. "I'm sorry."

She put her dress aside and dramatically said, "An apology

after all these years."

He flushed. A smile filled his mother's face. "My point is sometimes all we can do is survive what fate hands us."

He nodded.

"It seems fate has given you and Lisbeth another chance."

Thomas sighed. "I may have messed that up. I blew up on her."

She frowned, concerned. "What happened?"

"I bought a piece of property right outside of the city and proposed that we move there. She was hesitant, and then it became about everything that happened between us."

His mother gave him a stern look. "The two of you need to be open and honest with each other. Thomas, you can't keep things bottled up, or that will continue to happen."

"I know."

"You two will find your way," she said, smiling encouragingly.

"How do you know? I forced her to marry me."

His mother shook her head. "I don't believe you could have made Lisbeth marry you. It may have felt forced, but a part of her has always loved you. She and her husband were good friends, but there were no romantic feelings between them. To be honest, I think they both felt fortunate when Lisbeth became pregnant with Jeremy so quickly."

The thought of Lisbeth in bed with any other man made jealousy flare in him. His mother reached over and squeezed his hand reassuringly. "My point is that you have always been the only one for her."

"I've not been a saint."

His mother snorted. "I've read the serials. You were in a different spot than her, and you didn't know why she left you. Would you betray her now?"

Thomas flushed, somewhat embarrassed to be having this conversation with his mother. "Of course not."

"Talk to each other. Don't keep things bottled up. It will only cause more harm."

She was right, and even Lisbeth had mentioned that. He needed to be able to grieve everything he'd missed but also find a way to accept it and move on. He still believed they shouldn't dwell on the what-ifs of the past, but he couldn't continue to act unaffected—not if he didn't want to lose the family he and Lisbeth were trying to build together.

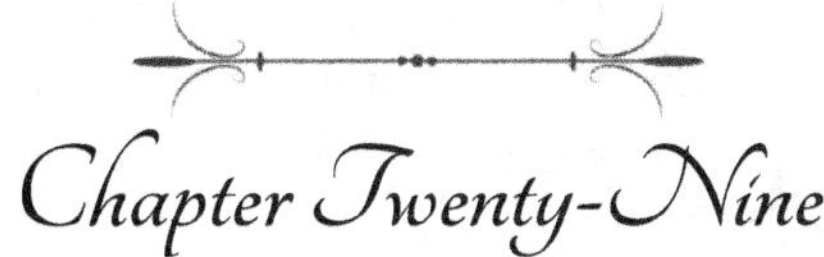

Chapter Twenty-Nine

LISBETH HADN'T SEEN Thomas since the previous day when they quarreled in the carriage. She stared at her reflection in the mirror. Tonight was Rose and Sinclair's ball to celebrate their marriage. Thomas would be escorting her. For a mad moment, she wondered if he would still accompany her. Lisbeth shook her head. He would.

A knock on her bedchamber door caused her stomach to dip. She sensed it was him. "Enter."

He stepped in and shut the door behind him. Their eyes connected in the mirror before his gaze wandered down her form. "You are beautiful, Lizzie."

She blushed. Lisbeth did feel wonderful in her gown tonight. It was a dark magenta dress that was tightened at her waist. Black crystals outlined the top of the deep neckline. She usually wore her hair in an elegant bun at her nape, but today she'd asked her lady's maid to leave half of it down in curls.

It had a less regal look but was just as elegant. She smoothed her hands over her skirts. "I thought I would try something different."

"You always look beautiful, but I won't lie. I'd rather take you to bed than go to this ball."

She walked to him and straightened his cravat. "Does that mean you aren't angry with me?"

"Can I speak freely?"

Lisbeth stared at him intently. "That is what I want more than anything. I know this is hard. It isn't good for us to pretend that it isn't."

He nodded and sat on the edge of her bed, and she joined him. Thomas was silent as if trying to formulate his thoughts. Eventually, he said, "It is still hard for me not to be angry that I didn't watch my daughter grow up."

Her heart clenched in her chest. She nodded and waited for him to continue.

"It is difficult for me to be in this townhouse and know I'm always in the presence of the duke's ghost. Someday this will all go to Jeremy, and I want that for him, but I need something for us to have with Alice, Jeremy, and our future children. I need a place that I've helped create. I plan for us to spend time at the townhouse. Still, wouldn't it be nice to have an estate right out of the city to escape to, but close by if needed?"

She nodded, knowing that for all of this to work, they needed something that was all of theirs. Lisbeth said, "Thank you for not insisting we abandon the only home Jeremy and Alice have ever known. I think you are right. We can have both. There is a ducal country estate, but it is over eight hours away. We only go there twice a year."

Thomas threaded his fingers through hers. "I would never deny Alice or Jeremy the memory of their father, but I think to be happy, we need a measure of change."

"We will tell Alice someday."

He gulped. Lisbeth sensed the emotions swirling through him. She added, "Both Nicholas and I wanted her to know."

Thomas took a deep breath. "In time we should, but for now I want Alice and Jeremy to allow me into their lives in their own time. When she is an adult, we will decide about telling her everything."

Her eyes watered, and she whispered, "You are a good man, Thomas Easton."

"I don't care if I'm good or bad. I want to be the man who gets to grow old with you and watch our children become adults."

"Nothing would make me happier, Thomas. I choose you. Let's end our thirty-day evaluation of whether our marriage will work. We will ensure it does."

They faced each other, and Lisbeth added, "You are my forever, Serious Thomas."

He rubbed a tear from her cheek. "It has always been you, Lizzie."

She fell into him, their lips touching gently and exploring. It was a kiss, not of wickedness or temptation, but belonging to one another. It was perfection.

Lisbeth pulled away, and Thomas frowned, looking around the room. "Morrison, the butler, told me you are redesigning the lord and lady suites of the townhouse. You don't have to do that."

Lisbeth held her hand out. "I'm doing it for us and our future. Nicholas and I used to discuss finding happiness wherever we could. He always hated the décor of this place, and I think my decision would amuse him."

Thomas rose from the bed and wrapped his arms around her. "Seeking happiness sounds like a brilliant idea."

She smiled up at him. "Shall we go to the ball now that we've solved all of our problems?"

His eyes clouded with desire. "I'd rather stay and celebrate our new happiness here."

Lisbeth laughed, her lower half going warm. "Soon, my love. This is for Rose."

The woman was like a sister to Thomas and a dear friend to her. They couldn't miss the ball celebrating her marriage to Sinclair and the upcoming grand wedding that was set to take place next month. Thomas sighed. "I suppose a night watching Benjamin gloat about marrying her off to a duke is worth it."

Lisbeth giggled.

⟫⟫⟩✦⟨⟪⟪

THOMAS SIGHED AS he stood with a gaggle of young ladies on the marriage mart. They had surrounded him. Lady Chloe and her friends were part of the group. He was still worried about the letters from C. He needed to meet with Devons to see if his investigator had heard anything. Perhaps the admirer had moved on.

"Mr. Easton, can you tell us a story?" One young lady requested.

He smiled and shook his head. "Tonight, ladies, I'm simply here with my wife to celebrate our friends' marriage."

A handful of the ladies groaned, but he slid between two of them and fled. It wasn't elegant or even polite, but he needed a reprieve. His wicked wife had seen him become inundated with questions and had disappeared. Thomas shook his head.

He glanced around, hoping to catch sight of her. Where had she gone? He stepped into the expansive, elegant foyer of Sinclair's house. Even this area was packed with people. He slid past the lords and ladies mingling everywhere, hoping to catch sight of her tempting dress.

Lisbeth had taken Thomas's breath away when he'd stepped into her bedchamber. She was stunning, and it had taken everything in him not to immediately wrap her in his arms and make love to her until all the anger disappeared from both of their beings. Still, he'd stopped himself. And, truthfully, he was glad they talked. They were in a much better place. A loud laugh caught his attention, and he glanced up to the second-floor landing to see Addie, Rose, and Lisbeth studying a painting. Sinclair had both the first and second floors open for guests. An expansive gallery was located on the second floor, and people went between there, the ballroom, and the outdoor gardens.

"I knew the two of you were meant to be," a gruff voice said from behind him.

He turned and smiled at Benjamin. "You always said that."

Benjamin beamed. "And I was right. Though I feel like I should be thanked for bringing you back together."

Thomas raised a brow. Benjamin liked to take credit for most things. His friend grinned. "I was the one who suggested to Lisbeth that she bring the ancient map back to Syria."

He laughed. "You did. What if we had hated each other?"

Benjamin shrugged. "I remember when I first met the two of you. You looked at each other as if there was no one else, finished each other's sentences, and were fiercely loyal to each other. It reminded me of my wife."

Thomas studied Benjamin. The man was in his fifties and cut a handsome figure. "Have you ever considered remarrying?"

His friend frowned. "I've had relationships and formed great friendships, but I'm not sure another marriage is for me. Rose's mother would want that for me. Still, one great love is enough for me."

Thomas glanced at Lisbeth. She was still staring at the painting with the other ladies. He suspected, like Benjamin, that he was meant to have only one soul mate. It had always been Lizzie—no one else.

Benjamin followed his gaze and chuckled. "I don't think you will reach her. How about a drink in the library?"

He frowned at his wife. The stairs were much more crowded now. "I suppose you are right."

They made their way through the crowd of people, but Thomas stumbled to a stop as several ladies screamed. A loud noise of something or someone tumbling down the stairs echoed through the foyer. He glanced up and saw that Lisbeth was no longer there, and people were surrounding a person now crumpled at the bottom of the stairs.

His heart hammered. It couldn't be Lisbeth. He pushed through the crowd with Benjamin right behind him. Thomas had to prevent himself from roaring in anguish when he spotted Lisbeth's gown swirling around her while she lay there with her eyes closed.

He dropped to his knees in front of her. "Lizzie, wake up."

She didn't move. This couldn't happen. They'd just found each other again. He leaned forward, and relief coursed through him. She was still breathing.

"Someone send for a doctor immediately."

He gently tapped on Lisbeth's cheeks. She mumbled, but her eyes refused to open. He heard Rose in the background asking everyone to return to the ballroom. The room emptied, and Rose dropped down next to him in her emerald and silver ball gown.

"Lisbeth, you must wake up," his friend said to his wife.

Thomas's eyes connected with Rose's. "She has to be okay. I can't lose her. Do you understand me, Rose?"

She squeezed his hand reassuringly. "Lisbeth will be fine. She is still breathing."

Sinclair said from behind them, "The doctor should be here soon. He isn't far."

Thomas nodded, squeezing his wife's hand. His voice cracked as he said, "Lizzie, please wake up. Alice, Jeremy, and I need you."

Chapter Thirty

LISBETH SAT IN her bedchamber with Thomas sitting next to her in a wingback chair. "You must get some rest."

He glared at her, and she rolled her eyes. The man had sat in the chair all night. He had to be sore.

"I'm not leaving your side until the doctor says you are fine."

She sighed. "Thomas, he said I was fine last night."

"No, he said he believed you were fine but would check on you today to confirm."

Her husband rubbed at the scruff on his face. Lisbeth had to admit he had a rakish appeal right now, looking rumpled and grumpy.

"I'm happy you didn't break anything," Rose stated.

She sat at the foot of the bed next to her feet. Her friend arrived early this morning with Sinclair. Lisbeth sighed. "I'm sorry I caused such a dramatic ending to your ball."

Rose gently squeezed her ankle. "I couldn't care less. You matter to me more than another few hours of dancing."

She frowned. "I hope Sinclair's mother wasn't too upset."

Her friend shook her head. "Everyone did what they were supposed to at a ball—see and be seen."

Lisbeth giggled. Rose was not the typical duchess. She doubted that her friend would ever prefer dancing at grand affairs to toiling over ancient text. Rose smiled. "I did enjoy the desserts and spending time with the ladies from the Historical Society for Female Curators."

Thomas snickered, but Lisbeth said, "That is a start."

Rose nodded. "Augustus's mother has asked me to join her as a patron for a charity that supports several orphanages. I think I will enjoy that as well."

"Good for you."

"Will you return to one of the excavation sites?" Thomas asked.

Rose blushed. Thomas and Lisbeth glanced at each other, both intrigued by her response. Their friend sighed. "We are not sharing this broadly, but I'm with child."

Lisbeth screeched and pulled Rose towards her. Her friend laughed, hugging her back. Thomas smiled. "Congrats, Rose. A mother and a duchess."

Rose nodded. "Yes, but we do plan to return to Syria after the baby is born, at least for a few months. My father, his mother, and his sister are the only ones who know for now."

Lisbeth squeezed her hand. "I'm honored you told us."

She leaned back against the bedframe, grimacing. Rose frowned. "Did I hug you too hard?"

"I hugged you. I'm fine, just sore."

"What happened?" Rose asked. "One minute you were standing with me on the landing, and then you were tumbling down."

Lisbeth shook her head. "I'm not sure."

"But it was an accident?" Rose prodded.

Thomas studied her intently and, at her continued silence, said, "Tell us, Lisbeth."

"Before I fell, I felt a push on my lower back. I'm not sure if it was intentional. There were so many people going up and down the steps, but it was a hard shove."

Thomas's eyes widened in alarm. "Why didn't you mention this last night?"

"I didn't want to worry you."

"I will ask Benson to bring in more guards. Devons's investigator still hasn't been able to locate who C is."

Rose frowned. "Is that your admirer who thinks she is your wife?"

Both Lisbeth and Thomas nodded. Rose said, "Please be careful."

"I think it must be an accident. Pushing me seems extreme," Lisbeth insisted.

"Still, we will hire more guards. Perhaps you should not attend the event for the epic."

Lisbeth and Rose looked at each other, shocked. She would do no such thing. If there were some crazy admirer, Lisbeth wouldn't let them chase her away from her work. She jutted out her chin and said, "No."

Thomas pressed his lips together firmly, his displeasure evident. Lisbeth would not hide. Rose looked back and forth between the two of them. "Why don't the two of you discuss this, and we can decide at our weekly meeting at Seely House tomorrow?"

Lisbeth looked at her husband and firmly said, "I'm fine." She then said to both of them. "We can make a final decision tomorrow."

Annoyance lingered on Thomas's face, but Lisbeth wouldn't hide because of one of his fans. She wasn't even sure if someone pushed her. It was only a suspicion. Still, she shivered because she had a vivid memory of two dainty hands pressing against her back as hard as they could.

Rose headed to the door. "I will see you both tomorrow."

After their friend left, Lisbeth turned to Thomas. "I refuse to hide because of one of your admirers. That is ridiculous."

"This C person could be dangerous."

"Thomas, I'm unsure if I even was pushed."

He sat on the edge of the bed. "I will not lose you."

The intensity and concern in his eyes softened her words. "Thank you for worrying about me, but I can't miss the event."

The conversation ended because Alice and Jeremy burst into

the room. Alice said, "Miss Ashby said we could finally visit you. Are you hurt?"

Lisbeth called them up next to her. "I fell down some stairs, but I'm perfectly fine. Thomas was there to see me home."

Alice smiled shyly at him. "Thank you, Thomas."

Jeremy snuggled into her, and she grimaced. Thomas looked as if he was about to say something to him, so Lisbeth held a hand up in protest. He wasn't in danger of damaging her or breaking anything. She would gladly take the cuddles.

Lisbeth listened to them explain their day, happy to be with her children even if she was sore. She glanced at Thomas, who was still frowning at her with concern. She mouthed, "It will all be fine."

He lifted a skeptical brow.

THOMAS SAT WITH Harston, Martin, and Lord Hawley at the Den. He was there to meet with Devons about the letter, but had bumped into them while waiting.

Mr. Martin said, "Are you sure you won't change your mind?"

He shook his head and explained, "I'm planning to host lectures at Seely House. I will have one for adults and one for children."

Lord Harston's lips pressed together in annoyance. "You should reconsider. Also, I'm not sure a lecture for children would be beneficial. Antiquities are not something that would hold their interest."

Thomas disliked Harston; he was a pompous ass. He wasn't sure why Martin tolerated him as vice president. He supposed he didn't have a choice. A body of their peers likely voted upon it.

He tried his best to keep his tone even and said, "My love of antiquities was developed when I was a young boy."

"Did you study it at school?" Harston questioned.

He shook his head. "No, my mother was a housekeeper for a lord. I used to swipe antiquity books from the gentleman's study."

Harston wrinkled his nose as if he found his explanation distasteful. Lord Hawley, who'd remained silent to date, grinned at him. Hawley had returned from somewhere in the East, where he was studying the ancient culture of the Assyrians. The man was always doing something.

Thomas smiled at him. "It is good to see you. I haven't seen you since we were in that bit of trouble in Tuscany three years ago."

Hawley laughed. "I'm still not sure how we ended up in the same city in the middle of a revolution."

Thomas had been there to help a friend flee. To this day, he wasn't sure what Hawley, scholar of all things ancient, was doing there. Tuscany was like a second home to Thomas. He'd always returned there between work. One of his dear, good friends, Messina, had needed help when he'd become a wanted man. Thomas has smuggled him out under the guise of being a professor of antiquities.

It was all over now. The quest to unite the region had failed, but whispers of unity still lingered in the area. Thomas suspected someday it would happen.

Hawley added, "I hear I should congratulate you. You are married to the Duchess of Lusby. Everyone is talking; it is apparently a love match."

Thomas smiled. "It is."

Harston rolled his eyes as if their conversation was beneath him. Hawley smirked at the man. "Harston, you do not help yourself by being uninterested in every conversation besides the one you want to have."

The lord turned bright red. Martin, always the pacifier, said, "He is just dedicated to making sure nothing interferes with the club."

Hawley sighed, and Thomas stated again, "I will not be joining the London Society of Antiquaries."

Harston stood. "I think I will find a game to play."

They all watched him storm off. Martin frowned. "He doesn't mean any harm. He is very dedicated to the London Society of Antiquaries."

Thomas studied the man. "Have you ever spoken with your daughter about the Historical Society of Female Curators? She is a key part of their success."

Martin flushed. "I allow her to participate."

Thomas found it sad that he wasn't more supportive, but he supposed he couldn't change that. His few conversations with Sarah Martin had been enlightening. She was a remarkable historian, particularly in the realm of art.

Martin stood. "I think I will join Harston."

Both Thomas and Hawley nodded goodbye. They didn't have a private moment together because Devons appeared.

Thomas nodded at him. Hawley stood, ready to depart. Devons shook his head. "Why don't you stay? I know you've just returned, but you may have contacts I don't."

Hawley looked at them, intrigued. "Does this have to do with my wife's club?"

Thomas said, "In a roundabout way."

Devons sat and sighed. "Easton has been receiving fan mail that has become increasingly threatening."

Hawley raised a brow. "Threatening to whom?"

"My wife. This person is upset and believes we should be married."

Devons added, "I've tried to track them down from their letters, but whoever they are, they drop their letters at various places."

Hawley frowned. "I'm not sure how you think I can help."

"You have interesting connections," Devons pointed out, not allowing him to play the part of a befuddled gentleman.

Thomas had to stop himself from laughing. He'd known

Hawley for a long time. He played the part of the bumbling historian well, but the man was more complex than that. Clearly, Devons knew that as well.

Hawley didn't deny Devons' words but said, "I'm not sure I can be of help. Perhaps it is truly just a love-sick admirer."

Thomas confessed, "My wife took a tumble down a staircase at the Duke of Lusby's townhouse. We believe she may have been pushed."

Devons frowned. "I will have my investigators increase their efforts."

Hawley shook his head. "I hope that isn't the case, Easton. Please let me know if I can be of service."

Thomas nodded, grateful but unsure if Hawley could be helpful. He needed to find C, whoever it was. He hoped the fall was an accident, but he wouldn't allow his fame to be something that harmed Lisbeth.

Chapter Thirty-One

LISBETH WALKED INTO one of the smaller exhibit rooms, where a gaggle of young ladies were perusing the artifacts on display. She'd only come in to review the inventory. They kept glancing her way and whispering.

Eventually, she said, "Are you enjoying the exhibit?"

The girls grinned, and one asked, "Are you Thomas Easton's wife?"

Unease filled her, but she refused to let it consume her. "Yes, I am."

They all giggled, and one of the ladies said, "You are so lucky."

The one woman who appeared older frowned. "Lady Chloe, that is inappropriate."

The young woman sulked. "Georgina, we are only having fun."

Lisbeth couldn't fathom that a young woman like this could be a danger. Perhaps the fall was truly an accident, and the letters were nothing but dramatic words from a young girl.

The woman, closer to her age, said, "I'm sorry. They are all enthralled with Mr. Easton's serials."

One of the girls giggled and said, "We visited your home and convinced your husband to sign our serials."

Lisbeth smiled at the girl's flushed cheeks. No, these young women weren't threats; they were excited about her husband, but not dangerous. She smiled. "My husband will be giving monthly lectures starting next month. You should attend. There is a small fee, but you can learn about his adventures and antiquities."

They all squealed, making Lisbeth and their chaperone cringe. They shook their heads at each other. Feeling a little more at ease, Lisbeth added, "He will also be at the reveal of the ending of the epic that will be shown in our grand exhibition room."

Lady Chloe turned to her chaperone. "We must go."

The slightly older woman said, "We shall."

Liseth smiled at them all. "I need to depart, but I hope to see you at the event for the epic in a few days."

They all nodded excitedly, except for the lady, Georgina, who Lisbeth suspected had the duty of escorting them about—poor woman.

What they didn't know was that the famous Thomas Easton was actually upstairs waiting on her with the rest of the board members of the Historical Society of Female Curators. If she were an awful wife, she would have ushered him down to talk with all his adoring admirers, but Thomas had been on edge about anything related to his fame since her fall.

In some ways, Lisbeth wished she hadn't told him her suspicions about falling at the Sinclair ball. The more time that passed, the more she wondered if she imagined hands on her back.

She entered the office to find Rose, Esme, and Thomas peering at documents, while Diana, Sarah, and Addie sat at their desks.

Thomas looked up at her, his eyes roamed hungrily over her. Her body hummed, and she flushed as the desire in her flared. He'd only just left her bed hours ago, but her need for him never seemed to subside. His lips tilted up at the corner as if he could read all the wicked thoughts in her mind.

The last few days, even with the fall, had been wonderful. Lisbeth felt as if they were finding their way. They were becoming a family—her, Thomas, Alice, and Jeremy.

She grinned at him. "Some of your admirers are downstairs."

He frowned, and she sighed. "They are just some young women hoping to catch a glimpse of you. Don't fret."

Addie smiled. "I'm so excited, Easton, that you will be presenting lectures here."

Thomas reluctantly turned away from Lisbeth and said, "I think it is the perfect way to spend my spare time. Lisbeth and I are building an estate just outside the city that will keep me mostly occupied. These lectures will fill the rest of my time."

Rose nodded. "You will be a great fit."

Addie giggled loudly. "I bet the London Society of Antiquaries is green with envy."

Thomas smiled. "They've asked me more than once to partner with them."

"You had no interest?" Sarah Martin asked. "They are a very prestigious organization."

Thomas glanced at Lisbeth. "They said I would have to ask my wife to step down from your board."

All the women gasped, and Lisbeth frowned. "You didn't tell me that."

He shrugged. "I never planned to join them."

"I would be furious if you did," Rose replied.

He laughed. "I know."

Addie said, "Are we ready to go for the event to reveal the end of the epic?"

Both Rose and Lisbeth nodded. Rose explained, "Lisbeth will explain how they found the last two tablets and then introduce me. I will reveal the rest of the story."

Thomas asked, "Is it necessary that Lisbeth present?"

The room went quiet. They all stared at him, shocked. Thomas flushed. "I have concerns that one of my admirers may harm Lisbeth."

Annoyance flared in her that Thomas had brought this up to the board members. The ladies all stared at Lisbeth, and Addie asked, "Do you have the same concern?"

She frowned at him before turning back to the ladies. "I suppose it is a possibility, but I would still like to present. It is important."

Thomas scowled, displeased. Lisbeth turned to him. "Thomas, when I said I was leaving London before the exhibit previously, you told me not to give up something I care so much about. You can't ask me to do it now."

"It wasn't dangerous then," he bit out.

"It is important to me that I stay and contribute," Lisbeth reiterated.

The ladies studied her, but each of them eventually nodded in agreement. Rose said, "We are with you, Lisbeth."

She was grateful to have these ladies in her life. Lisbeth beamed. Thomas sighed. "As you wish, but we need to ensure there are plenty of guards."

She smiled at him, not wanting to argue, knowing he was simply worried because he loved her.

THOMAS KNOCKED ON Lisbeth's bedchamber door. It was late, but he had to see her. She said, "Enter."

He stepped into the space, his eyes roaming over her. She was only dressed in a thin nightgown. His body started to hum. Desire pounded through him. He'd removed his jacket and cravat before visiting her.

She tilted her head and studied him. "I thought you were upset with me."

When Thomas left Seely House, he'd been angry and frustrated, but eventually, he'd calmed down. Ultimately, it was Lisbeth's choice, and he would support her. He shrugged and sat, removing his shoes. "I don't like your decision, but I moved on. Did you think I left to go sulk?"

Lisbeth flushed. He suspected that was precisely what she thought, and truthfully, he had for a moment. After that, he went about his day, which was busy but productive. He raised a brow. "Perhaps you thought I was off partying it up with my admirers, bemoaning my wife."

She gave him a pointed look. Thomas walked to her, grasping her by the shoulders. "I left to speak with Devons to see if the investigators had found anything. Then I met with some colleagues I've been writing to off and on for several years."

"I did think you were angry."

Thomas shrugged. "I was, but I quickly moved on. I told you how I felt, and you disagreed. I'm still concerned, but that is it."

"I'm sorry I jumped to the conclusion that you were off sulking."

He smirked at her. "It's because I behaved like an ass previously."

Thomas grabbed her hand and kissed her fingers one by one. She shivered from his light touch. He smiled wolfishly at her. "You and I are stuck together, Lizzie. Over the next thirty years, we are going to fight, laugh, cry, and I hope to spend countless hours in bed together. Every fight can't be the end of the world."

Lisbeth grasped his shirt. "How many hours exactly?"

"I mean, I'm delighted with at least half the day."

She grinned. "Half the day. I won't be able to walk."

Thomas would be fine with that. He brushed his lips across hers. "Good, then I can have you in bed the whole day. It is my mad scheme."

Lisbeth became lost in thought and frowned.

"What is it?" he asked.

"Will you miss exploring and being at the excavation sites?"

The question was out of nowhere. "Why?"

"Life is fairly predictable here."

He wasn't sure he agreed. Thomas's brows shot up. "Really?"

She blushed. "Usually."

Thomas wrapped his arm around her waist and was quiet for

a moment. He would never regret the last ten years of his life. It had made him a wealthy man, but only one thing had driven him to be as ambitious and so successful. "You have to know, Lizzie, that everything I ever did was to impress you, to prove that I was worthy."

She kissed him hard as if to take away any pain he might be feeling. "You always were."

"My point is that you and I both loved antiquities as children, but it was you who pushed us out to explore the world. I stayed working with antiquities because it reminded me of you."

Her eyes watered. "Thomas, don't say that. You must have hated me."

He pulled Lisbeth to his chest but didn't lie to her. "Some days I did, but I also appreciated that you'd given me a new life path. For our future, I don't care where I live. It can be London, Syria, or somewhere else as long as you, Alice, and Jeremy are there."

She looked up at him, warmth spreading across her body. "Make love to me."

Thomas groaned and walked them backward until the back of Lisbeth's legs bumped the bed. "I'm here to do your bidding."

They stared at each other, and desire thrummed through him. This woman was his wife. She'd be in his arms until they grew old. She smiled at him impishly. "Take my clothes off."

Enticed and amused by her demand, he leaned forward and kissed her neck. He softly said, "I like you ordering me about."

His hand grasped her gown and slowly slid it up. Once it reached her shoulders, he tugged it over her head and tossed it behind him. She giggled. He wanted to see what else she desired. "What now?"

She sat and scooted up on the bed, motioning to her most feminine area. "I want you here."

Thomas also wanted to be there, but he stayed where he was. Folding his arms across his large chest, he stared down at her hungrily. Her blonde hair fell around her naked form, and his cock twitched when she bit her pouty lower lip. Thomas suspected that shyness was taking hold of her. He didn't want that. His voice thick with desire, he gruffly asked, "There are so many ways I could be between your lovely thighs. Tell me exactly how."

Lisbeth widened her legs. "I want your mouth between my thighs. Make me moan with your tongue."

Thomas rubbed at his cock in his trousers. "Christ, that mouth of yours may destroy me."

His temptress smirked. "I want you naked, too."

He quickly disposed of his clothes and stood by the edge of the bed. Lisbeth was scooted a little further up. He stroked his cock as he looked down at her. She was lightly rubbing her little sensitive nub as her hips rocked. "I could watch you touch yourself every day. Do you like doing that, my love? What do you think about?"

A puff of air escaped her along with a moan. Lisbeth's eyes connected with his. "You."

The hunger in him raged at her words. He grasped her hips and pulled her down closer to him. Thomas didn't let go of her but held her tighter as his head dipped down to feast upon her. He lapped at her most feminine area as she bucked against his mouth. Her fingers found his hair as she moaned, "Thomas."

He teased her sensitive nub until her hip movements became frantic. She was so close. He licked and suckled as Lisbeth bucked against his mouth. Her body arched, and she let out a strangled sob. Lisbeth's body shuddered as she collapsed against the bedding.

She took deep breaths, and Thomas's eyes immediately went to her breasts. He reached down and ran a thumb over the tip of one. "You are beautiful, Lizzie."

"You always say that."

His hand moved from her breast to her belly, his fingers swirling over her skin. "I love you."

"I love you. Come here. I want you in me," she said, pulling him closer to her by crooking her leg behind his. He stepped forward so his thighs were pressed against the bed. It was the perfect height for him to pull her down and bury himself in her. Thomas grasped her hips and did just that.

Being inside her was a sweet perfection that would never get old. He slid out of her and thrust back in. She gasped, but desire sparked in her eyes. Thomas enjoyed this view of her. She was lying across the bed as he stood between her legs. His Lisbeth was a vision. She whimpered as his hand grasped her hips, holding her in place as he pounded into her over and over again.

The walls of her quim clenched around his cock, and he tilted his head back, groaning. His tempo picked up. This woman was his, and the thought heightened his desire even more. She whimpered, and his eyes flew open to see her face flushed. She was on the verge of climaxing again. He released her hips and played with her clit, making her buck frantically every time his shaft plunged into her.

She felt so good. He was so close. Their eyes connected, and Lisbeth whispered, "I want you to finish in me."

His blood pounded, and he drove into her harder. He nodded. "Climax again."

Lisbeth stroked her sensitive nub again, not slowing down with his thrust. She let out a loud whimper as the heightened ache within her shattered. Thomas thrust into her one more time deeply and stayed there, spending. The feeling almost made his knees buckle.

Eventually, he leaned down and placed his forehead on hers. "You are mine forever now."

She smiled at him and stroked his jaw. "I was always yours, Serious Thomas."

He laughed at his nickname and withdrew from her. Thomas joined her on the bed. Lisbeth cuddled into him. "I'm glad you are my husband."

"Me too," he said, kissing the top of her head.

They lay there for a few minutes, and Lisbeth said, "I want to tell the children about the estate you are building tomorrow."

He rolled her so they were facing each other. "Are you sure?"

Lisbeth nodded. "I want us to start planning our lives togeth-er."

Thomas kissed her. "Me too."

Chapter Thirty-Two

LISBETH SAT ON a blanket in front of the ruins on the property Thomas had purchased outside of London. They'd decided to take Alice and Jeremy there and reveal the news about building a new home. Nerves rumbled in her belly, but she thought they would be okay.

They'd agreed that they would spend time between the townhouse and the house being built here. Thomas had shown her the plans so far, wanting her input. It was going to be a stunning place with views of both the lake and the ruins.

She smiled as she watched Jeremy, Alice, and Miss Ashby chase each other across the field. Today, they'd taken the train, and it had been a forty-minute train ride and another ten minutes to the property by rented carriage that Benson had arranged beforehand.

Lisbeth smiled, watching Thomas and Benson speak. They'd become fast friends. Her guard had been with her for almost a decade, and she was glad he got on so well with Thomas, her husband. The word had once caused apprehension to flare in her, but not anymore. Lisbeth was hopeful and happy about their future.

Her mind drifted to Nicholas. He'd told her to be happy before he passed, and she and the children were. Nicholas would always be a part of her life and the children's, but there was also room for Thomas. She was grateful that he'd been able to see past the difficult choices she made so long ago.

When he'd forced her to marry him, she feared that his resentment would not subside and they were doomed to have a combative marriage, but she didn't believe that anymore. They were both dedicated to open and honest communication.

She glanced around. Lisbeth had been foolish to immediately deny Thomas an opportunity to build a home here. She supposed change made her nervous. So much had happened in the last year. She'd become a board member for an antiquities club, traveled to Syria, and become Mrs. Easton. Lisbeth could still use her title if she wanted, but did not feel the need.

For the first time in a while, things felt right, and even more shocking, she felt content. Thomas dropped down next to her on the blanket. "Benson and Miss Ashby are going to take a walk while we talk with the children. I think Benson is sweet on your governess."

Lisbeth's eyes widened as she peered at them walking towards the ruins. Miss Ashby shyly smiled at Benson, who looked at her in awe. She glanced at Thomas and smiled. "I had no idea."

He laughed. She studied her children. "They seem happy here."

Thomas nodded, holding her hand. "Good, I want us all to enjoy this place and the townhouse in London. I do mean that. I have no intention of erasing their memories of the duke."

Her eyes watered slightly. "Your compassion may be what I love about you the most. I still can't believe you don't hate me because of Alice."

Thomas stared at his daughter. "We have time to tell her the truth. The duke was her father for almost ten years. I want her to treasure those memories. I've made peace with that part of our past. I love you and the children too much to hang on to the bitterness."

She smiled. "I love you, too."

He leaned forward and kissed her. Jeremy dropped onto the

blanket and groaned. "Gross."

Alice frowned. While she'd warmed up to their marriage, she wasn't entirely comfortable. Lisbeth pulled out sweets from the picnic basket. "Sit, you two. Thomas and I have something we want to speak with you about."

They sat and waited patiently. Lisbeth was nervous, and Thomas squeezed her hand for assurance. "We are going to build a house here. We will stay between here and the townhouse in London. We will also still visit the estate in the north twice a year."

Jeremy's eyes went round, and he jumped up, yelping. Alice's response was silence. Nerves filled Lisbeth. The children had endured a great deal of change. She picked at some grass, and Lisbeth opened her mouth to speak, but Thomas shook his head. Eventually, she looked up and said, "I think Father would like us to live here too. He always used to say the city didn't give us enough freedom to run around the way he wanted."

Lisbeth had forgotten that Nicholas held those beliefs. Thomas smiled at her, and Lisbeth didn't see any resentment. She saw love and compassion. He said, "I think your father, the duke, was a smart man."

Alice smiled. "He was."

Jeremy frowned at them all. "Why are you all so serious?"

Lisbeth laughed. Thomas winked at her daughter. "I think we can make sure your room overlooks the ruins."

Alice nodded excitedly. Thomas and Lisbeth's eyes connected. They would be fine, but more than that, they would be happy.

THOMAS SAT IN the study in the townhouse, scowling at the letter that had been delivered in the floral envelope. Who was this person? It alarmed him that they couldn't find this girl. Lisbeth entered the room with Benjamin Calvert following behind her.

Rose's father was spending the day with them. Lisbeth noticed Thomas's expression and asked, "Is something amiss?"

He held up the floral envelope, and she sighed. "I can't believe no one can figure out who it is."

"Devons explained to me that the woman, whoever she is, is utilizing different mail couriers. He believes she is doing it intentionally to make it nearly impossible to identify her."

Benjamin frowned. "Are you still receiving strange mail from admirers?"

Lisbeth smirked. "He receives mail all the time."

Thomas flushed. "It is because of the serials. Still, this writer has me worried because her correspondence is growing increasingly hostile. We still aren't sure if Lisbeth was pushed. In this letter, she tells me that I need to cease spending time with Lisbeth and come home to her."

His wife sighed. "We are doing everything we can to identify her. We can't spend all of our time worrying."

Benjamin glanced back and forth between them, frowning. Eventually, he said, "I agree with your wife."

Annoyance flashed in Thomas. He wished he'd sided with him. Lisbeth, noticing his expression, said, "I can't be stuck at home because of this. It is wrong to show that we are concerned."

Still, Thomas was apprehensive. Lisbeth tilted her chin up stubbornly and complained, "Benjamin, he doesn't even want me to attend the event for the epic ending."

Their friend sighed. "I don't think you should let this stop you from doing what you want, but you should take care, Lisbeth. There are some dangerous and unwell people out there."

Lisbeth begrudgingly nodded in agreement and said, "I promised Alice and Jeremy I would help them hunt for artifacts in the garden."

Benjamin smiled. "I wanted to speak with Thomas, but I will join you shortly."

Lisbeth kissed the older man's cheek and then cast a glance at Thomas. "Stop worrying about things we can't control."

He sighed. "I will try my best."

She shook her head and departed. Benjamin sat in the chair across from him. "You seem settled here."

"I don't see myself traveling outside of England, to be honest."

The corner of Benjamin's mouth curled up. "You finally married your lady, and now you plan to retire. I think I always suspected it was Lisbeth who drove your ambition. What will you do now?"

Thomas stretched and grinned. "I'm building an estate for us right out of London, and to start, I will be giving lectures at the Historical Society for Female Curators."

His friend nodded. "I'm starting to sense we have become the old guard of antiquities, and it is our duty to help the new guard coming in."

He smiled. "I like that. Is that why you agreed to have Lady Esme and her chaperone join you?"

Benjamin nodded. Thomas frowned. "Watch Keaton around her."

"Keaton is a flirt, but he'd never mess with an innocent lady."

Thomas nodded, agreeing. Benjamin stood and said, "I just want you to know, I'm proud of you and I've been honored to work with you."

Thomas's eyes flicked to his face. The man affectionately smiled at him, and he had to swallow, finding himself getting choked up. He'd worked side by side with Benjamin Calvert for over ten years. He was like a father to him. His own died before he could remember him. "Thank you. You mean the world to me. Both you and Rose."

Benjamin nodded. "We know. You are stuck with us. At this point, we are all pretty much family."

"Thank you, Benjamin."

Chapter Thirty-Three

LISBETH STOOD IN front of the packed lecture room at Seely House with Rose and Addie. The chatter throughout the room was deafening. None of them had expected to have so many people. They had almost double what they had when they opened the exhibit for the cuneiform tablets. It was madness. Diana, Sarah, and Esme stood in the back of the room speaking with the Royal Commission for the Great Exhibition.

The commission seemed happy to be there, and Lisbeth hoped that meant they would be granted a space at the Great Exhibition. Excitement swirled in her.

"This is a bloody mess," Rose muttered under her breath.

Lisbeth giggled. "This is exciting. You and the club have made it."

Rose grinned at her. "I suppose you are right. It just feels cramped in here."

"All these people are here to learn about the ending to Belit and Sibri's tale. A story that is thousands of years old, and we only know because you were able to decipher the ancient text. It's amazing."

A blush formed on Rose's cheeks. "Enough of that."

It was true, but Rose would never be one to accept all the credit. A loud whistle from Addie caused the room to fall silent. She beamed at them all. "Please take your seats."

People shuffled around quietly. Lisbeth looked around for Lord Harston and was shocked to discover he wasn't in attendance. The man loved to attend their events and cause trouble. Perhaps this talk wouldn't be as combative.

She noticed one of Benson's associates standing with Thomas. They were both perusing the room for any dangers and watching her. Benson had arranged for a few more guards to be on hand, but nothing seemed amiss. Plenty of ladies approached Thomas to talk with him or obtain his signature. Lisbeth smiled, wondering how long he would be this famous. The hilarious part was that he didn't have any interest in fame.

Addie motioned for her to start. Lisbeth looked out at the crowd. "Thank you for joining the Historical Society for Female Curators for this event. We are so excited to reveal the end of Belit and Sibri's story."

A woman sighed. "We can't wait."

The rest of the room giggled. Lisbeth and Rose smiled at each other. Another lady raised her hand, and Lisbeth pointed at her. "Why did we have to wait for the ending?"

"That is an excellent question. Once Miss Calvert started deciphering the text, we quickly discovered we were missing the last third of the story. The club worked with the solicitor, Mr. Abbas, and the London Society of Antiquaries to find the rest of the ancient tale that was suspected to be on two tablets in a cave system in Syria."

"How did the London Society of Antiquaries help?"

Lisbeth smiled. "In their vaults, they had a very old map that gave us an idea of where to look for the tablets. Thomas Easton and I journeyed into a cave system to find the artifacts. Mr. Abbas was there as well. It was quite an adventure. Mr. Easton was swept away and pushed out into a river."

All the ladies sighed. Thomas from the back said, "Her Grace is being far too kind. She is the one who retrieved the last two tablets containing the end of the epic."

Ladies beamed at her, and one raised her arm. "Did you really marry Mr. Easton?"

More women giggled, and the noise sent a chill down Lisbeth's back. Thomas said from the back. "Yes, we are married."

A few ladies applauded, and some actually booed. Lisbeth refocused the conversation, growing uncomfortable. "Why don't we listen to Miss Calvert explain the end of Belit and Sibri's story? It's a wonderful ending, I promise."

Several ladies sighed. She smiled at Rose, who stepped forward and said, "Before I explain the rest of the tale, let's applaud the new Mrs. Easton on finding the tablets."

The room broke out in loud applause. Lisbeth blushed, and her eyes connected with Thomas's, who grinned proudly at her. It was good that she attended.

Rose stated, "The last two tablets are the most exciting, but let's do a quick summarization of what has happened so far. Belit is a guard, and he falls in love with the princess Sibri. The king says the only way he can be with her is if he obtains the golden fruit. Our hero sets off on his quest and encounters many challenges, but eventually he finds the fruit."

"He befriends the monster guarding it," a lady burst out.

Lisbeth and Rose both smiled at her excitement. Rose nodded. "Yes, and at the end of the third tablet, he is on his way to claim Sibri as his. The recently discovered tablets reveal he encounters several problems but overcomes them. His biggest battle is with the king. They've agreed to fight to the death, but in the end, Belit grants him mercy. The king allows him to marry Sibri. They rule their kingdom for twenty years."

People applauded. Addie stepped forward. "We have art representing the story and the deciphered text for the last two tablets in the exhibit room."

Men and women started to stand, excited to see the display. Happiness and pride coursed through Lisbeth. The club had accomplished this. She caught the eyes of Diana, who was walking with the Royal Commission for the Great Exhibition. She beamed at Lisbeth. Had they pulled it off? Were they to be given a space?

Addie looped her arm through Lisbeth's. "I think we've done it!"

$$\Rightarrow\!\!\ggg\!\lll\!\Leftarrow$$

THOMAS STOOD NEXT to Devons, grinning as he watched all the ladies of the Historical Society for Female Curators thank their well-wishers. They'd concluded their talk a couple of hours ago, but plenty of people still lingered to speak with them.

"Diana told me that the Royal Commission of the Great Exhibition offered them a place in the Crystal Palace that is being built."

He nodded. "I'm glad they were admitted. It would have been outrageous for them to be denied. They hold the only fully deciphered epic."

Devons nodded and chuckled. "When I signed on to work with them, I was skeptical how successful this club would be, but I am damn impressed."

"Me too," Thomas said.

"All of society is talking about some grand estate you are building right out of London. I suppose that means you plan to stay. I'm glad I will have another husband to spend time with, while our ladies are challenging the world."

"Agree."

"What are the two of you talking about?" Sinclair asked, joining them.

Devons grinned. "That we need our own husband's club for the Historical Society for Female Curators."

Sinclair nodded. "There are three of us now."

Thomas watched Lisbeth as she explained the details of the tablets to a young teenage girl. Sadness lurked in her eyes, and he suspected it was because she'd fought with Alice earlier. Alice had been excited to attend the event, but they'd decided to bring her when it wasn't so crowded. Just in case there was any validity to his admirer being dangerous.

She'd been so upset, but Thomas was glad they'd made her stay back. The place had been overwhelmed with a crush of people today. They could lose sight of her within seconds. Lisbeth smiled at him from across the room. He said, "Excuse me, gentleman. I think I will join my wife."

They nodded. Once Thomas reached Lisbeth, he kissed the top of her head. "I'm so proud of you."

She smiled. "Thank you. We obtained a spot in the Great Exhibition. They are calling the space being created the Crystal Palace. We will have to take Alice and Jeremy there to make up for not attending here."

"They would love that."

He glanced around the room and smiled. A memory flashed in his mind.

⤐⤐⤐⫷⫷⫷

Eleven-year-old Lisbeth flipped through the book about the ancient city of Palmyra, located in present-day Syria. The ruins had been discovered over a hundred years ago, and they were still finding new artifacts and secrets about the society.

Thirteen-year-old Thomas frowned at her. "You've looked at that book a dozen times. Why do you keep rereading it?"

She lifted her head and grinned. "Because someday, Serious Thomas, I'm going to discover something amazing, and the world will applaud me as an explorer and antiquarian."

He grinned at Lisbeth, completely enamored with his friend. Her eyes narrowed, and she frowned at him. "Are you laughing at me?"

Thomas looked at her, shocked. "Of course not."

Lisbeth looked at him skeptically. "Are you sure?"

He pulled her up from where she was lying on her belly, reading the book. "I promise I will always believe in you."

Lisbeth hugged him tight, and Thomas squeezed her back. She whispered in his ear, "Good, because I expect you to be by my side."

"Always, Lizzie."

She released him and charged out of the room. "Come on. Let's find some adventure."

⇥⟫⟪⇤

LISBETH, STUDYING HIM, asked, "What are you thinking about?"

Amused, he said, "I'm just remembering an eleven-year-old girl who said she was going to discover something amazing and the whole world would applaud her. She was right."

She smiled. "That was so long ago."

"It is a good memory."

Lisbeth looped her arm through his. "And here you are by my side as you promised."

"Always, Lizzie."

She leaned into him and said, "Let's go home. I think the ladies can manage without me."

Chapter Thirty-Four

LISBETH AND THOMAS walked to the door of the townhouse, laughing. The event for the epic had been a spectacular success. She was still grinning because they'd been given a spot in the Crystal Palace.

They would need to design a new exhibit for the space. She and the other board members had already started planning. As they reached the front door, it was yanked open. Morrison looked at her, a worried and terrified expression on his face. Fear clutched her heart. She and Thomas glanced at each other, alarmed.

"What is it, Morrison?" she asked.

He shook his head frantically. "The children are missing. I sent a footman to fetch you. He must have missed you."

Lisbeth shook her head in shock. This couldn't be. Why would the children be gone? "Perhaps they are hiding?"

Thomas ushered her inside and asked, "What happened?"

Benson sat in a chair in the foyer with blood dripping down his collar. Miss Ashby sat next to him with a bruise on her cheek. Lisbeth shook her head. "Tell us."

Hoarsely Benson said, "I was in the garden walking the perimeter when I was hit in the back of the head with what felt like the butt of a pistol. When I woke, Miss Ashby was tied up, and the children were gone. I'm so sorry, Mrs. Easton."

Miss Ashby wiped at her tears. "A woman, who I think has been here before, smacked me and then tied me up. I tried to fight her. I swear. She said she was keeping them until you spoke to her about her husband."

Lisbeth stumbled slightly, and Thomas grasped her arm, giving her support. It had to be the admirer C. She looked at him frantically. "How are we supposed to find them? We couldn't even trace her letters."

"Mrs. Easton, it was someone who'd been her before looking for your husband."

She didn't understand. A teenage girl had done all of this. "She was one of the young ladies here previously?"

Miss Ashby frowned. "It wasn't a girl. It was their chaperone."

Thomas's eyes widened. "Miss Sanders. She visited with Lady Chloe."

"Morrison, do you know who Lady Chloe's father is?"

Morrison opened the visitor book they kept by the door. "Lady Chloe is the daughter of Lord Towson."

Lisbeth knew the family. "They only lived a few townhouses down."

She rushed to the door with Thomas, Benson, and Miss Ashby following her. Benson winced, and she said, "Perhaps you should stay."

He shook his head. "I will not leave you."

Lisbeth continued to the townhouse that was only a five-minute walk from her own. She couldn't believe that such danger lurked close by. She glanced at Thomas, whose face was filled with remorse. "I'm so sorry, Lisbeth. If I hadn't returned—"

She shook her head. "Don't you dare say that. You are not the cause of this. This woman is not stable."

Fear clawed at her, but she didn't blame Thomas. The door was thrown open by another frantic butler. Thomas demanded, "We need to see Miss Sanders right away."

The butler looked at them frantically and said, "She isn't here.

Good day."

The man attempted to shut the door, but Thomas stuck his boot in the opening. "You will let us in and tell Lord Towson and Lady Chloe we must speak with them at once. Am I clear?

The butler gulped. "Yes, sir."

They entered, and he led them to an empty drawing room. Lisbeth hoped that Alice and Jeremy were here. They sat and waited. Minutes ticked by, and Thomas paced, becoming angrier and angrier. Benson and Miss Ashby sat silently. A sense of dread hung in the room.

Thomas cursed. "I will go find the man myself."

Lisbeth nodded. They needed to speak with someone right away. He started to storm towards the door when it was yanked open by an older man, followed by Lady Chloe, who was crying. Towson stated, "I'm sorry it took me so long. We were looking for my niece Georgina. She is missing."

Lisbeth added, "She has taken my children."

"I'm sorry, Your Grace. I'm not sure how this happened," he said, and they glanced at Thomas. "Are you Thomas Easton?"

A servant carried multiple journals and sketchpads into the room. Towson handed one to Lisbeth and one to Thomas. Lisbeth opened hers to find sketches of Thomas, the children, Miss Sanders, and then a drawing of her, knocked out at the foot of Sinclair's stairs. So, she had been pushed.

She stumbled backwards, and Thomas insisted, "Please get my wife a chair."

Lisbeth took a deep breath. She needed to pull herself together. It wouldn't do Alice and Jeremy any good if she fell apart. "We need to know what is going on and where she might have taken my children.

Lady Chloe sniffled. "This isn't her first infatuation, but after she came back from the asylum, she seemed so much better."

"What do you mean this isn't her first infatuation?" Thomas demanded.

Lord Towson explained. "My niece was locked up for stabbing a boy."

Lisbeth didn't faint but allowed herself to fall into the chair a servant had brought. Her children were with someone unwell and dangerous. Her heart pounded.

"Explain it all to us," Thomas bit out.

THOMAS COULDN'T BELIEVE what he was hearing. Fury and frustration surged through him. A mad woman had Alice and Jeremy.

Lord Towson said, "Seven years ago, my niece Georgina—she went by her middle name then, Cadence—developed a tendré for a young man who didn't reciprocate her feelings. We assumed she would eventually move on, but she started writing him angry letters about marriage. One night, she snuck into his house and stabbed him. Thank goodness, the young man lived, but we promised his family we would get her the help she needed."

"Why did you let her leave the asylum?"

"All the doctors said she was completely cured."

They'd been wrong, Thomas thought.

"My brother died shortly after she was sent there. He made me promise to look after Georgina. I didn't want to let him down. Everything seemed fine until recently. She'd always loved your serials, Mr. Easton, but she started talking as if the two of you knew each other."

Lady Chloe sniffled. "She was the one who wanted us to seek you out."

Lisbeth couldn't believe what was happening. She couldn't bear the thought of Alice and Jeremy being harmed. "Why do you think she took my children?"

Lady Chloe quietly said, "She told me today that we had to collect them. That you'd asked us to, but I knew that was a lie. I'd already told Papa that I suspected something was wrong with

Georgina. I went to fetch a parasol, and she locked me in my room. By the time the staff heard me, she was gone."

Towson said, "We were searching the gardens when you arrived. Georgina has always had a very vivid imagination. I hoped to find her out there, playing make-believe."

"Do you think she will harm my children?"

"I don't, but I'm not sure why she kidnapped them," Towson provided.

Lady Chloe said, "Recently, she kept saying that Her Grace should be focusing on her children, not Mr. Easton."

Lisbeth shook her head, still in shock about the woman's actions.

Thomas said, "I've never even written to her and only spoke to her once at Lisbeth's home."

Lady Chloe explained, "It doesn't matter what you've actually done. In her mind, she has built a whole fantasy. It is what she did before."

Benson asked, "Do you know where she might have taken them?"

Towson shook his head, but Lady Chloe said, "There is a wooded area in Hyde Park with some ruins that Georgina likes to spend time at. Maybe there?"

They all looked to the front door as Morrison burst through it. He rushed to Thomas. "Sir, this was on the desk in the study."

It was a floral envelope with the same strong perfume smell. Thomas ripped it open and read aloud.

Your Grace,

I insist you speak with me! Meet me at the ruins in the trees west of the Serpentine.

C

Lady Chloe nodded. "That is the area. Georgina likes to pretend she is some grand lady there."

Towson looked gutted. "I'm sorry. I thought she was better.

We assumed the letters she wrote to you, Mr. Easton, were questions about antiquities."

Thomas wanted to scream that the man should have watched his niece closer, but he wasn't sure if it mattered. Truly, all that mattered right now was making sure Alice and Jeremy were safe.

Lisbeth spoke first. "We can't dwell on that. We must go to Hyde Park now. I need to find my children."

They rushed out, and two carriages were already prepared. Lisbeth climbed into the carriage with Thomas, Benson, and Miss Ashby. The carriage quickly made its way over the cobblestone streets. To reach that side of Hyde Park, it was a twenty-minute ride.

Thomas squeezed her hand. "We will find them and bring them back safely."

Her eyes watered. "You don't know that for sure."

"We will bring them home," he said firmly again.

Lisbeth didn't respond. She appeared devastated. Thomas had hope, and it would be enough for both of them. He would not lose his family, now that he'd just found them. Fate wouldn't be that cruel. Thomas refused to believe that.

The carriage began to slow down. Benson said, "We are going to walk the rest of the way in. Miss Sanders is only expecting Mrs. Easton. We don't want to alarm her. Hopefully, she will release the children without any issues. Then Towson can collect her and make sure she obtains the help she needs."

Concern flared in Thomas. "You want Lisbeth to go to her alone."

Benson shook his head. "We will be in the perimeter to step in at any time."

"I'm going," Lisbeth said, her eyes blazing with protective-ness for Alice and Jeremy.

Thomas nodded, knowing that her mind was made up. "I will be with Benson. Please be careful, Lisbeth."

She looked at him frantically. "I just need them away from Miss Sanders."

Fear clawed at him that she might do something dangerous to ensure Alice and Jeremy could escape, but there was no other solution. Lisbeth had to go.

He kissed her. Benson frowned at her. "Be careful."

She nodded and took a lantern from him. Lisbeth walked towards the tree line, revealing only a hint of the ruins. Night was quickly approaching. He hated this.

Chapter Thirty-Five

LISBETH TOOK A deep breath. Her hand holding the lantern was shaking so hard that she had to stop and gather herself. She needed to stay calm no matter what. A girlish voice was chattering away, and she frowned, listening.

"Thomas and I will go far away and make discoveries together."

Alice flatly said, "He is married to my mother."

The girlish voice became screechy. "No, he isn't. It is a trick."

Jeremy whimpered, and Lisbeth stepped closer to see Alice push him behind her. She understood now why they hadn't run. Miss Sanders held a pistol in her hand. She scooted forward, and a leaf crackled under her foot.

Miss Sanders peered into the trees. "I see a lantern. Is that you, Your Grace?"

Lisbeth took a deep breath and joined them in the middle of the woods by the stone ruins. It was a building that still had three walls standing, but everything else was gone. Miss Sanders grinned at her as if she were delighted to see her. This woman wasn't well, and if she wasn't holding her children, Lisbeth suspected she might feel a degree of compassion for her.

Still, she had Alice and Jeremy to think about. Right now, all she cared about was seeing them safely away from Miss Sanders.

"I received your missive. I won't speak with Mr. Easton. He is yours," she explained.

Jeremy frowned at her, confused. "You are Thomas's wife."

Miss Sanders spun in his direction, along with the pistol. Jeremy whimpered behind Alice. Her daughter glared at the woman. Lisbeth stepped forward. "Please let them go. They have nothing to do with this."

"They shouldn't tell lies," Miss Sanders spat out.

"They are young and don't know any better. I promise Thomas is yours," Lisbeth pleaded.

She just wanted this woman to send Alice and Jeremy on their way. She studied Lisbeth and then glared. "You tricked him once into believing you were his wife. How do I know you won't do it again?"

The pistol swung back and forth as it dangled from one of Miss Sanders' fingers.

"I give you my word."

The woman scoffed. "What good is that? You are already an indecent and deceptive woman."

Alice snapped, "Don't call my mother those things."

Lisbeth cringed, both loving her daughter for her defense but also wishing she would, for once, not feel the need to speak up.

"Your mother is the worst sort of woman."

Alice and Jeremy's faces scrunched up with anger. Lisbeth pleaded, "How can I convince you?"

Miss Sanders turned back to her. "I don't know."

"There has to be some way," Lisbeth insisted.

Jeremy and Alice moved closer to the tree line from which Lisbeth had emerged. Perhaps they could make a run for it. Noticing movement out of the corner of her eyes, she swung back towards them and aimed the gun. They froze, and Lisbeth threw herself in front of them. "I will not let you hurt them."

Miss Sanders's face became angry. She screamed, "You have no control. I decide everything."

Lisbeth decided she would charge the woman and wrestle the pistol from her. She eyed her, trying to determine the best way to do it, but then Thomas stepped out of the tree line. "I'm right here, Georgina."

The woman's eyes widened, and then her face filled with pure joy.

THOMAS EYED MISS Sanders, who was looking at him as if he'd just confessed, he loved her. She sighed. "You came for me."

He glanced at Lisbeth, Alice, and Jeremy, who were huddled together. Lisbeth frowned at him with worry, but happiness shone in Alice and Jeremy's eyes. Yes, he was here for them. He would not allow them to be hurt. He tried to convey that to them silently. Thomas didn't care what happened to him as long as they were safe.

"Georgina, I'm here for you."

She scowled at him. "Don't call me that. You know I only like Cadence. My uncle made me go by Georgina. What an awful name."

Thomas smiled at her. "I agree, Cadence is beautiful."

She blushed and said, "I knew you would eventually come for me. I've been waiting so long, Thomas. I'm ready to be your bride and to see the world with you."

Alice wrinkled her nose in disgust, and for a mad moment, Thomas thought he might laugh. The entire situation was absurd, but his biggest worry right now was why his daughter seemed to have no idea how to hide her emotions.

He turned away from the family he loved more than anything and said, "Cadence, let them go. You don't need them anymore. I'm here only for you."

Happiness bloomed in her, and Thomas felt a sliver of compassion for this woman. It was apparent she desperately wanted love and that she wasn't well. Softly, he requested, "Please release them."

Her gaze darted between him and his family. She frowned. "How do I know you won't leave?"

"Because I'm here now. I could have not appeared."

The pistol swung back in his direction. It wasn't intentional, but the woman was careless with the weapon. It unnerved him, but he preferred for it to be pointed at him rather than Lisbeth, Alice, and Jeremy.

"We will have to leave right away. My uncle is likely looking for me. I locked my cousin in her room. She was going to tell my uncle that our love was unhealthy."

He nodded. "We will deal with that after they are gone."

She smiled at him one more time and then swung back towards Lisbeth, Alice, and Jeremy. "Leave."

Lisbeth pushed Alice and Jeremy in front of her, but she glanced back at him. He shook his head. "Leave. Cadence and I have plans to make."

He silently screamed at Lisbeth not to fight him on this. Thomas was grateful that in the darkness, Miss Sanders likely couldn't see the stricken look on Lisbeth's face. More firmly, he said, "Go."

She rushed through the trees, and when he turned back, Miss Sanders smiled at him adoringly.

He forced himself to smile back at her. "Cadence, may I have the pistol?"

Her demeanor changed, and she immediately became suspicious. "No."

Thomas didn't want to push her on it and hoped Lisbeth and the children would be on their way home. Lisbeth had left the lantern she carried earlier behind. He reached for it and held his arm out to Miss Sanders. She took it and said, "I knew you would find your way to me. When I started writing to you years ago, I felt such a strong connection between the two of us. I didn't tell anyone because they would have said it was just like Albert."

"Who is Albert?" he asked.

Pain flashed across Miss Sanders' face, and then she shook her head as if trying to make a memory go away. "It doesn't matter."

They made their way through the trees, but once they reached the other side, Miss Sanders stopped. Her uncle and the constables stood by two carriages. Lisbeth and the children were standing by another one further down.

Her look of adoration turned to pure fury. "You tricked me!"

"Your uncle is going to help you."

She stomped her foot as she still clutched the pistol. Her eyes went wild as she looked around. Lisbeth stood with Benson, who made sure to position himself between him and Miss Sanders. Thomas was grateful to the guard.

Miss Sanders screeched loudly and kicked him before taking off. He grunted and grabbed his leg. Her uncle and the constables chased after her, but she was too fast. She ran in a large curve, and Thomas realized she was trying to make her way to Lisbeth. He took off running towards the unwell woman. She suddenly stopped and raised her pistol, aiming at Lisbeth. No!

Chapter Thirty-Six

LISBETH USHERED THE children into the carriage, trying her best to keep them safe. Miss Sanders raced across the grass. Lisbeth wasn't sure where she was going, but then she realized the woman was avoiding the constables and heading directly towards her.

Benson charged the woman. She screeched and dodged away from him, running in a large arc. What was she doing? He continued to chase after her, but she'd been able to put some distance between them. The woman grinned at Lisbeth and pointed the pistol in her direction.

Lisbeth shook her head and whispered, "Don't do this."

There was no way Miss Sanders could hear her, so she wasn't sure who she was whispering to. She only had one shot; maybe she would miss Lisbeth.

Benson was charging the lady while Thomas was trying to get between the two of them. Lisbeth shook her head at him. She didn't want that.

Miss Sanders laughed crazily and pulled the trigger. A loud boom echoed through the waning light of day. Lisbeth hadn't been hit. She'd missed. She almost collapsed from the joy of knowing she would live, but then saw Thomas's crumpled form in the grass. She couldn't lose him. They'd only just found each other.

Benson, along with Towson, held the hysterical Miss Sanders. Lisbeth didn't have time to pay attention to any of that. She needed to go to Thomas. Alice stuck her head out the door, and Lisbeth said, "Stay in there."

Her daughter's eyes became watery. "Is Thomas okay?"

Lisbeth didn't want to lie to her, so she didn't answer. "Stay here."

She raced to where he lay, falling on her knees. Benson reached him at the same time and gently rolled him over. He groaned. Blood was covering his shoulder and spreading. Towson yelled, "A doctor is on the way."

Thomas groaned. "I don't feel good."

"That is because you jumped between me and Miss Sanders."

His eyes connected with hers. "I would do it again."

He grimaced and looked at Benson. "Is it bad?"

Benson frowned. "It looks like the lead ball went clear through your shoulder. You will be fine if infection doesn't set in."

Thomas nodded, and Lisbeth stroked his face. He smiled at her. "I love you. No matter what happens, I'm glad I had this time with you, Alice, and Jeremy."

Lisbeth shook her head. "Don't talk like that. You are going to live."

He smiled at her, but his focus was fading. "I promise to do my best."

An older man appeared at their side. "I'm the doctor. We need to get him to a place where I can clean his wound."

Thomas's head lolled to the side as if he'd passed out. Lisbeth looked at Benson. "I can't lose him."

"Come, Mrs. Easton," he said, and he escorted her back to the carriage with Alice and Jeremy.

She stepped in to find two tear-streaked faces. Lisbeth sat on the bench and opened her arms. They both darted into her embrace. "Alice said Thomas was shot."

"They are taking care of him now," she told her eight-year-old son who'd seen too much in his short life.

Alice sniffled. "We can't lose him. He just became part of our family."

Her words warmed her heart even though Lisbeth was terrified. They were a family now, and they couldn't lose Thomas. "I know. He is being cared for now. Have hope."

She squeezed them tighter, grateful they were unharmed. "I'm so sorry."

Jeremy lifted his head and scowled. "Why did she take us?"

Lisbeth sighed. "She is unwell. She thought she was supposed to marry Thomas."

Jeremy shook his head, and Alice said, "I tried to explain to her that Thomas was married to you."

She kissed the top of her daughter's head. "I know. Her uncle is going to make sure she gets help."

They both nodded and snuggled further into her. She forced the tears welling in her eyes to stop. Lisbeth had to be strong for Alice and Jeremy, but worry overflowed in her that Thomas might not make it. As her children fell asleep against her, she shook her head.

Thomas Easton could not die. The world was not so cruel. They'd loved each other since they were children. She would stay by his side until he woke up and knew they were waiting for him. Yes, there would be no dying for the man she loved.

THOMAS BLINKED HIS eyes. Where was he? He felt like he'd died, and his mouth was unbearably dry. As his eyes adjusted, he realized he was in Lisbeth's bedchamber. His gaze darted to the left, and he saw Lisbeth lying next to him on top of the blanket.

She clutched his hand, but other than that, she seemed to be deep in sleep. She looked exhausted. Her hair was spiraling across her face, and she had dark circles under her eyes. He was exhausted, but lifted his hand and brushed a curl from her cheek.

Her lashes fluttered, and then her eyes opened. She bolted up and stared at him. Thomas smiled. "Hello, Lizzie."

Her lips trembled, and she reached out and ran her hand along his jaw. "You are awake."

Thomas winced as he moved his shoulder. He remembered Miss Sanders had shot him, but after that, it was all darkness. Lisbeth bolted from the bed and rushed to the door. "Fetch Benson and the doctor. He is awake."

Thomas shook his head. "I don't want a doctor. I want you to join me back in this bed."

Lisbeth smiled as she wiped tears from her face. "You don't understand, you've been out of it with a fever for five days."

His eyes widened in surprise. Benson and the doctor entered the room. The guard's face filled with relief. He smiled at Thomas. "We thought we'd lost you, Easton."

The doctor beamed at him. "Your wife's steely determination that you would live seems to have proven true."

He glanced at her, confused. She shrugged. "We had another doctor at first who told me to start saying goodbye to you. I fired him, and Benson found Dr. Leroy. He has been much more helpful than the man Towson employs."

Dr. Leroy grinned. "Dr. Jules is a good doctor, but old-fashioned in some of his methods."

Lisbeth pursed her lips together as if she wanted to say more but was refraining herself from doing so. Thomas chuckled at her sour expression. The doctor smiled at him. "You are, indeed, feeling better, and your fever has broken. I think, Mr. Easton, you will be on your way to a swift recovery now."

He turned to Lisbeth and said, "He will need bed rest for the next week, but short of his fever spiking again, he should be fine."

"Thank you so much, Dr. Leroy," Lisbeth said.

The man smiled at her. "It was my pleasure."

The doctor departed, and Benson remained. He frowned at Thomas. "I'm sorry I didn't reach Miss Sanders in time. You should never have been shot."

Thomas frowned at the guard, who had become a friend. "You did everything you could. The lady isn't well. I hope her family is getting her the appropriate care."

Lisbeth nodded. "Dr. Leroy recommended a place for her. It is a few hours north. Towson left yesterday to escort her there."

"Good," Thomas said. Fury coursed through him that the woman had almost ripped his family apart. Still, he wouldn't dwell on it. He was alive. Thomas had everything he wanted.

He held his hand out to Lisbeth. Benson smiled at the two of them. "I will depart."

Thomas was already getting sleepy, but he said, "Thank you, Benson, for always being here for the family."

The guard nodded and departed. Lisbeth squeezed Thomas's hand, and he pulled her towards the bed. "Come lie with me."

She didn't fight him and lay down beside him. Still, she said, "I don't want to keep you awake."

He shook his head. "I sleep better with you here. I always will."

It was true. She nodded. Thomas's eyes drooped, and he fell into a restful sleep, knowing Lisbeth would be by his side when he woke.

Hours later, Thomas heard two little voices whispering. Alice said, "Did you know Mother snores?"

"No, I didn't."

Jeremy asked, concerned. "He isn't dead, is he? You promised he wasn't."

"Miss Ashby said he was recovering."

Thomas opened his eyes and quietly brought a finger to his lips. "Your mother is sleeping."

He glanced to his side where Lisbeth slept, snoring softly. Thomas winked at Alice and Jeremy. "Don't ever tell her she snores. She wouldn't like that."

They giggled quietly. Then Jeremy's face scrunched up as if he was about to burst into sobs, but he didn't. Instead, he whispered, "Can we lie down with you?"

Thomas choked back tears. He understood at that moment that this was his family. He was home. It didn't matter if it was the townhouse or their new country estate. He was right where he should be.

Thomas nodded. "Of course, but don't wake your mother."

They joined him on his other side. Jeremy bumped his shoulder, causing him to grimace, but he didn't care. They snuggled into the bed. Thomas was exhausted, but he watched the children fall asleep and then allowed himself to peruse his family. He was a lucky man, certainly more fortunate than any famous explorer could ever be.

Chapter Thirty-Seven

April 1851

LISBETH SAT IN the lecture room at Seely Hall. Chaos reigned around her. Today was Thomas's first lecture for children on antiquities. There was nothing sedate, serious, or sophisticated about what was taking place in the room. Children bounced up and down in their chairs as Thomas explained how to clean an artifact effectively.

Benjamin walked around the room, helping them. It was a fantastic idea that Thomas conceived while stuck in bed. It had been almost a month since the shooting. He was doing so much better.

Her heart ached as she remembered him crumpled on the ground in Hyde Park. She shook the devastating thought from her mind. Her Serious Thomas was right here, teaching and joking with children. He practically glowed, and Lisbeth suspected there was nowhere else he'd rather be.

She did hope that someday they would go on another adventure but was happy to live and enjoy their family in London and their new country estate for now. It would be another year until they could live there, but the whole family went every week to see the progress.

Rose dropped down next to her, and Lisbeth smiled. "How are you faring?"

Her friend shook her head. "I'm sick every morning. Augustus is beside himself with worry. This morning, we quarreled because he wouldn't stop hovering over me. Losing my breakfast is awful, but it is made even worse when your husband is leaning over you watching."

Lisbeth giggled. "He is just worried about you."

Rose nodded at Thomas. "I'm glad he is recovering well."

She smiled. "Yes, the doctor stopped by for the last time yesterday and said Thomas was officially mended."

"I can't believe what you all endured."

Lisbeth wished it had never happened, but in some ways, it brought her, Thomas, Alice, and Jeremy closer. They truly felt like a family. They still had to share with Alice the truth about Thomas, but had decided not to focus on it until she was eighteen. "Thomas is apprehensive about any of his admirers now and at first said he wouldn't respond to any more mail, but fortunately, he's changed his mind."

"And you support that?" Rose questioned, surprised.

"I do. Look at him with those children. He is inspiring the next generation of historians, explorers, and scholars."

Her friend nudged. "Don't forget, Mrs. Easton, you are doing the same."

They all were. Lisbeth was proud of that.

Thomas clapped his hands. "Now, to the gardens of Seely House. Mr. Calvert and I may have hidden some artifacts to find."

The chatter heightened as the children headed to the green space. Lisbeth stood just as Thomas reached her. "Are you ready to go adventuring, Lizzie?"

"Of course."

THOMAS SAT IN the study, reviewing the plans for the estate just outside London. They'd decided to call it the Majnun Estate. He smiled; perhaps it was a little dark, but it was an ode to the story that so many people had said seemed like it was about him and Lisbeth. He smiled. Thomas was no longer the madman but a man in love with his wife.

He studied the plans. To date, the foundation had been laid. Next, the kitchen and first-floor rooms would be designed and built. The second floor would come after that. As requested, Alice's room would look over the old manor ruins, and Jeremy's would look over the lake.

"Is this where you've been hiding all morning, Mr. Easton?" Lisbeth said, entering and locking the door behind her. His body hummed at what that meant.

"I'm never hiding from you," he said.

Thomas's eyes raked over his wife. Today, she was wearing a green dress. The neckline dipped down, hinting at the perfect mounds the fabric hid.

He smirked. "Did you come to distract me from my work?"

"Perhaps, I must spend the day at Seely House, so I thought I would visit you before I departed."

"Is that so?" he said, standing. His cock was already hard and ready to sink into her warmth.

"Yes," she said, her voice going breathless.

He pulled her to his desk, bending her over. A mirror reflected their image. Thomas loved its position and had used it to watch his wife more than once. She looked back at him, her eyes clouded with need.

He threaded his fingers with one of her hands and leaned down over her. "Did you want me to bend you over my desk before you departed?"

He pushed his cock into the back of her skirt. Lisbeth moaned and pressed herself against him. "Yes."

Thomas used his other hand to push her breasts out of the low top of her dress. His thumb ran across the tip of one, and Lisbeth arched back into him. "Please, Thomas."

His eyes glowed with desire. "You are such a wanton sight. Is that all for me?"

"Yes, only you."

He opened the flap of his pants and stroked his hard cock before flipping her skirt up. She wore nothing underneath. His palm caressed her bottom. "You are a wicked woman. Now I will think of nothing but what is under your dress all day."

She smirked at him in the mirror. "Good."

Thomas caressed her bottom some more and then gave her a playful smack. She gasped as his hands roamed down to her feminine folds. Lisbeth was so wet and ready for him. He positioned his shaft at her opening, and she whimpered.

He grasped her shoulders and slid deeply within her. Their eyes connected. "I love you, Lizzie."

"I love you, too," she whispered.

Thomas pulled out and thrust back into her again. Things went flying off his desk, but he didn't care. His eyes and focus were on his wife. She moaned and pushed against him every time he impaled her with his shaft. He released her shoulders and slid one of his hands between her legs without slowing down his onslaught of thrusts.

Lisbeth's moans became louder as his fingers stroked and teased her sensitive nub. He was close to spending, but wanted to watch her face fill with ecstasy when she came apart. His fingers pinched and circled the most sensitive part of her body. She panted loudly, and then suddenly she let out a loud, strangled moan. Her climax drove Thomas over the edge, and he plunged into her, spilling his seed.

They both lay against the desk. Finally, Thomas kissed her neck and pulled away. He found a cloth to clean them both. She pulled her skirts down and adjusted her top before standing and saucily grinning at him. A gasp of laughter escaped him as he fell back into his chair. She sat on his lap and brushed her lips against his.

Thomas smiled. "You will be the death of me."

"I didn't want you to forget me while I was gone."

He nuzzled her breasts. "I think you should do that every

time you leave. We wouldn't want you to be forgotten."

She giggled. Thomas wasn't a globetrotting explorer anymore, and he didn't regret those days, but this was the life he'd always envisioned and never thought possible. Yet, here they were.

Epilogue

LISBETH STOOD IN front of the stunning glass building with her arms looped through Addie's and Diana's. Rose stood behind them, wanting space as she was still nauseous from the human she was growing.

Addie grinned. "I can't believe we are setting up the exhibit today."

In one week, the Great Exhibition would open. They'd been given a spot right next to the London Society of Antiquaries. All the board members of the Historical Society for Female Curators suspected the men-only club would be very displeased about that.

They didn't care. Having the epic exhibit at the world event meant that they'd made it. Lisbeth smirked. They weren't the richest, most knowledgeable, or most well-known club, but their desire to succeed had propelled them to this moment.

Diana sighed, "I wish Esme and Sarah were here."

Addie shook her head. "Don't be sad about that. They will return before the Great Exhibition is over. Let them have their adventures. We will handle this while they are away."

Rose nodded. "Plus, we need them to find us more artifacts to display."

Lisbeth said. "I agree. I do hope that Sarah and the Count de Messina don't throttle each other."

Addie giggled. "When they met, Sarah was having none of his

charm, and he didn't look pleased to be corrected about his island's history."

They all laughed.

Lisbeth looked around at the women she'd barely known a year ago, but now were her dearest friends. "Shall we, ladies?"

They all nodded, and Rose looped her arm through Addie's. The Historical Society of Female Curators walked arm and arm towards the Crystal Palace with their heads held high and excited. They were damn proud to be representing the antiquities field at the Great Exhibition.

Thank You for Reading!

I hope you enjoyed Lisbeth and Thomas's story. I loved writing this second-chance romance. These two were just meant to be. The story of Majnun (the madman) and Layla is a well-known Arabic tale that dates back to approximately 684 AD. It was so much fun incorporating the ancient story into "The Explorer Returns."

The Explorer Returns is the third book in the Brazen Curator series. This series is about a group of ladies finding love while they try to one-up the men-only London Society of Antiquaries. Who doesn't love that! I hope you enjoy these women's happily-ever-afters as much as I loved writing them!

Always feel free to check out my website for new information on the Brazen Curator series.
Link: https://ramonaelmes.com

SO GRATEFUL

So many people have encouraged and supported me on my writing journey. I just wanted to take a moment to thank all of them.

To my mother and mother-in-law: Thank you for always being my biggest supporters and reading my books. You two are the absolute best. I'm lucky to have you both.

To my step-daughters and daughter: When I told you I was writing steamy romance novels, you were all in with your encouragement. I appreciate that so much.

To my siblings: Thank you for all the ribbing about writing porn and bodice rippers. I wouldn't expect anything less from all of you. LOL! I'm so lucky to have you to laugh with.

To Dave and Lisa: My first writing buddies and champions. Thank you!

To my girlfriends: How lucky am I to have all of you? Thanks for all your support and also for allowing me to bounce questions off you, whether they are historical, sex-related, or about the feels.

To Stephanie: Thank you for editing my books and giving me feedback so I can better understand the book world. I'm learning so much.

To Dragonblade Publishing: Thank you for working with me to get this series out in the world. I truly appreciate it!

To my Hubby: You are last but the most important. Thank you for telling me I needed a hobby that wasn't family or job-focused. The many hours I spend writing are all your fault. LOL! Seriously, though, I'm so lucky to have you and your support. You are in every one of my stories in some way—it may be a smile, an eye roll, or a snappy phrase. Love you so much. 143.

About the Author

Since stealing her first historical romance novel from her mother more than twenty years ago, Ramona Elmes has been all in on the genre. Her infatuation with the historical and steamy stirred her to write her own romances.

Ramona loves to write happily ever afters set in the Victorian era. She believes this period makes an exciting backdrop for fast-paced storylines, steamy moments, dramatic endings, and memorable characters.

When not creating ways to entice and torture her characters, she spends her days in Georgia coordinating her family's crazy life, refereeing pets, hiking, and reading on her front porch.

Reading is hands-down her favorite way to relax, and she is an avid reader of all romance subgenres. Give her a dramatic storyline, a grand declaration, and heart-filled steamy moments, and she is in.

To get updates on Ramona's books, follow her on Amazon, Facebook, Instagram, or her website.

Instagram: elmes_ramona
Facebook: RamonaElmes
Website: ramonaelmes.com
Amazon: amazon.com/stores/Ramona-Elmes/author/B08TTX6TJP
Goodreads: goodreads.com/author/show/21134562.Ramona_Elmes